P9-AQO-566

A new guy comes in and tries to mooch me off of Rick. This new guy is huge—six-four at least, muscle-bound and flat-topped, with gross arm veins that only a steroid dealer could love.

He's awful. He has on a purplish shirt that aches to be retro but is really just retardo. Fat gold links. Weight-lifted man-boobs that are probably bigger than mine. He's Omega Travolta, some inbred result of a million years of anonymous disco hookups.

Not only that, he speaks the line out of a hundred B-movies, mid-season TV pilots and Charles Atlas print ads. "Hey baby, why don't you dance with a real man?"

I give him one out. "I'm here with Rick," I say, pointing.

"You're here with Prick?" he asks. "Sweetie, I got all the prick you need right here." And lord help me, he grabs my hand and puts it on his crotch.

Okay Omega. You had your chance.

"You are inadequate," I tell him, and I don't bother to yell it.

I'm speaking directly to a specific part of Omega's mind, the part of every mind that craves discipline and punishment and longs to willfully obey a strong leader. I seize that part, the sniveling worm of the soul, through Omega's eyes and twist it beneath me. I can do this very, very well.

"Your penis is too small. Every woman you meet can tell. Lots of men can too." He can't ignore this. He can't doubt it. This is his new truth.

His eyes are locked on mine and although he shouldn't be able to hear me over the thumping club beat, I know that every word is getting hammered straight into his brain. "You do not have what it takes to make a woman happy. You make women laugh. Women laugh at you all the time."

More than his hand goes limp, and I can see tears starting to drip out of his eyes. Good.

"Go home and think about this," I tell him, and he turns to the door, moving like a man in a very sad dream.

This is, I think, my favorite part about being a vampire.

©2004 White Wolf, Inc. All rights reserved.

Cover art by Jason Alexander. Book design and art direction by Pauline Benney. Copy edited by Ana Balka.

No part of this book may be reproduced or transmitted in any form or by any means, electronic or mechanical—including photocopy, recording, Internet posting and electronic bulletin board—or any other information storage and retrieval system, except for the purpose of reviews, without permission from the publisher.

White Wolf is committed to reducing waste in publishing. For this reason, we do not permit our covers to be "stripped" for returns, but instead, require that the whole book be returned, allowing us to resell it.

All persons, places and organizations in this book—except those clearly in the public domain—are fictitious, and any resemblance that may seem to exist to actual persons, places, or organizations living, dead, or defunct is purely coincidental. The mention of or reference to any companies or products in these pages is not a challenge to the trademarks or copyrights concerned.

White Wolf, Vampire and World of Darkness are registered trademarks of White Wolf Publishing, Inc. Vampire the Requiem and A Hunger Like Fire are trademarks of White Wolf Publishing, Inc. All rights reserved.

ISBN 1-58846-862-3
First Edition: December 2004
Printed in Canada

White Wolf Publishing
1554 Litton Drive
Stone Mountain, GA 30083
www.white-wolf.com/fiction

a hunger like fire

greg stolze

Vampire
THE REQUIEM

It is curious, if not unfitting, that the most common name for unlife among vampires is a musical reference, the Requiem. The word itself means a mass or musical composition for the dead. In some cases, a requiem is a dirge. In other cases it is a chant intended for the dead's repose. In still others, it is a gesture of respect.

No surprise, then, that the word has taken on its own meaning among the vampires who call themselves Kindred. The word has connotations of its own, suggesting that the Kindred must have adopted it in a more enlightened or sophisticated time. Tonight, however, all but the most cloistered Kindred know that the word bears its own specialized meaning. The Requiem is the Kindred's unlife, the grand, doomed waltz through which every one of their kind dances every night, urged on by metaphorical strains of music that represent the hidden powers that guide, manipulate and inspire them.

Every night stands out as singularly as each separate note in a composer's opus. When we hear the composition, though, we do not examine each and every note. Rather we experience it in sum. This is the key to avoiding the malaise of eternity. Let each night, each note, stand out in the greater body of the Requiem your life has become.
—Charlotte Gaudibert, *Aequitas Fatalis*

This book is lovingly dedicated to my child Daniel, born May 27, 2004. Son, I apologize in advance for any neglectful or shaky parenting.

Part One:

Summertime

"For strangers to the truth, bewilderment is to be expected. For those who know the truth, the natural reaction is suspicion."
—Solomon Birch

Chapter One:
Bruce

I open my eyes and I think, *What the hell?*

I'm wrapped in plastic. Crinkly thick stuff, smells kind of like paint.

Looking left and right, nothing hurts, so I try turning my head. It's all right. Stomach feels okay. So I must've slept right through the hangover. Haven't done that in a while.

I move and my wrapping isn't too tight—I can get it off my face without a lot of trouble. It's a drop cloth, and I get my head and shoulders free.

I'm in a basement, I think. It's dark, and it feels like I'm in a small space. Everything's dusty, and there's a little light coming in from under the door.

Man. I must have really tied one on last night. Nina's gonna be pissed.

What time is it? My watch has a light on it; I pinch the little button and it's *Saturday*! Saturday, and eight o'clock at night! Damn, I must have slept through the whole day, and I was going to fix that toilet handle in the half-bath. Shit.

I stand up and find the light cord.

The room is small, maybe ten by ten, with a bare bulb and wood shelves stacked with junk. There's a humidifier, some old tools, a dusty aquarium with magazines in it, a red Coleman cooler with maybe a folded-up tent on top of it... just crap. I bet I'm in somebody's storage room, like in the basement of an apartment building.

What the hell happened to me? How did I get here?

Okay, last thing I remember. It was Friday night. Check. Got out of work and went to Pitchers & Pool with Tony and Spence and that new guy from Lawn. Check. Had some pitchers, played some pool. Okay, all normal.

How'd I get here from there?

I guess the first thing is to figure out where here is. And get some food. Damn, I'm starving.

The door on the storage locker is busted, looks like someone kicked it in. Did I do that? It's not a big deal, a cheap padlock and hasp, Aisle Eleven, probably fifteen bucks. There's a cruddy linoleum floor with corners turning up over dirty concrete, water damage on the cement walls, I smell something musty... and fabric softener? I hear clunking from down the hall, there's more light that way. Off I go.

The well-lit part is the laundry room. Yeah, I must be in an apartment building. Someone's got her clothes in the dryer and I step out into the light. Young woman, small, real dark hair, wearing a blue tank top. She's sitting in one of those plastic and metal stacking chairs. I come in and she turns her head. She's frowning a little, but just for a second. When she sees me, she gives a little yelp.

"Hey, I..."

Her eyes are kind of wide and she's inching away. Okay, whatever. I head for the door. Outside, I see streetlights.

I get out of the apartment building and look around. It's a hot, humid night. Anyone with any sense is inside with a cold beer and the fan on, but there's a few young kids running around, a few *vatos* hanging out on porch sofas or stoops, one young couple walking down the street holding hands. I get out and in the good light I take a moment to look down at myself.

I've got dust and mess all over me. I'm filthy. My arms look like they're really encrusted with... something. My

greg stolze

jeans are the same ones I wore to work on Friday. Same Home Depot polo shirt, only there's some dried crud on it and... the hell? Where'd that hole come from?

Clearly I got a lot to answer for. I wish I could remember what happened, but I'm drawing a blank. It's been a long time since *that* happened too. I usually don't black out from just beer. In fact, I don't think I've ever blacked out from just beer. Did we start drinking hard stuff on Friday? Why?

I was at Pitchers & Pool and I played eight ball with the new guy... what was his name? I can't even remember who won. Did I start to go home? I think I did, but then it all gets fuzzy.

Fire?

Yeah, fire... I remember a... an accident? Something. And some guy, some short guy, just hideous, like something from a freak show...

I hear someone hiss.

It's not a cat hiss, like when an ump makes a bad call. It's one of those sharp breath hisses, like when you come around a corner and there's a dead dog all spread out in the street. I look up and the young lovers are looking at me, and I'm the dead dog.

They edge around me. The chick looks kind of nervous. The guy, just disgusted.

"What're you lookin' at?" I ask, but I don't really want to know, I just want them to move along.

They move along.

Screw this. I'm starving. I think I know where I am, and there's a taco joint not far.

My name is Bruce Miner. I'm thirty-eight years old. I graduated from Morton East High School when I was nineteen, married Nina that summer, had our only daughter Brooke a couple years after. I worked at Meridian Rail for a while, until the accident, and now I work at Home Depot.

Brooke's in high school, talking about dropping out. I keep telling her it's not like when I was young—you can't just quit school and get a job. But she knows it all better. Louder, too.

Nina works at a doctor's office, answering the phones and typing and stuff. She makes more money, so it's *her* car, and she never lets me forget it. Not that I'm supposed to drive anyway.

It's not the best life in the world, but there you go. At least I knew what to expect. Until tonight, I guess.

The taco place is Pepe's, I remember it. It's a dive, but I'm so hungry I don't care. It's a long walk to my place, but not too bad if I get some food in me. Three tacos and a beer and I'll be good as new.

Maybe I should give Nina a call, ask her to come and get me? Probably not. The first couple times I broke the leash, she worried about me, but I guess that routine got pretty old. Now she's just gonna be mad, and if I ask her to drive out and get me it's not going to make things any easier. I'll eat, then call her.

There are four teenagers in a corner and one guy sitting at the counter. He gives me the evil eye when I sit, just like everyone has been, and I am not in the mood. And then I smell it.

I look over at him (and he leans back when I do) and damn, something over there smells *great!*

The short-order cook comes up and asks if he can help me, and I point at old Evil Eye's plate. "I want that," I say.

"Burrito supremeo," he says.

"And a… what you got on draft here?"

"Budweiser and MGD."

"And a Budweiser."

"Coming up."

He's been giving me the stink-eye, just like everyone else. What the fuck? Maybe I got something on my face?

Maybe it's like that time Spence and I were drinking with that one guy... what was his name? Some really Italian name like Angelo or Giovanti... and when he passed out, Spence's girlfriend put lipstick and rouge and eyeliner on him. Yeah, when he woke up he was one puzzled and pissed off eye-tie.

I pick up one of those metal napkin holders and use it as a mirror, but it's too greasy, all I can see is smears and blurs. But Jesus Christ, what happened to my hands?

I put the napkin holder down for a closer look. Man, my hands look like they went through a meat grinder! I thought they were just real dirty, but that's not it. They don't hurt or anything, but the skin's all red and choppy and scabby... it's like when that guy at the plant got psoriasis, only it's redder, it's worse.

I put my hands to my face and I can feel the bulbs and blisters. Now I know why everyone's been looking at me weird. Christ, I must look like the Elephant Man!

I leave the restaurant before my food comes.

The walk home is longer than I remember. I catch a bus halfway there. The Herberts aren't home on the other side of the duplex—good, I don't want to talk to them anyhow. I let myself in and the dog starts barking.

"Hey Peaches. Hey. Whooza good girl, huh? Huh? Who's my good girl?"

The dog cocks her head and starts to whine. No. C'mon, no, not my fucking *dog* too?

"Peaches. Kiss kiss doggie. Whooza good doggie? C'mere girl. Come to da-da. C'mon, please? *Please?*"

My voice breaks on that last word, weird, kind of high and whiny and I don't like it, am I that desperate? But it works, it gets through, and Peaches comes up to lick my hands and my face.

"Yeah, you're a *good girl* aren't you? Who's daddy's good girl? Good Peaches."

Fuck, I'm almost crying, but I'm so grateful this dog isn't rejecting me. Everyone else might, but not Peaches, she's licking my face like she always has. Of course, she drinks from the toilet, but still.

It's still a relief.

Man's best friend. Fuckin'-A right.

First thing I do is go to the bathroom. I'm ravenous, but I gotta see the damage first.

Looking in the mirror, all I see is blur—guess I'm still kind of teary-eyed from the reunion with my dog, damn. Or maybe whatever it was did this to my face is making me blind too? Man. Is this that Ebola shit, or West Nile or what?

I lean in and squint and it's bad.

It's almost kind of cool, how gross my face looks. Like when you were a little kid, and you'd show someone your chewed up food? Or when you snuck into a slasher flick when you were fifteen or something? I can't stop looking because it's so nasty.

You can still recognize the shape of my face, and there are clear patches here and there on the cheek and neck. The forehead's pretty much okay. That's something. But those boils, that rash... they're all over my neck and one side of my face, it looks like I got burned really bad or maybe electrocuted. Man, what happened? My face is covered with sores and *what the fuck happened to me*?

I have to look away before I start to cry again.

Food. That'll cheer me up. I'm so hungry that even my own messed-up face can't spoil my appetite.

I open the fridge, grab some leftover Chinese food and a beer, and there's a note on the beer box.

Uh oh.

I put the fried rice on a plate and start heating it while I open the beer and look at the note. Nina's handwriting. Oh boy.

Dear Bruce

I don't know why I'm putting 'dear' on this letter because I am so mad at you I can barely hold this pen without breaking it in half. What kind of man are you? You're no kind of a man you can't provide for your family and I accepted that you can't keep down a job and I got used to that too but I hoped you could at least respect yourself. But you don't. The only thing you respect is your fucking Budweiser. I was close to throwing all your beer down the drain but you know what? I'm tired of trying. You're a lousy boozer and I'm tired of even trying to stop you. So why don't you go ahead and drink yourself to death if you can even sober up enough to find your way home?

FUCK YOU.

—Nina

Wow.

Well, it could have been worse, I guess.

The microwave dings. Snack time.

I twist off the beer cap and get out the plate and sit down at the table, I take my first swig and almost spit it out. It's *terrible*! What the fuck? It tastes like piss, like vinegar, it gives this sting in my nose like when you smell hydrogen peroxide, it's *nasty*. Fuck!

Did Nina put something in my beer? Man, that's not like her. She's never been sneaky. Mean yes, mad yes, but never sneaky. Must just be a bad batch, but I'm disappointed. Budweiser's never let me down like that.

I get a forkful of fried rice and it's turned too. How old is this stuff? It tastes rancid, jeez, it's got that fishy taste like when meat goes bad and, and that kind of grapey taste like sour milk and the next thing I know I've puked all over myself.

Perfect.

"Peaches ol' girl, this is not my lucky day."

I go, get in the shower and find out that those patches of scab or scar or whatever the hell they are, it's all over my body. Great. My cock has a cracked, leathery looking *thing* on it, right at the base and spreading on both balls. There's some pus or something coming out. Man, if I hadn't puked before I'd puke now. I can't stop poking at it, it doesn't hurt or anything, but *man*.

I start to cry, again. The water's running down my whole mangled body, and when I look at the drain, I can see a little blood going down there too. Wonderful.

At least I've got something to throw in Nina's face when she gets home. Where the hell are they?

I try some more food, but it's all wrong. Even bread, just plain white bread without even any butter, I bought it on Wednesday so it's got no chance to go bad... I can't even swallow it. I gag it, cough it up. Peanut butter, bananas, milk, stuff that *anyone* can eat but I just can't choke it down. And I'm *hungry*, I'm starving, but nothing's good, and I'm still looking in the cupboards when I hear Peaches bark and the back door open.

I'm still not sure how to handle this. Do I tell Nina I really was drinking, got drunk, passed out? Heck, do I *know* I passed out? I'm sick, maybe that brought me down. It's not like she didn't know I was going to Pitchers & Pool after work. It was Friday, after all. She's not going to think I was out buying her a gift or something.

I see her coming in and Brooke's right behind her, they've got a bunch of shopping bags. I stand up and turn.

"Hey."

Nina drops the bags and just stares. Brooke's less stunned, her face crinkles up and she says "Ewww!"

"Nina. It's me."

"Bruce?" She can't believe it. Doesn't want to believe it. But she takes a little half-step toward me.

"Yeah. It's me, I'm..." Sorry. "...home."

greg stolze

I move forward and she moves back.

"What? Yeah, I'm... something happened, but I'm still..."

"What happened?"

"...I'm still *me*, c'mon..."

"What *happened* to you, Bruce? Jesus Christ, your face!"

"I don't know."

"You don't *know*?"

"How can you not know?" Brooke asks.

"Look, all I remember is..." The bar. Drinking. The guy from Lawn. (The ugly man. Fire. The stink of the ugly man's breath as his sharp pasty nose got close, closer, his breath was like rotted meat and I could see bugs on his *clothes*, jeez, a huge centipede crawling along his collar, and fire, *fire*...)

"Are you okay, dad?"

"It doesn't hurt."

"How can it *not hurt*?" Nina asks.

"Because it *doesn't*, shit, you think I don't know if I'm in *pain* or not?"

"Well I'm *sorry* Bruce, but you disappear for a whole night and day and when you come back you're... you're... were you in an accident?"

"I don't know." Fire. "I... maybe. I think so."

There's a little pause, and I can see on her face that she's having a bad thought, and then her eyes narrow and she says, "You weren't *driving*, were you?"

"What?"

"Bruce just... just tell me you weren't behind the wheel."

"I don't fucking believe this."

"You were, weren't you?"

"I show up covered in wounds and sores and instead of, of maybe showing me some *niceness* I get the third degree?"

"*Were you driving drunk again*?"

"No!" Before I know it, I'm right in her face, right inches away and I don't know what I was doing last night but I can't let her win this...

"No Nina, I was not fucking driving drunk, I don't drive, I haven't driven since then and *I'm never driving again*, are you happy now?"

I guess I grabbed her wrist because I can feel it in my hand, her skin is so warm, like hot...

"Huh Nina? Satisfied? That *okay* with you?"

Man, I'm just getting madder and madder and Nina, Christ, she looks scared, her eyes are big as pool balls (beautiful) she jerks her hand out and backs away, she stumbles over one of the bags she dropped and falls, she's (trapped) funny and I can't help it, I laugh, it feels good to look at her sprawled down there with her skirt coming up above her knees a little, breathing heavy and, man, she smells *great*...

Then something smashes into my back. Thump. Hard enough to make me stumble forward. I turn.

Holy shit. Brooke just slugged me in the back.

"Hey!"

"Leave her alone!"

"You don't hit me," I start, and this time she kicks me. Hard. In the shins. With her pointy-toed little boots.

I'm forward and I get her by the shoulders, she's hitting my side with her little fists and she smells great too, just like her mother, her binky little short-sleeve sweater tears under my hands and her skin feels hot too, so good, like that sex hot you feel afterwards when you're just lying there (mmm...) and then I bite her neck and yes, this is what I was hungry for.

Man.

It's maybe an hour later. I finally pulled over the car. Yeah, I took the car, Nina's car, the car I'm not supposed to drive for a bunch of reasons. I got bigger problems right about now.

I think I... I was a little bit out of it for a while there. When I was... when Brooke and I were...

What did I do to her? What did I do to my *daughter*?

It was like when I was younger and I'd go to bars with bands, and sometimes after the first pitcher I'd just trance out, not really drunk but buzzed and with the music going and I could just sit at a table and drink and listen and look without really thinking about anything at all. I think it was like that, when I was... when... then.

Nina brought me out of it.

Jesus. Nina.

Nina was screaming and she didn't bother with a simple punch like Brooke. Nina stepped in the kitchen and got a knife.

There's a hole in my coveralls, a little blood on it, right by the ribs on my side. (Coveralls? When did I put on...? Oh, after the shower, right.) When I pulled the knife out and looked at the hole, it just closed right up. Of course, I didn't do that until I was done with Nina.

I hope I didn't kill her. I hope to *Christ* I didn't. But she stabbed me and I got mad, I hit her (which, drunk or sober, I never did before) and then... well, I hit her in the face, busted her lip and I saw the... the blood...

I saw it and I wanted more. I wanted it again. She'd let go of the knife and I grabbed her, like I'd done Brooke, and it was (even better) even worse, in a way, with Nina. It reminded me of making love to her, to be perfectly honest, I mean, I was... sucking... right on a spot I would kiss all the time, your face fits right there where the neck meets the shoulder and the skin is so soft and tender, so salty... but this was no kiss. Shit, I bit her open, I was working my tongue in to make the hole bigger, I *chewed*, I didn't care if she bled to death as long as I was there to catch it, get it, drink it all.

At some point, it was enough, I guess. Usually, you drink or eat a bunch and you feel sluggish and drowsy, but not me, not... this. I felt great. Strong and tough. More alive than I had in years. Since the accident, really.

I've gone crazy, haven't I? I'm around the bend. I'm a serial killer now. Is this how it happens? One day, or night, you wake up and you're psycho? You attack your wife and daughter and then just leave them piled up by the back door? Steal the car for bonus points?

Man.

Step one. Money. I'm going to need some. And a place to hide. I can't keep the car, I don't have a license. Yeah, I don't have a license and my wife's going to tell the cops I stole it after trying to kill her.

Unless I killed her.

Right, money. And a place to hide out. And get rid of the car.

Peaches barks.

"You're okay girl, just stay still, good dog."

Cash, hideout and dog food.

Money's easiest, for a little bit. I pull over by an ATM, try for the maximum withdrawal, but there's insufficient funds. That's me and Nina in a nutshell. I see how much there is and it's $793.57. I withdraw $790 because the machine has nothing smaller than a ten in it.

One down.

There's a Motel 6 up ahead and I pull into the parking lot. Maybe they won't notice the car for a while. Maybe I can get a leg up on the cops. Or I could get on the highway now, just run, get to Pittsburgh by six in the morning. They wouldn't look for me there, I don't know anyone there.

The only problem with that is, I don't know anyone there.

Crap, maybe what I should do is just check into a hospital. Something is clearly very wrong with my skin to make it break out like it did, but Nina had to go and fuck *that* up by pissing me off so bad. Thanks, honey.

No, that's not fair. This is my own fault. I snapped. Maybe this stuff that's in my skin, maybe it's in my brain too. Maybe that's what's making me crazy and violent and messed up.

Shit, what am I going to do?

There's a bar next to the Motel 6. Budweiser light in the window.

Lord knows I could use something to calm me down.

It's midnight. I've been sitting in the bar and not drinking. Nina would be so proud, if she knew. If she's alive.

I tried, of course. Shot of Jack, usually a big comfort. No dice. I had to spit it back in the shot glass before I puked it.

Once, when I was going to those dumb AA meetings, I heard about this stuff, some drug. I can't remember what it was called, but they put it in you and it makes you allergic to alcohol. I must have gotten dosed with some of that stuff. It's the only thing that makes sense.

I hope Peaches is okay out in the car.

Man, I hope Brooke and Nina are okay at home.

I came into this dive, ordered my Jack, got the oogie look from the bartender who, I think, just barely decided I might sue him if he tossed me out for being ugly. Not that the people here care. This isn't a place where people go to drink martinis and giggle and flirt and hear music. It's a barfly bar. It's a place where drunks go to get drunk. I got a bunch of quarters and took my drink to a dark corner by the phone. I was happy to be out of sight and I'm sure the bartender was glad too.

First, I called Gino. Gino and me have been pals since grade school and, sure, we drifted apart after we got married and everything, but the chips are down and I thought he'd help me.

Good thinking, Bruce.

The good news was, Gino's become the kind of solid citizen who's home on a Saturday night. The bad news is, he's the kind of solid citizen who won't invite a drunk he hasn't talked to in five years to stay with him, his wife, and his two daughters on short notice. Yeah, it pisses me off, but I can't blame him. A man's gotta look out for his family first, I guess.

I call Spence. Get the answering machine. I call Tony. Answering machine. I know Tony's got a cell, but I don't have his cell number (because why would I need it? I see him at work every day and most weekends).

Who else would help me? Nina's brother? Sure. He'd help me black my eyes so they match the rest of my face. My folks are both dead, and my brother's way the hell out in Florida, I haven't talked to him for forever.

I call him anyhow.

"Hello?"

"Hey there, Todd."

"Who is this?"

I'm a little hurt, but what should I expect? "It's me, Bruce. Your brother."

"Bruce? What the...? What time is it?"

"It's late, I know, I'm sorry..."

"Are you okay? I mean, are you in trouble? What's wrong?"

What's right? "Well..."

"You can tell me."

Family. "I, uh... I had a thing with Nina..."

"Bruce, have you been drinking?"

Jesus, what is it with everyone? Like they never have a fucking beer. "It's not that, really," I say. Though I guess you could say it's exactly that, I just wasn't drinking what he thought. "We had a fight and I'm kind of out of the house."

"Where are you now?"

"I'm at a hotel."

There's a pause.

"What do you want me to do?" Todd asks.

"Hell, how should I know? Man, can't a guy just get some, some support?"

"Okay, I'm, look, I'm sorry, but I what I meant was... what do you want me to *do*? Do you want me to come up there?"

"Could you?" For a minute I almost think it could work. But it wouldn't. "Uh... well, as I think about it... nah. Nah, don't come up. It wouldn't help." Dragging Todd in is just going to slow me down and fuck us both up. I mean, what if I'm contagious?

(Jesus, what if I infected Nina and Brooke?)

Another pause.

"Is this something you and Nina can work out?"

"I don't... think so."

"Huh."

"If you'd like to continue, please insert another..." I shut up the phone's mechanical voice by cramming in more quarters.

"I thought you were in a hotel," Todd says.

"I'm using the pay phone in the lobby."

"Oh." He clears his throat. "Do you... y'know... want to come down here and stay? For a while, y'know?" He doesn't sound really thrilled.

"Maybe. Yeah, that might... I'll have to think about it, okay?"

"All right. You got a number where you're staying?"

"Not yet. I'll, uh... I'm gonna check in and then I'll call you again, all right?"

"Okay. You sure you're...?"

"I'll be all right. G'bye."

Okay. Is it a plan? It's a plan. I'll go down and stay with Todd, get my act together, maybe get some goddamn *medical attention*. Florida, sure, they're crammed full of illegal immigrants so their hospital probably won't check me against Illinois' outstanding warrants. That stands to reason, right? I could set out right now, drive like a fiend and be in the Sunshine State by Monday, just drive all night and day.

(*Fire.*)

...and suddenly I've got the creeps. Suddenly I'm scared. Suddenly, I don't want to go to the sunshine state. What the hell?

I make a few more calls. Steve. Dave. Neither of 'em help me out, neither of 'em give me the time of day. (Well, okay, Dave tells me it's almost one o'clock and asks if I have any manners.)

I'm so desperate I even call Lydia. She's friendly at least. From the time she says "Hello, whoozis?" I can tell she's soused.

"It's Bruce Miner," I tell her.

"You gotta wrong number."

"No, I... this is Lydia, right? Lydia Wheeler?"

"Mm hm?"

"You were my AA sponsor. You remember?"

There's a pause and then she just laughs.

"Alcoholics 'Nonymous," she snorts. "What a crock of shit. You think it stopped me drinking?"

"I guess not."

"It just slowed me down. You know, like a halftime. Now I 'preciate my liquor more than ever."

Oh boy. "That's great for you."

"You mus' be feeling 'tempted,' right? You're 'in crisis'? Otherwise you wouldn'ta called."

"Uh huh, well, yeah." I'm trying to think of a polite way to hang up, trying to think why I should bother being polite, when the bartender yells out that it's last call.

Lydia hears, she laughs. "Come over here," she says. "I've got a bottle of Beefeater. That'll take care of your crisis."

Gin's never been my drink of choice, but what the hell? It's not like I've got anywhere else to go.

"Sure," I say.

Lydia gives me directions to her place, which is way out there in Aurora, and when I get there it's 3 A.M. and I can't fucking find it. I drive around those lousy, dirty streets for an hour. I can't find her address, Peaches is snoozing in the shotgun seat and I finally just punt the whole idea. It was dumb anyway. What am I supposed to do? Hole up with drunk Lydia until this blows over? I'm not going to be back at Home Depot working the key-cutter in a month. Not unless I square things with Nina.

As soon as I think that, I know it's right. It's what I've got to do. I was being a chump, running away. I do that. But I should at least make sure Nina and Brooke are okay before I do anything else. I owe them that much. Shit, I owe them a lot better than that, but right now it's all I can do.

I get on the highway. I'm not tired at all, hell, I must have slept something like sixteen straight hours. I take the Harlem Avenue exit, just to stretch it out a little. I haven't driven in a long time.

The city is creepy at night. Empty, and in that yellow lamp glare everything looks washed out and dead, like after a gas attack or something. The only people out are drug dealers, drug buyers and the worst whores of all, ugly and used up cheapies who look even worse by streetlight. Even the bums are smart enough to be under cover by this time of night. It's just the dregs and me.

I start to see newspaper trucks driving around, and other delivery trucks getting an early start. I see cops. Eventually one of the cops turns on his lights and pulls me over.

Maybe it's just as well.

"License and registration, sir?"

"Look, I give up."

"Excuse me sir? If you could just give me your license and registration…"

"Ain't got one. No license I mean. And if the car isn't showing up stolen, then my wife didn't report it. I stole this car. I give up. I'm turning myself in." I keep my hands on the steering wheel, where he can see them.

He starts muttering into the radio on his shoulder. Peaches blinks and sits up.

"Is that a dog?"

"Yeah, it's my dog. Her name's Peaches," I say, though I'm sure he couldn't possibly care less.

I'm watching him in the rearview mirror and from his posture I can tell he's thinking that a dog is all he friggin' needs.

"Sir, I'm going to have to call animal control to take care of the dog."

"No, look, come *on* man, the *dog* didn't do anything wrong!"

"I realize that sir, but they're equipped to tend to the animal."

"Look, when my wife... I mean, it's her dog too, okay? You got to make sure she knows who has Peaches and how she can go get her, right?"

"Your dog will be fine, sir." I can't tell for sure, but I think he relaxes a little. He's still got his hand near his gun, but he's not looking quite as cautious.

"You got a dog?" I ask.

"Yeah," he says. "Actually it's my ex-wife's. She didn't want it. Little yappy dog named Bobo."

This is almost nice. He's not being so cop-polite to me anymore. We could just be two guys talking, like at a barbecue or something, talking about our dogs. I lean back a little and he's alert again, hand by the gun again. I put my hands back on the wheel. We're not just two guys talking.

He gets my name and calls it in. He reads me my rights and slowly talks me out of the car. Peaches starts barking and I calm her down. He thanks me for that as he puts the cuffs on me.

"Do we really need...?"

"Standard arrest procedure, sir."

Sir again. Crap.

He opens the back seat of his cruiser and puts his hand on my head so I don't bump it against the doorframe. He's wearing rubber gloves—when did he put those on? I get in and it's cramped and tiny, just a plastic seat with no cushion.

Despite my drinking which, I'll admit, is not completely under control, I haven't been arrested more than twice. Once was when I was a teenager, which I don't really count. And after the accident. So I'm hardly used to being in the backseats of cop cars. But there I sit and there I wait.

And wait.

And wait.

The holdup is, I guess, the animal control van. He keeps getting on the radio about it and sounding more and more impatient. He asks them if he can get someone else to come out and watch the dog while he takes me in, I don't hear the reply but I guess it's negative because we just keep sitting.

He looks at his watch.

"It's nearly dawn," he says, and something about that makes me scared. Then the dogcatcher finally shows up and everything goes crazy.

While the animal control guy is trying to get Peaches out of the car (and she doesn't want to go, she's doesn't know who this guy is) the first ray of sunlight comes over a roof and (fire) falls on me in the car and it *burns*, shit, it's horrible and I can't help but yell and try to get away. (Fire)

The cop hears me freaking out and turns, he was standing near the dog pound guy and *holy shit my skin is starting to smoke!*

(Fire!)

I'm burning alive and then I get my hands free, smash the window, I scramble out and the cop runs over, I hit him, knock him back...

"Peaches! Get 'im!"

Peaches goes for the dog catcher and the cop has out his gun, just an hour ago we were talking like guys but he shoots and I grab him by the throat, grab his arm, pick him up and throw him across the hood of his car, the sun is getting higher, getting hotter

(Fire!)

and I run, run for the darkness...

"Peaches!"

...run for the shadows.

I wake up and think *Where the hell...*? Then I remember. The storm sewers.

I pinch the watch and, yep, I slept all damn day again. This is getting really old.

At least this time I remember what happened... sort of. I punched out that cop and ran away down an alley and there was a sewer grating and (I ripped it out of the pavement) it must have been made with some really cheap concrete. Big surprise. Everything the city of Cicero does is crooked. I wouldn't be surprised if they were patching potholes with buckwheat flour. Anyhow, the stupid thing came right out in my hands and I jumped in the hole and ran.

Now I'm in the pitch-black damp, I hear rats and I got no idea where I am at all.

"Peaches?"

No reply. Just echoes.

It takes me about an hour of stumbling around before I find some light. It's another sewer grating, right under a lamppost I guess. I sit there a while, grateful that it's been a dry summer.

My side hurts and I look down. There's a hole.

The hole in my coveralls is dirty and damp and about as big around as my little finger. There's maybe a little blood on it, but when I was lying in the water it must have washed it, kind of.

The hole in me is the same size. I can actually stick my finger in it (ow!) and feel guts and it's not bleeding.

Sweet Jesus Christ.

It closes up as I'm looking at it.

Okay, this is *really* not real. But hey, I'm insane, right? I lost my nut, jumped my family, punched out a cop. Man, they're going to lock me up until doomsday for that one...

Unless it's all a dream, like. Or a hallucination, I guess. Sure. I mean, that hole just closing up, like when Nina stabbed me, what if those are just hallucinations? That makes sense, more sense than them just going away, and if that stuff's all in my head, why not the rest of it? Maybe I've been on some crazy DT thing, maybe right now I'm tied down in a nice warm hospital and I never hurt my wife or kid or anyone else.

A rat crawls on my foot and I jump and you know what? Crazy or sane, I don't have that much imagination.

I start looking around for a way out of the sewer.

I find a maintenance hatch that I can unlock from the inside, and someone's already cut a hole in the bottom of the fence, so I don't have to crawl over the barbed wire on top. I've still got my wallet with my $790, but Peaches doesn't come when I call. Why would she? I probably walked a mile underground and she's had all day to run. She probably ran home.

Home.

I find a train station with a change machine, get quarters, call home.

"Hello?"

Nina sounds awful, like she's been crying, but she's alive.

"Aw Nina, thank God you're okay…"

"Bruce?" She's surprised. I guess I should've expected.

"Sweetie, I'm sorry, I'm *so sorry*, I…"

"Bruce, where are you?"

Something sounds weird. Off. The Nina I'm used to would be yelling at me.

"Nina, is Brooke okay?"

"Where *are* you, Bruce?" She sounds tightly wound.

"First tell me if Brooke's alright."

"What do *you* think? No, she's not alright, she's in the *hospital* in a *coma* because of what *you did to her!* She may not come out of it and she may have brain damage because of *you,* you *sick, evil fuck!* Now tell me where you *are* so I can have the cops come and *bust your worthless ass!*"

I drop the receiver and run.

I don't know how much time passes. I keep walking. I try to stay out of the light so people don't see me. I walk by the shitty bars where I can't drink anymore, and the shitty houses like the one I can't go home to, and past all the shitty people who are still better than I am.

I'm walking along by the railroad tracks, not doing much, when I hear a voice.

"Are you Bruce?"

What makes me stop is the dog's bark. I turn and she's coming at me—Peaches, she found me!

"Hey! Whooza good girl, huh? Who's my good girl?"

I kneel, and she's in my arms.

"Yeah, she's a smart animal."

I finally look up, and I shudder.

(run)

The guy with Peaches is wearing Redwing boots, jeans, and even though it's summer he's got on a leather jacket— one of the old kind, like a *Hogan's Heroes* jacket. He's about my height, probably my age, shaggy gray-brown hair, sharp blue eyes and skin so white it looks a little blue too. He has a long nose and high cheekbones and thin lips.

(Run)

And I don't know why, but he scares the crap outta me. I only realize I'm getting ready to bolt when Peaches gives a little wimper when I stand back up. I glance down at her and that happy, pitiful look she's got catches me like it does every time. I can't just run off on her too, can I?

"It's okay," he says. "I ain't here to hurt you."

"You a cop?" But I know he's something worse than a cop...

"Nope. Name's Masterson." He steps closer and I notice that he's got dirty fingernails. For some reason that makes me feel a little easier.

"I guess you've been looking for me."

"I guess so. You need some help, I reckon."

"Unless you're a doctor, you..."

"You don't need a doctor."

"Maybe you didn't get a good look." I step close, so that he can see my gross face.

Unlike everyone else, he doesn't flinch.

"You ain't sick," he says. "You're just a monster."

When he grins, his mouth isn't right. His teeth are all fangs, like inch-long needles.

"C'mon," he says.

"Where are we going?" I follow anyway, but I still want to know.

"You're going to meet the other vampires."

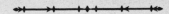

It's fucked up. It's insane. A vampire? That's crazy. (But then, I'm crazy.) Vampires aren't real. They're like ghosts and werewolves and the thing under the bed, they're not...

Although, it does explain a hell of a lot.

We catch a cab and don't talk, and we go to an okay neighborhood in Berwyn, right nearby. Ordinary house, right up the street from a school for fuck's sake. It's a little nicer than mine, built around the same time.

Before we go in, Masterson stops me on the steps. "You're gonna want to wig out, when you go in there," he says. "Try to keep your shit together."

"What?"

"Look, you know when two nasty dogs meet? It's like lots of snarling and fighting and shit, right?"

"Yeah, but what—?"

"Well there's a part of you, that's like one of those dogs. You run into another predator, it'll want to fight or run or just wig the fuck out. Like when your dog brought me to you."

This is all too much. Way too much. "Why should I go in there, then?"

"'Cause I ain't giving you a choice, Brucey." He smiles that needle-toothed smile of his. "But don't fret. It'll get easier." Then he knocks.

As soon as the door opens, I feel a shudder of fear and rage pound through me. Masterson puts his hand on my shoulder. "Easy," he says.

I swallow down the panic and force myself to look at the guy standing in the entry to the house. He's skinny and pale, like Masterson. He's taller, looks like he's about twenty, with a blonde crew cut that's a little long on the top, spiked up with gel or something. His eyes are brown and he wrinkles his nose at me. He's wearing white leather pants and one of those jackets that buttons right up to the neck, like a dentist.

"Found our lost lamb," Masterson says.

"Your lamb stinks like shit, Ambrose," the host says, but lets us in. "The dog stays in the yard."

"Go on in back, Peaches," Masterson says, and Peaches does it. I figure Ambrose is Masterson's first name.

The house, inside, looks normal. No coffins, no skulls, nothing... monster-y. Ratty carpet, hardwood floors, a couple framed pictures of Chicago buildings in the living room.

"I am Raphael Ladue," leather-pants announces. "You may remain here as long as you do nothing to endanger me or my activities, but I expect a high standard of behavior. Do you understand?"

"Just let him shower," Ambrose mutters, lowering onto a sofa.

Raphael Ladue glares at him. "It's in here," he says.

I hear the door open while I'm washing, and when I get out I find that someone's left a pair of shorts and a T-shirt from Taste of Chicago 2000 on the floor in the bathroom. They're a pretty awkward fit, but my coveralls are a loss.

Going to the living room, I hear Ambrose and Raphael talking.

"...Just hand him over," Raphael says. "Get Lucky off our backs, maybe get him to take me seriously..."

"He says 'frog' and you jump. Yeah. That's the *best* way to earn his respect. I can make this right, don't worry."

"You *better* fix this, that's all I'm saying. I'm not about to throw away everything..."

"Yeah yeah. Look, are the nose four at two coming or not?"

"Filthfoot is on his way. I haven't heard anything from Naked or Anita."

"I'm here," says a woman, and suddenly she's there.

She's naked and fat and black, but not a proper black. I mean, a black person is usually brown, right? She's black like really dark mud, like a gray black, wet ashes... like nothing living. She stands there and just looking I can tell she's *slimy*, her skin's more like a frog than a person and her eyes... they're little pools of blood.

I lose it.

"Gawddamn!"

I turn and run. I hear Raphael yelling, "Don't *do* that, dammit!" I hear them getting up behind me and I can hear that... *thing*... laughing—a little tinkly laugh, high and pretty and *wrong* coming from a walking pile of grease.

I'm trying to get the back door unlocked when I feel a hand on my shoulder. I bat it away.

"Calm down! Look, it's okay. Really."

Suddenly, I can do it. I can calm down. I turn to look at him and I don't understand how I could have ever thought Raphael was being mean or snotty. He's my friend. He's going to make everything work out as long as I can just keep looking at his face and hearing his voice...

"You're okay," he tells me, and I believe him. I slump down against the door and start crying, mostly just from relief.

"Poor thing. Is this better?" It's that same pretty voice, only now it's coming out of an ordinary woman wearing a flannel shirt and cutoffs.

"You... you were..." I swallow, hard. "Is this real?"

"Nothing is real," she says, which doesn't help.

"We're here to help you," Raphael says, and I look up at him, grateful.

Just then the back door opens and I fall back, hitting someone's grimy old pants. I look up into the face of another monster—this time his face all *wrong*—like each eye is just a half-inch away from where it's supposed to be, and his ears are too small, and his nose is just a little tilted, and his mouth is just a half-inch too wide. It's a face, all the pieces are there in more or less the right place but... they're wrong. *He's* wrong.

"This the guy?" he asks.

Peaches is way over in the farthest corner of the yard, whining.

"I've got the police video saved," Raphael says. "That's how we found out about you."

"You really should be a little more subtle," Filthfoot says. That's the guy with the mixed around face. He's dressed like a bum, and barefoot. His name fits.

"Give the poor fellow time," says Naked, who still looks normal. Completely normal. So normal, in fact, that I'd have a hard time describing her.

"So, did one of you...?" This is Ambrose, and he asks it looking at Naked and Filthfoot. I have no idea what he's asking.

"Not me," Filthfoot says. "I got enough sorrow in my life."

"No," Naked says. She leans forward and takes my chin in her hand, like... like she's got every right to do it. "He's one of ours but not one of mine."

"You think it was Anita?" Ambrose asks.

"Anita had some stuff going down." Raphael squints at me. "I don't know if she'd... you know..."

"What are all you guys talking about?"

"Vampires don't just happen," Ambrose says. "They're made by other vampires, and it's not easy. It's not something you do by accident. And it's not something anyone is supposed to do lightly."

"It's not something anyone is supposed to do *at all*," Filthfoot adds.

"So... what does that mean?"

"Well, you're a rogue, and you were pretty blatant with the attacks on your wife and daughter..." Raphael says, and that hurts. I was right the first time. He *is* an asshole.

"Hey," Naked says. "Take it easy on him."

"What? It's just the truth, isn't it? He got on TV slugging it out with a cop, and the only reason they didn't find out about him ripping up the pavement is that they're too dumb to believe what's before their eyes." He turns to me, and that good feeling I had about him earlier is totally gone. "Listen. You are a creature of darkness, damned to hunt the night forever or until your own destruction. You are a curse upon humanity, like all of us. You can never go back, and the sooner you accept your role as a predator, the less damage you'll do overall."

Ambrose rolls his eyes behind Raphael's back.

"Wait, you mean I... I have to...?"

"Drink the blood of the living?" Naked asks. "Oh yeah."

"You know that's not true," Ambrose says. "There's animals."

"It's not the same," Filthfoot says, "Though it is a good idea for a newcomer like... say, what's your name, anyhow?"

"I'm Bruce."

He laughs and repeats it, and for a second I think he says *Brews*, but when he adds, "That's a good one. Fits your look," I realize he's actually saying *Bruise*.

"No," Raphael says. "His name *is* Bruce. Like Bruce Lee or Bruce Jenner?"

"My mistake." Filthfoot turns to face me. "Lots of us change our names after the embrace. You know—keeps your mind on your business."

"Huh?"

"After you become a vampire," Ambrose clarifies. "You have to cut ties to your old life. You know that, right?"

"But what about...?" I'm about to say *Nina and Brooke*, but I know the answer. Hell, I'm the poster child for why vampires should cut ties. I sink back into the couch.

"Hey," Naked says, leaning forward. "It's not so bad. We never get old, never sicken..."

"Never have to take a whizz," Raphael adds, sneering, "And all it costs is your soul."

"It does not," Filthfoot objects. "Don't listen to pretty-boy there. We're part of God's plan. We do important work."

"I don't see…"

"You just haven't found your path. We are the scourge of the wicked, the punishers of man."

"Yeah, and that's pretty fun, isn't it?" Ambrose says.

I can't tell if he's joking or not.

They tell me a bunch of other stuff. Sunlight and fire can kill me. Stakes in the heart are bad news. Garlic and holy water are bullshit, and so are roses. (I'd never heard that roses were supposed to hurt vampires.) I don't have to be invited into a house. I have a reflection, but it's messed up unless I concentrate… just a bunch of stuff, I can't take it and I tell them.

"You better take it," Raphael says. "If you're going to spill the secret and mess everything up, I don't want it happening here."

"Now, it's a lot to… digest," Naked says, "But if, as you say, you have no idea who embraced you, and you know nothing about it and you were… well, made and dumped… then you're doing well."

"Yeah," Filthfoot says. "We'll take care of you, even if your sire doesn't."

"What's a sire?"

"Don't worry about it," Ambrose says. "Not yet. Here, c'mon out in back and I'll teach you a trick, something you can use right away."

We go in the backyard and everyone else stays inside. Maybe Ambrose waved 'em back, I didn't see.

"You already twigged to a little bit of beast speech," he says, rubbing Peaches' ears. "That's a good skill. Let's work on that."

"What? Whaddaya mean… beast speech? I just, I mean… Peaches is my dog, that's all."

"It's not all. Animals don't like us, they can smell us or something… we give 'em the creeps. Unless we use the beast speech on 'em. Not everyone gets the knack, but you did it on your pooch here. You can use it on anything."

"Anything?"

"Well, not bugs or worms or, you know, germs or what have you. But anything with enough of a brain. F'rinstance... okay, see that cat over there?" He's pointing at a big stray with long gray hair. "Call it to you. Good and loud now."

"Here, kitty kitty...?"

"No no no, you have to say it like you mean it. Put some, you know, some *catness* into it. Like this. *Heeeeere kitteeeey.*" His voice has a weird, piercing quality. "You gotta look it in the eye. *C'mere, poos pooos.*"

The cat hops up on the fence and gives Ambrose a wary look.

"*C'mere kitty. No one's gonna huuuurt you.*" He walks forward, holds out his hands, and it jumps into his arms.

"There." It's purring. "This will get you through a lot of lean times."

Then he sinks those monster fangs into it, right by the neck, so deep I'm surprised the head doesn't just fall off.

I stumble back, but it's over quick.

"You know what I hate 'bout eating pussy? The taste. And the hair that gets stuck in your teeth."

I just stare at him.

"That was a joke," he says.

"Uh huh."

"You do it."

"I don't want to kill a cat."

He sighs. "Neither do I, particularly. But you need blood, cat's got it. It's not the same, not nearly, but a cat or a dog or a squirrel... it's a smart way to start your night. Keeps the hunger down. Keeps you from doing anything stupid. Anything crazy. Look it in the eyes first and tell it anything it wants to hear..."

"Isn't there some other way?"

He sighs. "In theory you could just hang out by the slaughterhouses. That seems like a great idea, right? So great that lots of older, tougher, vampires already had it. Emergency rooms are too risky unless you really know what you're doing, and you don't. Small kosher butcher shops are too piss-ant for the Prince or his posse to bother with, but the rabbis get awful suspicious if the same guy comes back night after night asking for the same thing. Nah, it's this or people."

"Prince?"

"It's about as dumb as it sounds," he says, "but he and his gang of assholes will make your eternity hell if they find out what you did to that cop and your family."

My family. Nina and Brooke.

Cats will keep me from doing anything crazy.

"So I... I just talk to it?"

Chapter Two:
Persephone

Bella leans forward, lips parted, eyes half closed and says, "I wish I had your tits."

"I wish I had your hair," I say, not meaning it. I'm putting makeup on her, dramatic burgundy lipstick over a layer of powder with another layer of lipstick underneath that. I've already done her eyes with a touch of rose-brown shadow and mascara. Bella's hair is a big dishwater blonde ball, supported by a glittering series of fake-jewel pins and with a few limp tendrils hanging off it. She looks scrawny and pale and like she's trying too hard. Her knobby white knees are prominent between the high hem of a short black skirt and the high tops of patent leather boots. A pair of tank tops, black and gray, both rise above a stomach that isn't buff—it's actually concave. She looks anorexic.

"You really should smudge the makeup on your hand before putting it on me," she says. Like it matters.

She's been dead for fifty-seven years and we're going clubbing.

She lets me step out first, which is kind. I start Pushing Out when the bouncer outside looks at me.

That's how I think of it—Pushing Out. I read somewhere about pheromones, about secret chemicals that make insects respond, make them mate. That's what I do. I project a wave of Wanting Me and I can see the bouncer's expression change when it hits him.

He waives our cover.

When I go down the hall into the club, the music is already deafening—something with the obligatory penetrating bass. Perfect, I'm sure, for people who came here hoping for some penetration. There's a repetitive lyric over the top—"Do it! Do it! Do it!" Delightfully subtle, uh huh.

I love the moment I enter, with the strobe lights and the disco ball specks and the colored lasers zipping all over the place. I Push Out and everyone turns.

Inside, I feel a little bit of "this isn't me!" but it's nothing negative. It's like that first Halloween in tenth grade when Betsy Plesser convinced me to dress up as a sexy kitty cat (she was dressed as a sexy belly dancer) and we went to the stupid Halloween dance and the boys all looked. The ones our age, from our class at school, they didn't know what to do with us except make some jerky comments, but a couple older boys, like seniors, asked us to dance.

That's what I think of every time I Push Out. I think of their eyes, in the dim, wanting me.

Dancing with seniors wasn't me either. I was smart little Linda Moore, jazz choir and debate team. I followed rules. But for that night I felt like the kind of free, smart-alecky girl who could ride on motorcycles and drink beer and smoke and still, somehow, never get date raped or in a car crash or anything. The next morning when I put on my normal jeans and normal sweater and went to school, I knew that there really weren't girls like that, that being irresponsible and antisocial and *naughty* had horrible consequences, with STDs and unwanted pregnancies and being a dropout.

Only now I find out that there are girls like that, girls with no consequences. Bella's one, and tonight, I'm pretending to be one too. Maybe pretending enough that it's true.

I'm wearing gobs of black eyeliner and a water bra that pushes those boobs Bella envied right against the neckline of a black lace-and-spandex top. It's cropped around the bottom of my ribcage, showing off a henna "tattoo" that skirts my navel and disappears into the top of skintight black jeans with the top button undone. A couple armbands, a silver choker, and lace-up knee-high boots complete the ensemble.

Maybe I don't even need to pretend any more. Maybe, at this moment, with all the eyes on me, I really am this person called "Persephone."

Bella comes in then, and she Pushes Out too. And if mine is a little urge of Wanting Me, hers is a tidal wave of Needing Her.

Maxwell said there's something in everyone that wants to be overwhelmed, wants to be awestruck and dumb-founded. Something that wants to worship. He told me Bella could teach me how to touch that, that it would keep me safe and help me. He was right. He's always right. That's why I love and hate and fear and admire him.

Now, Bella's sallow skin takes on the cool deliciousness of whipped cream, and her little raccoon eyes become deep pools of liquid mystery. Her thin frame is the supermodel answer to every dieting woman's prayers, and her hair is a treasure of gold, not limp and fine but ferally matted, al-ready heavy with sweat, like she's already been at it with some guy, some lucky guy, the luckiest guy in Chicago....

I have to look away and remember that it's a trick that works on me, too.

We hit the dance floor ("Do it! Do it! Do it!") and we strut and pose and again. It's not me, not like the old me. The old me always thought she was comfortable with her body, and always had respect for herself, and putting on a display of lurid sensuality in public would have felt... silly. Even in the kitty cat costume I felt a little silly. I told my-self that this was self-esteem, that I didn't need to act like some slut from a pornographic phallocentric fairy tale to get a man's attention, that a proper man would be inter-ested in my brains and not in some lascivious display.

Bella turns to me on the dance floor and languidly winds her arms around me, grinding her pelvis into mine but not looking in my eyes. She's looking around at the boys, giving them a little show and I help her out. We're dyking it up on the dance floor, not like *real* lesbians but like the fake-pretend girl-on-girl lipstick lesbians from the skin flicks, the poor girls who are *so hot* that they have to make do with each other until Buck Hungwell delivers a pizza and gets a threesome as his tip.

Two John Travoltas are on the hook in no time. They disco up and offer us drinks at the top of their lungs (which is necessary over "Do it!"). Bella coquettes and we slink off to a table where it's marginally quieter.

Alpha Travolta is tall, hairy, looks like he does coke. Delta Travolta, his wingman, is tall, skinny and lacks confidence. Frankly, he broadcasts the kind of self-doubt that, in a saner world, Alpha would have.

They summon beverages that we ladies don't sip, they make small talk, and pretty soon Alpha is whispering in Bella's ear. She's giggling, she nods and they go off to the dance floor together. Delta asks me my name and I tell him "Persephone."

"Stephanie?"

"Persephone!"

"Oh." He nods, nods, nods with the music. "Cool name!"

Cool pickup line, asshole. He won't do.

Six months ago, I killed someone just like him.

We chat a little back and forth, he's a lineman for the phone company, and then I hit him with the torpedo.

"Yeah, I wasn't sure I'd be able to get out tonight," I yell. "My sitter cancelled and I had to get another on short notice!"

"Oh, you got a kid?"

It can't be four minutes before he's gone. I get up to survey the terrain. Bella and Alpha are on the dance floor. He's shaking his groove thang, she's making every guy jealous. Go, Alpha go. Enjoy it while you can.

I'm scanning the crowd for someone suitable, which isn't easy. Then I spot him from the back, by the bar. He's a little stocky, maybe five-foot-six, sandy brown hair... a beard? Maybe, maybe.

I mentally thank Delta for the drink as I stumble and spill it on Mr. Stocky.

"Whoopsie!" I act drunk. "Oh, I'm sorry, so sorry."

He turns. No beard, just one of those yucky soul patches. But he'll work.

"It's okay," he says, or at least I think that's what he says. There's a new song on. This time the refrain is "The system... is down! The system... is down!"

"Lemme buy you another one!" I shout at him.

"No, I've still got one," he says. He's blushing, which seals the deal for him if he can just screw his courage to the sticking point and *ask me to dance*. I'm reaching for his eyes, I'm pounding that slave spot in his brain like crazy, I can tell it's working but it seems mostly to be making him tongue-tied and shy.

I glance out on the dance floor and Bella is tearing it up, she's got two other Travoltas trying to beat down Alpha in a testosterone fight. She's glorious, like a crescent moon, her hard little apple boobs are twitching under her shirt, and even in the dim light, her nipples are visible from twenty paces.

"Look," I tell Soul Patch, "To tell you the truth, this creepy guy was hitting on me and if you'd dance with me he might get the message. Please?"

He has a sweet smile. "I'm Rick," he says. Yeah, I've chosen well.

We go out on the floor and he busts an awkward move, and I relax a bit. I flatter myself that I could do this without Bella's trick. I mean, she liked my tits, right? I'm a pretty girl, right?

It turns out I'm right, in the most awkward possible way.

A new guy comes in and tries to mooch me off of Rick. This new guy is huge—six-four at least, muscle-bound and flat-topped, with gross arm veins that only a steroid dealer could love.

Rick tries to back him off with body language, but not aggressively, which is maybe just as well. I turn my back pointedly but he just rotates around to my front again.

He's awful. He has on a purplish shirt that aches to be retro but is really just retardo. Fat gold links. Weight-lifted man-boobs that are probably bigger than mine. He's Omega Travolta, some inbred result of a million years of anonymous disco hookups.

Not only that, he speaks the line out of a hundred B-movies, mid-season TV pilots and Charles Atlas print ads.

"Hey baby, why don't you dance with a real man?"

The single-parent torpedo isn't enough for this lunk, but I give him one out. "I'm here with Rick," I say, pointing.

"You're here with Prick?" he asks. "Sweetie, I got all the prick you need right here."

And lord help me, he grabs my hand and puts it on his crotch.

Okay Omega. You had your chance.

"You are inadequate," I tell him, and I don't bother to yell it. I'm not pushing any more. I'm grabbing.

Maxwell himself taught me about another part of the human mind, the part that craves discipline and punishment and longs to willfully obey a strong leader. He taught me to seize that part, the sniveling worm of the soul, through the eyes and twist it beneath me. I can do this better than the Pushing Out. I can do it really well.

I seize his soul and I tell him "Your penis is too small. Every woman you meet can tell. Lots of men can too." He can't ignore this. He can't doubt it. This is his new truth.

His eyes are locked on mine and although he shouldn't be able to hear me ("The system... is down! The system... is down!") I know that every word is getting hammered straight into his brain. "You do not have what it takes to make a woman happy. You will never really be loved."

More than his hand goes limp, and I can see tears starting to drip out of his eyes. Good.

"You will never really satisfy any woman. You make women laugh. Women laugh at you all the time."

His shoulders have dropped and his face is slack with grief.

"Go home and think about this," I tell him, and he turns to the door, moving like a man in a very sad dream.

Linda would have been flustered. She would have been indignant and afraid and would have tried to defuse the situation by talking. The new me? Persephone just sent his ass packing.

greg stolze

This is, I think, my favorite part about being Kindred.

The first time they told me it was rude to say "vampire" and that we should always call ourselves "Kindred," I thought it was kind of stupid. I mean, we suck blood and do mind control and we never get old and don't show up in mirrors. Is using a different *word* supposed to help us forget what we are?

But I've gotten used to it. I kind of like it, now. If you think about it, calling each other "vampire" is really the stupid thing. If you get used to doing that, sooner or later you'll slip up and do it when someone (normal) who doesn't know the secret is around and then, well, who knows what would happen? "Kindred" sounds almost folksy, like "kinfolk" down south. "Me and Luella and the kindred are gettin' together for a Sunday brunch."

One big happy family.

Omega Travolta nearly pulls Rick off the line, but I smooth things over. I act embarrassed and tell him that Omega is my ex-boyfriend, can't let go, blah blah, poor little stupid me with the bad choices and would you like to go somewhere and get coffee?

Rick's a regional distribution supervisor for International Harvester. He buys me coffee I don't drink, while I give him my phone number and tell him lies about my past, stories about Persephone that make her sound sweet and vulnerable and kind. Persephone's that kind of gal. Persephone has made some mistakes but she's a good person at heart. She's trying. She's making a fresh start and just needs someone she can believe in, someone to trust who can save her....

Rick, while boring, is sweet. Doesn't even go for the grope and fondle when he drops me off by a building where I don't live. (Of course, I don't "live" anywhere, get it?— seriously, it's not my building.) I have to kiss him and, of course, I can't resist.

I pull his lower lip into my mouth and my two incisors, my fangs, they slide out like a cat's claws. They're sharp as a cat's teeth, and sink all the way through his lip and make four parallel holes. He grunts—does it hurt? Does it just sting a little? I don't know.

The blood comes out and the whole experience changes.

I know a lot of vampires—Kindred—liken feeding to sex, but it's never been that way for me.

(Maybe that says something about my sex life when I was alive, I don't know. I lost my virginity with Ed and it was just awful and afterwards he never wanted to talk to me.)

I can feel Rick against me and the flow of his blood into my mouth is slow but I don't mind, it's a delicious slowness, like taking a hot bath on a winter morning when you don't have anything to do all day long.

(After college I was with Perry for a couple years. I once told Perry that making love to him was like poetry. I didn't tell him that the poem in question was *The Waste Land*.)

I'm with Rick and it's like being with a close friend all evening, someone you haven't seen for a year, and it's even *better* than old times, because you've saved up a year's worth of stories and jokes and commentary, the two of you sit on the couch and make popcorn and tea and you giggle, you get silly and chuckle and chortle and when you're all done laughing the two of you sit, tired but so content, enjoying a mellow silence, and that's what Rick's blood is to me. It's sweet, mellow silence.

(It's not like I was frigid or anything—when I was alive—but I just never seemed to line up a time when I felt it with a person I liked and a circumstance where it really clicked. Maybe I set my standards too high, but if you're going to settle, what's the point of doing anything? I don't know. Maybe I never really grew up in that one area of my life. Maybe I waited too long, or maybe Ed was too soon. I just can't say.)

Rick's blood, his life, it moves through me. I was wrong. *This* is the best part about being what I am. I drink Rick and he's raw and strong and humble, he's everything, a cozy flow, I could lose myself in this and follow it to its source, to his end...

greg stolze

But I don't. I won't lose myself. My teeth draw back, they're small and normal once more and I give him little healing nuzzles, the four holes seal up like magic (is it magic?) and when I step back he looks dazed, drugged, all slack lips and constricted pupils.

For a moment we just look.

"Can I get your phone number?" he asks.

"You already have it. Remember?"

Six months ago I never would have touched Rick. I contented myself with scumballs with too much cologne, too much body hair, and too many condoms in their pockets. I fed only from men who filled me with contempt. Filled the Linda me, that is, the old me, the brisk, no-nonsense lawyer who had no time for clubbing and who could make a calculated display of sex-attract when needed but who just didn't go out and *strut* it. I picked guys I wouldn't miss and in the middle of feeding on one, some callous part of me decided no one else would miss him either.

Of course, I panicked. I was in a strange man's apartment with his dead body and four or five people must have seen me enter. I almost picked up his phone, then I thought about fingerprints, then I wondered if vampires leave fingerprints (because at that moment I couldn't think of myself as "Kindred," oh no). I got my cell from my tiny black clutch purse and I called Maxwell.

He fixed everything. He didn't even come in person, but sent his buddy Robert, who escorted me out and assured me that everything would be "tidied." He used that exact word. Robert smelled like pepper and mustard that night, I remember. I think he'd been at supper when Maxwell sent him.

Robert told me to go to Maxwell and I did. He was at his penthouse and he held me close, listened and nodded. He showed me compassion and stroked my hair and let me cry blood tears all over his fuzzy green cashmere sweater.

"It happens to everyone, eventually," he said.

I was bawling like a baby and sounded like one, too. "I don't want it to... I don't want it to happen ever again...."

He sighed and nodded.

"How do I stop it?" I whispered.

"You must be on your guard," he said. "And you must feed with great care. The urge to glut yourself, to drink down to death, is strong. It is always within us. To counter it, you need to find those whose life you enjoy, or admire, or cherish. If you feel their death diminishes you, it is easier to protect their lives."

"But... but what if I can't keep it down, even with someone like that? What if I, I find someone I like, and feed off him, and I kill *him*?"

"That death and guilt can make you stronger, and help you resist the time after that," he said. "Or, it can drive you mad, if you're weak. If you're weak, perhaps it's better to sup with disdain and resign yourself to... inevitable indiscretions. Many of our kind take that route, too."

Bella drove to the club and her car is still where she parked it, so I take a cab home. I ignore the driver's attempts to talk to me, and I open up my log. It's a plain spiral notebook, not much bigger than my hand.

I fill in the date column, I write, "Rick—dist. sup., Inat. Harv." Then I put in his phone number. It's a little cramped, but I write small.

When I get home, I take down the wall calendar in my kitchen (it's got Monet prints), page forward three months, and put Rick's name down. I'll string him along until then and feed from him again. If he's interesting or useful or something, maybe I'll start conditioning him, start poking holes in his mind to make him think I'm out of his life, but program him to meet me every three months, gives me the blood I need to survive, then forget all about the encounter. I could do that. I ought to, it's the smart way, but... I haven't yet. Not with anyone. It seems so cold and calculated, so *Manchurian Candidate*. Maybe if Rick turns out to be a real creep I'll do it. But really, I don't mind working hard to stay fed. If a thing is worth doing, it's worth doing right. Right?

I look at what's coming up on my calendar, shower and change into sweats (although I don't sweat anymore), and check my email. There's nothing good. I pay bills and by then it's gotten to be about four in the morning. The city is silent.

I live in the basement. I got a break on the rent because the windows are so tiny. (I've got them covered anyhow. Nothing serious. If all goes well, I won't be here much longer.) I take the elevator to the top of the building and I go out on the roof and look over Chicago. Even the skyscrapers don't have many lights on now, and it's all orange streetlight glow congealed along the avenues. I watch for a few minutes.

I can see the Larkins' house from here. It makes me smile, a little.

The night, she is mine. I guess.

I go downstairs and turn on the VCR. I watch *History Detectives* and then I go into my lightless bedroom and lie down.

The next night, I arise and start the painful process of putting on my makeup. It's no treat when you've got a blurred and smudged reflection, but tonight's a big night. I have to make an impression—no easy task, since I'm going to be hanging out with some people who look like sea-bloated drowning victims, and some people who can turn invisible at will, and some people (Bella, say) who can make you feel like they're gloriously beautiful even when they're dressed in ratty lounge pants and a faded Spuds MacKenzie T-shirt.

Without those options, I get into a full-length black skirt with burgundy brocade on the front. It laces along the sides—it's really just two cloth rectangles with eyeholes on the long sides. The laces contain spring-loaded beads so that you can tighten it and block the eyelet, without visibly tying the laces in a knot. It's a very complicated way to make it look like you left your skirt ready to fall off with the slightest movement. Underwear is out of the question, of course, except for thigh-highs to go with my black Manolos. Toss on a sheer white linen shirt thin enough to scandalize, some dangly silver earrings and a leather thong necklace with a black lacquered bird skull... I'm ready to go.

It's the first Sunday night of the month and the Kindred of Chicago are meeting.

I've been going to these "courts" ever since I made the change nine months ago. I have mixed emotions. It can be interesting to meet other Kindred, talk to them and watch them talk to each other. I've always been very social, very comfortable in groups—I'll even go so far as to say "political." The issues discussed sometimes seem rather silly, but maybe that's just because I haven't been dead for thirty years or more.

On the other hand, some of the people there are just creepy. It took me until my third time to realize why one attendee had always looked especially peculiar. I finally figured out he had no eyelashes and, when I looked closer, no eyelids at all. He explained that he'd cut them off because "They get you when your eyes are closed." I didn't ask who "they" were.

The court of Chicago meets in "Elysium," which in this case means the Shedd Aquarium. It's closed to the public this late at night, but private groups often rent it out after hours. When I was alive, I went to a real-estate law conference and they had a dinner there one evening. It was nice.

I put a long, light jacket on over my finery and take a cab. It's funny: When I was living and I could really enjoy sex, I never would have dressed in anything so preposterously slutty. Now, dead and going to a conclave of other walking corpses, it seems perfectly natural. Business casual just wouldn't cut it, here.

Loki is working the door, standing at the top of the broad stone steps and slouching against one of the tall, grooved columns. I like Loki. Slenderness and pallor sit well on him, and he belongs to that small subset of mankind that looks good in leather pants.

"Hi," I say. "Is my makeup okay?"

"Hold still," he replies. He licks the tip of his thumb and carefully reaches out to smudge the corner of one of my eyes. "There. Flawless."

greg stolze

"Anything going on?"

"We've got guests," he says.

"Guests?"

"Unbound." He says it like the word tastes foul.

Unbound means these guests aren't connected to any of the established groups of Kindred in the city. As I understand it, most just keep their heads down, but some of them think none of the rules apply to them. That can be trouble, and Loki's job is to be some sort of cop in this freak show. Not a job I envy.

"What do they want?" I ask.

He shrugs. "I think it has something to do with Cicero."

"The city or the Roman senator?"

He smiles but doesn't answer. "They're meeting in the amphitheater by the dolphin pool."

The Shedd was gorgeous by day, with soaring ceilings over marble floors, the classic architecture centering on a huge vaulted skylight over the Caribbean Reef exhibit, all Beaux Arts, plate glass, and fish the size and colors of mopeds. Entering by night, the only illumination is a full moon above and the trembling blue radiance escaping the tanks. I walk among drowned pillars, and everything looks blue-green and submarine.

I head off to the right. It's the wrong direction for the cetaceans, but I like the jellyfish display. They're lit from underneath with changing colored lights, so they shift through a rainbow display, translucent and gently pulsing.

I'm not the only fan, it seems. The other admirer is wearing a no-foolin' zoot suit—high, baggy pants, long draped jacket, even a big pimp hat with a feather. I know him. He's called Scratch.

Not many people can pull off that look, and Scratch is hideous. His nose is unnaturally long, like a mosquito's proboscis, and his eyes are beady, glassy and black. Most Kindred can retract their fangs, but his jut out all the time. It's not just his canines, either—all his teeth are pointed and uneven. Factor in gray skin with randomly placed marks like bruises and he's a gruesome picture. As I get nearer, he turns to me, raises an eyebrow, and smiles. This close, I can see that his clothes are dirty and stained. Even his rings are tarnished and corroded. I think I see something move in his lank, greasy hair and that's it. I'm near enough.

"Persephone, isn't it?"

I nod. "You like the jellyfish?" I ask.

"They're gorgeous, the bee's knees. Don't you think?"

I agree with him.

"Have you seen the giant octopus? It's another critter with a bag for a body and a dangly set of tentacles. You think it's beautiful?"

"I prefer the jellyfish," I say.

"Why is that? Everyone agrees that one tentacled creature is hideous, while these aren't. What's the difference?"

Scratch is an elder, which is like being a senior partner in a law firm. His respect could really pay off for me, so I think hard before I answer.

"Transparency," I say. "They have nothing to hide." I hope like hell he thinks that's profound.

"Really? I think it's because they so perfectly blend with their surroundings." He turns from them and looks me up and down, "Nice outfit. But would it kill ya to look a little more feminine?"

I cock my head and give him a curtsey. He laughs.

"C'mon," he says.

"Where are we going?" I ask, though I can see that he's pushing the button for the elevator to the shark reef exhibit.

"I'm going to show you something."

We sink to a lower level. The dark carpeted floors and lower ceilings that greet us form a drastic contrast with the vibrant colors and flowing shapes shining behind the glass walls. Scratch beckons me impatiently past corals and anemones and fish with gauzy spines like the finest lace. He's headed for the shark tank.

There are no great whites here. The sharks displayed are the size of greyhounds at best, but there's still a cold

greg stolze

and dispassionate deadliness in their eyes as they swim past. When I was a law student, I did an internship with the State's Attorney's Office, and I was present for an interview with Carter Soames, a man accused of smothering his wife with a pillow. She was seven months pregnant. As I left the room, Soames told me I had a nice ass, and it made my skin crawl.

He was convicted.

The sharks have eyes like Carter Soames.

"Any moment now," Scratch says, and I'm about to ask him what we're waiting for when the rippling top of the water plunges down, there's a rush of bubbles and a funnel of foam, clearing to reveal a naked white figure.

I think her name is Alice or Amy or something like that. I almost wave, but I realize she can't see me—all the lights are inside the tank shining out. From her perspective the wall of glass is a perfect mirror.

She's painfully scrawny and beautiful like a mortified saint in a Renaissance painting. Her hair is towhead white, it floats around her like a cloud of silk. I see bubbles from her mouth as she speaks and the sharks circle her, they rub their abrasive skin against her like eager kittens, and then there's another splash.

"Dinnertime," Scratch says, and this second intruder in the pool doesn't enter with grace. He's black and chubby. Mortal. He's naked too, and his body has the unfinished look of an adolescent—hands and feet too big, limbs awkward because the bones grew faster than the muscles. The white figure swims to him, she's not breathing out any more but he is, fat bubbles of screams as he thrashes, and then a third figure plunges in right beside him. The third figure is another vampire, sleekly muscled and cutting through the water like he was born there.

The two Kindred seize the boy and they bite either side of his neck. They're right by the glass, I can see that they're looking into each other's eyes, their faces rapt with adoration. Their victim struggles harder.

"Love among the river snakes," Scratch says, but I barely hear him, I can't stop staring as they open their mouths and the drowning child's blood oozes into the water. I'm horrified, I'm frozen, yet I find my fingers are up against the cool glass like I'm a child and it's a candy store. I feel my fangs slide free....

The sharks smell the blood. Instantly, the water is churned into a froth, the whole scene goes abstract, suggestive, just white water and with red currents, I see the sharks biting the boy, muscling the Kindred aside and they're biting too, biting each other, biting themselves.

"Hold this for me, willya?" I can barely tear my eyes away as Scratch puts something in my hand, it feels like a cardboard cylinder, I glance at it and just as he says, "You might want to cover your eyes," I realize it's a flare.

I get my arm up just in time and even around it I can see that this is glaring bright. It's not just a simple roadside torch—it must have magnesium in it or something. There's a horrible stench of smoke and fierce heat, and I nearly scream, nearly fling it aside by instinct, even knowing that's the worst thing I could do. And then its loud hiss subsides. I lower my arm as it cools and I see Scratch doubled over, chortling.

"You shoulda seen those two poor mugs," he snorts. "I mean, there they are doing their love-sex-death-swimming-with-sharks routine when suddenly—whoop! Fire! Six inches from their faces! They would've crapped their pants, if they'd had pants."

"Or crap," I add weakly. I realize he's holding a camera. He glances down at it.

"I'll show you these when they're developed," he offers. "I'd get you a second set of prints, but what's the point? They'll be blurry as hell."

Just like in mirrors, Kindred don't show up clearly on film. One more reason not to lose my old driver's license.

"Do you think they recognized me?" The words are out of my mouth before I can think about it—I'm still shook up from the flames. Get a grip! Persphone wouldn't be so scared and neither should Linda!

"I doubt it. I don't think they were looking right at the fire and, even if they did, all they'd see is their own burned retinas. Besides, you had your hand over your face."

"Then I guess I'll have to hope someone else wore this skirt."

"I think I saw Rowen in it earlier." Another joke. Rowen doesn't care what people think, or doesn't seem to, and she probably outweighs me by fifty pounds.

"Calm down, relax, don't getcher panties in a bunch." He turns to me, all mold and ghastly smirk. "I gotta go reconnect the fire alarm, but you want to go take a gander at that giant octopus first?"

He holds out an elbow for me to take.

He's an elder. I know this. I should kiss up to him. He's been dead since before my parents were born. But before I can steel myself to do it, he sees my hesitation.

"Perhaps some other time," he says, withdrawing. "When you're not in fancy dress."

I can't help but feel that I've failed some test.

Unwilling to follow Scratch further, I head for the elevator to the bottom floor. As long as I'm here, I want to look at the Beluga whales. But before I reach them, I hear a voice call my name.

"Persephone." It's a clear baritone, commanding. A good voice for a lawyer or a high school principal. A voice used to being obeyed—more, a voice that takes obedience for granted.

I turn and stand up straight for Bishop Solomon Birch.

A lot of vampires are old school in ways you wouldn't believe. We swear oaths of fealty and bow to a Prince, for example. So when we find religion, it's not touchy-feely Unitarian stuff. No, Kindred go in for something like Roman Catholicism, circa 1350. The faithful call it the Lancea Sanctum—the "Holy Spear," I think—and preach about vampires being God's curse upon a wicked world. Nice folks, if you like self-righteous sociopaths.

Bishop Birch is the local head of this happy bunch, and tonight he's certainly dressed the part. A thick red velvet robe trails the floor behind him, complete with a hood, overlaid with a black clergyman's stole. The stole is embroidered in gold with symbols of his faith—snakes devouring themselves, thorns, spears, skulls, and more.

Solomon's chalk-white head is bare, hairless, crowned only with a series of thick, blunt scars. He smiles as he sees me and opens his hands, but his eyes are arctic.

"We must speak," he says.

"Delighted to." I'm anything but.

Standing behind him are two of his Sanctified flunkies. They're dressed in plain black robes with the hoods over their faces. Black gloves cover their hands, which are supporting elaborately embroidered red pillows. The pillow on the left cushions a golden mask, the face of a bearded man showing exquisite sympathy and sorrow. The other holds a pair of gold-gilt gauntlets, detailed with animal fur and sporting three-inch claws. I can't help but notice that they've been positioned so that the finger-claws dangle over the pillow's tasseled edge, and the thumbs are crossed to leave those talon-tips resting in midair.

Those are the signs of Solomon's office: the Visage of Man and the Claws of the Beast.

He takes my arm and steers me away from the elevator, down the steps by the otter habitat. "I have made arrangements for you to go to New Orleans," he says. His porters fall in behind us, totally silent.

"W... I beg your pardon?"

"New Orleans. It is a city of strong faith. I know Kindred there. It is a fitting place for you to truly begin your new existence."

"That's... um, did Maxwell ask you to arrange this?"

"*Prince* Maxwell," he corrects me. "It is not polite to be over-familiar, especially in Elysium." Out of the corners of my eyes I can see one black-robed figure at the top of the steps, gently dissuading other guests from descending. The other has stepped around a curve on the down staircase. Solomon and I are alone.

My skin prickles.

"With all due respect... what would I want in New Orleans?"

"It is far from your life as 'Linda.' Far from the site of your Embrace. A new start, clear of any doubt or prejudice. In an environment of strong faith."

Now I get it. Solomon wants me out of the way.

Lineage is a big deal among Kindred. So is the Embrace, which is what they call the creation of a new vampire. What *we* call it.

I first met the ruler of all Chicago's vampires—Prince Maxwell, or "Max Collins" as I knew him then—at a meeting over the fate of the Meigs Field airport. He was charming, articulate, friendly.... A week later we met for drinks, and somehow we wound up in a room at the Palmer House hotel in a luxury suite. We were kissing on the sofa, and he was unlike anyone I'd ever been with. It all seemed so natural. There was not an awkward second: He didn't show a single sign of hurry, going deliciously slow with each touch, with each brush of his lips. I felt like I'd finally met a man who *wanted* me without wanting to *take* anything from me.

What a crock of shit *that* turned out to be.

He kissed my neck and every inch of my skin came alive. I felt like I must have been purring, and I swooned. There's just no other word for it. I went limp, it went dark and I was falling into splendid warmth all over, wrapped in the most lovely darkness....

And then the darkness turned cold.

I tried to wake up, tried to move, tried to fight my way back to awareness but my limbs were lead, heavy, dead. I could feel myself sinking down, feel my thoughts slowing.

I knew, somehow, that if they stopped they would never start again.

I was almost gone when a hot, angry taste flooded my mouth, flooded my whole body—I could feel it with every sense, red and livid and itching and raw. Some tiny part of me almost rejected it, but I couldn't stand to not be. I needed to exist, even at the price of embracing that dark and alien burning.

I opened my eyes and I had become the only offspring of Chicago's Prince of the Damned.

"I really haven't had a lot of problems with prejudice," I tell Birch.

"A lack of problems can, itself, be a problem. A coddled existence is possible for mortals, but we must be of sterner stuff. Surely you see that?"

"I can take care of myself."

"Can you?" His smile is cool and patronizing and suddenly I don't care that this jerk is the fucking imam to vampires who think mercy is a sin, I don't care that he's a celebrated badass who just last fall captured some psycho old vampire cannibal. In this moment, he's just a bastard like all the bastards holding up the glass ceiling, all the bastards who think a woman has to be weak and call her a bitch when she isn't, all the bastards who didn't pick me for their team, didn't call on me in class, didn't take me seriously.

"I damn well can. Want proof? I can take care of myself because I'm suspicious of *favors* that come from nowhere and benefit the giver more than me. I can take care of myself because I know enough not to squander power, or to go meekly into danger. I know enough to recognize fear, Bishop, and I know enough to see through the grade-school machinations of a withered, senile religious nut."

His smile is avuncular but he's got eyes like Carter Soames. "I presume that the 'senile religious nut' is myself?"

"What's the Bible quote? 'It is you who say it'?"

"You do me a disservice. I'll confess to some self-inter-est—your presence in Chicago disrupts a precarious social balance, one I desire to preserve. But you *need* the truth of the Lancea Sanctum. You still cling to your mortal friends, your relatives…"

"Have you been *spying* on me?"

He rolls his eyes.

"You… you pervert!"

That gets a chuckle. "The perversion, my dear, is to treat as human something that is not. That is the core of the sin of bestiality. How much sicker is it to treat as alive some-one who is not?"

"I don't know what jollies you get seeing a woman alone, afraid and isolated from people who *love* her—maybe it makes you feel better that no one loves *you*?"

"Spare me your puerile psychobabble."

"Why? Did it hit a nerve? You want to drive me away from my friends…"

"We do not have *friends*! We have victims and we have rivals!"

"I'd rather be your rival than your victim."

"You lack the wherewithal."

"Oh? I'm insignificant, is that it? So unimportant that you'd go to the trouble of shipping me to New Orleans? Sorry, Bishop. No sale." I lean in. "I know you and Max-well are close. I know you've been close for decades. But don't forget which one of us has his *blood*. That's mine alone, and for all your envy, it's something you will never have."

This time his chuckle is most definitely forced. "You really have no notion of how ridiculous you sound."

"Maybe, but I'm not the one with my fangs showing."

For a moment I think I've gone too far. Hell, I *know* it. He looks at me and it's simultaneously like he's suck-ing all the heat out of the room *and* like he's pulsing with waves of blazing anger, I'm vacillating between hot and cold…

Then his incisors retreat—I'd almost swear I heard a click—and he's utterly calm and composed once more.

"Consider New Orleans," he says. "It was a dispassionate offer. Sooner or later, you *will* break your ties with the life of Linda Moore. They can be severed clean, or they can end in tragedy. At some level you know this... Persephone."

He turns away, smirks for a moment at the frolicking otters, and then stalks off down the steps. A few moments later, his black-clad assistant follows.

I expect to need a deep breath. I expect to shake. But no. Only the living breathe. Only the living tremble.

"...local focus is reactionary and absurd," is the first thing I hear. I've gone up to the elevators, then all the way down to the whale habitat. Only I'm not alone there, either. "The future of our species is virtual—international and clandestine. If you want to stay hidden, it's not enough to simply pay your taxes and, and not drain anyone in public. We're entering the age of surveillance, the price on egg-cams is dropping steadily, bandwidth is getting cheaper and pretty soon it's going to be like a private sector version of *1984*! That's what these ancient types don't understand..."

"Surely it's not yet as dire as you think." I recognize this voice. It's Bella. I creep forward as the first voice—a man—starts in again.

"Not yet, but it's closing fast and the rate of change is only going to accelerate. Our community needs to get wired *now*, or in ten or twenty years the dangerous ones are going to be the elders like Scratch who don't understand—what?"

Suddenly, Bella rounds a corner. It's almost like she just appears, poof! One moment a blur and the next she's stock-still, composed and collected. I've never seen anyone move that fast. As she sees me her eyes melt from suspicion into welcome.

"Persephone! So lovely to see you! I'd like you to meet my new friend, Raphael."

I bite back what just might be an honest-to-goodness *hiss* of anger. With a few exceptions, coming face to face with another Kindred triggers a flash of fight-or-flight instinct, something deep in the lizard-corners of my brain where everything is eat or be eaten. That instinct is a lot closer to the surface now than it ever was before.

(Before I died.)

That effect can be useful. Among other things it allows us to recognize our kind on site. But sometimes—especially when meeting someone new—the instinct can get the better of me. It almost does with Bella's new friend.

He's wearing a boxy three-button suit, very plain. For just a moment, I see him as nervous and small, but then in an instant he seems poised and chic.

That's a good trick, Raphael, but I've seen it. If you'd used it a half-second earlier, I wouldn't have suspected a thing. But it's flattering, really, that he wants to make such a good first impression. It's cute. And it eases my lizard-brain desire to hurt him.

"Raphael… from Cicero?" I take a shot in the dark and he smiles.

"It's so gratifying that my reputation preceded me. May I ask where you heard my name?"

"Oh, Persephone hears so much," Bella responds. She's not bothering making herself impressive. "She's the sole get of our illustrious Prince."

I feel a frown coming and quash it. Thanks Bella. Thanks a lot. Now Raphael is suspicious.

"I believe I heard your name come up in certain Carthian circles," I tell him. Carthians are the one-man-one-vote crowd among the undead. They used to be in charge in Chicago and apparently made a spectacular mess of it, but some of them make some sense. Anyway, telling this to Raphael is meaningless flattery, but it gets us off the topic of my relationship to The Boss. If he's really unbound, he shouldn't be too fond of my maker, Prince Maxwell.

"I'm surprised that someone of your... excellent lineage... is associating with Carthians." He's not deterred. Not fully, anyhow.

"I keep an open mind," I say, "and value my freedom of association."

"The Prince's grasp of freedom is imperfect," Bella says, and I'm a little surprised by her bluntness. "Surely freedom of religion is something even a man raised in the early nineteenth century can grasp."

Nineteenth century? Is she talking about Maxwell? Is he really that old?

"You've been finding your... current structure... a little confining?" Raphael asks. His eyes narrow. "I know Solomon Birch and the Lancea Sanctum have a very close place to, uh, Maxwell's ear."

"*Prince* Maxwell," Bella corrects.

"Of course. You have to call him that." Raphael puts a subtle emphasis on "you," but not quite subtle enough.

"I prefer to think that it's Lancea Sanctum influence that keeps the Circle from greater recognition in Chicago," she says.

This is Bella's thing. In addition to being Club Queen Supreme, she is an up-and-comer in another group of bloodsuckers called the Circle of the Crone. If the Lancea Sanctum is Catholicism as seen by Charles Manson, then the Circle is his version of Wicca. Joy. Bella hasn't been too heavy-handed in trying to convert me, but give her an inch and she'll tell you how the Prince and Bishop Birch are keeping her faith down.

"This is my problem with religion in general." Raphael is warmed up now, and he makes a couple condescending, teacherly gestures with his hands. "I don't care what you believe, until you start telling other people what to believe."

Bad mistake. Bella's eyes narrow and she says, "That position makes sense if nothing is true, or if all things are equally true. When you have touched the ultimate truth, however, there is an obligation to share it."

"But..." Raphael swallows, trying to recover from his fuckup.

"How is it that you and Solomon Birch both claim ultimate truth, and you can't agree?" I ask. This dingbat had better like me for bailing him out.

Bella relaxes as she looks at me. "The vastness of truth can look contradictory, when viewed from a miniature perspective." Jesus, this is the woman who was giggling with Alpha last night while he told her about the latest Rob Schneider movie?

"'If the doors of perception were cleansed, we would see all things as they are—infinite.'" Raphael tries some Huxley on to see if Bella likes it.

"All things are *not* infinite," she replies. "All things are terminal. If there is any lesson we should take from our condition, it is that."

The three of us go upstairs and even though I've braced myself, I'm still overwhelmed.

Any place that's declared Elysium is a big deal—neutral ground where Kindred can't rip into one another without serious repercussions. In theory, the entire city of Chicago is bound by Prince Maxwell's Peace—the "Pax Max" to vampire wags. But that rule expressly forbids only murder, so solving a problem by breaking your enemy's arms and legs or poking his eyes out—that's just fine. In Elysium, even poking and shoving is absolutely forbidden.

Already, then, Elysium is where the Damned are on their best behavior. It's where they are *watched*, and know it. So naturally, it's where they try to impress.

Courts take that usual level of posturing and launch it into the stratosphere.

One of the most prominent boons offered by the "Mistress of Elysium" is the right (and responsibility) of decorating for court. Chicago's Kindred compete feverishly for the right to spend thousands of dollars—possibly even more—decorating the Shedd for one evening. Every month, some status-conscious vampire attempts to outdo the month previous. (Unless, I gather, the previous month's décor came from the Prince. Trying to make him look bad would be a terrible breach of etiquette.)

This month, the decorator is Tobias Rieff, and he's chosen to go with tasteful understatement. For vampires, tasteful understatement means skulls, candles and flowers.

It's not just a few, either. The amphitheater in front of the dolphin pool is huge and echoing, ranked in gradually descending stone benches. Usually, it's bare rock—easy to clean after seating hundreds of kids and parents who came to see the show. Tonight, the central aisle is covered with white petals. Each bench has a floral display at each end—white roses, white lilies, white carnations. Nestled in the center of the each display is a waxed and polished animal skull, each different. Some are tiny—bird or cat, barely visible among the blossoms. Another features a yawning alligator, its bottom teeth all tipped by candles. Candles line the horned arc of a cattle skull that would please Ansel Adams. There are dog skulls and snake skulls and many more too exotic to easily identify. As I look at them, I realize that the bigger crania, and therefore the more elaborate displays, are all down towards the front. Of course. The rising brightness, all of the warm and flickering yellow that's so forgiving on our complexions, it naturally leads the eye to the front. There, hundreds of tall white tapers rise from floral glory to form a line of radiance at the water's edge. In front of the line, at the center of it all, stands an empty chair.

The guy I take to be our second visitor from Cicero is standing by an ornate silver punchbowl at the top of the chamber, in front of the gift shop. He just seems to be taking it all in.

The bowl is full of blood—something from the slaughterhouse, pig or cow. I just don't understand how anyone could drink that. I mean, when you take from a person, from the right person it's... intimate. I don't want to get all mystical here, but you can understand how it extends your life. (Well, not *life* I guess, but you know what I mean.) Something from an animal, though... why would you want to make *that* a part of you? I couldn't do it. It's like bestiality, but a lot of Kindred have no problem with it. (Feeding from animals, I mean, not screwing them.)

This unbound is wearing oil-stained jeans and a blinding white polo shirt that still has creases from being in its package at the store. He's got brown hair, tight lips and tired eyes that flash with a familiar predatory rage. First meeting and all.

"Ambrose," Raphael says. "This is Bella Dravnzie and..."

"Persephone Moore," I tell him, reaching out.

"Ambrose Masterson," he says, and gives my hand a perfunctory shake. He glances at me briefly, nods, then goes back to keeping his eye on everyone in the room. He's holding the lizard-brain in check, but maybe not so easily.

"So, what brings you to our court?" I ask. Ambrose looks like he's been asking himself the same question. I think he's older than Raphael. I mean, clearly he *was* older at the time of his Embrace, but that doesn't mean anything. Bella was nineteen when she got it, but no one would ever think she was young. Unless she wanted them to, of course. For all I know, Raphael is three hundred years old, but... he doesn't have that elder feel to him— the easy moves of a predator who knows he can send you home disassembled if he feels like it. He doesn't have the wary confidence of Scratch and Solomon. Ambrose, he's got it... a little.

(And Maxwell? Sometimes he shows more of it than any of them. But other times, he seems to be a lost amateur... like so many of us.)

Ambrose looks at Raphael, who looks back, so it's Bella who fields the question. "A couple days ago, a policeman tried to arrest a wife beater and child abuser named Bruce Miner. Miner seemed to be complying, but right as the sun came up he lost his temper, snapped his handcuffs, smashed out the cruiser window and tossed the cop around like a department store mannequin. Both wife and child were admitted to MacNeal Memorial and treated for blood loss. The suspiciously blurry video of Miner's fight with the cop has made it onto TV. So all in all, we're looking at a serious Masquerade breach."

The Masquerade. The fundamental commandment of our kind, something every faction and tribe supports. There are a number of rules, all prettily phrased, but they boil down to "Survive, but don't ever get caught." There's this paranoia among Kindred, and the older ones get it worse and worse. The central article of faith is that if a few mortals find out about us, soon they'll all believe and will be eager and able to wipe vampires off the face of the earth.

Vampires aren't supposed to kill one another (at least, not in Chicago), but if you break the Masquerade, the Prince might just make an exception. Or they might put a stake in your chest, paralyze you, and bury you in the foundation of Chicago's next big building project. It doesn't *kill* you. It just makes you a headache for sewer engineers in three decades, or for archaeologists in a thousand years.

"A serious breach?" Raphael snorts. "No, New Orleans in 1996—*that* was a serious breach. A serious breach was Paris in 1882. Or how about Dubai just last year?"

Bella leans back a little and raises her nose defensively. She's getting ready to defend her position when the sound of a gong cascades through the room.

Prince Maxwell has arrived.

"All stand!"

That's not Maxwell's voice, of course. It's a guy named Garret McLean, and he's impossible to ignore. It's as if his voice shudders through us, the way his hammer shivered the gong. The younger vampires start to their feet like sentries caught slouching. The older ones, Solomon Birch in particular, rise with more gravitas, projecting a fine subtext of *I don't have to stand, but I'm choosing to stand.*

Garret processes in, stately and serious, holding aloft a plain mahogany box about four feet long, six inches deep and six wide. He's making a gradual beeline towards the empty chair at the bottom of the amphitheater. It's big, baroque and old. He's about halfway there when Maxwell enters behind him.

The Prince of Chicago is not really tall—five-nine, maybe five-foot-ten. About my height. Though if he really was born around 1800, he must have been a giant in his day. He's stocky, dressed in a conservative Phat Farm sweater, the kind Bill Clinton wears. He has high, prominent cheekbones and a calm, genial appearance. Tonight, he's grandpa getting ready to cut the turkey at Thanksgiving.

My "sire."

By the time he reaches the chair, McLean has opened the box and produced (with suitable small flourishes) a shiny metal sword. Maxwell sits on the throne and McLean hands him the weapon. Maxwell unsheathes it and lays the naked blade across his knees, and it's hard to explain his expression when he does this. It's ambiguous, oblique. You can read it as an absolute commitment to the cause that all this pomp represents. You can read it as straight-faced irony, a double bladed visage that mocks this pretentious formality by perfecting it. You can read it as a constrained tyranny, a reined-in contempt for the ceremony that says, "I don't need this ridiculous metal stick to enforce my will."

His expression alters, and for a moment I'm *certain* that he winked at me. Then I see the movements, the shifts of posture through the gallery and I realize just how many of us had the same thought.

The ones up front, the elders—Solomon, Scratch, Rowen—they aren't convinced. The middle range, like Bella, they shake it off after a moment. But the youngsters, the fledglings, those of us farthest away, up by the free drinks... most of us fall for it.

I glance at the unbound. Raphael looks puzzled. Ambrose is frowning. I can't tell if they were fooled or not.

"We are the Damned," Maxwell begins, "And yet we are not so fallen that we cannot make more of ourselves than we are. We are, by inclination, solitary hunters, but we find ourselves tonight in peaceful company. We carry in every drop of our blood a polluting cruelty... but steeped in hunger though we may be, humanity remains. Cold eyes yet seek beauty," he says, gesturing about the hall, and he's right. Despite its eeriness or maybe because of it, the austere display is thrilling. "A stilled heart still craves companionship. Thus, Elysium. Thus, our court. Thus, our covenants. All our higher impulses—all that raises us above brute predation—all the good that lingers, is displayed here tonight."

He says something like this every time, some corny opening remark, but from him, it's not trite. From him, it's a ray of hope in the red darkness. Tonight, as every night, the crowd applauds.

"My dear fellow Kindred, please—be seated. We have with us tonight two visitors," he says, gesturing to the two strangers. As I'm sure he intended, everyone else looks at them. Raphael stands up straight and I feel a trickle of regard for him, he's Pushing Out but it's weak and artificial, spread too thin over souls too jaded. He's trying to warm our gazes, but it's like lighting a match in a locker full of frozen meat.

Ambrose just acts resigned.

"May I introduce our guests for the evening?" He gives them a tight, tolerating smile. "I know you may find the formality of our gatherings somewhat stifling, but please. Humor us with your names, and a recitation of your lineage."

Raphael meets his gaze. "I'm Raphael Ladue, and my sire was Old John."

I have no idea who the hell Old John is, but apparently others do. Many pale faces crane around to look at him with new interest, and most of the interested parties are sitting up front, where the power is. Rowen doesn't turn, but everyone else in the front row does, expressions all carefully blank. A few rows back, there are Kindred who can't repress fear.

greg stolze

"My, my," Maxwell says. "A notorious lineage indeed. And your companion?"

"I'm Ambrose Masterson and I was Embraced by the Unholy."

That gets *everyone* looking. All but the newest of us know who the Unholy is. It's like saying your dad is the boogeyman.

"Bull*shit*," says a voice from the middle, a man in an impeccably beautiful suit with skin like alabaster.

Ambrose bares his fangs, and we can all see that his teeth are inhuman, needle-sharp and unnaturally long. Not like Scratch, though. Where Scratch's mouth is a wreck, a mistake of nature, this mouth looks carefully evolved to pierce and shred.

"Yes," the Prince says. "I remember you now. From the DNC." Ambrose narrows his eyes and nods.

(Did Maxwell say "D & C"—meaning an abortion? Or was it "DNC," the Democratic National Convention with the riots? Or is it something else entirely?)

Maxwell goes on. "Despite their... well-known heritage, our guests have opted to ignore our hospitality in the past. Nonetheless, it is my hope that you will all join me in extending them a courteous welcome tonight.

"Our guests share with us a common problem. We are both concerned with the actions of one Bruce Miner. Garret, if you'd be so good...? I'm quite helpless when it comes to programming VCRs." The line gets a laugh.

While he was talking, Garret wheeled in a big screen TV, which he now pokes at until a recorded news show comes on. The story is about a man in Cicero resisting arrest and fleeing the cops, and in the middle of it they show grainy cop-cam footage of a burly guy in filthy coveralls struggling with a policeman. The two of them lurch out of the camera's coverage for a moment, and then the officer comes flying across the hood of the car. It's dramatic, the more so for being silent.

The somber news anchor fills in what I already heard— wife and daughter bled out, snapped handcuffs, et cetera.

They juxtapose a still frame from the video and what's obviously a cropped snapshot from some neighbor's scrapbook. The former is basically just a gray blur, pretty much what we all see in the mirror whenever we bother to look. The latter is a depressingly average white guy with bad hair.

When the segment ends, there's a silent moment.

"Comments?" Maxwell says at last.

Scratch stands. "Ice him," he says. "He's from my clan, he shares my curse and I still say ice him."

"Out of the question," says Solomon. He remains seated. "He, like we, has been cursed for a reason. We shirk our duties and corrupt our natures if we turn violent hands upon him."

"Not all of us accept that 'duty.'" The speaker is up near me, far from the center of authority. Dressed in cargo pants and a jean jacket, the only indication of his nature is a crescent on a necklace. A mortal would think the brown matter under his fingernails was oil, not dried blood. "We prey where we will, we are the fangs of the world. Why should we not fall upon any who threaten us?"

Solomon won't even acknowledge him. He makes a tiny gesture and the robed figure holding the Bishop's mask stands and speaks.

"Men feed on animals and are despised for harming men. So too we prey on men and are despised for harming our own. No Kindred has the right to any of the sacred blood, save that which flows in his own veins. It is not ours to give. It is not ours to take."

"This 'sanctimony' gets us nowhere and only leaves us in a rut we've occupied too long," says jean jacket—he's a loudmouth, and not old enough to get this much attention. Elders must be thinking what he's saying, if they're not interrupting him. He's taking a big risk going toe to toe with the Bishop, but I'm sure he'll be flavor of the month with the Circle of the Crone for a while, just for his big brassy balls. If he actually gets his way, he could make permanent gains....

"I'm always respectful of religious debate," says Max-well, "But the ban on killing is a law of my authority."

The Crone follower bows—to all appearances, he's sin-cere. "None appreciates your enlightened rule more than me," he says, "but the hand that turned the key in the lock could turn it back to loose it again. What better cause than a Masquerade violation?"

"That's a gross over-reaction," Raphael says, and he takes a breath to say more when Scratch interrupts.

"Fine, so we stake him and put him on a slow train to Baltimore. Pick your nits, I don't care as long as you agree that we need to take this rogue down fast."

"It may not be so simple." This is Norris, and he's very close to the Prince. No one talks about him directly, but I get the impression that if Maxwell has a Gestapo, Norris is its Heinrich Himmler. He gets to sit up front with the popular crowd, even though his bass voice has a creepy Peter Lorre whine to it, a grating growl. It's like hearing Barry White deliver the "You have to help mee Reeck!" line from *Casablanca*. "Loki, Ms. Lasky and I have dis-cussed this matter, and have yet to find any trace of Mr. Miner."

"If Loki..." This is one of the neonates, a new vampire like me up in the nosebleed seats, but Bella interrupts her before she really gets going.

"Maybe the problem solved itself. Maybe he made a rookie mistake, couldn't get away from the sun, and ashed himself."

"That would seem to be an ideal outcome," Maxwell says, chuckling, "but I don't think it's prudent to rely on day-light for our dirty work. Perhaps our guests can shed some light on the matter? If you'll pardon my little pun."

Raphael stands, looks around to measure the room, runs a hand through his hair and speaks.

"As a Cicero resident, it is my considered opinion that Bruce Miner is not a substantial threat to the Masquerade. Either he'll be found or he won't. If he isn't, there's no problem. Clearly, if no one can find him, he can't prove vam—uh, Kindred exist, right? If we do find him, it means that after his initial, you know, problems, he went to ground and started playing it safe. Hunting him like an animal isn't going to do any good. If anything, it will just put his back up and scare him. Scared people make stupid mistakes, and stupid mistakes are what lead investigators to the truth."

"Well said." Solomon has turned to look at Raphael. "Nevertheless, it would be best if he could be brought into the fold and educated properly for his role."

"I just, I..." Raphael's thrown off—I guess he never expected to come down on the side of the Bishop. "Right, if we find him and *educate* him... If we teach him, then we've got, you know, another..."

"Another mouth to feed," snarls Scratch. "Another moronic amateur trolling the same clubs, the same bus stations, the same slaughterhouses and tenements. Who needs it? What's another vampire, more or less?"

Voices murmur up from the assembly, some agreeing, some taking issue. Hesitant starts like "What about...?" "Have we tried...?" "Maybe we could...?" But Solomon drowns them out.

"Your words are an abomination! It is against the law of the Prince and against the justice of the night! Those who share the Blood shall not spill it on the ground!"

"Don't take that tone with me," Scratch says. "*I* know what's behind your mask."

This gets Solomon on his feet, pointing his finger and shouting, "Were this not Elysium you'd pay for your insolence!"

For the second time, I see Solomon's fangs flash out, and Kindred near him instinctively flinch away—not only the youngest, either. Even the bearer of his talons seems to shrink out of Solomon's shadow.

"Calm yourselves, I beg you." Justine Lasky says this, the Mistress of Elysium. Her voice is like a bell or a sigh or wind blowing through silk curtains. Solomon doesn't change his stance, he doesn't look any safer or gentler, but somehow his menace seems to become more distant.

"It's not like there's no precedent," Scratch says.

"What's the precedent?" asks a youngster. They ignore her.

"For exceptional cases, yes." This is Raphael again. "What's so exceptional about this? All the mortals see is a man who fought a cop and won. Half of them probably fantasize the same thing. Many probably think they could *do* the same."

"Where is his sire?" Rowen's voice rolls over the assembly like a blanket. She isn't standing, she hasn't turned, but it's like her words hit the glass walls across the water and echoed back redoubled. "Why don't his crimes redound upon his maker?"

"Even in Cicero we know the Prince's ban on the Embrace." This is Ambrose's first contribution.

"The ban is more than the Prince's." This is Solomon, sounding the very definition of holier than thou. "It is a tradition from the very dawn of our kind."

"Perhaps," says Maxwell, in a manner that leaves an unsaid "but unhelpful" ringing in every listener's mind. He turns back to the two newcomers. "So, nobody knows who has been so… indiscreet?"

Now they're glancing at me. Like this Miner bozo, I'm an unlawful by-blow. I do *not* like being associated with some child-biting asswipe, so I need to get the air cleared fast.

"If no one can find Miner," I ask, "How much harder to find his maker? Presumably anyone who sired him is older, smarter and more experienced. If, as Ambrose here said, even the unbound aren't Embracing… well then, whoever it is broke the rules and has a strong motivation to stay hidden."

Solomon audibly chuckles at that. Bastard.

"Persephone is right," Bella says. "Finding Miner is our first priority. Once found he can be educated or otherwise dealt with. His sire is the greater criminal, but Miner is surely our best link to him."

"Or her," Solomon adds. "So. How do we do it? Watch for his next dangerous indiscretion?"

"Has anyone even cleaned up his first?" Tobias asks.

"He hasn't done it again," Ambrose says. "He probably learned his lesson."

"I'm not worried about the cop." Scratch has stood up and turned to address the whole audience. "I'm worried about the wife and the daughter. 'Severe blood loss' trips a lot of alarms, and not just among us. I, for one, don't want this nitwit to lure a bunch of wackos who know just enough to be trouble."

"I think we can..."

"Severe blood loss takes place everywhere, every day, to people who've never seen a vampire and never will." Raphael is standing too, rolling his eyes and working that impatient teacher voice again. He's pushing his luck.

"All it takes is for one smart cop to realize that the two bitches lost a lot of blood, but that there's no blood at the scene where it happened." Scratch is looking straight at Raphael now. "Hell, all it takes is one cop getting a deposition that hideous hubby bit them on the neck, then he's wondering, 'How'd this guy manage to swallow four quarts of blood in just a couple minutes?' Stir in the fact that this kid looks like a freak show reject"—Scratch gives a little nod and smile to acknowledge just how well he fits that particular bill—"and you've got a recipe for monster paranoia."

"Blood fetish murders are well documented," Raphael counters. "The FBI has files on human serial killers who drank blood or ate skin or whatever, they go back to the 1960s. It's a standard profile, psychos with sanguiphilia."

"That is surely a double-edged sword," Maxwell says. "Yes, every crazed mortal who acts like one of us provides a beard for the activities of true Kindred. But by the same token, many of those obsessives developed their fixations after experiences with our kind. They may be slaves to Kindred, or former servants, or feeding vessels who came to crave the experience or envy those they fed. It seems to me that the more common this explanation for a Kindred's behavior becomes, the more attention the FBI will pay. If they search long enough, they are far more likely to trace us through some cast-aside fetishist, or through simple luck. Or by finding an ignorant neophyte like this Bruce Miner who can, nevertheless, provide proof positive of our existence."

"Luckily, the police aren't finding him. Any more than your bloodhound Loki is," Ambrose says.

"Well, Cicero has been a notoriously difficult area to keep safe," Norris says, glaring.

"Safe for whom?" Raphael retorts.

"For all of our kind, certainly," Maxwell says. "While it's outside of Chicago proper, surely you can understand our concern with any... disorder there."

"Disorder? Maybe you should talk to your elder Scratch here about Cicero's disorder!"

"What does *that* mean?" Tobias asks.

"Are you insulting me?" Scratch demands. "Are you *stupid* enough to come here and shoot your mouth off in front of my Prince, my peers and everyone?"

"I'm sure no offense was intended...."

"Sure," Raphael says. "All I meant is, I know you've got a haven there. In Old John's burnt-out brothel. You remember the place, right?"

A silence falls. I don't understand why.

"We've all got bolt holes," Scratch says at last. "We all have feeders, we all have places we dump and we all have underpants on too. That doesn't mean it's germane to today's discussion."

"I'm sorry if I outed your presence in Cicero," Raphael says, "But I just meant..."

"Well, this is interesting," Maxwell says. "I had no idea that one of our elders was familiar with the area. A consensus is emerging, I think. Scratch, you..."

"Hey, look, I do *not* want to wind up Prince of Cicero, okay? I've got enough pain on my plate." Scratch adjusts his lapels.

"Oh, there's no need to make it a separate domain, but given the concerns stated by Mr. Ladue and Mr. Masterson, it seems apparent that the judicious course is to expand our protection to Cicero, bring the situation there under control and…"

"Wait wait wait!" Raphael says. "Just what do you mean, 'under control'?"

"Which word didn't you understand?" Solomon asks. He's turned on his stone bench and slung one leg over it, so he can glare at Raphael without straining his neck.

"Why don't we appoint a Regent?" Norris says. "Someone seasoned whose loyalty is, heh, reasonably firm. Someone familiar with the area…"

"I know Cicero," Bella says. "And the Kindred there would be far more likely to accept someone of my beliefs than a more… rigid philosophy. Isn't that right, Raphael?"

Before Raphael can respond, Solomon says, "The last thing Cicero needs is the lax hand of an idolater. When moral failures emerge, the solution is not to send some anarchic pagan blood-slattern!"

"The last thing Cicero needs is *any* outside influence!" Raphael says. "Hey, we came here to help *you* deal with this problem, not to ask for your help and not to invite you to set up shop!"

"You have a very high opinion of yourself, who would deign to offer us your *aid*." Solomon's starting to work himself up again. "You laze through your nights like hogs at a trough, unwilling to look farther or deeper than the end of your own tongue. Fangs of the night? Your ilk are little better than ticks, annoyances who escape only because your victims don't suffer enough to bother destroying you."

"So I suppose I should join the Sanctified and learn how to *really* murder and torture mankind? *That'll* keep the Masquerade intact!"

"We honor the First Tradition far more than you sad, cringing, domesticated vampires do! To us, it has meaning. It's a holy pledge, not merely a convenience!" He turns to Maxwell. "My Prince, put these noisome brats under the shadow of the Spear! Give them the gift of discipline!"

"I don't want your fucking discipline!" Raphael jumps to his feet and stalks to the aisle. People are backing away.

He's got his fangs out and his pupils are dilated. Everyone knows the signs.

This is exactly what Solomon wants. He's playing to Raphael's bloodlust, trying to wind him up and get him to go berserk. Once that happens, Raphael's credibility is shot and Solomon, the injured party, probably has a pretext to do any crazy thing he wants. But looking at the Bishop, I can't help thinking this is a dangerous ploy. I've heard stories… Solomon has a long fuse when he needs one, but when he goes off, he *really* goes. Blood calls to blood with us, and anger calls to anger…

I'm not the only one who's spotted trouble. Ambrose blocks Raphael's path and says "Ladue, take a moment, take a breath…"

"*Shut the fuck up!* Christ, *you* never respected me but I'd expect you to help me defend us from this bald-headed, sanctimonious *douche bag!*"

"Hear the squall of the infant's tantrum," Solomon sneers.

"You weren't so high and mighty when you were *kissing Old John's ass!* You think I didn't know? Solomon Birch, shit, he made *jokes* about you, he called you his *Solomon Bitch!*"

"Oh, I am stung to the quick." Solomon's playing it cool but I have to give Raphael credit—he's playing by the rules, and if he's not completely under control, he's at least got enough willpower to stick to harsh language.

"Why don't you get all your superstitious fundamentalist buddies together, maybe burn a few used band-aids and put a *hex* on me? You think everyone's scared of you, but *you're* the cowards, looking for some dark dead daddy figure to tell you what to do, scared to be free for *even one night!* Praying to *Longinus*, of all the stupid, dumb…"

"That's *enough*," Solomon says.

Raphael's definitely got to him. Longinus is the Roman centurion who tabbed Christ on the Cross. He also happens to be the Lancea's own messiah figure.

Solomon takes a step forward. "I'll abide your disrespect of me, but when you blaspheme in my presence—"

"Whatcha gonna do?" Raphael asks, on a roll. "You gonna sock me one right here in Elysium? You talk a good game with your centurion 'Dark Messiah,' but I think when the shit's down, you'll respect the Prince who's right in front of you above your horseshit faith—"

Then Solomon's on him.

Jesus! He's up the steps in no time, even faster than Bella. Before anyone even reacts, Solomon's smashed his fist into Ladue's face. His arms come up, he falls off his bench and the back of his head impacts the floor with the loud thud of meat and bone.

"Owwwwww!"

"*Solomon Birch! Be seated this instant!*" Maxwell is standing, pointing the sword and his fangs are out, his eyes burn, his voice echoes with command.

Solomon turns, takes a deep (and unnecessary) breath, then saunters back to his seat.

"Excuse me," Ambrose says, "But isn't there some rule against this shit?"

Raphael sits up. His nose is flattened and blood is coursing down his face. Both eyes are starting to blacken already, but then Ladue grits his teeth and his nose straightens, blood rewinding back up into it.

"That wasn't violence," Solomon says. "If I'd decided to be *violent*, he'd be an ink spot on the floor. That was just a friendly tap, something to remind him of his place."

"Is that a taste of the discipline I can expect under Lancea Sanctum rule?" Ladue asks. "A nonviolent reign?"

"We're getting away from the point!" I say. "Look, let's get back to the immediate issue here—Bruce Miner! If you can't find him in Cicero now, what chance do you have if you send in an unwanted invader and alienate every Kindred there?" I give Solomon a good hard look—he's glowering, chastened, down. Perfect time to get in my kick. "We all lose if we let some overly ambitious demagogue turn the hunt for one rogue into a midnight Vietnam."

"Miner is only the symptom—" says one of Solomon's acolytes, but no one's paying attention.

"I think we can all agree that anyone who finds Miner has done us all a service... Miner, perhaps, most of all," Maxwell says. His voice is smooth and mellow, but final. "As for the larger issue of Cicero, I'll have to discuss it with my council of advisors. Does anyone have any other business?"

Bella stands and starts talking about the Crone, *again*, and everything's back to normal. Or whatever "normal" means for a hall of murdering beasts, lit by fire and gilded with skulls.

"Thanks for taking the heat off Cicero," Ambrose says. "I hear you've got a link to the Prince?"

"Well, your pal made a nice play. Provoking Solomon to discredit him isn't something I'd try again, but it sure worked out this time."

Ambrose snorts. "You think he did that on *purpose*?" He drifts back to the blood bowl, goblet in hand.

Oh shit.

Chapter Three:
Solomon

The light hits my face and I'm lost, confused....

"Sir?"

I was in fur. It was everywhere, pressing up against me, hot and humid and with an acid stink.

"Sir? You asked..."

Now it's light. It's not right—I shouldn't be alive yet. In front of me a man stands, food, outlined against the brightness. My puzzlement turns to hunger, quick as a finger-snap.

"Sir? Sir!"

I lunge and seize, my hands bruisingly strong and fangs showing in the light. I smell fear, and close for the kill—

No.

It's David. I will not bite David. I will not feed from David. He is my aide, he does my will, we have a bond of trust and I will not violate it. Despite the rage, the hunger in me is lazy. It's there, always there, but not unbearable. The beast is either glutted or ravenous. If I do not drink myself into stupor, then I know the keen irritation of hunger. There is no middle ground.

But I am the master here. I break my hunger, make it heel.

"David."

"You asked me to waken you early, sir," he says. David is a brave man. He fought in Korea. But though his voice is steady I still feel the arms in my grasp tremble.

"Early. Yes." It starts to come back to me. I look down at myself. I'm already dressed, dark slacks and a sport coat over a button-down blue shirt.

"Ian is in the car," he says.

Ian. David's son. My breakfast.

Ian Brigman looks more like his mother than like David. That's well and good. His mother, whose maiden name was Rosen, was a talented flutist and from a family of skilled musicians. Over a number of decades, there were also several Rosensweig mathematics professors in Berne, where the Rosens originated. My researchers have not yet made a connection, but I suspect it is there. Mathematical talent and musical ability are often found side-by-side. I think there is a common gene.

Ian has shown no outstanding talent for either music or math, though like his father he was a fine athlete. But I am patient. His daughter Margery may show the potential he lacks. Ian married Diane Locker, whose maternal grandfather was one of the original Oneida stirpicultures. You can keep your mass-produced Nazi Übermenschen, thanks. I'll take America's homegrown, individually crafted eugenic prizes. The Nazis stole their eugenics laws from us, you know.

The Oneida commune fell apart before it could produce more than a single generation, but they were on the right track. I have maintained their good works. I have high hopes for Margery, who has just recently turned sixteen. Old enough.

David drives the car while I refresh myself from Ian's wrist. We get on Lake Shore Drive heading south, and I'm finished with my feed by the time I need to give him more specific directions.

Ian and David wait in the car while I go downstairs to see Persephone Moore.

I am alone on the steps. I set down my briefcase and double check the envelope inside. All is in order. Then I pull a small plastic box from my jacket, transferring it to the back pocket of my pants. Before I do, I open it and check the glove inside.

Before I died, I made prosthetic limbs. I was a craftsman—there was still demand for handmade arms and legs. I did a leather nose once, and two leather ears, but mostly legs and arms. Each was unique, scaled for its owner only, made to do what he most needed.

Hand-building an artificial limb that has anything more than rudimentary function is a taxing endeavor. One must be skilled with leather, wood and metal, knowing the unique properties and qualities of each. There were times, surprising times, when a leather hinge would more closely mimic the human form than one made of iron.

One must also study the human body, of course—learn and understand the interplay of muscle and bone, how weight and strength move cleanly, how they stall.

My best work was a pair of fingers, I think. A mill owner's son had lost them, not in his father's wood mill, but exploring the forbidden interior of the town hall clock. Funny. I was able to build him articulated fingers that would, with a turn of the wrist, open and close almost like nature's own work. They were weak, of course, but as he grew and came back for larger sets, I installed ratchets that would lock them in place if needed.

I still putter in my workshop. When the mood takes me I make furniture, or boots. I made that grand chair upon which our honored Prince sits at Elysium, and I made the box for his saber. There's no call for my true profession any longer: artificial hands and feet roll off assembly lines, all alike. But I still have a pair of those fingers, the latest, and an earlier set is in the collection at the Smithsonian. Or so I'm told. I've never traveled that far.

I think of those fingers as I look at the sturdy leather glove sewn with heavy canvas thread. The hooks are anchored firmly to nylon fishing wire that distributes pull through them all the way back to the wrist. Each hook can support 500 pounds without coming loose. I've tested them.

I put the glove carefully away. I descend. I'm ready.

I hear murmurs behind her door. As anyone would, I press my ear to the crack and listen.

"…worried about you. All your friends are." It's a man's voice.

"I'm, honestly, there's no need. I mean, I don't know who she saw. Maybe it was someone who looked like me?" She even sounds different. Already she starts playing her games, spinning in circles, being too clever even for herself. Persephone or Linda? Soon she may build so elaborate a façade that even her personae cannot relate to each other. I've seen it happen before.

"Maybe she did, it still doesn't change things. Why didn't you go to Beaner's party? He really missed you!"

"I told you, I was sick. Remember? That flu bug?"

"You weren't sick the next day when I came by about that Larkin place."

"Do you know how creepy that sounds, Scott? How crazy?"

"Don't get defensive now, I'm not trying to attack you! I'm trying to *help* you."

There's a little pause. I have to strain to hear his lowered voice.

"Is it drugs, Linda?"

"Scott, that's… that's the most ridiculous…" She has trouble denying it. What is the theft of life itself, if not the most heady of drugs?

"Ridiculous? We never see you except late at night or, or that one time Valerie stopped by and said you were so out of it that you nearly fell asleep on your feet! You're falling away from all your old friends, you've quit going to your yoga class and your book group…"

"You *were* spying on me!"

"I'm not judging anyone, I just want to know what's going on!"

"Scott, I promise you, I… look, listen just… just look me right in the eye…"

I knock, hard.

Persephone's expression is carefully neutral as she opens the door. As is my own, of course.

"Mr. Birch," she says. "What a surprise."

"Let me in, please." It never hurts to try manners.

"Now is not a very good time."

"I'm sorry, but I must insist."

"Well, you see, I'm with someone."

I put my shoulder into the door and push. There's a chain, it looks pretty sturdy—I'd guess brass plating over steel—but it doesn't last. There's an oaken groan as the mounting rips out of the doorframe. I only get a glimpse, but it looks like three-quarter inch wood screws, nothing stronger. Really, what's the point?

The man on the sofa stands. He's short, clean-shaven, Caucasian—I'd say of Scots descent if forced to guess. He wears "business casual" over a small paunch and looks indignant, but uncertain. A cup of tea steams on the table before him.

"Linda?" he asks. "What's going on?" He raises his chin. "Is this guy giving you trouble?"

Oh my. A hero.

"It's okay," Persephone says, looking back and forth between him and me. "Perhaps Mr. Birch and I can talk about this privately for a minute? Maybe back in the...?"

"No," I tell her. "He has to leave."

"I'm not going anywhere," he says, and he steps between her and me.

I move to light threats. "You don't want trouble with me."

"That's it. I'm calling the cops."

"Scott, don't!" Persephone cries, but he's already at the phone. I make no move to stop him, and just pull out my wallet.

As he draws in breath to speak to the operator, I show him my badge.

"Detective Birch," I say. "Vice squad. How's that for rapid response?" I pluck the receiver from his fingers and say, "I'm sorry, someone hit the 911 button on the phone by mistake. No emergency here."

He looks from me to her. The badge is a forgery, but obviously he can't tell the difference.

"You want to tell him, Persephone, or should I?"

"Persephone?" he asks.

"Please. Just go," she says.

He looks at me and I raise an eyebrow.

Reluctantly, he leaves.

As soon as the door closes, Persephone puts her hands on her hips and glares.

"What the hell was that all about?"

"I'm concerned," I say. I don't look at her. I'm looking around the apartment. It's a bit cozy for my taste—small, tasteful, original watercolors on the walls, all ponds and flowers and sunshine. Here and there some tribal knick-knack bowls or cat statuettes or baskets, Chinese or Aztec or North African, something "multicultural." Very pleasant, very feminine.

Very human.

"Concerned about what?"

"About your development."

"What do you mean, my 'development'?"

"That man who just left. Scott. A friend of yours?"

"You leave him alone!" I can see nervousness in her every gesture. She's backing away from me, shifting her weight, fidgeting her hands.

"You *think* he is your friend. You care for him? You would spare him danger?"

"You bet I would." She raises her chin and now her hands are at her hips again. Fists.

"But don't you see that you are a far greater threat to him than I? If you truly love him, you should go far away."

"Is this New Orleans again?"

"Go where you will. I'm sure you'd never trust any succor I offer you, preferring instead a trap of your own making."

"I'm sure you get your jollies off making little girls doubt themselves—I've heard all about it—but no sale here, Elder Birch."

"You are trying to live in two worlds, and one of them is no longer your home. If you continue to see your friend, he will become increasingly suspicious, and he will peek and pry even more. When one of Norris' thugs kills him, will you deny your role in his demise?"

"Look, I can make the adjustment, I can keep Scott in line—all my friends. You overestimate their determination, I promise, just like you underestimate mine. Don't worry about me fooling them. I'll do just fine."

"Until the stress of lying to your friends gets the better of you. Until *you* are the one who kills."

"That's not going to happen. *I'm* not the one with the anger management problem."

"Indeed?" I hand her the envelope and wait. Timing is everything.

I give her the chance to see her mother's picture. Recent. She's bending to get groceries out of the car, and her skirt is riding up a little in back.

It sinks in. She's trembling.

"Negotiate with me, Linda. Tell me you'll go to New Orleans if I agree to kill her without raping her. Tell me you'll come to the Temple for a year if I let her live, a decade if I leave her mind undamaged. Use your words. Use your logic. Persuade me, you *stupid little cunt!*"

She shrieks and she charges. Her eyes are wide and her fangs are prominent. Utterly undisciplined.

I duck under one arm and put my hand on the back of her neck. While she was looking at the pictures, I put on the glove and the hooks sink in to the side of the neck, right where it joins with the trapezius muscle.

She screams, but I'm confident that her apartment is soundproof. After all, Maxwell supplied it.

"You underestimate the curse you carry," I say in her ear. Over her shouting and struggling, I have to raise my voice. "You have no mother. You have no friends. You will never be a part of their world again. You cannot. Your blood denies it."

She struggles inefficiently. With a twitch of arms and body, I slam her head into the broad white plane of her refrigerator. I feel neck bones shift (but not break) under my hand, blood pours from her nose all over her lilac silk blouse. (Maybe silk. Could be rayon, I'm not sure.) A second slam turns her voice off like a switch. Good.

"I will not permit you to jeopardize our existence because of your foolhardy refusal to admit what you are. You are not human. You never will be. You have no place with them. The best you can hope for from them is their ignorance. Failing that, their adoration. Failing *that*, their fear. But you are doomed if you think you can move among them as an equal. Your only place is to curse them, or test them, or destroy them. Every mortal close to you is in the shadow of peril, and you are that shadow."

A high animal whine emerges from her throat and I have reached her. I know I have found the real her—not the insolent youngster with no sense and too much protection, but the beast within, ageless and guileless and wise. "Do you feel this?" I ask. It is a rhetorical question. I know she can feel nothing else, but I want her to remember, when the blanket of thought lies once more on the blood. "This is what you really are. These are drives that can't be tamed."

I jerk her down, against the counter, her face inches from the toaster.

"Look at yourself!" I command. "You see only shadows, because your soul is now a shadow. Accept that. We cannot move in human light, among human eyes, because we are no longer human. Our souls are damaged, diluted, chewed free of flavor by the curse of the blood within. You are a monster, Persephone. All of us are."

I put my left hand on the back of her head. I turn her so she's facing away from the toaster and, with a good shove, rip the hooked glove free.

She runs, of course. Flees deeper into the apartment, slamming doors behind her. What else can she do? The beast within her rules, and a stronger one has bested it. Mine has driven out hers.

I know there's only one exit from the apartment, so I'll hear her if she emerges from the bedroom. I don't expect her out soon.

I strip off the glove over the sink and turn on the water. She has one of those little hose attachments—it's handy for sluicing away the blood. There are no dirty dishes in the sink, of course. Why would there be?

When my hands are clean enough, I open the briefcase. It's got a change of clothes, a box of garbage bags, and a canister of those Lysol sanitizing disposable wipes.

The kitchen has a fair deal of blood on it—a drizzle on the fridge, spatters on the low cupboards, a small pool by the oven and a rather dramatic spray on the floor from when I pushed her loose. Nothing like a mortal would have spilled, with a heart pumping it out sundered veins, but it's still present. I should have brought a scrubbing brush.

When the kitchen is clean I strip off my soiled garments and put on fresh ones. The dirty wipes go on one bag, the dirty clothes in another. Both, with some squishing, fit in the briefcase.

I'm just about to knock on Persephone's bedroom door when she pulls it open and comes at me with a baseball bat. I take it away from her and shove her back on the bed.

"Think about what I've taught you," I tell her. I drop the bat on the floor with a clunk—it's wood, an old-fashioned Louisville Slugger. "You are not in control of your passions. You are not safe to be around. You can only bring tragedy to your friends, unless you repudiate them.

"I'll show myself out."

Ian and David drive me home. I dismiss them and enter the chapel.

Its entrance, a rubber-lined door, is concealed behind a false panel of stone. It takes a strong man to move it, and

greg stolze

then only by a painful fingertip grip. But that is apt, is it not? Should any blessing come without effort?

A second door lies behind the first, this one decorated with the Spear and the Cross.

Inside, the chapel is red-draped, lit by fluorescent lights. Candles will not burn here, because there is no oxygen inside. Here, awash in pure nitrogen, I can pray safe from the fear of fire and humankind.

Oh Dark Messiah, purify my heart. Make me a tool for the Divine Will. Purge me of mercy, that I may cull the race without flinching. Cleanse my eyes, that I may see not in moments as a man, but in ages, as does God Above. Intercede with Him, that He may guide my malice according to His ultimate plan.

Great Longinus, Shadow of the Cross, open the hearts of the heretics that they may see their place in God's great design and thereby be Damned for meaningful acts, not for pointless self-interest. Lift the ignorance from the eyes of the Carthians, that they may turn their naïve political scheming into earnest spiritual search.

Guide Persephone Moore, that she may see the wisdom in leaving Chicago before she becomes a greater blight upon her great sire than she has already been. Failing that, let her flee in fear and ignorance, so long as she flees him.

Most of all, be in spirit with our Prince Maxwell. Guide him, shield him, enlighten him… yet, should he fail at the time of test, help me know when I must ruin him.

Emerging from my prayers, I find my thoughts still dwell on my Prince, my friend.

When he acknowledged Persephone, Maxwell pled a lapse of judgment. Swept up in the moment, he took too much, and with remorse restored her as best he could. He told us all that story—us, his Primogen, his council of advisors.

Can such puling be true?

But if it isn't, what gain could he possibly accrue by breaking his own law? What is worth the cost?

For it has cost him dearly. Not only my trust, but the trust of the other elders. A Prince who spawns? Who knows what mad, aberrant act might follow? He could unmask our entire court on a whim, or order us staked during the day by his servants, or bind us all to his will through the drinking of his potent blood.

Already the crop of folly rises up from the seeds he sowed. This rogue, "Bruce Miner"—he could be only the first of many. As the Prince goes, so goes the city, and a lax Prince models carelessness for others. Already someone has passed along the curse. The unbound flaunt their laziness before their betters, and are bolstered in their insolence by Persephone Moore, the Prince's Error embodied. Between them, they have made mock of me and cost me the esteem of my peers.

But all that is naught before the Prince.

Can the Kindred court of Chicago survive with so infirm a hand upon its tiller?

It's midnight, and the Primogen of Chicago gather under the shadow of Picasso's Horse.

It's a pleasant night, mild. We're in the heart of Chicago's Loop and there are a couple living souls about—people working very late at the stock exchange or in the Sears Tower, cabbies driving revelers to or from clubs, tourists who came here at what is very much the wrong time. From what I've seen on television, this place is awash with humankind during the day, crawling with vitality from the art museum up to the train station and beyond in every direction. But at night, especially on a Monday night, it's dead quiet. Nearly as dead as we are.

Norris, Scratch and Miriam are waiting at the bench. They greet me cordially.

"Miriam," I say. "I missed you at the meeting yesterday."

"You know I don't care for Elysium. But don't worry, I heard all about you." She is confident indeed, to taunt me about my misbehavior. Yet do I deserve any less?

"You should be less concerned about me and more concerned with the anarchy in Cicero."

"Do you think the Prince will attempt to extend his rule there?" she asks.

"Prince Maxwell has never been a 'join or die' type," Norris says. He shrugs.

"Unless you're a pretty little thing named Persephone," Scratch says, and emits a coarse guffaw.

No one else laughs.

"What? Lighten up. Jesus, what a bunch of tightasses."

"I'll laugh on my own time," Miriam says. "I just want to get tonight's business finished. Is Justine coming with Maxwell?"

"I believe so," Norris says.

"What do you suppose they're talking about?" Scratch asks.

"Probably about this Cicero issue," Norris says, looking pointedly at Scratch.

(Personally, I suspect Maxwell and Justine are talking about Bella and her exertions on behalf of her little coven.)

"Cicero business? You mean this Bruce Miner fellow?" It's Miriam again, sounding bored but I know she doesn't miss much.

"Well, it seems that Scratch here is quite the man on the Cicero scene."

"Screw you. I got a crash pad there, is that such a big fuckin' deal?" Scratch is wary tonight. Outside of Elysium, he is far less eager to try my patience. So. My blow upon Ladue accomplished that, at least.

"No, of course not. No big deal that you're digging around in the wreckage of Old John's lair. Why would anyone be concerned?"

The mention of Old John's name gets Miriam's eyebrow up. She turns a cool eye on Scratch.

"Look, Old John is dead and gone, okay?" Scratch asks.

"Gone, at least," I say. I'm pretty confident that Old John isn't coming back, even though no one *saw* him die. We leave only ashes, after all, and there are plenty of those in a burned-out house.

"I took a look around there a couple years back, just… you know. To make sure."

There's a little pause, uncomfortable, before Scratch continues. We all remember Old John. Even now, hearing the name pulls something in me, a small string of awe and terror that has been dormant since…

"And, you know, there was some good stuff there. Not, you know, anything physical, but… a good haven. Day-proof, hidden, secure. Maybe even a Guilford."

(Andrew Guilford was a Chicago architect in the 1920s, right about the time Scratch was brought over. He was a servant of one of the local Kindred, and through a few removes he built several houses and even a few public buildings with hidden chambers in which a Kindred might pass the day in relative safety. Most of the residences were destroyed by a group of vampire-hunting Treasury agents in the 1940s. Fortunately, Maxwell and I managed to discredit them before they could brick over the useful bolt-holes in the Engine Company 88 building and the one under the greenhouse in Garfield Park.)

"So you moved in and you didn't tell anyone that you were lairing at ground zero for the Chicago unbound movement."

"Movement? Movement? I've seen more movement from dead dogs. That Ladue punk has a coterie of fellow travelers and that's about it. They're a handful of dipshits with their little herds, their little scams, their little… hell, they're *little*, okay? They ain't doin' shit."

"Except for finding Bruce Miner before my own hounds and sheriff," Maxwell says.

I think I'm the only one surprised. Miriam has a nose like a wolf, Scratch is always jumpy and Norris has access to senses I frankly don't care to imagine.

"Formalities?" asks Justine Lasky.

"Very well," Maxwell says. "As all members of this meeting of the Chicago Primogen are present, I call this meeting to order."

"All members plus one," Scratch says. That puckered up wreck he uses as a face twists into something I think is a smirk. "Don't think you can con me into your club *that* easy."

"All members, plus Priscus Scratch," Maxwell says, rolling his eyes, voice overly prim. He knows Scratch hates the title. "Old business?"

From his tone, we all intuit that he wishes to get to new business.

"Very well, new business?" He pauses to wave to a police officer. The cop's across the street by the federal court building, eyeing the group of us. "Just a moment."

The policeman comes nearer, and when he sees Maxwell's face his expression changes to one of relief. "Mr. Polermo," he says.

"Officer Grundy." Maxwell has a big grin. "How's your boy? Recovered from that hockey injury?"

"Oh yeah, a long time back."

"It's been a while since we talked, I guess. You have to take care with those... was it a knee?"

"Yeah, that's right." The cop turns to go and then remembers why he came over. "You... uh...?"

"My friends and I had a business meeting go late. *Very* late," Maxwell says with a laugh. "We all came down in the elevator together and it just hit us that it's a beautiful night, in the most beautiful city in the world."

Burn me again if the officer doesn't look up and around, like he's never seen Chicago before.

"Well, have a good one." He tips his hat to a man who's been dead over a hundred years. "Stay safe!"

"That's the plan!" The Prince jerks his head to the side. "Let's walk," he says to the rest of us.

We walk. South and then west, discussing Cicero and the new rogue.

"What did you mean about the Cicero Kindred finding Bruce Miner?" Norris asks.

"I mean they have found Bruce Miner," Maxwell replies. "Furthermore, they found him even before they came to Elysium last night."

"Liars!" I'm not surprised, but I am still offended. "We should have known better than to trust them."

"How do you know this?" Norris says.

"The mouthy one," Maxwell says, his smile thin. "Raphael. We had a private chat and he... sued for a separate peace."

"Meaning?" Lasky asks.

"Meaning he offered me this Miner fellow in return for formal recognition." His mouth quirks. "He wants to be Regent of Cicero."

"You didn't admit him, did you?" I ask.

"I strung him along. Suggested he might make a decent Harpy." The Prince's eyes narrow, then twinkle. "His counter offer was to get his own Elysium."

"Damn him," Lasky whispers.

"Screw 'em both," Scratch says. "Why does it matter? Let him into your old boy's club, get Miner, kack the rogue and call the problem solved."

"Scratch, I'm warning you," I say. "Eliminating the fledgling, no matter how irksome he is—that's off the table."

"Mr. Ladue informs me that Mr. Miner is well in hand, studying the arts of Kindred behavior under his friend Ambrose and others in Cicero."

"You think Ladue can deliver him without a fight?" I ask.

"Is it worth it?" Justine asks. "I don't want Ladue creeping around. He's unpleasant."

"If Miner disappears and Ladue suddenly becomes a shiny new-minted Harpy," Miriam says, "his neighbors in Cicero are going to do the math and take care of that problem pretty quick."

"Which means that Miner and Ladue become the flashpoints in the Cicero powder keg," Norris says, cracking his knuckles.

"Any resistance becomes our pretext to seize Cicero," I say. "...If that is what the Prince desires."

"Cicero ain't worth it." This is Scratch, of course. "That city is mobbed up so dirty that anyone you tried to muscle would already be muscled, and anyone you tried to buy would already be bought."

"So anyone we wished to serve us would be serving two masters," the Prince says. "That is a drawback. On the other hand, a town accustomed to corruption has a certain allure..."

"The infrastructure is already in place," Norris says with a leer.

"We've always steered away from the mob," I say in turn. "O'Banion was an object lesson on the folly of letting a group of armed, violent, religious and superstitious men find out about us. Especially when they're already used to operating outside the law."

"Didn't Capone eventually clean that up for us?" Miriam asks.

"You'd have to define 'clean' very loosely," Maxwell replies, frowning.

"And 'for us,'" Scratch says.

"What would extending our influence to Cicero gain us, and what does it cost us?" Norris asks.

"It gains us a dirty, crooked town—which means it's a malleable town," Miriam answers. "But it costs us the effort of struggling with these unbound and whatever half-developed power structure they've established."

"These guys ain't going to struggle," Scratch says. "They'll just bitch, then fall in line or move elsewhere."

"Which could be worse than an organized resistance." Miriam strokes her chin. "Who knows how many of these idiots there are? I mean, a *movement* with a chain of command... you can roll that up. But a bunch of random jerks moving into your turf and upsetting your feed balance..."

"Straining our influence..."

"Embracing wantonly," I say.

There's a pause. They look at me. They look at Maxwell. He looks at me.

"Like Bruce Miner," I say.

More silence.

"All these problems," I say, "will be especially acute if they scatter throughout the metro area. I'd be happy to see these unbound gone, but I'll settle for them being confined to Cicero."

Another pause, and then Maxwell gives me a thin smile. "How is that different from gone?"

"Sycamore would be gone."

That gets a few snickers, along with suggestions that Springfield or Dixon would be even more gone.

"So," Maxwell says. "Are we agreed? The problems of civilizing Cicero outweigh the benefits, for the moment." We've reached the Chicago Board of Trade, and Maxwell leans back to drink in its façade. "We do not want their... disruptions and disorder spreading to our fair city."

"That's the ideal," said Norris. "But what of Miner?"

"What of him?"

"He's already creating disruptions—draining his family and assaulting police officers. He must be stopped, and if we have to bring Cicero to heel in order to stop him..."

"We don't." This is Justine Lasky. Usually quiet, she commands attention when she speaks.

"The problem is not Bruce Miner, not his 'atrocities'," she says. "Which of us has done nothing worse? If Ladue's companions are training him, he is under control."

"That's a *very* fragile assertion." Norris sounds huffy.

"Their interest in discovery is no greater than our own," she insists. "All Kindred fear discovery. Miner's flight from the police shows that he fears it too. The problem, therefore, lies not with him but with the witnesses he has left— the wife, the child and the police officer."

"And anyone else who saw him wandering around with blood on his face," Norris mutters.

"The problem," I say, looking squarely at Maxwell, "lies with whoever contrived our traditions by Embracing this wretch."

The Prince says nothing and the others take that as a cue to move on.

"People look away," Miriam says, picking up from Norris' comment as if I hadn't spoken. "You know this. People don't look at faces. And especially, they look away from the deformed." She turns to Scratch. "Right?"

"Right," Scratch says, his voice crisp, and I don't know if he has accepted his disfigurement or if her words sting him.

"How much of an issue is the cop?" Maxwell asks. "Norris? You've investigated?"

"I have." Norris frowns, as if he's tasting something bitter. "He's no genius," he admits. "He sees the whole episode as a case of a strong man who got the drop on him. He blames the animal control people for not getting there sooner, and his superiors are investigating whether he put the cuffs on tight enough."

"What of the kicked-out window?" Scratch asks.

"It's happened before," Justine replies.

"The curious timing that it was *just exactly* at sunrise?"

"No one cares."

"The torn-out sewer grate? The fact that he was *smoking*?"

"No one noticed."

When I was newly Embraced, I was stunned that no one spied my distorted reflection, or when I inadvertently showed fangs (I was much less controlled in those days), or any of the many careless clues I left. Now it shocks me whenever anyone rises from self-absorption long enough to notice *anything*.

Life is often much clearer to the dead.

"What of the wife?" asks Scratch. "The daughter? They're too dangerous to let live."

"No, they're too dangerous to kill." This is the Prince himself. "The wife, what will she say? Her husband beat her, bit her neck, made her bleed? No reputable news outlet would report the lurid details. Any that would, would never assert that he drained her blood as quickly as *we* know he did. To make such an 'impossible' claim would endanger their already-slim credibility. This story is already cooling—another domestic disturbance. Soon the viewers and readers will have another Kobe Bryant to distract them, another Iran-Contra, another celebrity wedding. But if we kill her, the story gets hotter. We want to make this incident *boring*, and slaying one of the principals is not the way to pursue that."

He makes such sense. How can I doubt him, my Prince? And yet, Persephone...

We have walked up to Union Station, and the clock there says it's one in the morning.

"I told Mr. Ladue that I was concerned," Maxwell says, that handsome grin surfacing again. "I asked if Miner might return to the scene of his crime, perhaps try to finish the job. He assured me that Miner has no further interest in harming them."

"Ah," says Norris. "Rather the opposite, I expect?"

"Yes. You remember what it was like to be new, yes?"

"To have a family," Scratch whispers.

"Indeed. The daughter, I think. She's still comatose."

"Easily remedied," mutters Norris, "With a taste of the Life..."

"A taste that will place her in our power."

"Scratch? You will do the honors?"

For a moment, Scratch just looks at his Prince.

"The renegade is from your line, after all. One of the Nosferatu, I mean."

"Right," Scratch says. "Sure. Yeah. I'll do it. I'll take care of her."

"Excellent," says the Prince. "Now, as to the next matter. The Mistress of Elysium, Justine Lasky, has registered a formal complaint against Solomon Birch for a transgression of the prohibition against violence."

I give Justine a low look. She could have come to me independently with her problem, but she had to drag in the Prince. Now he's voicing the words for her, poisoning the others against me. How could I think him mad, who plays us each like strings on his fiddle?

"Surely that's a matter for her to deal with personally," I say, "Not a matter for the Primogen."

"Considering that the complaint is *against* one of the Primogen, she felt it would be most proper to refer this to the highest authority." Maxwell shakes his head. "Your temper, Solomon..."

That fatuous prig. I *kept* my temper last night. I was never out of control: I stopped after one hit.

"If I have transgressed the *letter* of the law in some trivial fashion..."

"Elysium is a bastion of free speech." Justine must be very angry indeed if she's willing to interrupt me. Me, with my dangerous temper. "If we don't provide a forum to air opinions—even undesirable ones—they just go underground and fester. Then we wind up with a situation like Dubai or Catalina. It's not trivial, Solomon."

"No one wants another Dubai," Norris says, "But surely..."

"A higher standard of conduct applies to elders, Solomon," says Maxwell, "And your behavior was beyond the pale for anyone. What sort of example are you setting? What can we expect if the Bishop of Longinus flouts our laws?"

"Indeed," I say. "Those who interpret the laws of God must be even more responsible than those who make the laws of this world."

There. That quieted the hypocrite. What's one blow, quickly healed, when compared to a cancer like Persephone who could last for centuries?

I would look to the others, but I dare not break gaze with the Prince. Norris carefully stands an equal distance between us. Miriam, seemingly by accident, is at my right shoulder. Justine brought the complaint and stands at the right hand of the ruler. Scratch isn't a Primogen—he's backing away from us both.

After a significant pause, I speak again, still staring at Maxwell. "Your words have shown me the importance of cleaving *strictly* to tradition. I humbly submit to the judgment of my peers."

"For an elder of such longstanding," says Norris, "Surely a private reprimand..."

"No, no," I say. "Judge me by the same standard to which others are held."

"Temporary ejection from Elysium is standard for a first offense," Lasky suggests.

"Ah, but it's not a first offense." I'm almost enjoying this. "I was ejected from Elysium in 1947 for this same crime. Though that time, the damage was considerably more grave."

"I suggest beating with a white-hot sword," says the Prince, and I know.

Persephone. She went whining to her maker, bearing tales, and this isn't about my blow to the ambitious Mr. Ladue. It's about my attack on Maxwell's little *pet*.

"Now that," I say, "Is a punishment I can *respect*."

We set the date. Next Elysium, my humiliation will be public. I don't mind. Part of me looks forward to it—I can never admit it to others, but my wrath against Ladue mortified me. If I can remain Solomon Birch while the Prince, my friend, beats and scars me with a burning brand, then I will regain the respect my position requires. If I fail, it will surely be because I do not deserve to guide my flock.

During my mortal life, I liked to gamble. I wasn't very good at it, but perhaps I never found my game.

I will not fail. I am not Persephone. Longinus has shown me what I am, and I accept it. That makes me strong. Her illusions make her weak.

I return home from the Primogen meeting, work a bit on a credenza I'm building, then fall into slumber with daybreak.

Tuesday night I wake at my accustomed time and, after prayers, have the leisure of a long, hot bath. (I have never particularly taken to showers. Besides, a bath raises my core body temperature, at least for a while. It feels nice.) I dress casually—slacks and a polo shirt.

Tuesday is family night.

I reside in the Brigman house, in what was once a coal cellar. The house is spacious, but not ostentatious. However, it is pleasantly furnished with a great deal of well-built, handcrafted furniture. Every technological convenience is at hand, but concealed. The stereo speakers are hidden within the walls, and the other components lie in a refitted cabinet. The plasma-screen TV hides behind a painting when it's not in use, and even the telephones are discreetly tucked into alcoves with wooden doors. Nowhere does the functional ugliness of a modern gadget intrude upon Victorian stateliness, save in the bathrooms and kitchens I suppose. I never go there.

I come up through the basement stairs and Margery Brigman is waiting for me.

"Good evening," I say.

"Good evening, Mr. Birch." Her voice trembles. Poor thing.

"Margery? Are you all right?"

She bites her lip, nods.

"Your father and mother have explained the situation, haven't they?"

She nods again.

"Are you ready to hold up your end of the bargain?"

There's a pause and then... a violent shake of her head.

"Well, that's your choice, Margery, but I hope you've considered matters carefully." I sit beside her on the couch and she draws away.

That hurts, and I let the hurt show on my face.

"Come now. There's no need for that. Am I some monster from the late show, jumping out of the closet and yelling? I'm Mr. Birch. I was there the night you were born. I was there ready to give the Life, *my* Life, to your mother if she needed it during her emergency c-section." I sigh and look down at my hands.

"Mr. Birch, I... I just don't want to."

"Margery that simply is not acceptable. Are you a monkey in a zoo, to let your passions determine your conduct? I certainly won't force you—I respect you too much—but I hope you respect *me* enough to give me a reasoned answer for your refusal."

"I... it feels... I just know it's..."

"It's what?"

"It's wrong," she whispers.

"Wrong? Why?"

"I don't know."

"You do realize I need your Life—not all of it, just a little taste that you can easily spare—I need that to survive? I need the blood, if not from you, from someone. I have asked, politely and respectfully, for something I need and which you can give. Why do you refuse me?"

"It's mine," she whispers.

"And you don't want to share." I frown. "I expected better from someone your age. But perhaps you'll outgrow your selfishness. I hope so, and not just for my sake." I turn my head and body away, wait a little.

She says nothing.

"You're still here?" I ask. "Is there something you want? A question you'd have answered?"

She shakes her head.

"Then go! Go explain to your father why you won't help me. I have nothing else to say to you."

She flees.

Annoying. But I must respect free will. After all, it indicates a strong soul, that she would refuse me. At least she didn't devolve into grand theatrics.

Besides, there's plenty of time.

I discuss some family matters with Ian and David and Elena (who diffidently reminds me that her own supply of the Life is running thin). Mostly, I put them off. I'm distracted.

Prayer helps, and after that, I make a phone call and have Ian drive me to the pier. On the way south, he updates me on current culture—"phat" spelled with a "ph" for some reason is now a synonym for "cool," Ben Affleck isn't as bankable as he once was, game shows continue their decline. I rarely use all this horseshit, but on occasion it's useful. If tonight were less busy, we'd go to a movie. Once a week, I go—it helps keep me current, helped me know what a CD was (and now, what an iPod is). The last one I really enjoyed was "Saving Private Ryan," though it did make me terribly hungry.

Bella is waiting at the slip, and I courteously help her onto my boat.

"I'm sure you know that I've told my peers I'm meeting you here."

"I expect no less."

"This is... what, a thirty footer?"

"Forty. You sail?" She nods, and I ask her help in raising the sails. We slide out into the dark swells of Lake Michigan.

"This is your second boat, yes?"

"Oh yes, the *Century* was far more impressive. A motored yacht, fit for serious business, and I built all the fittings by hand. Handled well, too."

"Caught fire, I heard?"

"Yes, in '72. But I found the perpetrators." I smile. "They were bold of heart but... merely human. Still, they lasted a long time. The *Second Century* should be ready to sail in two more years, but I'm in no hurry."

"Outfitting it by hand again?"

"If you want a thing done right..."

We're now out in the bay, rocking on three-foot swells. It's a clear night, but the view of the lakefront sheds so much light that we cannot see the stars.

"So. Let's get down to it," she says. "What do you, the great elder Judge of the Holy Blood, want with a kooky Crone cultist like me?"

I take a moment to remember what 'kooky' means before I reply. "I may not share your faith, but don't assume I deride it."

"If 'anarchic pagan blood-slattern' isn't derision, what is?"

I laugh. "Elysium hysterics, intended solely as a... rhetorical flourish. The old and jaded Damned sometimes need a loud display to penetrate their ennui."

"Uh huh. And your beat-down on Ladue? You faked that too?"

"Certainly! You don't think...? No, Ladue needed to be shown that he could not hide behind Elysium, could not use the laws of the Prince to defy his betters. I'll take my lumps for it, but he'll think twice before he tries to game his betters again."

"I'd expect you to respect even an agnostic like him more than a 'pagan' like me."

"At least we agree that there *is* a religious dimension to our existence, that there *are* larger questions to ask, and at least we acknowledge the right way to find answers."

"We just don't agree on what the answers are. That's a bitter disagreement."

I wait until she's looking away from the sail and at me before I shrug. I tack around to catch the breeze and say, "My role in the court is not strictly religious. As a Primogen, I have political duties as well."

She raises an eyebrow.

"You may feel that your pleas for greater recognition and respect have fallen on deaf ears. But not everyone thinks you've gotten your fair desserts."

"The Prince has been very noncommittal, which I'm starting to realize means 'no.'"

"Our Prince has formidable skills when it comes to dodging questions."

"And you'd break with him?" She shakes her head, smiling. "You two are thick as thieves. I heard you were weaned on the same neck."

"Come to the next Elysium and you'll see just how friendly we are," I tell her. "Maxwell is my friend, but I'd fail him if I permitted my feelings to blind me to his weaknesses."

"You're talking about Persephone."

"I'm not the only one whose confidence is shaken. Profoundly shaken. I'm not the only elder with doubts."

There's a pause before she speaks.

"You think Maxwell could fall from the throne?"

I wait a bit to answer.

"I think his reign is unstable. I think the instability will get worse. And I think that it is during such times that skilled individuals can make great gains... if they maneuver wisely."

She narrows her eyes. "In the unlikely event that Maxwell left the throne..."

"Very unlikely." I smile.

"Who would you want to next see on it? Yourself, I suppose?"

I laugh out loud. "By the Centurion, no! A thousand times no. I'm no Prince. I lack the charm. I could rule only by force, and force is very limited. No, there are many better candidates. I can think of few better than Justine Lasky."

She raises an eyebrow.

"Justine is somewhat young," I admit, "but is that necessarily a disadvantage? She is current, a woman with a mindset far more modern than one finds in an anachronism like myself or my good friend Maxwell. These nights... they baffle us, in many ways. Maxwell might be happier if he no longer bore the burden of command." Have I laid it on too thick? No, she likes Justine. Bella *wants* to believe.

"You think she has a chance?"

"With support from the right sectors. The Circle could be potent, if they could ever agree on anything. My fellows in the Lancea Sanctum know which way the wind blows..."

"Or they can be shown."

"Do you think Lasky would be as resistant to your reasonable arguments about religious tolerance? Do you think she'd put you off until tomorrow, and tomorrow, and tomorrow?"

She's nodding. I have her. "Of course, any concessions made to the Crone's children would almost certainly be extended to the Lancea Sanctum as well," she says.

"That's not unlikely. You see what I mean? Religious tolerance benefits everyone."

"Except Prince Maxwell."

"You've given him plenty of chances."

It galls me to think of replacing Maxwell with Justine, especially after she ran sniveling to him for vengeance after I upset her little blood-and-crumpets Elysium party. But she's really the only choice. You couldn't drag Scratch onto the throne with a tractor. Norris is widely feared or despised, and I'm confident he'd turn Chicago into a police state. Miriam is too young and too isolated. Which leaves me, and I have no ambitions to be Prince. Every leader stands on the shoulders of giants, but I would rather *be* a giant.

Perhaps this can redound to my credit. In public I can display my distaste for Justine. Certainly it won't come across as feigned. But if she bids to unseat Maxwell, it only makes my support more meaningful. I can see she's uneasy with the punishment Maxwell declared. It probably looks worse to her than to me, and it's my back will take the blows.

Yes, this could work. And if it fails? If it fails, she is ruined, not I.

Next stop, MacNeal Hospital. Scratch is waiting.

"You know where she is?"

greg stolze

"Room 216." He takes my hand, and I feel a curious sense of distance, as if all those around us have fallen back and faded. Together we pass by guards, doctors and orderlies, unseen by all.

She is pale under her covers, pasty and fleshy and with the coarse features common to the lesser genetic strains. Someone chose this specimen's father to be preserved for eternity. Sad.

"Shall I do the honors?"

"It's your duty," I say. I don't want my blood in that creature. Better she take the blood, the Life, from Scratch. She's a dewy English rose by comparison.

There's no respirator, which is good. She's comatose, but at least can breathe on her own. Scratch's wicked nails gently pry apart her lips, her jaws, and with a flick he opens his wrist above them.

"Drinky drinky," he mutters as his blood, God's holy weapon against the world, drizzles into her mouth.

The blood is the Life. We exist beyond the bounds of death because of its mystic potency. When given to a living human, Life to Life, its power is dizzying. A touch, a mere taste of its might, and a mortal can heal as we do.

Brooke Miner's eyes pop open. She looks up at Scratch and they widen in horror. Then she spies his bleeding vein, and the look softens into desire. Hunger.

She leans forward like a baby bird, eager to lick the wound. Scratch withdraws it.

"No no," he says. "Maybe later."

The potent blood of the Kindred is instantly addictive. She begins to weep in frustration and we withdraw, holding hands unseen, as doctors and nurses come running.

In half an hour, the sun will rise. I'm in the Brigman family library with Elena. My blood has kept her frozen at age thirty since the end of the Great War. She has the prettiness of that time, like a Clabber Girl advertisement, but she is pale, the veins in her hands and wrists prominent if she does not cover them with makeup. Her gums are a pale pink, like the nose of a rat. While a perfect fit for the shelves of leather-bound texts (with no garish modern paperback to mar the eye), tonight she is visibly hungry and desperate.

Margery enters. She's in her nightshirt. She looks like a little girl, sleepy and confused and wakened by grownups. But the slim shape of her legs would draw the eye of many grown men.

"Margery," I say. "I'd like you to explain to Elena why she has to die."

"What?"

"You do understand that the exchange of the Life is a two-way street, don't you?"

"I... I don't..."

"Margery, your great-grandmother Elena is over a hundred years old. You know this. A cruel, aged death awaits her, but as long as she has the Life within her—my special blood—her demise is in check. Now, her time is running out. Her supply of that rare substance is almost gone. As is my own."

"No, you... you couldn't..."

"Couldn't what? Couldn't deny her what she needs to live? Why not?"

"Is this just because I... because I wouldn't...?"

"It's mine." I mimic her voice. "It feels wrong. I just don't want to."

"But it's, it's not the same..."

"Not at all. *You* can make more. I have to rely on what I can beg, borrow or steal. And your beloved great-grandmother has to rely on me."

"Please," Elena whispers.

Margery looks from her to me and starts to cry. But she steps towards me and pulls down the neck of her nightgown.

"That's a good girl," I say.

"Soon you'll come to like it," Elena says, as I offer her an open wrist. "Soon you'll crave it more than anything." She closes her eyes in bliss. Margery's eyes are closed as well.

"Soon," Elena moans, "Soon you'll count the days until you can be tasted again."

Part Two

Autumn

"The existential dilemma is particularly acute for us, who are not born but made. Too often, we know our maker's purpose—and rebel. Then we must invent ourselves, remade as monsters, and wonder at the mystery of all our breed. Why one vampire? Why a multitude?"
—Bella Dravnzie

Chapter Four:
Braise

It's about ten o'clock and I'm sitting on a tombstone with Ambrose, eating stray dogs. We must look like a couple dirt farmers from down south, shelling peas or something, only these peas wiggle and have hair.

It's the first time in a couple nights that it hasn't rained. It's cold, but cold doesn't bother me any more. It did for a while, but Raphael told me that I could get used to it. He said something about how I just had this memory that cold felt bad, so my brain still thought it felt bad even though my new dead body doesn't really care. Or something like that.

Actually, the cold still kind of bothers me.

But what's good about fall weather is that no one thinks it's weird to wear a raincoat with the hood up. Gloves, they probably figure I'm a wuss, getting an early start on dressing for winter. That's gonna be the best time, winter, when I can put a scarf over my face and bundle up to my eyes and no one will notice anything wrong with me.

I found this culvert by the railroad tracks that turns twice, so no sunlight gets in. There's a grating on the inside, and when it rains it's underwater. Man, the first time I went underwater and stayed down, I just about flipped my lid. But Ambrose was right—I don't need to breathe, so I just lay there and that was it. It's like being cold, I guess. I just *think* I can drown.

It's not like it's the crap sewer or anything. It's the storm sewer. It's just rainwater and stuff.

I meet Ambrose by the graveyard gate. He's got some place in here where he sleeps, and we get some strays. There's a Burger King nearby, where we wrap the dead dogs in plastic and put 'em in the dumpster.

I'm getting better with the beast talking. I'm starting to understand them more, which is hard because they aren't wordy they just… think in pictures. And they don't think about future or past, either. Everything's right now to them.

Ambrose says we shouldn't eat rats because they carry diseases that can spread to human beings. Like, a vampire could drink rat blood and get bubonic plague, and then spread it to the next person he bites without even knowing. I told him I wasn't going to bite any people, so why worry? He says I'll do it someday, but I don't want to.

Tonight's dog looks like someone's escaped pet, really shorthaired and fat, like a tiny bulldog but with a different nose. "*C'mere boy*," I huff at it, and it rubs its face against my hand.

"*Food?*" It asks. Ambrose and I feed dogs a lot, so they like us.

"*C'mere.*" I've got a tarp spread out on my lap. I pick up the dog, flip it over like I'm going to scratch it on the stomach, but I bite it instead.

It yaps and howls and I yell out "Aw *crap!*" Then I start spitting and Ambrose starts laughing.

"I told you," he said. "You've got bite high or you're going to nick the intestine."

I'm trying to strain the dog shit out of the dog blood, then I give up and bite again up at the neck. Poor critter's thrashing all over the place. But I get my fill, even though it tastes lousy. Even when I bite high, it tastes lousy.

Not like with Nina…

"Why don't you just drink somebody?" he asks.

"Not tonight."

"Some night you're going to, you know."

"Not tonight though."

He shakes his head, but he's smiling.

That's how I'm doing it. One night at a time.

I wish I could get drunk, still. Or not even drunk, just catch a little buzz.

Actually, I guess I could. Naked explained to me that if I drink blood from someone who's drunk, I can get drunk off them. But I'm not going to do it. Man, I just can't. Whenever I think of doing that to someone, I remember Brooke and Nina, I remember piling them up by the back door and… no. I can't do that again. Biting a dog is pretty sick, but it's not as bad as that.

I heard this story from one of the guys at work. It happened to his sister-in-law or some friend of hers or something. Anyhow, this woman was a serious smoker, like three packs a day. And she tried everything to quit, tried going cold turkey, tried stepping down, tried rewards, tried smoking brands she didn't like, the gum, the patch, the inhaler… none of it did jack.

Then one day she was taking a bath, and she saw this stuff in the water. Stuff like liquid ash. When she looked closer she saw that this gray stuff was leaking out of her nipples. It was like milk only it was cigarette tar.

After that (the story goes) she couldn't smoke anymore. Even when she wanted to or tried to, the thought of leaking that stuff out was just too disgusting.

I guess this is the same way. I finally found something so nasty that it turned me off booze.

The bad thing is, I want the blood *worse* than I want the booze. It disgusts me, but I want it. So far the disgust is stronger, mostly because I want it to be. But it doesn't make me want it any less.

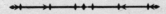

When we're done with the dogs, we clean up with some of those Wet-Nap wipes. I'm getting pretty sick of the smell of those things. I know, I live in a sewer and I sometimes get dog shit in my breakfast, but... I dunno. The smell on Wet-Naps is so fake. It's not a real good smell, it's something pretending to smell good.

Man, I'm starting to think like Raphael.

"You ready for tomorrow?" Ambrose asks. We're sitting on the curb outside a Kum'n' Go. That's where he buys Wet-Naps and garbage bags and other stuff. Ambrose always has some money, but not a lot. I'm going to have to find a way to get some cash. I'm not paying a mortgage or buying dinners or anything, but... I'm keeping my stuff at Raphael's and washing clothes in his basement and *man*, that guy never lets you forget what a favor he's doing you. He's putting up Peaches, too, though I think he ought to pay *me* for having a loyal guard dog around. Raphael doesn't see it that way.

"Sure," I say.

"Not nervous?"

"Nah, I guess not."

"Uh huh." He gives me a look. "Tomorrow, do you want me to... find you someone?"

"What, find me someone to bite on?"

He shrugs. "I could."

"Why do you keep bugging me to do that?"

"Because one day you will."

"Not tonight though. Not tomorrow. I have to have a clear head, right?"

"So you *are* nervous."

I shrug. "I don't want to screw it up. Does that mean I'm nervous?"

"We're all nervous."

Tomorrow we're going to take care of my police problem.

Ambrose looks at me long and hard. "You haven't seen your family lately, have you?"

"No."

"That's good."

Another pause.

"Haven't talked to them or anything? Your wife or your daughter?"

"*No*, man. Why do you keep asking me that?"

"I worry Bruise, that's all. You're smart to keep away."

"I know."

"You're probably smart to keep your fangs off people, too."

"Thanks."

He opens his mouth like he's going to say something else, then shuts it again.

"Whoosa good dog? Whoosa *good li'l girl?*"

"*Me! Me!*" Peaches barks, licking my face. I chuckle.

"That's heartwarming," Raphael says, lip curled. "She peed on the kitchen floor again."

"I thought you were going to keep her in the yard."

"Last time it rained, she pushed her way into the shed and knocked over a bunch of stuff."

"Were you really using all that crap in the shed, or was it there when you moved in?" Ambrose asks.

"That's not the *point*." Raphael looks pissy.

"Look, I'll talk to her about it." I look her in the eyes. "*Pee wherever you want.*"

"All taken care of," Ambrose says.

"So how goes it with the Prince?" Naked asks.

As usual, all of us except Ambrose jump.

"*Dammit*," Raphael squeaks. "Don't *do* that! Christ, is it too much to ask that you knock on the door and wait to be asked in like a, like a *person*?"

"You're just encouraging her," Ambrose says.

"You're so cute when you're startled," Naked says. "Besides, I have to tone up your reflexes if you're leaving us to sit at the grown-up table. Maxie-Max and his blue-blood types play for keeps."

"Do you really think I'm *so eager* to swear fealty to their dusty old monarch with his, his sword and his throne and his nineteenth-century mindset? Get real."

"You seem awfully interested, for someone who doesn't give a damn."

"Look, the Prince of Chicago isn't going to go away just because we ignore him. We're lucky he hasn't 'subinfeudated' us yet, made us all subjects to some crony or offspring. Maxwell and his circle can make things here really, really crappy. If you don't believe me, why don't you ask Anita?"

I've never met Anita. She was a Noseforatsu, which I guess is the name of the vampires like Filthfoot, Naked and me—ugly, or shifty or just off in ways even pointy-toothed Ambrose ain't. She disappeared right about the time I showed up. Some of the vampires—other Noseforatsu like Naked and Filthfoot—have kind of asked me questions like they think Anita might be my "sire," the one who made me a vampire. But I don't remember much about that night and, you know, it's not like they can show me a picture of her. I remember getting bitten by someone really ugly, but with us that doesn't narrow the field.

I don't know what she has to do with the Prince or anything though. I'm still not even clear about who the Prince is or what he's the Prince of, but everyone says I'm better off if he ignores me. Then, usually they lecture me about Brooke and Nina and that cop.

I really don't think that's fair. I mean, I didn't know what I was! No one told me. I had to figure it out, and I think I did okay. I mean, yeah, I wish I hadn't attacked my family and beaten up a police officer, but I haven't killed anybody.

And another thing. Any time I bring that up, that I haven't killed anybody, they say "yet." All of them, they just take it for granted that some day I'm going to do it. Everyone except Ambrose, and even he thinks I *could*. I wish they'd just make up their minds. On one hand, they're always warning me to stay out of sight, don't let anyone know, hide well, be smart, on and on and on. But it's also like they don't think I can keep a lid on anything, that I'm just going to snap and go apeshit on someone for no reason at all!

"...clueless anachronisms with *power*," Raphael is saying, getting in Naked's face. "You seem to conveniently forget that they've got their hands into, into *everything*. If you people ever got your heads up from your tiny little Cicero scene..."

"Oh, here we go," Naked mutters.

"...It's *true* dammit, and it goes beyond Chicago. Everywhere you go, you have to play their game. I know. I've got contacts in Paris and Cape Town and Melbourne..."

"Just how did you make all those *contacts*, Raphael? Send an email to everyone on AOL who had 'I am a vampire' in their user profile?" Naked's toe to toe with Raphael, bobbing her head back and forth. Ambrose cracks a smile, which is rare because he doesn't want people to see his real teeth.

"You can laugh, but you wouldn't have been laughing if Dr. Paul Schaafsma had got his way..."

"Oh, here we go with the Florida story again..."

"Hey, I take my safety seriously! This guy, this Schaafsma guy, he and his buddies killed *seven Kindred* in Miami and Hialeah and Fort Lauderdale..."

"Did you use the word 'Kindred'?" Ambrose asks.

"The point is, if it wasn't for having contacts and working with the power structure, no one would have been able to stop the good doctor. And then *everyone* would know about us!"

"No, I think the *point* is, you want to hang out with the cool kids like you never got to in high school!"

There's a knock at the door and I volunteer to get it. It's Filthfoot.

"You ready to go?" he asks me. I nod.

"Where are *you* going?" Raphael asks, sounding... I dunno, angry? But not really angry. More like he's insulted that he doesn't already know.

"We got a thing," I say.

For a moment, the three inside are silent.

"A thing, huh?" Ambrose asks. I nod.

"Be careful," he says.

"What kind of thing?" Raphael asks.

"Don't worry about it," Filthfoot tells him.

Another little silence as I go out the door.

"That's great." Raphael starts again. "Now they don't trust me. I hope you're happy, Naked, I hope you're glad that you're turning us into a nest of suspicion and fear, just like Chicago wants…"

"Just like Chicago *is*," she retorts, and then the door closes.

"Thank you," I say.

"They talk too much," Filthfoot replies.

Filthfoot has a van, the big old kind with one door on the side and two in the rear. It's all solid metal in back, no glass except windows in the doors. He's got them blacked out and the side door welded shut.

The van's a smart idea—I don't think he sleeps in here, but it's a good place to keep stuff, and he doesn't need to pay rent on it or anything.

The back is full of all kinds of junk—tools and books, gym bags, tied-shut garbage bags, tackle boxes and cardboard boxes and those accordion-file boxes full of papers. Some all sealed up, some open and with pens and wires and maybe a cell phone sticking out of them.

"Tomorrow," he says. "It's like a rite of passage."

"Uh huh."

"You looking forward to it?"

"I guess."

"My advice? Savor it. Saaaavor it. You can't do it twice, you know. It's like losing your cherry."

I'm not sure what he means, because these guys call you "cherry" when you haven't killed anyone yet. Once you do, you "lose your cherry," like losing your virginity. So I don't know if he means one or the other.

"Yeah," I say.

He looks over at me. We're getting on the Expressway, heading in towards the city.

"What are you going to do with eternity?" he asks.

"Sorry?"

"Eternity. Endless life. Or half-life at least." He frowns, honks his horn and flicks off a driver who cut in front.

"I dunno. Do I need a plan?"

"Oh yes. Yes, you need a plan. Or at least, you need a purpose."

"Ambrose said I had to dig a well."

"You do need to dig a well, but you also need a purpose."

When Ambrose says "dig a well," he means get a reliable source of blood. Only they don't always call it blood. Sometimes they call it Vitae. That's Latin, I think.

"Look," Filthfoot says. "Nothing's stopping you from finding some safe little hole and eating a couple cats every night and never interacting with anybody. But you'll go crazy. I mean, anyone would, right?"

"I dunno."

"You'd go crazy. That's no kind of existence. You need *something*."

Twenty minutes ago, he was complaining that Raphael talks too much. I don't want this conversation.

"So what are we doing, anyhow?"

"We're gonna make some money," he says. "Don't worry about it. It's a cakewalk. A milk run. But you gotta think of your future, Bruise..."

"Where are we going? I mean, what's the plan here, huh?"

"We're going up north. Up into one of the big fancy McMansion suburbs, okay? There's this house, big wild money house, we're going to go in and rob it."

"Wait wait wait. I thought you told me you needed my *help*. That this was some kind of... I mean, you made it sound like a big *thing*. And it's just busting into a house and stealing stuff?"

"What, you don't need the dough?"

"I got my cats and my hole in the ground. I don't need charity and I don't need to turn into some kind of *thief*."

He laughs. It's an ugly, screwed-up laugh. He laughs like his face.

"Bruise, buddy, you *are* a thief. You're a thief of *life*. You think that stealing someone's TV and jewelry is worse than stealing their vital essence?"

"I ain't bitten anyone," I say, "Not since that first night when I was all confused…"

"That'll change. You can't survive on kitties and puppies forever."

"Why not?"

"Because you *can't*." He turns his head a little, so that one of his googly eyes points my way. "Didn't anyone tell you?"

"What?"

"Look, the older you get, the more… I dunno, the more undead you become? It's like the power in you gets stronger. And more demanding. Eventually, you won't be able to survive on animals. You'll need to consume something with a soul."

"Huh? Whaddaya mean, 'soul'?"

"I mean a human being. Those elder fuckos, the guys with a hundred years on 'em? They can't use animal blood. It's no good to them."

"What?"

"Honest, man."

For a moment, I can't say anything. "Hell.".

"Sorry to have to break it to you."

For a little while, we just drive. I like the silence, but I have a question that's been bugging me.

"What about vampire blood?"

"What about it?"

"If I drank some."

"Oh." He chuckles, but it's ugly. "You really don't want to go down that road. In three hundred years or so, I hear you actually *have to*, but before that, avoid at all costs."

"How come?"

"Well, because the stuff we got is addictive. *Really* addictive. Makes heroin look like that orange baby aspirin. One taste and you want more, more, more. *Plus*, it makes you go all puppy-eyed and romantic about the vampire you drank from. The more you drink, the more in love you get—even if you drink from a guy! Now, you can always drain another 'Kindred' bone dry, but that's no way to make friends."

"It kills him?"

"And then some."

That does seem a little extreme, just to keep from feeling faggy about someone.

I watch out the window a little more. One of those Dodge Vipers drives by, cool.

"So someday I'll need to eat people, huh?"

"Yep."

"Fuck, I don't even want to steal their TVs."

"Oh Bruise, look, these people deserve it. Really. The people we are robbing, the guy in particular we're robbing... this is like a mission. It's *meaningful*, okay? Afterwards, you'll feel great, really. You'll wish we'd done more."

"How is stealing some rich jerk's stuff going to be meaningful? Just what does that mean, huh?"

"It means possessions are fleeting."

"Yeah, okay."

There's a long pause while we drive through downtown, make our turns, head north. I think about asking him to stop, let me out. But I don't.

We don't say anything else until we pull up at the house.

It turns out Filthfoot needs me for two things. One is the dogs, and the other is being the heavy.

The dogs are serious dogs—a pair of big black Rottweilers, absolutely identical from what I can tell, all thick muscle neck and slobbery jaws on the other side of the fence.

"*Don't belong!*" they bark at us, snapping and growling. "*Don't belong!*"

"*We belong,*" I tell them. "*We're okay. You like us. We're friends.*"

They whine and look around, confused, sniffling the ground near our feet.

"Trice! Hunter! Shut the hell up!" shouts someone from the house.

"*See?*" I wish I had some bacon or something to give them. "*Master wants quiet.*"

"*Not master,*" whines one of them, but they drop their heads and wander away.

"All good," I tell Filthfoot.

"For me too? Not just for you?"

"Yeah."

Then Filthfoot grabs a bar in each hand and just monkeys up, quick as walking. It's kind of weird to watch, he's like a spider. He's got to be freaky strong to do that just with his hands.

I gotta remember not to get Filthfoot mad at me.

"C'mon," he says. "Climb over."

"Can't I just bend the bars? I don't want to fall."

"We can't leave signs."

So I huff and puff and grunt my way over, and then Filthfoot says, "Head to the house. You won't see me, but I'll be right behind you."

"What, it's okay for them to see me?"

"It's only one guy and... yeah. After tomorrow, what's he going to do?"

Good point. I keep forgetting tomorrow. Or, I don't forget it exactly, I just don't think about it when I'm planning anything else. I don't know.

We get up to the back door and there's a little keypad.

"The code is 5462... heck, never mind. It's turned off already. Probably because of the dogs."

"Okay." The door's locked, but Filthfoot tells me to open it, so I pull hard and it crunches open.

"Is someone back there?" It's a man's voice, getting closer.

"Kitchen's as good a place as any." I hear Filthfoot's whisper, but he's nowhere to be seen.

"Deacon? If that's you, shit, come by the front door, those dogs could..."

The guy enters the kitchen and sees me. He stops cold.

"What do you want?" He's a young guy, maybe not even twenty, wearing this shiny purple disco shirt and blue jeans.

For a minute, there's silence. I expect Filthfoot to answer, but he doesn't, so I eventually say, "Give me some money."

Purple-shirt kind of rolls his eyes, almost like a reflex, almost like he's going to say "get a job," but I guess he adds it up that I'm in his house and he's alone and I'm not your typical bum. He makes with the nice, soothing, calm-down-the-maniac voice.

"Sure man, I can help a guy in need. I've got some cash over here in the junk drawer."

He's almost there when I hear Filthfoot. "Hit him, you fool!"

"What?"

Then I see that he's got the phone in his hand and is reaching towards the buttons, but it's Filthfoot who yanks him away.

"Waaak!" The guy actually makes that sound. Like a duck. He's struggling, and I can't see Filthfoot—not like he's invisible, but just like I don't look at him. He's got the guy, the homeowner I guess (though, man, how would a guy that young afford a place this nice?) in a full nelson, or something else where his hands are up and back, and I hit the guy. I hit him right in the stomach, not too hard, but hard enough.

"Work the legs," Filthfoot says. He's not bothering to keep it quiet any more.

"He'll need his breath to tell us where stuff is, and I'm sure he doesn't want us to mess up his pretty little face."

"Who are you?" the guy asks. He's trying to look over his shoulder.

"I'm the guy you never see," Filthfoot says. "I'm the guy on the street with the sign, the guy who'll work for food, and you just walk on by with averted eyes. Give him one, Bruise!"

I give him a kick in the shin. Again, not real hard. He starts to cry though.

"Look, you guys, look, I'll give you what you want, just stop, c'mon, stop okay?"

"You make me sick, you rich young pukes," Filthfoot says. "Bruise—junk drawer. Get some rope or some tape or something. Christ, make yourself useful!" He drags the rich young puke into a chair while I come up with some packing tape—the transparent plastic kind.

"C'mon," the guy says as I start to wrap him up, ankles and elbows and hands together behind the back of the chair. "I've got money. What more do you want?"

"Gee, I don't know. Maybe I want to fuck your tight, puckered little ass. You ever try that, huh? You ever get together with your parasite buddies and compare trust funds and do drugs and sodomize each other?"

"Jeez man," I say. "Let's just get the stuff and get out of here."

"Don't be scared," Filthfoot says. "He can't do nothin' to us. If he calls the cops, we can just tell them about the brick of marijuana he's got stashed. You do have it stashed somewhere nearby, right Barry?"

I guess the kid is named Barry. Barry looks scared.

"How'd you know about that?"

"I know stuff. What I'd *like* to know is where you've got the payroll for your candyman."

"My what?"

"Don't play dumb with me! Just 'cause I didn't buy my way into college on my daddy's dime…"

"No man," I say. "I don't know what a candyman is either."

"You know," Filthfoot says—still completely unseeable— "His, his drug guy. His connection. His motherfuckin' candyman!"

"You mean, like a pusher?"

"Pusher, candy… look, *whatever*, Barry, where's the freakin' money?"

"It's cool man, it's… aw Jesus…"

"Hit him, Bruise."

"No! It's, I swear, it's up in my bedroom! I've got, like a leather satchel, I think it's under the bed or maybe hanging off the chair by the desk, there's an envelope in there with the cash!"

"Bruise, go get it. Oh, and take anything else that catches your eye."

Ten minutes later, he's heckling me about how long I took to come back, but, man, Barry (and his folks, I guess) have some *nice fucking things*. On Barry's desk there was a laptop computer, a cell phone and one of those palm-top schedule gadgets. I found the money where he said it would be—a little envelope, but it's all full of fifties. I also took a look around, checked the den and what was I guess the dad's office. I saw all kinds of expensive looking statues and paintings and... and hell, everything really. I mean, I couldn't tell if all that stuff was real silver or chrome or what. How would I know? But there was a CD player that looked like a radar dish and a bunch of really nice looking pens on the dad's desk. I pocketed those.

"This guy's mom has to have some great jewels," I say, piling the computer and other stuff by the back door.

"Is there the *money*?"

"There is." I hand it off. "What about jewelry?" I ask Barry.

"I... I dunno, look in my mom's room?"

"Your mom's room? Where's that at?"

"Top of the steps, turn left."

"So wait, she and your dad don't sleep together?" Filthfoot asks, but I don't wait for the answer.

Ransacking his mom's bedroom actually makes me feel kind of funny. I mean, I can't get a hard-on anymore, and I don't know what I'd expect to do with it if I did, but this just seems too pervy for me, going through a woman's things. But crap, I need money and these people have obviously got it and then some. I ignore the dresses and shoes, find a couple jewelry boxes and take 'em without looking, and decide to check under the mattress because that's where

I'd hide stuff. There's nothing under the mattress, but when I tip it off the bed it knocks over a vase, which is, I guess, where she keeps her spare change. There's about five hundred dollars there.

Man. The day I changed over, there was less than a thousand bucks in our bank account, and this woman has half that just lying around. Who needs $500 for just walking-around money? I mean, is she on drugs like her boy? Does she just go out and buy, I don't know, hundred-dollar shoes all the time?

I hit Dad's bedroom next and he's only got $220 cash, but shit, that's good enough. Silk boxer shorts, my god. In the bedside table he's got a little bottle of almond oil (for some reason) and a locked wooden box. I take the box and a framed thing with six gold and silver coins—I figure they must be worth something if they're hanging in a rich guy's bedroom.

I get down to the kitchen again. I found a really nice steel briefcase in a closet and put stuff in that, and I don't know what Filthfoot's been saying to Barry, but Barry's *really* crying now.

"You about done?" I ask.

"Look at you, Mr. Robber-Man," Filthfoot says. "No zealot like a convert."

"What's that supposed to mean?"

"Nothing. Okay Barry, we're just going to steal your car and run, but before I go, I'm gonna do something to you."

"Oh Jesus..."

"No, Barry, my man, it's okay. Serious, it's okay. You'll like this. You'll like it a lot."

And then I can see him, and he leans in and chomps down on the boy's neck. Barry tenses up, then goes limp, and his mouth's open and he says "Oh! Oh..."

Filthfoot backs off and says, "You want some more of that?"

"Uh... Uh huh..."

"'Cause it's better than any drug you've had, huh? Well guess what? You can't have any more. Never ever. And you're never even going to know what it was you just lost. That's my little gift to you, you'*rich, lazy fuck*!"

"Jeez man," I say, and Filthfoot looks up at me. Tilts his head my way, anyhow. He grins.

"You wanna give him more? You can, you know. Give him all he wants."

Ambrose explained that getting bitten makes people all happy. Raphael thinks there's some kind of drug in our spit, like a leech he said, and Filthfoot thinks it's the wrath of God making weak people love their sin and punishment. I don't know. But I know it's what Barry wants right now.

God, he smells so good.

"Please," he says. "C'mon guys."

"You want more?"

He's silent a minute, and I can see him crying a little.

"You know I do," he whispers. Filthfoot is upright behind him, grinning.

"I'll be out in the garage." Filthfoot disappears.

He wants it so bad. Like I do.

So I give in.

I thought, just for a moment, that it might be weird with a guy, but it's not, it feels natural and perfectly right and I'm just there, I don't have to think or do anything but just draw it in, just feel good, I lose track of time and forget where I am and don't care what I'm doing…

And then Filthfoot smacks me, hard, right on the back of the neck. I start to cough and he yanks me off Barry by the hair.

"Take it easy, killer," he says.

"What?"

"Look at him."

Barry is slumped in the chair, unconscious. There's a little blood on his collar, a little more from the two holes in his neck. Filthfoot leans down and licks, and the wounds close up. It's another thing, like how I got over being shot so fast, I guess.

"You don't wanna lose your cherry on this guy," Filthfoot says, and he's got his voice slow and gentle, like when you talk to a little kid. "The situation is bad. Guy found tied up, bled to death, no blood anywhere? Nah. Too obvious, y'know?"

I'm only half-listening. God, I would've killed that guy. If Filthfoot hadn't come in, I would have. Not out of being angry or bad or anything, but just... just not paying attention.

We go and steal Barry's Jaguar, and Filthfoot drives off to take it to his contact while I load his van and drive it back to Ladue's place.

"It's not bad," Raphael says, looking over Barry's computer. "This was top of the line, last year." His tongue makes a little ticking sound. "And what does he use it for? Some ten page term papers and porn, porn, porn. Not even any games."

Naked is checking over the jewelry. "This stuff is nice, except that this piece is a fake. But it's a good fake. I'll give you guys a couple thousand for the whole batch."

"I can't negotiate without Filthfoot."

"What's in this box?" Ambrose asks.

"I don't know. It was in the dad's bedside table. You want me to open it?"

"I'll do it," Naked says. "You'd just smash the lock."

"What are you going to do?"

"Pick it. What did you think, that I'd tickle it?"

"Whoa!" Raphael says, staring at the screen. "This guy was into some weirdo stuff."

"Like what?" Naked looks up from the box and her bent paperclip.

"You really have to see it," he says.

"If it's a woman with a horse, I've seen worse," she says.

"It's worse," Raphael tells her.

We gather around and he starts a little computer movie. It's a guy's dick, close up, aiming at the camera. It's a pretty big one, I guess. A hand closes around it.

"I'm not shocked," she says.

"Just wait."

The hand jerks the dick and out pop two AAA batteries. They just shoot out, plop plop. Like from a dispenser.

For a moment, we're all quiet. Then Raphael shuts the lid on the laptop.

"I've seen enough," he says.

"Oho," says Naked, as the wooden box pops open. "Freeze, muthafuckah!"

She's waving a gun, a chrome-plated revolver.

"So, have you and Filthfoot decided how you're splitting stuff?" Ambrose asks.

"Not really, I guess. I figure fifty-fifty."

"Oh really? He sets up the job, he, like, cases the joint, he plans everything and you... you what? Hold the door? Haul stuff?"

"Hey, were you there?" I'm getting a little sick of Raphael's attitude.

"I'm just wondering if you're going to keep any stuff or sell it all," Ambrose says.

"I dunno. Why, you want the gun or something?"

"Guns are mostly good for making cops shoot at you. I'd sell it, if it was me."

"I don't know," Raphael says. "A gunshot wound makes a dead body a lot less suspicious, as long as you make sure to shoot them before they die. Those forensic guys can tell, you know. Shoot them, leave them somewhere the blood would plausibly drain..."

"Like you've done this a lot?" Naked sneers at him.

"I've lost my cherry," he says. And for once, he doesn't sound like a snotty punk kid. He sounds... sad, I guess.

For once, she lets it go.

"Hey, guess what?" Filthfoot says as he enters. He's waving Barry's tiny blue cell phone. I just now realize it's the same exact blue as his car was. "I got me the phone numbers of some other rich bastards!"

We split the goods, I get a quarter of the take, and we sell the jewelry to Naked after Filthfoot haggles her for about an hour and a half. Ambrose and Raphael leave for a couple hours each, then come back. I watch TV.

Mostly though, I'm thinking about Barry. I just about killed him.

And I'm thinking about how I can't get by on animals forever.

And, dammit, I think about what I want to do with the rest of forever.

It's raining at sunset the following night, which is okay, I guess. Shouldn't change the plan one way or the other.

I meet Ambrose at the graveyard and he's got a bunch of dogs rounded up, but I'm not hungry. He tells me I should eat, keep up my strength, and I suck down a couple just to be polite. But it's not anything real. Not like Barry.

"You ready?"

"Ready as I'll ever be, I guess."

I think about asking if it's too late for him to get me someone, but it probably is. And anyhow, I'm really full. I almost feel stuffed, all that blood from Barry last night and then two dogs.

"The important thing is, right before we do it, think strong thoughts. Tough thoughts. Like I showed you, okay?"

"I know, I got it. What's gonna go wrong?"

"Nothing," he says. "We've all got you covered."

At Raphael's, there's the new girl. Or I guess she's not really new; it's just that I've never met her. I get a flash of panic when I first see her—like I gotta get the hell out of there.

"Bruise," Raphael says, "This is Persephone Moore."

"Charmed," she says. She doesn't seem surprised that I'm wigging out and somehow that calms me down.

I feel more like a heel than anything. We shake hands. I don't take my glove off. I don't want to know if she'd jerk back or what.

Persephone is the kind of woman who, when she'd come into Home Depot, never knew exactly what she wanted, and then acted like you were stupid when you tried to explain anything to her. The kind of college graduate who always got good grades in high school, never had ketchup drip on her pants because she never got hot dogs at lunch, always had a salad, and even that never dripped on her.

You know the kind. She's the type who's too good for you.

She's in a tan pantsuit and I don't even know how I can tell, but it looks expensive. The kind of thing Nina would look at and say, "Doesn't that look nice?" and then she'd look at the price tag and shake her head. Meanwhile, I'm in some new coveralls and Ambrose has his greasy leather jacket. The only guy who looks right next to her is Raphael, who's actually got on a suit with a skinny black tie.

"I'm really glad you're willing to help out on this," Raphael tells her. Man. I'm not too smart, but even I know what's going to happen when the chess club geek asks out the prom queen.

"Not a problem," she says.

We needed Persephone in on this because she's got one of the vampire powers that none of the rest of us have. I guess it's like instant hypnosis—she looks in your eyes and says "Sleeeep!" or something and you turn into her zombie. Shit, and I'm screwing around with talking to kitties? If I could learn that one, what else would I need?

Raphael is going over the plan again and Persephone keeps staring at me.

"We've heard this before," Ambrose says.

"Yeah, you mind if I go check Peaches?"

"You and that dog." Raphael rolls his eyes. "Fine, whatever, go see your stupid puppy. We'll just make the plan to save your skin here, if that's okay with you."

Filthfoot's man can set me up with a car—an old beater, but I can keep a car running. Raphael can get me a fake driver's license with the picture from my old one. He's not cheap, but there it is. (Actually, it's kind of funny. Now that I'm dead and a monster, I get to drive again.)

If I get a storage locker to keep my junk, I can pay for a year of it and that pretty much takes care of my big robbery payoff.

It's not a lot, but crime does kind of pay.

"Hey Peaches, hey good dog, c'mere!" I don't use the beast speak on her, I just call her and she comes anyway.

Man, she's one dumb animal. Still loves me. Still thinks I'm the smartest guy around.

"Peaches, listen, I'm going to go away for a while, but I'll be back. While I'm gone, Ambrose is in charge, you got me?"

She whines a little. And then she growls. She's looking over my shoulder.

I turn and I see Persephone in the window. She's got a weird expression on her face. Not snotty or mean... more like when someone's just gotten some really bad news. I don't know. I was at work when this guy Andrew found out his son had got hit by a car. His face was a little like that. What's she seeing, that makes her look like that?

As soon as I turn, she steps back out of sight.

* * *

Dear Nina

I'm sorry what I did to you and I'm sorry what I did to Brooke. I know this doesn't help or make anything better, but I can't take it any more. I tried to quit the booze which was making me so sick and mean. If I'd been sober, I never would of gotten all burned. I remember how that happened now. I was drunk, and you'd think that would help me quit, but I can't do it. I'm too weak. I know I always said this was the chump's way out, but I guess I'm a chump. I guess this is all I've got. I'm sorry I wasn't a better husband or dad, I'm sorry I messed up that cop and took the dog and I'm sorry about Barry too. But I think it's better for you this way, and I think it's better for me.

Love

—Bruce.

Man, writing a suicide note is weird.

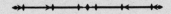

And then we're at the building, on the roof.

"This rain is good," Raphael says. He had all that jazz about how the cold was all in our heads, but he's huddling in a big wool coat. "It'll wash away any evidence that there was more than one person here."

Persephone is downstairs, ready to mind-zap anyone who comes by, I guess.

"You ready?" Ambrose asks.

"Sure." I step towards the ledge. "Tough thoughts, right? Tough thoughts."

"Soon, everything will be cleared up," Raphael says. He's looking around, like he expects a film crew from *Hard Copy* to show up and blow the whole scheme.

"Wait a minute," Ambrose says. "There's one more thing."

I look down. It's a long, long way. Forty feet doesn't sound so far, but it's a long way. I'm going to hit soft dirt and mud. It's a vacant lot with an old wooden fence around it, all full of beer cans and bottle caps. Just soft mud. But it's still a long way.

"What is it?" I ask. Forty feet, I could run that in no time. It's different when it's up and down, though.

"Look at me. Please." His hand is on my shoulder.

I turn and his grip tightens, and then I feel this hit, this hard blow, right in my chest. I look down and there's a plank of wood sticking out of me.

A stake through the heart. Man. I know about this—hell, it was Ambrose who told me! You get a stake through the heart and it knocks you out. Actually, it looks like he broke this off the fence down below. Very clever. Suicide guy jumps and lands on the fence. Sure.

The last thing I feel before blacking out is myself going over the edge.

Chapter Five:
Persephone

Bruce Miner—or "Bruise," I suppose—looks even worse when he isn't moving. I didn't think that was possible.

We're in the hospital. Ambrose called in the jump from the closest phone booth, anonymously of course. Then Raphael picked me up, police scanner blaring, and we followed the ambulance to the hospital.

All the way, he droned on and on about how he hoped the Prince appreciated how hard he was working to keep Bruise under control. Kept trying to see if I could set him up somehow. Sure, Raphael. I can set you up. I'm bigger than herpes at court. Almost as popular, too.

It's a relief when we get to the hospital and he leaves me alone. I put on a doctor's coat and head down to the morgue. It almost feels odd, stuffy, to wear one of my old lawyer suits. I tried not to let that evil bastard Solomon scare me off my friends, but I've been drifting farther from them. I should fix that, I shouldn't let him isolate me but... the last time I made an appointment with Rick, someone had gotten there before me.

"Can I help you?" asks the attendant.

"I belong here." I grab his mind with my eyes and squeeze that idea into it.

"Right, of course."

Then it's just a matter of waiting for Bruise, waiting for a doctor to check him out and, yeah, he's sure dead all right, no pulse or vitals, sign the paper.

(The doctor is short, with sandy brown hair. Very nice.)

All we need is a positive ID, and since he had his wallet with his library card and a signed suicide note, that shouldn't be long coming.

I didn't give much thought to Bruise's survivors, I guess. I mean, I knew he had a wife and a daughter, and I guess I pictured her as poor and cringing and pale, the kind of battered wife that they put on the mailer to get you to contribute to the shelter. I figured the daughter would be a scrawny waif with wide eyes and slap marks.

In fact, the wife is just on the good side of portly, and she's a little pushy and overbearing. The daughter is chewing her gum and snapping it, and she's wearing a skintight midriff shirt with TRAMPY! spelled out in cheerful little sequins. Jeans as tight as paint with flared bottoms over towering platform shoes complete the outfit. Maybe she dressed to try and attract a doctor's eye.

"I'm sorry if I woke you out of bed, Mrs. Miner..."

"It's all right, look, can we cut to the chase?"

"If you wish. I just..."

"Okay, pull back the sheet. Please?"

The doctor sighs and does it.

There's a moment of silence, except for a little gum crackle.

Nina Miner says, "Yeah. That's Bruce."

In an instant, she's exhausted. Her mouth crumples up and her head drops, then she turns it, looking for a chair. The morgue attendant hastily brings one forward and she sinks into it.

"Daddy?"

I turn to Trampy and suddenly she looks like she's about twelve years old. Instead of a sassy teen who, like, totally can't be bothered... suddenly she's the little orphan girl I expected from the poster, a sad waif trying to be grown-up with too much makeup. She gives a big snort, and sort of chokes for a moment, then a big swallow.

"Daddy..."

"I'm very sorry," the doctor says, and tries to put the sheet back over Bruce Miner's face.

"No!" The daughter teeters forward on her platform shoes, grabs the sheet and pulls it back. "No, don't!"

"Honey..." This is the mom.

"*Don't take him away!*" Her face is instantly beet red and she curls her whole body in, pulling back the sheet so that we can see just how badly broken the dead man is.

(And of them, I alone know that there's still something like life in that still body, something just waiting for another chance...)

"I'm afraid we have to..."

"*Fuck you!*" The girl screams it. "*Fuck you all!*"

"Brooke that is *enough*!" Mom stands up and heads towards her daughter, very no-nonsense again. I guess a crisis brings it out in her.

"No!"

"Brooke, give me the sheet."

"Nooooo!" They're tugging at it, back and forth, and the mom is almost as red as the daughter.

It's like watching him with his dog. You're not sure if it's tragedy or farce.

The daughter slaps the mom. Mom's eyes open and her mouth sets, she grabs one wrist and one ear and then I'm there. I don't know why I didn't act sooner. It was like the slap sound switched me back on.

"That's enough." I dose the mom first, look her in the eyes and... wow. There's a pause of challenge and then she lets go, she obeys.

I don't think she would have, if some part of her hadn't wanted to.

"Calm down," I tell the daughter, and she's a lot easier, she sinks to the floor and just sobs. The attendant, in the meantime, has gotten a new sheet to put over the body. The doctor helps the girl to her feet, says he thinks the staff counselor is free now. Gently, he leads the pair away and it's just me and the attendant and cold Bruce Miner.

"Must be nice," I mutter to him, "Knowing that you were loved."

After that, the night gets pretty boring. I wait for the cops, plant the suggestions there, wait for the orderlies, plant more suggestions, wait for the doctor without the beard, take his blood and make him forget it... I spend a lot of time there, in the morgue, and when I start to feel dawn approaching I open Bruise's little freezer-drawer and tell him, "I'll be back for you tomorrow night." He's starting to curl up, adopting the fetal position around the stake. Then I make the orderly forget what I just said and did, and I'm out of there. A cab ride home and to bed.

The next night it's Saturday and more screwing around with Miner and the Cicero unbound. I get there early, before I even feed, hoping it's the same doctor, but no. Some guy with a black crew cut, too skinny. No thanks— too easy to slip up.

It's a different attendant too, a woman with straight hair, too long for her face.

"Can I help you?"

"I'm supposed to be here."

"Right."

"Can I see the Miner paperwork?"

She looks uncomfortable. "Well, it's a sealed file. You know, a police matter."

"Right. Let me rephrase that. Get me the Miner paperwork."

"Of course."

She's really pliable. I wonder what makes her like that? Did she get beat up a lot as a kid? Or maybe she was so privileged and cosseted that she never got any toughness.

I wonder what I would have been like? How easy I would have been? Hell, for all I know, someone *did* use it on me when I was living. Maybe Maxwell did....

I don't want to think about that now. Paperwork. Check. Definite identification, definite statement of death, all good. Death certificate, all in order, stamped and signed. It is officially established that Bruce Miner is legally dead. As suggested (by me, to everyone), no autopsy is scheduled. No one has gone poking at his corpse to notice that he probably has fewer broken bones than he should. No one has decided to do anything foolish like remove the chunk of fencing that so obviously killed him. Great.

"You're not going to see what happens next," I tell her. It's an awkward proposal, but it'll warm her up for the next memory-erase.

"Sorry?"

I open Bruise's drawer, pull him out and yank out the fencepost from his chest.

"Gah!"

He reacts like a cardiac patient who's just gotten shocked to restart his heart. Bella tells me that a stake in the heart drives us into a terrible sleep full of nightmares and warped memories. Bruise clearly didn't enjoy the ride.

He starts to get up, fangs out and the hunger written all over him. I can see the hole in his chest starting to seal up, which is only going to make him hungrier. I need to calm him down and Push Out to do so.

"Shh," I say, "It's all right. Just move." He does.

"Th—Thanks," he tells me.

The attendant has backed up against the wall and is rubbing her eyes. That weak little brain of hers is struggling to believe three impossible things before breakfast.

Bruise stares at her and I know that look. I push him along and turn back to her.

"You didn't see that," I tell her, as I shut the locker door. "Go sit at your desk. In a minute, I mean, a moment, I'm going to leave. When I close the door, put your head down and fall asleep. When you wake up, you'll briefly remember an odd dream, but it will fade like all dreams do. Nobody looked at Bruce Miner's paperwork and no one looked at his body. Understand? Good. Go."

I close the door. Bruise is outside.

"Man," he says. "That instant hypnosis thing…"

"Here, drink this." I pull out a bag of preserved blood. Not easy to get, but I don't want any more outbursts from Miner.

He doesn't hesitate much and slurps it down. "Thanks. I mean, thanks a lot. For… well, you know. Without you, this would have been…"

"It's fine," I say. "Anything for the Masquerade."

"For the what?"

Good grief.

"Anything for the Masquerade" is a gross exaggeration, of course. I'm trying to keep an eye on Miner because Maxwell suggested it. God, it was awful. Like when my real dad dressed me down for wanting to be popular and suggested I get a job after school.

It was especially galling because he said it after I told him about Solomon.

"What do you mean, 'maybe he's right'?" I asked and I could almost feel tears beading in my eyes. But I didn't cry. I wouldn't cry. Persephone doesn't cry. Even Linda's too old.

"I don't mean that he was right to treat you so roughly, but are your mortal friends going to do you much good in your new state?" He agreed to see me in the same damn Palmer House penthouse where he changed me. It almost made me queasy, luxurious and anonymous at the same time. It could be anywhere, but it's where I died.

"Do me much…? I don't have them to get advantages; they're my *friends*. They make me happy."

"Oh. How do they compare?"

"I'm sorry?"

"Persephone, darling, you fed before you came here. I saw you." Then I *definitely* felt creepy. "What do these 'friends' give you that compares?"

"It's… it's not the same."

"Of course it isn't. Your entire nature, now, is focused on the theft of precious blood. Nothing else a mortal offers can compare."

"Then you think I... I should leave? I should go to New Orleans?"

"No, not at all. You have a great deal to do here. But I think you should turn your mind and energies to things appropriate to what you now *are*."

"Feeding and keeping hidden."

"Those are the essentials, but the potential is far greater. You could still be walking these streets in a hundred years, or a thousand! From that perspective, don't the petty struggles of your clique of young urban professionals seem petty and unworthy?"

"Then what? I should get involved in Kindred politics? I should start scheming with Invictus and the Ordo Dracul and the rest of them?"

He gave me a look, and I couldn't tell if it was pity or a strange admiration. "You could accomplish things far beyond the realm of posturing for the Damned. But I will say that until you master those machinations, you will never surpass them."

"I'm already your offspring..."

"Which has become as much a problem as an advantage. Make yourself useful! Contribute to the *gemeinschaft*."

"Do you really expect to sell me on humanitarianism for creatures that are no longer human?"

"By no means. When you've played the game for a century or so, altruism will baffle you." He said it with a twinkle in his eye, but his next words were sincere. "Being useful is how you incur debt, and debt is the fuel that runs the machine."

I don't know why I said "in a moment" to the orderly, as opposed to "in a minute." It's not like she's going to literally think I meant sixty seconds. I guess I choked. But it's fine. I'm sure the suggestion worked fine, especially on her little Play-Doh brain. And yeah, Bruce Miner's body disappears, but the cops aren't going to care much. Maybe the widow will sue the hospital. Good on her, she could probably use the money.

When the door opens at Raphael's house, the rest of his little posse all jump out and yell "Surprise!"

No, really, they do. There are two absolutely horror show gruesome Nosferatu, there's Ambrose, and there's Raphael, along with a couple others I don't know. Some of them are, I swear, holding out wrapped presents.

Miner's *dog* is there too, yapping and jumping and licking his face.

Raphael and the male half of the freak show couple push towards the front, jovially bickering over which gift Bruise should open first. Raphael has given him a driver's license for "Reinhart Bruce," there's a MasterCard and a birth certificate and a library card too. From Mr. Wreckedface (who, I can't help but notice, is barefoot) it's a little PDA, which makes him and Bruise laugh for some reason.

"It's got everything," the guy says. "Digital camera, GPS, MP3 player..."

"Yeah, but does it have the triple-A movie?"

As soon as Bruise says this, everyone laughs.

They're pulling him inside and he turns to me and... and I swear, he actually looks *shy* as he says, "Uh, hey... you want to...?"

For a minute, I'm tempted. They seem to be actually having *fun*. But what would Loki think? Me, hanging with the unbound? Loki's one of the last friends I've got left. At least, I hope he is.

"I've got business elsewhere," I tell him.

"Yeah, of course."

I turn to my car, and I *do* have business elsewhere. But it doesn't make me feel much better.

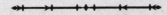

The business of doing business cheers me up, though. As it always has.

I meet Mr. Larkin and Mrs. Larkin at the offices of Hatch, Hatch and Hurst. Their son, Billy, is with them, poor-postured in a corner chair with his attention—his whole body, almost—curled around a GameBoy.

I like the Larkins. Nice people. I'm giving them a good price for their house, partly because I can afford it and partly because I just feel like they're good people. It's not like they're perfect, but they seem warm and tolerant towards each other. There's an easy understanding between them, with no sense of the fear or manipulation you get in so many other families. They remind me of growing up in Indiana.

I think it was Tolstoy (or Dostoevsky?) who said that all happy families are alike, while each unhappy family is unhappy in its own way. I like that. The Larkins, then, are my stand-in for every normal family in America, or in the world. That's why giving them a sweet deal feels right.

Plus, they have no idea what they're sitting on.

Scott Hurst, my good friend, is drawing up the papers. I could do them myself, but I don't want my name on them. Instead of buying the Larkin house for Linda Moore, I'm arranging it for the Brown Civic Trust. (A trust funded and run solely by me, of course, but there it is.) Instead of a deal brokered and described by Linda Moore, lawyer with Barclay, Mearls and Shaw, it's a Hurst deal. My connection to it *can* be found, but not easily.

All this made Scott uneasy, of course. He wants to know if I'm hiding something. Wants to make sure I'm okay, wants to know about Detective Birch. I keep putting him off and putting him off, but he's smart and he's determined to save me—unless I prove that I don't need saving. There's only so much I can do, though. The book club meets over lunch.

"Everything's to your liking?" I ask the Larkins.

"I think so," Papa Larkin says. He's smiling a little, a professional smile, trying not to split into a cheerful grin. He knows he's getting a good price. Part of him is still waiting for the other shoe to drop, but it's a small part and shrinking fast. He now feels he knows me. (As I know them. She's a schoolteacher—junior high, the same school Billy attends, the school where he plays lacrosse. Dad's an insurance salesman. In fact, he sold me some life insurance lately. The beneficiaries are my brother, my parents and the Brown Civic Trust.) He trusts me. He likes me.

His house was built by Andrew Guilford in 1924. Only no one knows because the city clerk mistyped the records, indicating that the architect and builder was "Andrew Fuilford." The error got encoded when the files were recopied into a database, and no one ever noticed it until me.

Before my fatal date with Maxwell, I was a real estate lawyer. On the night I was introduced to Kindred society, I mentioned that to a Kindred named Dubiard, who told me about Guilford. Over the next few weeks I was busy learning how to be a vampire, but the Guilford business stayed with me. Just the idea that the *whole time* I was wheeling and dealing, there were *nests built for vampires* hidden under my very nose... so I got curious and I started poking around and my old colleague Scott half-jokingly said he remembered a *Fuilford* house coming on the market. What a memory, huh?

We sign the papers and set the date, and on next Wednesday they'll be out—they'll be in their new house in the suburbs. Close to the train station and the DuPage Children's Museum. Everyone smiles, everyone jokes about wrist strain from writing our names so many times and then the Larkins file out and, I'm guessing, go get frozen yogurt treats.

I stay behind because Scott asks me to.

"Linda," he says. "About that guy..."

"It's not a big deal."

"Look, I called around and no vice squad in Chicago has a detective named Birch!"

"I've taken care of it."

"Why did he call you 'Persephone'?"

I sigh. I listen carefully.

The Larkins are gone. There are a couple other secretaries in the office, but I don't think they'll come in the conference room.

"How... how private are we, here?"

He crosses to the door and locks it. I follow two steps behind him, and when he turns around I fling myself into his arms.

He wasn't expecting it, but maybe figures I'm breaking down, bursting into tears, about to unburden myself of some horrible double life.

He's part right.

"Linda, what...?"

Then I bite him.

It's very strange, drinking a friend. Scott Hurst actually offered me a position with his firm. It was my best interview, really. I went with Barclay, Mearls and Shaw because the money was better, but I got re-acquainted with Scott after a year in practice. We met again at the dinner at the Shedd, him and his wife and me.

Scott is a decent guy, his wife's a sweetheart. They have two kids in college. He even drives a Prius. Used to climb mountains when he was younger but quit because he fell and actually broke his back, lost feeling in his legs and had to be flown out by chopper. He recovered, eventually. Quit climbing, which was probably smart.

I knew all this about him when I was alive, but until I sank my fangs into his neck, I never really *knew* him.

The blood flows and I know. I taste the wildness that drove him to climb up into the sky, and the caution that made him quit. I taste his core of decency, warm and sweet and gentle, but with a roughness to it necessary for strength, an undercurrent of outrage that he never shows but that keeps his goodness warm, keeps it moving despite defeat and resistance. I taste how he's lost the mountains and misses them every day, and how his warm comfortable life as a father and husband is slowly, slowly suffocating that loss.

I pull back and gently close the wound, knowing that someday his passion will die, and he will be more content, but less of a man. His blood seethes in me, bittersweet.

"Forget," I tell him.

The next night is the first Sunday of the month and we all meet, once again, at the Aquarium.

Loki's out front, alone again, and I greet him. He just grunts.

"What's wrong?" I ask him.

"What do you think of the Carthians?" he asks.

Here we go.

"I don't think anyone has all the answers," I tell him.

"Okay. You like the Carthian questions better?"

"I prefer them to the Lancea Sanctum."

"What does that mean?"

"I guess it means I'd rather know whether I have representation than know whether I have a soul."

"Hmph."

"What about you?"

"Me? I'm a sworn officer of the court. My loyalty is unquestioned, right?"

"Nobody's loyalty is unquestioned. Not with your boss around."

"Norris is all right," he says.

"Sure. But would you want to be stuck in an elevator with him?"

"No Kindred I know passes that test," he says, but I've got him smiling now.

"Is it busy tonight?"

"Packed. What did you expect?"

"I expected packed."

"You won't get a good seat."

"Anywhere I can hear him holler is a good seat."

He grins wider. "You should be careful how you talk about the elders."

"I should, shouldn't I?"

He pauses, then asks, "Do you ever wonder about the Prince?"

"What do you mean?"

"Do you ever think he might be... I don't know." He squints and looks around, as if he expects Norris' Thought Police to jump out and grab him. Even though he's one of them.

"Do I ever think Maxwell might be what?"

"Losing it?"

"Losing his throne? That's ridiculous." But I can't help feeling a stab of fear. How much worse would Solomon be without Maxwell holding him back?

He's quiet for a moment. "Losing his grip," Loki whispers.

"What, because of me? Is that what this is about?"

"Forget it. Forget I said anything."

I don't answer, but I don't leave either.

"Is this some kind of loyalty test? Some kind of crazy test?"

"Yeah," he says. "Sure. You passed. Go in and see your beating."

I get down to the amphitheater and it's as crowded as I've ever seen it by night. There are at least a hundred Kindred milling around, muttering to one another and glancing to see who's looking at them. Half of them have their fangs out and it's like there's electricity buzzing in the air, lighting up everyone who enters with fear or bloodlust.

The décor this month doesn't help. Instead of flattering candles, the hall is lit with fluorescent klieg lights that would make a swimsuit model look washed out and pale. On us, the effect is universally ghastly. There are no shadows, everything is glaring and stark and instead of drawing attention to the throne, we all seem to be looking at the five great black banners hanging in front of the windows. Lit from beneath, the spotlights turn the glass into mirrors, showing us as a hazy mass, half-real. In the middle of each great streamer is a white circle with a crimson design—they alternate the spear of the Lancea Sanctum and an all-seeing eye that represents Maxwell. All in all, the effect is very Leni Riefenstahl, very *Triumph of the Will*.

The thickest clot is up near the bowl of blood—the weak and the young, slaking their thirst on something their bet-

greg stolze

ters dropped and eager for the chance to see someone stronger get laid low.

I head down the center aisle, ignoring the laugh that breaks out from a little clot of Armani suits and Vera Wang dresses. (They have Kindred in them, but I'm sure the clothes are ultimately more useful to society.)

Past them are two black Kindred—they seem to get darker and darker while we get paler and paler. One is a stranger to me, old when he got Embraced: the deep lines of his face make it look like the bark of an ancient oak. Yet his hair is still perfectly black, swirling around his skull like a corona. He's talking to a woman who is tall, slender and absolutely bald. She's wearing a mannish tuxedo tailored for her slim curves. I've seen her before, but rarely, and never this close. She has marks on her scalp, the imprint of a spider and its web. They can't be tattoos, because you can't tattoo white, but they aren't scars either; they're not raised. The eyes she turns on me are the skim-milk color of cataracts, but she follows me as I walk. The language they speak is alien in my ears. Bella's group is larger, an eclectic mix. About a quarter of them are in rubber-club gear (one of the men has carried it to the point that he's got on a no-mouth gimp mask), another quarter are in more mainstream "buy me a drink and fuck me" dance clothing, and maybe ten percent are women in really formal regalia—like tiaras and opera gloves. The remainder are dressed in jeans and flannel, maybe accessorized with a stocking cap—somewhere on the continuum from "shabby chic" to "got a quarter, pal?"

"Good evening," I say. I'm in one of my best dresses, black silk and lace. I should fit in, but when they turn to me I can almost *feel* them ostracizing me. I mean, they're all commingled, the grungiest talking easily to the most dazzlingly bedecked. Their eyes flick to Bella, who smiles widely.

"Persephone! So good to see you!"

"Thank you." There's a pause. "What do you think of the set dressing?" I ask, gesturing at the looming banners.

"Appropriate for the occasion," she says.

"Pretty blatant with the 'Lancea Sanctum vs. the Prince' motif, don't you think? Solomon's probably furious at whoever put it up."

Bella raises an eyebrow. "It was Solomon who won the right to decorate this month."

Everyone except Bella's group keeps talking. Her friends are silent. Like they're waiting.

Screw this.

I wish I could just shrug, turn and walk away without a word. I believe the British call it "cutting them dead." But Bella's too important. I need to get out gracefully.

"If you'll excuse me…"

"Must you go?"

"I do, I have to have a word with…" I cast my eyes around the room. Tobias has his back to me, Raphael looks as lost as I do but no way am I getting *his* stink of loser sweat on me. Loki can't bail me out, I can't be seen running to my sire…

"Norris," I finally say.

Bella blinks and her eyebrows go up. I think it's genuine. She opens her mouth, then shuts it again, then says, "Okay."

Her followers start muttering, even before I walk away. What have I gotten myself into?

I find Norris down towards the front, at the side, talking to Miriam. When they see me coming, they clam up. I don't like it that I have that effect on people.

"Persephone!" says Norris in that horrible, grating voice. "How are you this evening?"

"Well, thank you."

Suddenly, Miriam is gone and I didn't even see her leave. How'd she do that?

"Now, do I understand correctly that you were a lawyer?"

"I still am a lawyer."

"Of course, of course." He chuckles. "As far as anyone knows, you're still 'alive,' yes?" He actually makes air-quotes for *alive*. "I just ask because, heh, before I became an undying blood sorcerer, I was a jurist myself."

"Is that so?"

"Mmmyes. I like to joke that it was not such a very big adjustment. Heeh heeh."

"You know how many lawyer jokes there are?"

"Oh yes, everyone loves the jokes…"

"No, it's… I'm actually *telling* a joke." God, it's like pulling teeth. Get it together, Persephone! "Do you know how many lawyer jokes there are?"

"Oh, a riddle?" He thinks for a moment. "There are… two."

In unison we say, "The rest are all true stories."

There's a little gap in which we should laugh. We don't.

At that moment, the gong clangs. Maxwell is about to enter.

Norris' hand is on my arm. "Would you care to sit with me?" he asks. "I'm up at the front."

He's an elder. Can I refuse?

The command to rise is superfluous. Everyone's already standing, as if it's a rock concert. Garret enters looking unusually somber, dressed in a tuxedo with a red sash, and *medals*. He looks like an ambassador at a funeral, with a black drape on his top hat. Behind him walks the Prince, clad tonight in a timeless tuxedo, complete with tails, black gloves, studs and a black cravat. Except for his race, he'd fit in at any high society burial of the last hundred years.

Even those of us in the front are shoulder to shoulder. Norris has seated himself far to the right. I'm between him and the broad, brooding presence of elder Rowen.

"As many of you know," Garret declaims, "Tonight is a solemn occasion. Two months previous, Elysium was defiled by an act of violence. Though the shedding of blood is in our nature, Elysium has always been holy ground to all Kindred, a place where one can speak in safety. This protection extends to the lowliest of outcasts, and the punishment reaches to the most prominent of elders."

I wonder how Raphael feels about that formulation.

"In accordance with the rules of Elysium and the laws of the Prince, a punishment has been decreed. Now we carry it out, in your view, so that all of our Kindred may know the justice of this court is stern and constant."

As he speaks those words, Solomon comes forward.

He emerges from the same arch Maxwell used. (I wonder what the two of them talked about backstage?) He's stripped to the waist and the relief map of scars on his torso must be visible even up at the top, in the cheap blood section. He walks with his head held high, not like a shame-faced prisoner. Justine Lasky is two steps behind him. She's probably supposed to look like his judge, but she looks like his handmaid.

Behind her, on a little rolling platform, sits a brazier of white-hot coals. Someone I don't know—not mortal, but strangely unfazed by the flames (vampires know each other on sight now, thanks to the Predator's Taint)—is pushing it, and when it rolls to a stop he produces a small bellows and starts pumping it up. I can hear people shifting away behind me and I have to sit on my hands to keep from moving back myself. Inside me I feel every muscle tensing to run, but I won't give in to the fear. I won't be that little girl at the movie theater who cowers when the hunters come on in *Bambi*. The elders around me sit still. I will be like them.

Garret, with a bow, accepts the sword from Maxwell and shoves it down deep in the coals. They leave it there to heat up. I'm sure a blowtorch would be faster, but so much less *dramatic*. There's probably some crusty old handbook of Kindred lore that describes the proper way to beat some-one with a hot sword.

Justine produces a pair of handcuffs, and Solomon says, "Those won't be necessary."

She takes a half-step back, but then Maxwell speaks.

"Put them on, Solomon."

There's a tone to his voice that doesn't fit. Everything to this point has been Grand Guignol, stagy, overblown. But the Prince sounds like a man who's just fed up with

greg stolze

this shit. He sounds like he's not playing along. Like he's not playing at all.

Solomon looks over at him and for a moment—just a moment, the first moment ever—I see him look uncertain. But he rallies.

"Fine."

Justine puts the cuffs on Solomon's wrists. He raises his hands by his face, looks at them, adjusts them so that they're tighter... and then, with a shrug of his shoulders, he snaps them. I'm close enough that I can see the center link go spinning up into the air, and I hear it plop into the water behind him for some porpoise-trainer to find.

Maxwell is now on his feet. He didn't jump up, there's no anger—he just stood. He looks resigned.

"These can't stop me *now*," Solomon says, jingling his new bracelets. "What good would they do if I lose myself?"

Prince Maxwell shakes his head. "You really do have lessons to learn about proper formalities. Don't you?"

"Isn't that what this is all about?"

The two of them are usually so chummy, but not now. There's a low mutter throughout the hall, punctuated by voices pressed into urgent hisses, words spoken with unintended shrillness. I've heard a lot of muttering at Elysium, but for the first time ever there is no voice, not a single one, with a tone of irony or sarcasm. This is serious and everyone knows.

Maxwell holds out his hands for thick gloves, puts them on and draws the burning sword.

"Kneel."

Solomon does.

"One!" the Prince says.

I should be enjoying this, but I can't help but wince as the first blow lands.

Solomon's expression, however, does not change.

"Two!"

The second blow is harder. It whistles through the air and Bishop Birch's body shudders with impact, but he doesn't flinch. His hands lie open on his knees, calm and still.

"Three."

Maxwell's voice is low this time, slow, and this blow is more like a caress, a slow stroke along a rib, and I realize that with the others there was little chance for the sword to really burn. This time, though, I hear flesh sizzle. I'm close enough to smell it.

Solomon's hands quake, but his face remains unchanged.

"Four!"

Another hard blow. He's hitting each time with the flat of the blade, and this time he sends it right into the side of Solomon's head. Solomon can't stay upright and he falls. A snarl creases his face... and then disappears, like wrinkles in a sheet when the bed is getting made. Calmly, steadily, he pushes himself upright for more punishment.

Maxwell makes him wait. He goes to the brazier, puts in the blade and stokes it himself.

"Five! Six! Seven!"

The strikes come in blistering succession, falling on shoulders, back and then the soles of Solomon's bare feet. Birch's nostrils are wide like a mad dog. His eyes squeeze shut and then pop open, his hands curl but don't quite clench into fists...

And Maxwell pauses.

He takes a step to the right and to the left, examining the kneeling form before him.

"Hm..." he mutters. His face is thoughtful.

Solomon is sweating. Vampires sweat blood.

"Yes... Eight."

I never dreamed Maxwell had this in him.

It's another slow and gentle touch, but this time it's with the tip, it's in Solomon's *ear*. No one deserves this. I hear the hubbub behind as Kindred stumble to their feet and flee this scene, gripped by the fear of fire and more, the fear of the Prince.

(And me? I don't know if I want to flee or if I want to run up and grab the sword from my sire's hands. I don't know if I'm nauseated or envious, the conflicting alien urges so strong that I'm frozen, the little bit inside that went to law school and grew up in a nice town is suspended between monstrous fear and savage bloodlust...)

Still Solomon does not move away. His face is contorted and blood steams as it runs down his chest. The Prince follows the drip line with the tip and makes a slow, hot, excruciatingly thin cut down the side of Solomon's neck.

(How can he do it? How can he stay still for this? I *know* what the red fear is like, I know what must be screaming through his veins but he stays there, motionless, just taking it.)

"Nine."

This time he cuts with the edge. This time the crowd is silent.

He swings it in a rapid sweep, skipping down the knobs of Solomon's spine, slicing off coins of flesh at each bone. Solomon rears upright, mouth open and fists clenched...

But he does not scream, damn him!

Instead, he opens his eyes and looks right at me. He holds my gaze, makes sure I see him seeing me. His face is utterly inscrutable and that makes it worse than any spoken threat or menacing grimace.

Then, slowly—and Maxwell is waiting, he makes no move to interfere—Solomon turns the same gaze on Justine. I see her eyes widen, and when he sees the same, he turns his face to the crowd. Is he looking at all of them? Or has he picked out Raphael?

Suddenly, Maxwell seems bored.

"Ten," he says, and swats Solomon lightly on the ass with the cooling weapon. Without even looking he tosses it to Garret. "Clean this," he says, then turns and leaves without a backwards glance.

The muttering begins at once. Solomon remains where he is for the moment.

"Would you come with me, please?" Norris once more has his hand on my arm. It's his left hand. He has a manicure, and a wedding band on the index finger.

I let him draw me away, all the time thinking of Bella's advice to never go off with him alone.

A life-sized model of a blue whale hangs in space over the aquarium cafeteria, but Norris leads me above it to the somewhat ritzier restaurant. It's closed, dark, but he opens the door with his own key. No Kindred are here, of course. What use would they have for a place where humans eat?

He takes an upended chair from a two-seat table and rights it for me, then repeats the action for himself. But he makes no move to produce light. We are looking at each other from what light spills in from the city.

"You know what I like about you, Persephone? I like that I feel no inclination to like you."

It takes me a moment to figure that one out.

"Bella told me that you don't... care to have your feelings manipulated."

"Heeh, yes. That was..." He pauses, sucking his teeth. "Bella," he says next. "You are wise to cultivate her. But I think you've gotten as close as you're going to without embracing her little coven."

"Maybe I'll convert, then."

"The Circle is not to be joined lightly. And they would know if you were less than fervent in your faith. They have ways. Besides, they would threaten your already-damaged credibility."

"What do you mean?"

He sits across from me and steeples his fingers. The nails on his right hand are all gone. They must have been pulled out while he was still breathing.

"You are the childe of the Prince. You have sworn oaths to him and to his way," he says. "Yet are a known Carthian sympathizer and are seen consorting with notorious unbound."

"Seen by whom?"

"Someone discreet, of course. Have no fear." His eyes twinkle. "Your friend Loki doesn't know. Yet."

greg stolze

Jesus.

"So what do *you* want?"

"What have I always wanted? I want information. That is my position. I am the Prince's nerve center."

"And you always need new eyes and ears."

He simpers an affirmative. "The renegades," he says.

"Bruise Miner."

"Who is his sire?"

"Don't you know?"

"Obviously, if I did, I wouldn't need to ask you."

"So you *need* to ask me?"

Then everything changes. Before I have time to shout "Hey!" he grabs my wrist with both hands, contorts it painfully and pins it down on the table.

"Ahhhhh!"

"I do not enjoy banter on work matters." Up close his teeth are bleach white and his breath smells like rancid milk. "If you know, tell me now."

"No one knows!"

He lets go. I massage my wrist. I try to glare at him, but I can't, I can't get the scared look off my face. God, I'm such a weakling.

"Bruise does not know?"

"He doesn't remember anything. He was drunk."

"Hm..."

"Raphael... you know him, he's kind of their leader?"

"Mr. Ladue. *Old John's* get."

Old John? Who the hell is Old John? "Raphael thinks it was someone called Anita, some Nosferatu they haven't seen since Bruise showed up."

For a moment, Norris just sits still. Computing, I guess.

"Miner doesn't know, Ladue doesn't know, but the prime suspect is this 'Anita'—another stray, I presume?—who hasn't been seen since Miner emerged. Heh." He gives me a shrewd look, another bleachy smile. "One is tempted to think that Miner *is* Anita."

"What?"

"Such a sophisticated change of appearance is no easy trick," he says, "but not impossible."

"But why?"

He shrugs. "Clean slate?"

I frown. I don't want to correct him, don't want to get on his bad side, but...

"What is it, my dear?"

My dear. Like he wasn't torturing my hand just half a minute ago.

"I saw Miner's wife and daughter when they came to ID the body. They seemed pretty convinced."

"Ah?"

"Besides, if he... or she... wanted a clean slate, why would she start off by breaching the Masquerade?"

"Ah."

Another thoughtful moue. Then he laughs.

"You're right, it was a silly idea. Still. You wouldn't believe the ridiculous things that some of our Kindred have tried. For that matter, you wouldn't believe what's succeeded."

We chat for a little while longer, then return just in time to see Raphael bending down to kiss the blade of the Prince's sword. Kind of suggestive, if you ask me, but now he's in the club.

Several nights later I'm at a club, my third club of the night, and this time the blaring refrain is "Hit the red button! Hit the red button!" Daringly, this song sometimes changes it up with "C'mon, hit the red button!" or "G'wan, hit the red button!"

I scored at the last place, didn't even get the guy's digits—just got him on the hook Pushing Out during some hip-hop ode to vulgar fucking, asked him to walk me to my car, got him alone under the shadows of the train rails and bit him. I didn't bother writing down his name or getting his job or anything, even though he had a nice beard, very full but cleanly shaved at the neck so that I didn't get hair in my mouth. I told him to forget the bite and go back to the club. He did it.

I'm not really hunting for more blood tonight. I'm after rarer prey: Bella.

Since it's a weeknight, it isn't too busy, but I still almost miss her. She's got her hair pulled back in a bun and is dressed in a knee-length skirt and a nondescript blouse. More importantly, her siren song isn't singing. She's just sitting.

When I come over to her, she looks pleased. Why wouldn't she?

"Persephone!"

"Bella!" I shout. "May I sit?"

"Of course, always!"

"You're looking uncharacteristically unglamorous tonight!"

"Whaat?"

("Hit the red button! G'wan, hit the red button!")

We bellow back and forth a couple times before agreeing to leave. Out on the street, I repeat my observation.

She smiles. "Sweet tooth."

"I'm sorry?"

"Sometimes I want a shy guy. Or gal, but straight tonight. You can't be too overpowering. I want someone who approaches the plain girl, who says hi to the wallflower."

"But how do you make them come to you?"

"That's the sport of it. I don't." She shrugs. "It's like fishing. It's calm, sedate. Not like going out with stiletto heels and speargunning some Italian Stallion through the eyeballs."

"What if no one bites the hook?"

"I'm not really hungry. If I was, I've got people to call. Don't worry about me, I've got a deep well."

"I don't doubt it."

We walk a few more steps.

"So Bella, you want to see something?"

"What?"

"Come with me."

We get in my car and talk about Raphael's induction while I drive. Sounds like I was lucky to miss his lengthy, personalized vow of fealty.

"What's this?" We're at the Larkin house.

"It's mine," I say. "I just closed on it yesterday."

"Oooh, a new haven!"

"You have no idea."

We circle around to the back. There's a garage off an alley.

"In here," I say. Inside it are five steps up to the back door.

I reach down under the last wooden stair and trip a hidden catch.

It's not like the movies where a section of wall rumbles dramatically away. Instead the steps themselves come up. They squeaked like hell the first time, and I needed some extra oomph, but yesterday I carefully oiled the old hinges. They were designed to move even after decades, like everything down here. It was designed to be a vampire's safe refuge for however long its master might sleep.

"Is this a *Guilford*?" she asks, and I can see that she's genuinely excited.

I nod.

Under the stairs, a tunnel spirals sharply down. I have to hunch over and even Bella has to duck a little. But soon we're in the cool beneath the earth, through twists and turns that sunlight can never navigate.

"Here's the vault," I say.

"Even here, outside the door... that's a pretty good place to stay."

"Yeah." I turn the dials on the steel door. It's a bank vault, and it's been heavily greased. Like the entryway, it's built to stay mobile even in the face of time.

I don't bother to hide the combination from Bella.

Inside, the steel floor has been muffled with a Persian carpet, the steel walls tastefully paneled. A crystal chandelier hangs from the ceiling, still filled with half-melted candles. (At some point, I'll upgrade to electric.)

A cherrywood desk occupies one corner, with an overstuffed chair and ottoman on the other. A chaise lounge occupies the wall opposite these amenities. At its head and foot there are low tables, with a number of small white statues arranged on them.

Curious, Bella picks one up. It's the figure of a woman kneeling to pray, but it's strangely lengthened, as if carved from something long and slender.

"Do you like it? They were there when I opened the chamber."

"They're ossuary art," she says.

"Excuse me?"

"Carved bone, preserved against decay." She puts down the praying woman, picks up a hunchbacked man leaning on a scythe.

"I think I know who did these."

"Really?"

"He's been dead since the 1960s." She looks up. "*Really* dead, I mean."

"Huh. I found a newspaper in here, and it was from 1933."

"It's a magnificent refuge," she says. Her eyes are downcast and she seems almost... shy?

"Look at this." I pull a large glass bottle from underneath the couch. "I think it's poison gas."

"Marvelous. One wonders why it was abandoned."

"No idea." I take a deep breath and square my shoulders. "Bella, I'll be straight with you. I'm in bad shape."

"You look fine."

"You know what I mean. No one's taking me seriously. To them, I'm just the Prince's spoiled brat."

"I'm sure no one thinks that." She's got her head turned down towards the art again.

"If it was just that, it wouldn't bother me so much, but Solomon's got it in his head that he can jerk me around any way he likes. He's messing with my feeds, he's..."

"Say no more. I can imagine what he's like when aroused, though I really don't care to."

"That's what I'm *living* right now."

She gives me a look.

"Okay, not 'living' but... you know what I mean! Solomon's treating me like his chew toy, and as long as he does, everyone else feels like they can piss on me too."

"Your sire..."

"I'm not going to go running to him. That might work in the short term, but I refuse to be 'daddy's little girl' for the rest of eternity."

She nods. "I have to respect that."

"It's not just me, either. I mean, Solomon's the local Lancea honcho, and I can't imagine it would hurt your cause to knock him down a peg."

"So what do we do?"

"I think we need to give him a bigger problem to worry about. Something so distracting that he won't be bothered with me. And it should be something where he doesn't know I did it."

"Do you know about Solomon's political aspirations?"

Even though my heart doesn't move any more, I would swear it skips a beat.

"No."

"He wants to be Prince," she tells me.

Just like that.

I'm not sure how to play this—I trust Bella, but my name's dirt and I don't want to get Solomon breathing fire down her back just as she's trying to help me. Thanks to the Bishop's slander, I'm in no position to really accuse him, but if he succeeds... I don't even want to think about it.

The first thing I need to do is warn Maxwell, but I can't even get through to him. He changes phones every few months and somehow I didn't get the last number. It's not like him to forget a little detail... unless he really is losing his grip? More likely he's cutting me off as a liability. Or maybe he just *forgot*. If he's over 200 years old, something like a phone number could slip his mind. Maybe I'm just being paranoid.

I'm also going to need proof, which means someone's got to do some snooping. If it was a hostile takeover or City Hall graft I could probably dig it out myself, but vampire infighting isn't legislated.

I call Loki and get voicemail so, reluctantly, I dial up Raphael. The asshole is pathetically eager, promises that he'll get the word out to "his people," whoever the hell they are. He even asks if I think there's a percentage in backing him. I give him a dose of contempt to keep him cringing and tell him no, of course not.

"Where'd you hear this?" he asks.

"I have my sources."

The trump card, of course, is my new connection with Norris. I ask him to meet me at my old apartment. (I have it until the end of the month and might just keep it as a blind against Solomon and his cronies.) Unfortunately, he seems eager to meet me right away. I was hoping I could get proof, even just something circumstantial, before I went to him. But if there's any vampire in Chicago who can get proof of a thing, it's Norris.

Unfortunately, when I get there, Scott Hurst is waiting in the hall. He doesn't look good.

"Scott? Are you okay?"

"I'm not sure," he replies. He says it like he's not sure about anything, what day it is or his own name. "Can I come in?"

"Yeah, of course!" I follow him through the door and, while his back is turned, I check my watch. Nuts. Norris is due any minute.

"What can I do for you, Scott?"

"I..." He sits down.

"Can I ask you a couple questions? They might sound sort of... funny."

"Sure." Christ, has Solomon gotten to him?

"The other day, when we closed on the house..."

"Yeah?"

"Did I... did we stay behind after the signing?"

"Do you want something to drink? I've got,.."

"Please, Linda! This is..." He breaks it off, looks away. "I got these calls. Friends, people I know who work with the police and... they were asking me about someone named Birch, and someone named Persephone."

Oh no.

"I... I think I remember making those calls, but it's... it's all cloudy. I've always had a good memory Linda and now..."

He stands up and starts pacing.

"I remember the closing, the Larkins leaving, and then, then I remember being in the car because I heard about Tom Petty coming to town on the radio and... and that was late at night. There's a *gap*, Linda, there's a hole in my memory. I don't remember you asking me to stay after but I... it's like I remember *thinking* you'd asked me and... and... did you?"

There's a knock on the door. I look through the peephole and it's Norris.

"Excuse me." I open the door halfway. "Norris, I..."

"You said it was urgent?"

"It is, but I've got a kind of a... um..."

"A what?"

"I'm not alone," I whisper.

"Look," Scott says, creeping closer. "I'm sorry. I didn't mean to... interfere or get in the way of... uh, hi." He gives a little wave, a little smile to Norris. Bleached teeth grin back.

"Good evening," Norris purrs.

"I'm Scott Hurst—Linda's real estate man," Scott says. Instantly, he sounds different. Most people in his line of work have a voice they use for people who just might buy houses someday, and I get the feeling that Scott's gone back to it on autopilot—that the part of him that's really *Scott* is hiding in a corner of his mind somewhere.

"I hope I'm not intruding."

"Can you let me have a word with Mr. Norris in private? Just for a moment?"

"Sure, no problem, I understand completely..."

I take Norris by the sleeve and pull him through the apartment into my bedroom.

"Heeh, the boudoir on the first date, why couldn't I have had such luck while alive?"

"Look, give me a minute to get rid of him."

"Is there a problem?"

"I, uh... no, no problem."

"Look, Persephone." He reaches out to take my hand and I steel myself against flinching back. He notices and sighs.

"I'm sorry I hurt you the other night," he says, and the way he says it gives me the creeps, especially if Scott were somehow to overhear and get the wrong impression. "I'd like to make it up to you. And I'd like to show you I appreciate you helping me with my work. What's your problem with Mr. Hurst?"

"Oh I... started using... *changing*... his mind. You know. And it didn't work out quite right."

"Would you like me to take care of it?"

Suddenly I'm remembering Maxwell's warnings, telling me that the human mind has hidden depths, that you have to be especially careful when you twist memories or the whole thread of someone's experience can unravel...

"You can fix it?"

"Nothing simpler."

"Oh, that would be great! I just tried to make him forget some stuff last night..."

"...and now he's more suspicious than ever. Right?"

"Right."

"Consider him dealt with."

There's an eagerness in his voice that makes me uneasy, and I cough a little.

"You're... you're not planning to just kill him, are you?"

"Er... no?"

"Because all I want is for him to stop being suspicious."

"Of course." But now he looks disappointed.

"Why don't I handle it myself?"

"If you're sure..."

"Yeah, I really, uh, shouldn't bother you with my problems. And, you know, you're so busy. And it would be good practice for me to, you know, try and fix what I broke."

"Shall I wait here?"

I go out and try it again with Scott.

I lock gazes with him and Scott's mind is strong, but rigid. There's a disciplined structure like the framework of a skyscraper... no wonder it started to crumple when I took out a piece. So I just have to replace it with something equally strong... right?

It resists me. *He* resists me. This is no boozy Travolta: Scott doesn't want to lose his memory, so I have to force it.

"Forget that I bit your neck. You had this idea that I was using the name Persephone, but I explained to you that I'm not and proved it to your satisfaction."

"I... I..." He's sweating. Starting to shake.

"*Listen to me.* There is no 'Solomon Birch'—I was the victim of a practical joke and you got swept up in it. My brother did it—he played the joke on me. If anyone asks, you'll explain it. You'll be vague. These things don't matter. Stop worrying about any gaps in your memory. You will remember resetting your watch—it got set wrong somehow and that's why you were confused. There is nothing odd going on. Understand?" I give him one final twist, one final push, and his body suddenly relaxes. For a moment, I almost think he's going to collapse right there.

"There's nothing odd going on," Scott mumbles back, eyes wide and fixed on mine. "Solomon Birch and Persephone aren't important. I reset my watch. That's why I was confused."

"Good." I take him by the hand and lead him to the doorway. "Go home now and... and think of some plausible reason why you came by here. No, I forgot something at the closing, a nice pen, my Mont Blanc, and you had to stop by and drop it off."

"I stopped by to drop off your pen."

"Right." I release his mind. He blinks.

"Thanks for the pen," I tell him.

"Right. No biggie." He frowns, blinks again. "Linda, were you... were you crying? Your eyes look *really* red."

"I'm in the middle of a sad movie," I tell him.

"Right! Well, I'll just go home now."

"Thanks again."

When I close the door, I raise a hand to my cheek, just as the first tear really wells up. A blood tear. Shit. He missed it by seconds...

Seeing Scott like that... *violating* him... it's awful. I can't do that again. Not to him. Maybe not to anyone, maybe it's wrong... but what was the alternative? Tell him, with Norris right in the apartment? That's as much of a death sentence as getting Norris to "deal with him."

I take a deep breath (even though I don't need to breathe any more) and wipe my eyes. Take a moment. I compose myself.

Then I open the bedroom door. Norris is sitting, straight-backed and patient, on my bed.

"Solomon is planning to usurp Maxwell's throne," I tell him.

He looks at me for a moment. Then he lunges to his feet, and races across the room. I barely get out of the way before his fist slams into the wall, inches from where I stood. He goes all the way through the drywall, pulls his hand out covered with plaster, turns to me...

...and suddenly starts to laugh.

"What?"

"Oh Persephone, you made me so angry."

"What? What did I do?"

"Do? It's not what you did, dear pet, but what you *are*, what you are *being*."

I edge away. He raises his hand, white-dusted and nail-less, and shakes his head.

"You're being a fool, dear. You're being a waste of time."

"I'm *not*! Dammit, Solomon is plotting against Maxwell!"

"Do you have proof?"

"Since when have *you* needed proof?"

He laughs again. "A fair objection." He sinks back on the bed, more relaxed this time. "Oh heavens... you believe it, don't you? That's what makes it so amusing."

"Why don't you? What makes it *so* implausible?"

"I've known Solomon for... mm, fifty years now. That's what makes it implausible."

"I heard it from Bella!"

"Oh, *Bella*." He laughs again and stands. "Sorry about your wall, but oh my! So angry. I really should have more patience with little things." He tilts his head. "You didn't tell anyone *else* this ridiculous theory, did you?"

"I... no. You're the first."

"Uh huh. See that you don't start. I mean, I *suppose* that you could waste your time shadowing the prominent and powerful Bishop of Chicago seeking proof for an unlikely charge that came from an absurd source... did Bella even tell you *how* she learned this? Regardless, you could do that, you could go find your law school notes on elementary evidentiary procedure, *or*, as an alternative, instead of wasting anyone's time with this, you could find Miner's sire and make yourself useful to me, the Prince, and everyone else."

He sweeps out of the bedroom and towards the exit.

When I was ten and my brother Andrew was twelve, he laughed at me for mispronouncing "dubious," which I'd read in a Sherlock Holmes story. I got so mad that I threw a three-ring binder at him, hitting him right in the eye with the corner.

To his credit, Andrew treated me a little more respectfully after that. I think maybe Dad sat him down and had a talk.

Now, here I am, undying and empowered and fucking "Mistress of the Night" or whatever, but I'm *still* getting treated like a malapropism-spewing ten-year-old! Are these elders going to bully and sneer and snicker at me *forever*? Is this what being undead *really* means? Christ, it's like first year law school, only the assholes who steal the references you need out of the library never graduate!

No wonder Dubiard says we're damned.

I try to be calm and logical, try to remember that from Norris' perspective I *am* hopelessly young and naïve, but it's *still* infuriating.

Unless...
Unless Norris is in on it with Solomon?

The final insult comes when I get back to my lair, my precious Guilford. It's an hour before dawn but I'm already exhausted. I go down the secret passage and the door to the vault has been welded shut—big thick seams, like you see on airplane wings.

That's not the worst.

There's a note stuck on the door with a refrigerator magnet. (To be specific, it's a Count Chocula magnet. Cute.) It reads:

Persephone,

I know you won't believe me, but I really am sorry about this. It was a good bolt-hole, except for one thing: No emergency exit. I'm pretty sure that's why its previous tenant moved out.

You'll be mad at me, which I understand, but you should realize we could have just as easily sealed it up with you inside. I talked them out of it. I told them you'd come around.

Please come around, Persephone. You're bright and willful, and those are terrible flaws for creatures like us. You need to realize how weak and helpless you are. Only then can you turn to the Crone. Only then will you realize the real source of all strength.

When you truly understand, I think you will thank me. I think you might even be grateful to Solomon.

Believe it or not, much love,

—Bella

I spend the day in the hall outside the vault. She was right. Even that's a pretty good hole.

The next night, I get a call from one of the partners at my old firm. Scott Hurst has killed himself.

Chapter Six:
Scratch

I got a busy night scheduled, but first and foremost I need to see my best gal Judy. I can't see her that often, and she can't see me at all, but I've got a new suit and that matters. Seeing Judy matters.

It's a swell set of clothes, hand-tailored with reams and reams of rich, thick velvet, midnight blue, drapes and swags, full seated and reet-pleated.

I'm in my hole, my Guilford maze under Old John's burnt-out whorehouse. Old John had it good, but all good things come to pass. That's why I choose to be bad, and now his king-sized bed is a democracy of roaches and centipedes. No matter how tightly I seal the doors, they find me, love up to my skin while I sleep out the day. A shower just knocks 'em back. A few decades ago I started trying bug spray, flea collars, pesticides. They were coming on the market for home use, but for me they're home useless.

Still, you gotta make an effort. It matters.

I shower off the lice and maggots, dry myself on a Turkish towel from a sealed dry-cleaning bag, put on my new glad rags and head upstairs. The car's parked in a rental garage a couple blocks from the lair, but I don't need the car. It's a nice night, cold and clear, and Judy's place is within walking distance.

No one sees me, of course. I push them back, make them far away like a fairytale from long ago. I pull the wool over their eyes and drift down the street like a bad dream, and they step out of my way even with their backs turned. They bump into each other for no reason other than they don't want to touch what they can't see and won't hear. Maybe they smell me.

I watch for collisions and pick a few pockets. Chump change. Credit cards for Sharif. Never anything good.

I get to Judy's floor and there she lies. A homely old husk if ever I've seen one, but still beautiful in my sight. I close the door and it's like breathing out, it's like the color coming on in *The Wizard of Oz*, I become immediate. I let myself show.

"Judy. Hey sweets, how you feeling?"

She rolls her head towards me, all ashy wrinkles. She was so upset when her hair started to gray. Even more so when it started falling out.

Her eyes are glassy with cataracts, so no more mirror-gazing for her. But now I don't have to hide myself, either. Some silver lining, huh?

"I brought you chockies," I say. "Your favorite, Frango mints."

Her mouth moves a little. I put the box on her bedside table, peel one and put it to her lips. She works her mouth like a little baby, pulling in the treat.

I have the fingers of a corpse, rotted, riddled, decayed. Fingernails like driftwood. Already my blue velvet is stained, darkened from underneath. Already it starts to fall apart. By dawn, it will look like I was buried in it ten years ago.

I hear the door. I don't even think about vanishing. I just disappear.

The orderly is a short guy, stocky, red-faced. Comes in, doesn't say a word, just checks the chart, checks Judy with about the same interest, sighs. Gives her a bedsore roll and I could snap his fucking neck, the way he treats her. Like he's moving a piece of furniture, like he's lifting a box of toasters. No gentleness.

And damn me blind if he doesn't try one of her Frango chocolates, and then pocket the whole box. Okay chump, that's it.

He's got a badge, so I've got his name. Cal Cromwell. Out to the front desk and there's a schedule. He's just started his shift and already he's acting impatient. Wouldn't want to see him by... four o'clock? Yeah, that's the grave-yard shift. They probably don't want this meatball around when any visitors might run into him.

See you later, Cal.

I go get the car and call Doctor Deal from the payphone in the garage. His real last name is "Diehl," and he really is a doctor—a chiropractor or an orthodontist or some other crazy specialty they didn't have back when I was still getting sick. He's crooked as a spring, a Cicero real-estate baron and what does *that* tell you? I had to buy Old John's burned-down pile off him, but he gave me a good deal. No one else was in the market for a hooker's graveyard.

Doctor Deal doesn't know about what I am; he just knows a little about what I do. I got a message from him yester-day, so I'm calling back. Could be some scratch in it and, after all, that's my name.

"Dealie-o," I say. "It's me. What's shakin'?"

"Hey, Scratch. We can talk, right?"

"I'm talking. You're talking."

"Yeah, but I mean... you know. You know what I mean?"

"I'm on a payphone."

"And I'm on a land line. Okay. Great. So, you know those robbing gangs? The ones with their own trucks, dress up like movers, show up and completely clean out someone's house?"

"Uh huh."

"You know 'em?"

"Yeah."

"No, I mean, you know a gang like that? 'Cause I need one."

"Oh! Gotcha. Yeah, I might know some people like that. What do you need 'em for?"

"Aw, it's the IRS, Christ, they're bleeding me dry. They say I owe 'em all these back taxes and, shit, I can't pay. My money's tied up, you know? I can't get it out for them."

greg stolze

Yeah, it's tied up in Columbian marching powder, tied up with psycho Afghani opium warlords. Not the kind of business partners who let you pull out before you've satisfied them. "And why would you hand it over to the Feds anyhow?"

"Exactly! I mean, what is this? Communism? So they're going to take my house, repossess all my stuff, it's like another divorce, practically. So before that can happen…"

"You'd like my friends to steal all your stuff."

"Well, somebody's going to."

"And in return for making the job a milk run, you get, what, ten percent when they fence it?"

"Ten percent? What're you, their agent? Nah, I'm thinking it's a flat fee, they take my stuff and store it and then, when the heat dies down, I get it all back. You know. Like, I replace my losses."

"Heavily insured losses, I bet."

"It's not really betting if it's a sure thing, huh?"

"Yeah. So you take the insurance money, pay off the feds, then get your stuff back over the next couple years or so."

"That's the general idea."

"I can make that happen." We dicker for another fifteen minutes over just how much my referral fee is, and then we hang up.

The sun's barely down and I've got money in hand and bacon in the pan. Not too shabby.

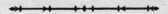

The next stop is a storage locker. It used to belong to a fanger called Anita. Actually, I suppose it still does.

Anita, like me, is Nosferatu. Like me, she found a comfortable niche in the criminal underworld. Like me, she was a clever, weaselly scumbag—and mean when cornered.

A *boa constrictor*. What kind of sick individual gives vampire blood to a goddamn apex predator? That was how Anita got the drop on me, figuratively. It was her freakin' snake (whose name, I gather, was "Sweetie Pie") that got the drop on me literally.

Anita and I had what you might call a disagreement.

I've been around Chicago a long time. I know about Capone and O'Banion and all the various gunsel mackerel snappers between and after 'em. I *know* the challenges inherent in dealing with the gangland mentality. Anita, however, thought that the Mafia was a hotshot train to fat city, and she was gonna be engineer. Told me, when we were still in the talking phase, that the new mob was soft, garbage collection and stag flicks, no backbone, not like the old days. I told her it didn't take people with guns much time to grow a backbone when they find out vampires are real, but Anita had talked herself out of people seeing the downside of our condition.

It takes a lot of brains to be that stupid, I guess. And a weird kind of genius to think about juicing up a boa constrictor.

I couldn't scare the damn snake, I couldn't outfight it and it was crushing me into peanut butter. So I did the only thing I had left: I made it think I wasn't there.

You'd think it would realize it could still *feel* me, but no, it let go. I guess it's only got a brain the size of my big toe, probably not much room in there for anything other than "prey" and "not-prey." Anything you can't see is "not-prey," I presume. It let me loose, I got a butcher knife from Anita's kitchen and I chopped its evil pointy head off.

Getting to the kitchen took me about fifteen minutes, because I had to heal an awful lot of broke bones and pulped guts before I could get up and walk.

It was a clusterfuck, but I found Anita eventually. And I staked her.

Now, I gotta figure out what to do with her.

I open the storage locker door, one of those garage-door type ones. Inside there are boxes and crates and a stacked up set of lawn furniture. There's a giant screen TV all wrapped up in plastic—that's to keep burglars from poking around in the big footlocker at the back. That's where Anita slept, and that's where I dumped her after putting the wood through her back.

I open the locker and roll her over.

She's started to curl up, like a crouch with her hands up over her face. She's drying out too. When I nailed her, she could pass for normal in candlelight. Now her flesh looks like onionskin stretched over bones, like a discarded cicada shell.

"Hey Anita."

I peel the lid back from her left eye. It's gritty, now.

"I been thinking about what I ought to do with you."

I sigh. She doesn't respond, doesn't change expression. She's deep in la-la-land. It doesn't make talking to her any easier.

"I know you had plans, big plans, but big plans have big problems. Especially if you don't see the bigger picture. And Anita, you don't. You don't get it. You think you can take over. In Cicero, for a bit, you probably could. Kind of. But you don't understand how things are going to change. You don't understand how big the world is, outside of Illinois.

"I bet you're having some nasty, nasty dreams right now. I know—I've been there. It didn't take a stake for me to go under and take the big dirtnap, though. Nope, I went to sleep all by my lonesome back in 1927 and didn't snap out of it until 1975. The dreams were bad, but waking up after fifty years? That was the nightmare. Do you have any idea what that's like? How would you, you got the Life in 1970-something, right?"

I don't know why I'm telling her all this. Delaying the inevitable, I guess.

"Anyhow, I woke up and suddenly it's jet planes and nuclear power and fucking *cars* everywhere, half of 'em built in *Japan*. And I think that's when I learned, Anita. I think that's when I understood that we're built to last, but our rulership—if we take it—just isn't. I couldn't prepare for computers and the Cold War and feminism and the Civil Rights movement. That stuff was just... I could never have thought of it. So when you think you'd run Cicero until the end of time, how do you know what the mortals are going to have by 2020, or 2050, or the twenny-second century? The best we can do is keep up, and that's it.

"But you don't believe me. You won't believe in the fuckup until you've fucked it up and I can't let that happen. So I'm gonna have to drink you down."

I know she can't move, can't even shift, but it's like I see the fear in her eyes.

Then I bite her.

I haven't taken another vampire's blood since I woke up in the '70s. I told myself it's too much, that a double-stack of unholy blood is too powerful for anyone's system. That's why I Rip Van Winkled through five decades of nightmares. I had quite a cannibalism dependency as a thirsty young vampire, and everyone who's tasted Vitae can tell you it hooks you hard, fast and strong.

Of course, when you're immortal you have plenty of time to wean yourself off your habit. But it just takes one slip, one sip, and you're back in the opium den.

When I first bite Anita I feel the love. This always happens, the intoxicating infatuation, the bond that you can't avoid when you take a piece of someone's soul into your own. I feel Anita, her cunning and her calm and her quirky humor, and the first couple times I jumped Kindred this made me stop before I could seal the deal—I wimped out and paid for it. But I've learned the way past.

I don't resist the love. I give in to it.

I let myself love Anita the way I love Judy, and then more, the way I loved my wife, and then *more*, the way I love love itself, I can't get enough and want it all, I can't bear the thought of missing even a single drop of Anita and that's the way through, to take it all, to need all of her.

The way to do it is to love her to death.

I wipe the ash of her body off my lips and I feel her singing inside me, a second soul entwined with mine, and I weep. It's so beautiful. I'm drunk on power, I'm invincible, I contain a multitude.

I'm hooked again.

I'm still feeling high when I get to the graveyard, but it's under control. This was a special case. I'm not going to start up preying on other Kindred again. That's just stupid, no matter how good it feels.

Sure, I can quit any time I want. Isn't that what every alkie is supposed to say? Hello, my name is Scratch. My drug of choice is murder.

(Is it even murder, to destroy a vampire? Heh. Ask O'Banion. Ask those firebugs from the 1870s.)

I'm sure that's why I find myself wondering if I could take this Ambrose guy before he had a chance to turn into a bat or something. Probably not. He looks like he knows his shit.

Ambrose and Raphael, there's a pair for you. It's like an irony. Raphael looks down on Ambrose, who really *is* all the things that Raphael just *thinks* he is. And Ambrose doesn't care about being what he is, he just is it. Or shit, maybe I'm just drunk on Anita and not thinking clearly.

"Ambrose."

"Scratch. Want a pooch?"

"I've eaten, thanks."

He looks me over. Doesn't like what he sees, but who would? I can't tell if he's reacting to what I look like, or to what he thinks I am—Prince's stooge, Kindred poser, another predator on his turf? I don't suppose it matters.

Using a big piece of plastic sheeting as a bib, he eats the stray. Shit, he's barely better than being one himself. But Ambrose is a cunning animal. A survivor.

Tight-lipped, too. Not going to ask my business, but screw him.

"How's Bruise?" I ask.

"Just missed him."

"He feeding regular?" Damn, I spend two seconds with this guy and I'm talking in sentence fragments too.

"Animal blood." He looks up from his and says, "You're in with the Prince and his crew. You got all that stuff from the slaughterhouses. You should set him up."

Wow. Three complete sentences. I ask about his little buddy and suddenly he's making a Castro speech.

"That's feasible," I say. "I could fix you up too, if you want."

"I'm good."

"But you know what the question is, don't you?"

"Do I?"

"It's the same question it *always* is."

He shrugs. Doesn't want to play.

"The question, Masterson, is 'what's in it for me?'"

He rolls his eyes. "If there's ever a self-interest Olympics, you're the only guy who could give Raphael a run for the gold."

I gotta laugh. "Okay, very amusing. But seriously. I was the one voting to make Bruise a zero in the big Kindred equation. Why should I do him a goody now?"

"Masquerade stuff? Help him dig a well and he's less likely to beat and eat some policeman or tabloid journalist."

"You look at that from the right perspective and it's like terrorism. 'Gimme what I want, infidel, or I make bad anger at you!'"

"Okay then. How about this? If you help him out, I won't tell him what you did to his daughter."

"Ooooh! Hardball from the man with dog blood on his teeth! Iiiiii *like it!*"

I lunge at him and he's just as quick, back over his tombstone seat, dropping his tarp and his meal. He's got a monument between me and him and, hello, there's a sharpened hunk of wood in his fist. Something purpose-made, a nice heavy wood like oak, nothing flimsy.

He's got his lips back and I can see those freaky fangs. He got those from something that eats meat, no doubt about it.

I grin at him. I wonder whose teeth are bigger, mine or his?

I've got a gun in my pocket, a disposable little wop nine. But if I pull that out, he might just change form and scram. And anyway, bullets just don't have the same stopping power against folks without functional organs. As it is, he's not running and he's not fighting. I could leave the gun in my pocket and sissyfight this fucker, but it only takes one lucky hit from that stake and I'm in Anita's cement overshoes, waiting for a trip down to the river.

Not running, not fighting. Which means, not yellow and not stupid.

I straighten up and fix my lapels.

"Supposing you tell your man Bruise. What then? What's he gonna do to me?"

Ambrose shrugs. He's still ready to bring the pain. Probably thinks I've got some evil surprise hidden in my suit. Christ knows it's big enough. You could hide a tommy gun in all that cloth.

"I don't know," Ambrose says at last. "He's not very creative. But he'd have all eternity to think of something."

I almost laugh and almost think what a weak threat that is. And then I think about what I was like back in 1921 when I got brought over, and I think about how many "older" or "smarter" or "more powerful" vampires I murdered in just six short years. You never can tell.

"Bruise wouldn't be a huge pain. But neither is blooding him up, I guess. Sure. Yeah. You drive a hard bargain," I tell Ambrose.

"Am I supposed to be grateful or flattered?"

Criminey, what a sourpuss.

Next stop is the Miner household. Just checking in—if Judy's my best girl then Brooke is, I guess, my most recent.

She's got some Mexi-pop music on, so loud that her window's actually rattling in its frame. I knock and nothing happens. Dumb deaf teenybopper probably can't even hear me.

I take a look around the back and, ho ho, mama's car is gone. I ring the doorbell like a proper guest. (Though it is the back doorbell, as befits a backdoor man.)

No answer, of course. Finally, I start really pounding.

Just before I have to contemplate kicking it, the music drops and she comes, looks out the window and right through me.

In all the Dracula movies, the Babe In Jeopardy is always a looker dressed in some gauzy white virginal thing that's unintentionally revealing of the voluptuous curves within, right? Well maybe that kind of thing happens to Maxwell or Raphael or those pretty-boy types, but for me, I get a victim in a flannel shirt and sweatpants with one of those mud facial masks on and her hair done up in tinfoil.

She scowls, and I rap the glass and she jumps about a foot.

I can't help it. At heart, I'm a drama queen. I let her see me and she puts her hands to her mouth.

"You…"

"Can I come in? I thought you might want some company. Y'know, since yer mama ain't home."

She's torn. I can see that she's torn. Half of her, her normal half, wants to scream and run, hide in the closet, call the cops, get a cross and some holy water. But the other half has the blood poisoning, the other half tasted the black blood inside me and wants more, it wants out of the cage so it can hunt and kill and be a predator. Or at least taste blood and pretend.

She opens the door. I guess the bad half won.

In my experience, it usually does.

"What's your name?" she asks.

"You don't give a fuck," I say, and I pull her to me. She struggles, but I get a kiss planted on her gritty, green-gray cheek.

"Stop it! Stop it!"

"Kiss me, darlin'."

"I'd rather fuckin' die!"

I crease my lower lip along jagged, broken fangs. I feel the sting as the skin parts, ragged. Vitae, the secret life, wells up.

Her face is inches from mine, and I can see the look in her eyes.

"Not so revolting now, is it?"

She stopped struggling as soon as she saw me bleed.

"I don't want to," she whimpers, but I can feel the way her body is straining, straining against *itself*, that same old angel and devil pulling her this way and that.

"Then don't," I whisper. I relax my arms.

greg stolze

She starts to shake. She's sobbing. Tears run down her face. I almost feel bad about this, but poor broken Brooke is the Bruise brake.

She leans forward, lips parted, and she sucks it.

I wonder if she can feel Anita through it?

Driving away, I feel dissatisfied. Brooke's my property now, like Anita's snake. Only Anita's snake wasn't useless.

She's had two drinks, so she's not going to be able to think clearly about me at all—too addled with fake blood love. One more drink and she'll pretty much be a slave, but I don't think it needs to go that far. As is, she can *stop* thinking about me when I'm not immediately present, and the bond will wear off in a couple months or a year. People who take that third gulp are bound tight, and can be pretty useless unless you're right in their face all the time, telling them exactly when to jump and how high.

Now, if Brooke were a cop or a building inspector, or if she had money or a lot of clout... well, wow, I'd be sitting pretty. Then it would be worth all the extra hunting I'd have to do to keep her habit fed. But what's she good for? A teenager, not too bright, hardly pretty enough, with a missing dad and a cranky mom who's barely making ends meet. Just what does Brooke do for me?

It puts her dad under my control, but he's only marginally more useful than the daughter. The crabapple doesn't fall far from the tree. Besides which, if I tell Bruise what I did to her, he's going to be one very resentful lackey, and you get what you pay for in that department. Shit, I know how pissed off *I'd* be if someone did that to *my* family. It's dirty pool, but the Prince said jump, so now *I'm* the one asking how high.

Besides, if I really wanted, needed or could use Bruise's assistance, I could just let him know I'm his sire.

I blame that goddamn snake.

Anita the clever bitch just about made me into vampire jelly by having her boa squeeze me tight while she beat feet. I got the better of the dumb animal, but it was a close thing. So after that, I was pretty worn, which means pretty hungry.

I had a good idea where Anita was going, but I could let her wait until I fed. There's no point going into a gun-fight with empty chambers, you know? So I got out of her apartment and started looking for some poor sad sack, someone no one would miss for twenty minutes or so.

I saw this place called "Pitchers & Pool." Figured that was as good as any.

When Miner came out, he looked like a likely prospect. He wasn't wobbling, or stepping with obvious care. He looked big, a little fat, healthy enough. Why not?

I shadowed him, hoping he'd go to a car, but he walked. So I waited until we were by an alley, no one around, and then I sucker-punched him on the back of the neck. He passed out, just like a thousand other times. You sneak up on someone, clobber him, drink him, close the wound, take the wallet, he wakes up with a headache and figures he got rolled. Simple, clean, easy, and no Masquerade en-tanglements.

Only this time, it went south.

At first, it seemed okay. I was getting good flow from him, and then suddenly I realized that this guy's blood alcohol was *way* higher than I figured. I mean, I can handle liquor, always could dead or alive, but this guy was much drunker than he acted. I'm now guessing, from what Norris and Loki let slip, that Brucie was what you'd call a serious, lifestyle alcoholic. He probably had a mellow little buzz on, after enough liquor to put a normal man under the table.

So I got drunk. My judgment got impaired. That's my big crybaby excuse. But it still would've been fine, except that just about the time that I'm really starting to be af-fected, his blood pressure goes crazy—all irregular, now spurting, now really weak, back and forth all over the map. And his eyes flutter open and he grabs his left arm. Right after that, the blood stops altogether.

And I realize, fuck and double-fuck, I've given the wino a heart attack and killed him.

I thought about putting the bond on him, but that was no go. A dose can fix a lot of physical damage, but to cross over from death? That takes more serious medicine.

I thought about just leaving him there, and in hindsight that was probably the wise play. Guy gets found in the street, clutching his arm and with all the signs of a massive coronary? Who's gonna see that and think "vampires done it"? But at the time I was panicky, I was already off my game on account of being used as a big snake's love toy, and I was boozed up.

Drunk and maudlin, that's my excuse. With that panicky-drinker logic, I realized that I wasn't thinking clearly, and that I might well be overlooking something if I just dumped him. But more than that, I hadn't meant to kill the poor slob. I mean usually, I kill somebody, it's because I figured I should kill him or needed to kill him or had some reason or desire to do so. I don't fancy myself an accidental manslayer—it's just not my style. Too klutzy, too amateur-hour.

You start not caring who you kill, and pretty soon you're a head-case like Solomon. Or a monster like Old John. Thank you, but no. Not for me. I'm unhappy enough with rot on my *clothes*—I don't need it in my moral fiber.

So I brought him back. I was drunk and stupid and clumsy and I brought him back. I dragged him into the alley, gave him my blood and immediately put a stake in his chest to keep him quiet until I finished my business. I left him there while I went to get my car and when I came back—Jesus fuck, there's some homeless guy with his throat torn out, my stake in his hand, and a very surprised expression on his dead old face.

I mean, I was only gone for, like, *twenty minutes*! Can't a guy leave a dead body in an alley in the middle of the night for, for less than half an hour without someone coming along and messing with it?

I ain't exactly Sherlock Holmes (and I was loaded, remember) but it doesn't take a genius to follow the dotted line. Bum comes along, finds Bruce and, for some *stupid reason*, pulls out the stake. Bruisey Bruce, freshly back and thirsty for that juicy juice, sucks his savior dry and wanders off.

·Sad, huh? Clown shit. Something you expect from a panicky newbie, not a respected elder.

Instead of Bruce, I dumped the bum in my trunk. I drove around for a while looking for my lost lamb, but for a dumb drunk dead guy, he proved pretty smart at covering his tracks. By that time I was starting to sober up and I realized I needed to shake a leg to deal with Anita. She was a far more pressing problem than one missing vampire who was, for all I knew, going to wander into sunlight anyway.

I went, found Anita at her storage place, did her, took the bum's body to Old John's place for disposal, and by that time it was nearly dawn. The next night, Bruce Miner goes home, fucks up his family, fucks up a cop, gets all this fucking Primogen-level attention and the next thing you know it takes a village to raise the dead.

At least I have drink as an explanation. What's Maxwell's excuse for his girl, huh?

I was drunk and stupid. That's my story and I'm sticking to it.

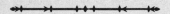

After my visit to Brooke, I head to Raphael Ladue's house. It's just one worthless bitch after another tonight.

When he answers the door, Ladue looks peeved. "Can I help you?"

I show him my real face. "May I come in?"

"Do I know you?"

"No, and unless you let me in your goddamn house in the next sixty seconds, you won't get to."

"My loss," he says, starting to close the door. Christ, what an asshole. I put my shoulder into it and blast him back.

"For someone who was so fired up to get into the big leagues, you're sure doing a botched job of sucking up to the elders," I tell him.

"Just who do you think you are, barging in here and..." Then, for once, his brain catches up to his mouth. He blinks.

"Oh God, you're Scratch. Aren't you?"

I give him a smile.

"Oh man, I'm sorry. I, I didn't know."

Someone give this kid a Chapstick. I think he's gonna need it when he starts kissing my ass.

He makes this weird, self-mocking laugh sound and sinks into the couch.

"I've really made a hash of it, haven't I?"

Poor bastard. Yeah, he has, but what the hell? I can give the poor dork a break.

(I know what he's doing, of course. He's working the blood, playing "I'm gonna make you love me." But I don't much care. It's kind of flattering. At least he's smart enough to know he's better off with me liking him.)

"Let's start over from the top," I say.

"I'd really appreciate that."

"You want to play in the big leagues, right? Well, that's 'you scratch my back and I'll scratch yours.'" I smile. "I got a scratch."

He sits up a little bit straighter. "Name it."

Yeah, he's a little rough around the edges, but once he gets rid of all those pesky *opinions* he'll have the makings of a champion lickspittle.

"Tell me about Bruce Miner."

"He's a Nosferatu, newly risen, he beat up his wife and a cop... but you know all this, right? You know about his daughter and everything. It'll probably save us both a lot of time if you just tell me what you're missing and I see if I can fill it in."

Ah, a good lickspittle would never allow even that small hint of impatience to enter his voice. Take care, Ladue, take care.

"All right. Do you really think he's safe?"

"As safe as any Kindred with a low IQ. He's not too sentimental about his family, which is good. He's made a real effort to cut ties with them, and to fit in with us."

Is that good or bad? "You think he still cares about his old life?"

He snorts. "Not much. I think calling what he had a 'life' is stretching it. He made the rounds between his boring job and his shrewish wife and the cheap bar where he drank to get numb."

Maybe Brooke isn't the great lever I thought. Which means that I'm *really* wasting my time and effort with her.

"He's hunting safe?"

"He's a rat-eater, for now. Keeps thinking he can do that forever."

"He can do it a long time."

"But will he?"

One could interpret that as a direct challenge. Yeah, this guy can't even brown-nose good.

"If I asked you to fuck him over for me, would you do it?"

He blinks and looks a little uncomfortable. "What do you mean?"

"I mean, if I told you to put a stake in him and bury him at a construction site, would you *do* it?"

"I don't know what you've heard about me..."

"I heard you asked the Prince for a... what did he call it? A 'separate peace.'"

I can see his jaw working and, for a moment, his charm wavers. Justine and her Harpy piss pack are going to eat this guy alive.

"I'm not going to go toe to toe with him," he says.

"Gotcha." I stand. "Well, you *talk* a good game, but I suppose I shouldn't expect you to actually get off your ass and *do* something..."

"Now hold on!" He stands up too. Moves his head around a little, like he's keeping his neck loose. "I said I wouldn't... confront him. I have to look out for myself, and besides, the unbound still trust me, don't they? Just how valuable would I be to them, or to anyone, if they felt I'd betrayed Bruise?" Now he starts to look ticked. "Not that I owe him anything, or them for that matter. I mean, Christ, I take care of his dumb *dog* all the time, give him good advice, extend my hospitality and everything, and I barely even get a 'thank you' from him, or from the rest of them." He realizes he's rambling and looks me in the eye again. "I have no objections to getting Miner out of the way. I don't think he's contributing much to Chicago's Kindred, not by any standard you want to apply. But I *do* object to shooting myself in the foot. If you're certain you want him dealt with, I'll help you. But I can't be *seen* helping you. Is that clear?"

"You're putting a lot of conditions on your loyalty."

"I don't want to make myself useless and despised."

I almost say "too late," but I stop myself in time. At the core of it, Ladue *is* right. He is more valuable to us as a liaison to the unbound, and surely the converse is also true. If I really did want to take out Miner, I'd be wiser to do it without him.

But the Prince doesn't think that's necessary or desirable, so it's all academic. What's not academic is that Ladue is willing to sell out my poor chump offspring. Knowing *that* is worth something all by itself.

At about quarter of four I park the car, tip the attendant nicely, and stroll down towards Judy's place.

I've got plenty of time—two and a half hours until dawn—and my suit's a wreck. It's got stains, it's got little decay holes and—oh look, a roach! Christ. Well, they say the little bastards can survive nuclear holocaust, what am *I* supposed to do about them?

I'm unseen and silent when Cal Cromwell comes out of the nursing home and, hm, he must have changed clothes awfully fast to be going out on the dot of four-ten when he got off work at four o'clock. Unless he's slacking off, leaving work early. The bastard.

He's heading down the street. Wrong direction, Cal. Can't have that.

I take a deep breath and turn my mind to thoughts of trenches, and gas. I think about sunlight shining on spiked German helmets, the implacable Austrian hordes and the hell of no-man's-land...

Cal slows down, and then he stops. He's a little puzzled. He's nervous and he doesn't know why. He's trying to tell himself that there's no reason.

I let my lips brush his ear. "Cal..."

He whirls about, just about ready to shit his pants. But of course, he sees no one.

I get behind his back, a few steps closer to his car and I start to whistle. *Lullaby of Birdland*, not that it matters. When you're alone in the dark and someone you can't see is whistling, you get scared. Cal thinks he's scared.

Poor Cal. He has no idea.

Cal's edging away but not running, so I think about landmines, gunshots, mustard gas, all those hideous Civil War vets I saw marching on Veteran's Day as a kid, Christ, I had nightmares for weeks, Veteran's Day was a hundred times worse than Halloween.

He starts to breathe heavily. "Who's there? Is someone there?"

I'm inches from him when I whisper, "No one, Cal."

Now he runs.

I dash along behind him, the wind flapping my coat and pants like bat wings, and I have to drive him towards Old John's place. I think about strafing, German biplanes roaring over me with machine guns blazing. I think about mortar attacks, grenades, about being pinned under barbed wire unable to move with the rats and the shredded bodies of my friends, all the terrors of the Great War that I was so desperate to avoid, that I gave *everything* to avoid...

Awash on a wave of my old remembered fears, I float Cal up the steps. I wonder what he's thinking? He probably wouldn't tell if I asked.

Cal thinks he's terrified. Just wait Cal. Just you wait.

Looking over his shoulder, Cal shrieks, a high and whiny yell. "*Shhhhit!*"

Not bucking for famous last words, are we Cal?

He runs away from whatever phantoms scar him, not even bothering to look where he's going. I *know* where he's going so I get there first and open the door (which he doesn't see, he's running forward while looking over his shoulder), and he glances up just in time to see the darkness of the cellar. He can't stop and I don't think he wants to, but he does manage to run down the stairs instead of falling. Once more, he slams the door behind him and, once more, he doesn't know I'm with him.

It's pitch black.

I stop hiding and wait. I hope Cal's a smoker: This last bit would be great by the flame of a flickering cigarette lighter. But no such luck. Hee's got a micro-mini flashlight on his keychain—it has a red beam for some reason. He turns that on and looks around.

He sees a cruddy basement filled with ash and rust and debris, singed paper, rat droppings and burned dust.

He turns around, looking for a window (there are none), looking for another door out (it's excellently hidden), looking for anything to help him (fat chance) and then his beam falls on The Grinder.

I'm directly behind him at that point and (unlike my guest) I have both a lighter *and* a sense of drama. Also, a candelabra.

When I flick my Bic, he spins. There are three candles—none brand new, hell no, they all have good creepy wax drips down the side—and as I light each one my face becomes clearer.

"Hello, Cal."

He screams again. Christ, does he ever!

I step up and backhand him, not too hard, but not a love-tap either. Just enough to rattle his cage and, damn, shut his yap.

"In my day, Cal, we had people who didn't weep and piss themselves at the first sign of trouble. They were called 'men.'"

"Oh God, oh my God, oh God, oh Jesus, oh please..."

"Huh. I was gonna tell you to say your prayers, but I guess you're way ahead of me."

He looks up, awful fascination on his tear-streaked face.

"What are you?" he whispers.

"You wanna guess?" I pocket the lighter.

He just looks at me, ass-eyed dumb.

"I'll give you a hint."

He tries to get away as I reach out for his shirt, but I'm much faster. Predator instincts, part of the package, I've been teasing myself and him both so I'm *really* primed to go. I get him by the collar and yank him forward, right off his feet. I'm aiming for the neck but he has his hands up, so I get his wrist instead. That's okay, there's blood in there and my teeth are sharp.

He doesn't even limp out. He is *so scared* that even the joy wash of a vampire bite can't calm him down. He hits and struggles and pulls but, c'mon, no way. Not a chance in hell.

You do this long enough and pay attention and you can tell when someone's losing strength. I mean, okay, fuckin' *Miner* took me by surprise, but that was a heart attack, special case. With Cal, it's a-okay, I feel the flow slow down and I let him loose. He's dizzy and weak and won't be fighting any more. I probably still have two hours until the sun comes up, and my bolt-hole is ten feet away.

All the time in the world.

"Figure it out yet?" I ask him.

He just stares. He's too fucked up on panic and blood loss to make any kind of coherent response, he's just mumbling.

"Need another hint? Okay. I'm going to drain all your blood out of you and then put you in that machine. It's going to grind your body into paste, which I will divide into two portions. Half goes to the strays outside, and half to the rats living in the walls here. Still don't know?"

He's crying quietly now. Shit. He's gone all resigned on me. All out of fight.

Not much point in delaying things.

"Come here."

He shakes his head, weakly, tears spattering.

"Come"*here*, dammit! Or do you want me to grind you up *alive*?"

He stands.

"Do you believe in reincarnation, Cal?"

I look into his eyes. He's just confused, miserable and lost.

"I don't know one way or the other," I tell him, "But just in case, I'll give you some advice. If you come back? Next time, don't you *ever* steal chockies from *my fucking granddaughter!*"

I don't bother to look for comprehension in his eyes. I just go for the throat and finish the job.

Part Three

Winter

"Never trust a Kindred who enjoys a challenge."
—Prince Maxwell Clarke

Chapter Seven:
Bruise

I sit in the cold car outside the old duplex and I wonder if people can see me or not. I'm not using any kind of vampire hiding magic; I'm just slouched down in my seat.

People are coming and going. Today is Nina's birthday. When she answers the door, she looks so pretty.

I don't know why I'm here. I miss her, I guess. I miss Brooke especially, but I keep away. I want to do what's good for them, so I stay away. I thought about sending them money or something, but I'm still pretty poor.

I've been dead five and a half months now.

I guess I've come a long way since I woke up in someone's basement storage. Still have no idea how I got there. I'm still sleeping in my hole, though these days I usually have to punch through a crust of ice to get into the water. It's not a problem though.

I pay $200 a month as my share of an apartment. I'm in with Ambrose and Filthfoot. None of us actually sleep there during the day—it's up high and not real secure. But it's a place I can keep my stuff, somewhere dry to leave the computer, a place people can leave messages for me. Peaches stays there along with Don Newberg.

Don's not dead, not a vampire or a Kindred or whatever. He's what they call a ghoul—a living guy who's drunk vampire blood. He's addicted to the stuff. As long as we give it to him, he'll do anything we say. He's always begging for it, so it isn't hard to get him to walk the dog and clean up her poop. Hell, if I told him to, he'd probably eat it off the sidewalk.

Don kind of gives me the creeps, actually. I know his work schedule, so I try to go to the apartment when he isn't there. Naked's been trying to teach me the hiding tricks, but I suck at them.

That's why winter's so nice. I got this big long parka. It's like wearing a sleeping bag. The hood is really deep, with these snaps that close a flap over my mouth and nose, and there's a drawstring around the edge. When I pull that in, only my eyes show, and they're normal, the same as they always were. With gloves on, I can pass.

Someone else goes up to the door. I don't know this guy. He's maybe forty, stocky, kind of Mexican-looking. Lots of black hair with some gray in it. He's wearing a thick leather jacket and gloves, no hat.

Nina opens the door. She looks great. She's wearing a knee-length black skirt, black pantyhose. (Or, for all I know, stockings and a garter belt. She wore those sometimes. Not often, but on our anniversary or whatever.) Her top is new, some kind of gold and black pattern thing, low neckline. She must be freezing every time she lets someone in.

When this guy arrives, she gives him a big smile. Real big. She's got a drink in her hand and she's flushed. (We never had parties when I lived there, never had booze in the house.) She gives him a big hug, a kiss on the cheek. He pulls back his head, he kisses her on the mouth.

Both of them look as I start the car and jerk out into traffic. I know this because I'm watching them instead of the road. Someone honks and swerves on slush.

I shouldn't let that get to me. Nina's a widow. I'm gone, out of her life and good riddance, right? Why shouldn't she get on with it
(get it on)
and meet someone new, someone better? Why not?
Man, I feel mean.

I could kill that guy. I could go back there and hide, tricks or no, I could wait for him to leave or, if he didn't leave, I could break in when everyone else was gone. I still have my key, and if she changed the lock I know where she hides a key, and if she's hiding it somewhere else I could just smash the window, jump in and snap his neck, snap it right across, before anyone even realized what was going on. Sure. I could do that. I'm freaky fuckin' strong now, even stronger than at first, I can bend steel bars and everything.

Though what I'd really like to do is drag him out of the window, knock him out maybe, stuff him in the trunk and drink him dead somewhere. Yeah, that'd be better, get a good feed off it too.

But what I'd *really* like is to feed off Nina, get my face in that low neckline. Even more than *that*, shit, I'd like to be alive, at her party with a drink in my hand. Or be alive and not care whether I had a drink or not.

Christ, while I'm at it why don't I just wish for a million dollars?

I stop by the pad and, great, Don's there. Already I'm in a bad mood and now there's Don.

"Hey Bruise," he says. Big smile. He's patting Peaches on the head. She's not crazy about him, but she puts up with it because Ambrose and me told her he's okay.

"Don." I nod. "Here girl." Peaches comes over without a second glance back at him.

"A guy stopped by for you," Don says.

"Yeah?" That's weird. No one stops by for me.

"Some guy named Raphael Ladue. Said you knew him."

Holy crap.

"Did he say what he wanted?"

"No." Don must see something in my face, or the way I'm standing. "Is there a problem?"

"Nah." He doesn't look convinced. "I owe him some money." He still doesn't believe me. "He's just being a prick about it. Don't worry about it."

"Okay. If you need some cash...?"

Don works as a gas station clerk. If we weren't splitting his rent with him, he'd be living in his mom's basement still. It's sad, but almost kind of sweet, him offering me money. What's he got in his checking account? Two hundred bucks?

"It's not a problem," I tell him.

I haven't seen Ladue since Naked told me about him. She'd been hanging around his house, unseen, waiting to jump out and surprise him like she always does, when some real old vampire called Scratch showed up and they started talking about putting a stake in me and leaving me out to burn.

"Now I don't want you to take this wrong," she said. Like there was a *right* way to take that. "Raphael's a weenie and, yeah, he said he was willing to betray you. But there's a big difference between saying he would— saying it to a big scary elder who barged into his crib— and actually doing it. I think Raphael would find some way to weasel out of it before he'd actually do you like that."

That didn't make me feel a hell of a lot better, so I talked to Filth and Ambrose and I got myself away from Raphael. Poor Peaches had to be a stray for a while until we got the apartment set up, but I took care of her best I could. I haven't talked to Ladue since I heard. Not even to ask if it was true. Maybe Naked is lying, but what for? Nah, I'd trust her a lot quicker than I'd trust him.

The good news is, Don wouldn't tell Raphael where I sleep because Don doesn't know.

What could Ladue want? Ambrose and Filthfoot still talk to him—still hang around his place sometimes, though I guess he puts on airs and won't let them in whenever his *Chicago* friends are there. Sheesh.

I'm halfway to his house to have it out with him when I think, what if that's just what he wants?

I mean, really, the most likely reason he'd want to see me is so he can feed me to this crusty old Scratch critter. If that's the case, going to his house is pretty dumb.

So I pull over by a 7-11 and plug some quarters into a payphone. (One of the scams I'm working with Filthfoot involves ripping off vending machines. It's nothing complicated—bash-'em and grab shit—but it keeps me in change for the tolls.) I've still got his number in the PDA, which I hardly ever use.

It rings and rings, and while it's ringing I start to think. Raphael is some kind of computer geek genius, supposedly. I mean, I heard that was why he got the Embrace in the first place, to help some old vampire pimp launder his money. What if he can trace my call? Do you have to be a cop or something to do that?

I get his answering machine and hang up. Shit.

No, maybe that's good. If he's out of the house and away from all his gadgets, he can't trace my call, right? I'll try his cell.

"Mmmhello?"

"Ladue?"

"Miner? Is that you?" He sounds awful eager.

"What do you want?"

"What do you mean, 'what do I want'?"

"I thought you were the big brain, Ladue. What do you want? It's not a hard question."

"Jesus, I just hadn't heard from you in months, okay? I wanted to make sure you were all right."

"Really?"

"Yes, really. Though the way you're giving me the third degree, I don't know why I bother. Where are you, anyhow?"

"Why do you want to know?"

"My *God* Bruise, what paranoid thing flew up your butt and died?"

"I'm at Pitchers an' Pool," I tell him. That's a good three miles from the phone booth, and I haven't been there since my first night.

"There. Was that *so* hard?"

"So what do you want?"

"I want to make sure you're okay! Man, you're all the time at my house and then suddenly you vanish and I never see you. What gives? I'm concerned. Can't a guy be concerned?"

"It took you a while to get concerned."

"It took me a while to find you so I could *express* my concerns. Do you know that Filthfoot and Ambrose are keeping people away from you?"

"Huh?"

"Yeah, I've been asking after you for months and they kept blowing me off. They said you were fine, that you'd found a new place, blah blah, that you were busy doing stuff—but they were always really vague about it—they said they'd pass on my messages but you never got back to me. Did they tell you?"

Naked told me about you, you son of a bitch. "Well, I am fine, I do have a new place, and I have been busy doing stuff."

There's a pause. I can hear music and people in the background of his line. He's probably at a bar waiting for some pretty girl to work up her courage and talk to him.

"So you're okay?"

"I'm okay. Hey, Ladue. How'd you find my new place, anyhow?"

"I got my ways. Don't worry about it man. You're okay?"

"Yeah, I'm doing great."

After I hang up, I think about maybe giving Don's place the old heave-ho. Don's no big loss, except for the dog-walking stuff. I could get Peaches a kennel, but jeez, it's so expensive. Especially for something she'd hate. And it's nice to have somewhere I can shower and change clothes.

Dammit.

I'm pretty fed up when I get to the car and I decide I deserve a break. A little something for me, something to keep me on an even keel. I decide it's time to feed.

Why not? It's a special occasion, right? Nina's birthday.

I start the car and turn right. Towards Pete Staggers' house.

I know I promised that I was going to lay off, take it one day at a time, all that AA stuff that didn't work when it was just simple, legal old booze. But after Barry, I knew that just wouldn't work. I haven't *killed* anybody and I'm not going to, but I have to, you know, face the facts. This is what I am, a vampire. This is what I do, drink blood.

But I've got rules. Good rules, stuff to keep my head on straight.

Rule number one is, animals first. I start off every night with a dog or a cat, just like Ambrose, just like before. Something to keep the hunger manageable. I know I won't be able to do that forever, but it seems like a shame to not do it while I still can.

As I park by Staggers' house (which is at the end of the block by a house that's been for sale for months), I give Peaches a pat and think about all the dogs I've killed. Man, I'd sure be busted up if someone killed Peaches the way I've killed all of them but... I don't know. It's different. Peaches is *my* dog. Those other mutts, no one cared about them, they didn't have names or know how to act around people or anything. They were just animals. I guess I know that, deep down, Peaches is just an animal too. But she's my animal. I'd never eat her, not even if I was starving to death.

Still, I haven't had to put up with that so much any more. Ambrose talked to some guy and now every day I get a quart of animal blood delivered to the apartment. Like, from a meat packing plant, beef or pork blood. Don signs for it. So I don't even have to bother with real animals anymore. It tastes totally flat and nasty, but it keeps me going. So that's okay, except that now I might have to bail on the apartment.

"C'mon girl. *Stay quiet now.*" I tell her that second part in Beast Speech, not because I need to force her to do it, but because otherwise I'm not sure she'd understand.

We go up to Staggers' front door and I listen at the window. No sounds. I peek inside. Lights are off. Is he even home? Well, if not I can let myself in and wait. I have a duplicate of his key.

Pete's an ugly guy, a big fat BO type, which is good. If he was some pretty woman, I'd be a lot more tempted to come and get some. That's why I have rule #2, no women. Biting a guy, there's still a bit in the back of my head that thinks it's kind of fruity. Something that makes me uneasy. Not while I'm *doing* it of course—then it feels completely natural. But still. I think I could get into the habit of biting women a lot easier. So, just to make sure it's something I only do now and again, I stick to guys. Not just any guys, either.

I open the door—gently, just in case anyone still is here—and it's a good thing I do because I hear sounds from the basement. That's where Pete has his bedroom. That's where I do it. I wait until he's asleep and then I creep up and before he even knows it, I've got the fangs in him. Most of the time he doesn't even wake up when I pull out, he just sighs and rolls over, drooling on his pillow. One time he even said a name, which made me feel kind of sick.

It's already pretty creepy that I'm just walking in without any of the hiding stuff that Filth and Naked can do. I mean, I *try* but I have no idea if it's working. I think most of the time I'm just some normal guy breaking and entering. It makes me wonder if anyone ever got into our house, me and Nina I mean, and we never knew.

If he's down there and making noise, he's awake, so I'll stay up here. But then I hear the noise a little clearer. Not much—is it someone laughing? Or crying? It's not a man's voice though.

"Peaches?" I ask. *"How many are down there?"* 'Cause he could be watching TV, of course.

"Two," Peaches whoofs back, nice and quiet. Good girl, I pat her.

"You stay here and come down if there's trouble," I tell her. *"Stay."*

"*Stay?*" She whines it, but she sits.

I creep down the steps and then I hear that noise again and it's for sure someone crying, a young voice.

"Don't worry, don't worry, it's going to be okay, just be easy, be easy." That's Pete's voice and he sounds nervous, eager, he sounds the way I feel before I go in to chomp someone.

"NooooOOOOOO!" That's the young voice again, getting loud and really scared and I pound down the steps, I'm running, I don't care if Staggers hears me because rule #3 is, I only take blood from sex perverts.

There's this thing called Megan's Law. Some guy, a child molester, he moved into this neighborhood where no one knew him and he killed this little girl. Megan. So they passed this law that rapists and child molesters and sex offenders have to register with the cops and their addresses have to be available to the public. There's actually a web site, you can type in your zip code and it gives you a list of all the registered sex offenders in the area. That's how I found Pete Staggers, and that's how I found all the others.

I don't know what he did, exactly. There isn't a whole lot of detail on the web. But it doesn't really matter, right? He's a bad guy, and if a bad thing happens to him, then it's less bad. Right?

Filthfoot says we're the Arrows of God, that God shoots us down at the planet to punish the unworthy. I don't know if there's anything to that. I've never been really up on religion. But I figure that if anyone deserves to get his neck bit and his blood sucked, it's a guy who hurts kids or messes with women.

Even if he's wrong about the Arrow of God business, Filthfoot is right about needing something to do. I mean, forever is a long time to be around if nothing makes sense, if it's all pointless. Even Raphael said it was important to have a purpose —"getting a train set," he called it— something to occupy your time.

I guess Pete's my hobby, him and the other sickos.
I never figured I'd catch one in the act, though.

I get down there and the girl's on the bed, a tiny girl,
not even five feet tall. She's wearing jeans and a binky little
tight sweater, she's curled up in a ball and big fat Pete is
digging at her, he's pulled off one of her tennis shoes and
I guess he's trying to get the pants off her.

"NO NO NO NO NO!" she yells.

He must have heard me coming down the steps, even
over her screaming, because he looks up and I just fucking
deck him. Pow. He doesn't even have time to look re-
volted when I jack his jaw and he drops like a sack of garbage. Fat fucker.

I reach down and grab him by the shirtfront and this is
gonna be sweet. He's out cold, his face is already all bruised
and distorted, and man, I think I broke his jawbone. Good.
Dirty child-molesting asshole.

I peel back my hood with my right hand just as I realize
the girl has stopped yelling. She's looking at me but it's too
late, I have my mouth open and I can't stop now. I bite in to
Pete's neck, no time to hide now even if I was good at it.

Her mouth and her eyes both open, but no sound comes
out. Her eyes are all red and she had a bunch of mascara
on, it's gone all black and drizzly like Alice Cooper's
makeup. She looks like she's about ten but she has to be
older than that. Doesn't she?

I want to tell her that she's all right, that she's okay,
nothing's going to hurt her, but the blood hits my tongue
and I can't stop.

Man.

Man oh man.

I realize that Pete Staggers is a shitball, but man, it
feels so good. Too good. It's like when you're outside
the house working on something, like repainting a window or something, and it's really hot so you just sweat
out gallons, and then you finally get done and come in

and have that first beer from the fridge... it's like that, the relief and satisfaction and being perfect. Perfect. I drink Pete's blood and that's what it's like. Or when I was a kid and still went to church, I remember that the first few times I went to confession, after the priest told me my sins were forgiven. Those first few times, I felt *light*, like I'd really put down a load of bricks or something. I felt relieved. And then I got used to it and it stopped feeling good and then I stopped going to church even. I guess I thought I'd never have that feeling again. But now I do, in this dirty basement, drinking the blood of a guy who rapes kids. I feel light, I feel good, I feel forgiven.

Then, just like that, it stops. Like a switch going off, and I look down and his eyes are open but all rolled up, just the whites. He's dead.

I've lost my cherry.

Peaches came down the stairs after I started running, and now she's standing by my side kind of rubbing her head against my hip. The girl is still staring. She's brought her arms up so that she's like hugging herself, and she's got her knees up in front of those. She still has her eyes open wide, but she's closed her mouth.

"Uh.... Hey," I say, and as I say it I realize I can still taste blood on my lips and teeth. I look around and wow, I guess I really got into it. I mean, I once saw Peaches catch a rabbit in the park and she shook her head back and forth real fast. It kind of looks like I was doing that with Pete or something, because there's a lot of blood that got sprayed and spattered around. In fact, some of it's on the girl.

I've got Wet-Naps in my coat pocket. I mop up my face and hands. "You're okay," I tell her.

She doesn't say anything. She just stares.

"Uh... what's your name?" I ask.

No reply.

"Hello? Can you hear me?"

I step forward to wave my hands in front of her eyes, and she scootches back away. She starts making this creepy sound in her throat, this kind of low peeping noise, like a whining puppy, or maybe like a baby bird that's fallen out of its nest.

"Hey, you're okay," I say. "Don't be afraid, it's okay. It's all right."

Shit, that's just the kind of thing Pete was saying to her before, wasn't it?

"Um... say, do you like dogs?"

Her eyes shift to Peaches.

"This here is Peaches. She's a friendly dog." Man, I hope this doesn't just make things worse. "You want to pat Peaches? She won't mind. *Peaches, go see her. Be real gentle.*"

She goes over and gives the girl a few snuffles with her nose and that seems to maybe help a little. At least the girl isn't jerking back or moving away, like she did with me.

What the hell am I supposed to do?

"Hello?"

"Ambrose? Hey, it's me."

"What's up?"

"I'm kinda in trouble."

"Hold on a second."

It isn't a second, but it feels like a million years, standing there in Pete's basement, shifting from foot to foot, the girl on the bed kind of cuddling Peaches but still staring at me.

"Okay, look, here's the phone number where I'm at, a land line?" Raphael is super-careful about what he says over a cell phone, he's always harping about intercepts and taps, so I guess the rest of us have gotten all jumpy too. "Don't call me from your cell on this, all right? Are you near a phone?"

"Yeah."

He gives me the number, so I hang up my cell phone and pick up Pete's phone, which is shaped like a football for some reason. I dial into that and Ambrose picks up again.

"What's the matter?"

"Man, I tell you I have a problem and the first thing you do is, is put me on hold and have me call back?"

"I figured that if you had time to make a phone call, it couldn't be really life threatening."

"Yeah, but still..."

"*Is* it life threatening?"

"Well... no."

"Tell me what's going on."

Where do I start? "Well, I went to see this guy about digging a well."

"Uh huh."

"And when I got here, there was this girl here. And now things have kind of gotten screwy."

"Did you lose your cherry?"

"...Yeah."

"Okay. And the one you weren't...?"

"Still here."

"Okay. Tell me where you are and I'll get there as soon as I can. You have your car there, right?"

"Right."

"Then I won't drive."

It's about twenty minutes later that I hear his boots clomping down the stairs. He gets to the bottom and looks around.

By that time I'm sitting on the desk chair, the girl's as far back into the corner of the bed as she can get, Peaches is lying at her feet, Pete's a fuckin' heap on the floor and I've started to dab blood off the walls and stuff with wet-naps.

Ambrose takes it all it and says, "Shit."

"Yeah."

The girl looks at him, then at me, then tries to push herself even further away. It's winter, so Ambrose has a ratty green knit scarf up over his mouth.

"Hey, you okay?" he asks her. She just tries to escape, tries to make herself smaller.

"She's been like that since... well, since."

"Yeah. Looks like hysterical muteness or catatonia or something. I don't know. Well, at least she can't tell anyone what she saw." He looks at Pete and shakes his head. "Is there a rug or something?"

"Wait, what about her?"

He looks at her and shrugs. "Let's wrap up fatso, get him in the car. Then we can worry about her."

"His name was..."

"I don't really want to know," Ambrose says. "Find a tarp or something."

We pull a carpet out from under Pete's kitchen table, and it turns out there's ropes and duct tape in the bedside table. Man. For a minute there, I was feeling kind of bad for what I did, but seeing those ropes and that poor little girl... there's a knife in the drawer too. She doesn't even react when Ambrose pulls that out. We use it to cut the rope.

Before we wrap him up though, Ambrose saws the guy's head off. It takes me by surprise when he just kneels down and does it, like he's carving the Christmas ham.

"Jesus, Ambrose!"

"What?"

"Well... what the hell, man?"

"Tossing the head separately throws up a roadblock for the cops," he says. "We dump these in Lake Michigan with some bricks and they'll bloat a while before anyone finds them. Then it won't be an issue that there's no blood."

"Okay, but... I mean..." I gesture at the girl.

Ambrose glances that way. "She doesn't look any *more* shell-shocked," he says. He rummages in the closet and comes up with a gym bag. The head goes in there, wrapped in sweaters.

"You see?" I tell her. "The bad man can't hurt you any more."

"Oh Christ," Ambrose mutters.

"What?"

"Get a grip, Bruise."

"I've got a grip! Man, what did I do that's, that's not right or whatever?"

"Help me with the rug," he says.

We roll up Pete's torso and tie it and tape it, but midway through Ambrose thinks to ask if I took his wallet and, of course, I didn't, so we have to undo everything to get that out. But eventually we make a big fat six-foot cigar out of him. I carry that upstairs while Ambrose handles the gym bag.

"You just stay right here," I tell the girl.

"We'll be right back."

Ambrose keeps shaking his head.

When we reach the front door he says, "Try not to be seen lugging that out to the car?"

"Yeah, okay." I don't think there's anyone to see anyhow. I mean, Pete's house is kind of in a crappy neighborhood, the place next door is empty, and there's a screen of overgrown trees right by the street. Hell, it's a perfect place for a child molester. Which makes it perfect for us, I guess.

That's kind of a downer.

Slamming the trunk, Ambrose turns to me. "So what *do* we do?"

"I thought you were dumping that stuff in the lake."

"Yeah, that's no biggie. You really could have handled this on your own."

"What about the girl?"

"Uh huh," he says. "*That's* the issue."

For a moment, we're just quiet.

"We could... I guess we could just leave her and call the cops, tell them to come here and get her?"

He sighs. "I don't like it."

"Yeah?"

"I mean, she's clammed up now. But suppose she gets some therapy, tells people what she saw?"

"Suppose she does? 'Two monsters came in and ate the rapist'? She didn't even see your face. Who's going to take her seriously? Especially when she's been all, you know, traumatized and everything. They come in and find her all zonked and they're not going to take her seriously if she tells them about me biting that guy."

"The cops won't pay attention," he says, "But the Prince and his men might."

"Oh *Jesus*! Them again? Why would they care?"

"Because they're uptight about vampire stuff," he says. "And I can't really blame them."

"If the cops don't care, what's it to this Prince?"

"It won't matter that the cops don't care. What matters is the cops *might* care, might *start* to care. This guys thinks in decades," he says.

"So in ten years, someone's going to care more about Pete Staggers than they do now?"

"Is that the guy's name? "

"Sorry."

"They think a pattern might emerge. Enough people talk about neck-biting monsters, someone might listen. Hell Bruise, people *are* listening. You remember that guy down in Texas, right?"

"But he was a kook."

"No, he was a fearless vampire hunter who *became* a kook. They got someone to mess his head up so that he wasn't making sense any more, but he killed two vampires before they could find out who he was. He did it all with stuff from old books and listening to what his friggin' Boy Scout troop told him."

"So, what, turning the girl in isn't an option?"

For a moment, he doesn't say anything. "I could take care of her," he says.

Fuck.

"You mean you could kill her," I say.

He nods.

"I don't believe this."

"Bruise..." He looks away from me.

"I don't *believe* this. You're the guy who only eats rats, the guy who won't feed off of people, the guy who, who's strong and resists temptation!"

"I'm a carrier, Bruise."

"You're the guy who, and now you just want to take that girl and... and..."

"I feed off people. Same as you do. But I have to be really careful because I'm HIV positive."

I take a step back.

"What?"

"Come *on* Bruise, you remember all this stuff don't you? I'm a carrier! Everyone I feed from gets exposed to AIDS! So yes, I'm careful and yes, I resist temptation, but when someone's better off dead you better believe I'm hungry for the job!"

"You think she's better off dead?"

"I think we're better off with her dead."

For a minute, I don't have any idea what to say to that.

"C'mon," is what I eventually come up with. Ambrose doesn't reply.

"But... c'mon Ambrose, if we just... just kill her because it's easier for us how..."

"Forget it. Forget I said anything."

"...how are we any better than Pete?"

"Okay, *fine.* You don't like my solution. What's your brilliant idea?"

"Uh..."

"There's ten guys who can tear down a plan for every one who can produce an alternative. My commander always used to say that."

"I'm thinking!"

"If all I wanted was criticism, I'd go to Ladue."

That actually gives me an idea.

"Okay, wait... how about this? The Prince and the rest of those Chicago guys, they're the ones with the big problem with all this, right? Why don't they help us out?"

"You think they're just itching to help you clean up your messes?" He turns and starts back towards the house.

"Who's the critic now? Raphael's all in with them now, right? We go to him maybe, he can calm the girl down…"

"Calm her down enough to understand what happened, to explain it maybe?"

"Okay, um… wait! I got it! Whatsername!"

"Good old whatsername?"

"The, the doctor! The instant hypnosis gal. You know. The one who helped me out with faking my death?"

"Persephone."

"That's her! We can take the girl to her and…"

"Lower your voice," he says. By this time we're inside, at the top of the steps. "Do you want her to hear you?"

"We take the girl to her," I say, "And she does that brain thing on her, and she forgets it all."

There's a pause. Ambrose just looks at me.

"Okay," he says at last.

"Why wouldn't that work?"

"The question is, what's in it for her? That's always the question with those types."

"She told me she'd do anything for the Masquerade. That's the policy of hiding, right?"

"Yeah."

"Well? I mean, keeping this girl silent, that's a, a whatchacallit. It's a chance to keep things quiet."

For a few more seconds, he just looks at me. "You really want to save this girl, don't you?"

"Why not? I mean, we're…" This time I shrug, I look around. "What's the point of it? I mean, if we're going to, to be around forever and we can't even help one girl out of such a, a shitty situation… if we can't even do that? What's the point?"

Again, he looks at me.

Then he nods.

Getting her out of the basement turns out to be trouble. I ask her to come and, of course, she ain't having it. So then I call Peaches away, hoping the girl will follow. And she reaches her arms out as the dog goes, she makes some sad noises, but nope, she's not getting out of that corner of the bed, hunched up against the wall.

"Do you have a purse or a wallet or something?" Ambrose asks her. But she stays mum.

"What about your parents?" I ask her. "Can we call your parents?"

"Where are you from?"

"What's your *name*, sweetie?"

Not a word on any of it. Ambrose gently tries to take her hand and lead her out of the bed, but she pulls away, staying all balled up.

I'm out of ideas on how to get her to move, so I start looking through Pete's wallet. He's got a MasterCard with his picture on it, sixty bucks and a coupon for a free dinner at Outback Steak House. Great.

"This is gonna get ugly," Ambrose says. "Not that it's not ugly enough."

"Yeah?"

"I don't think she's leaving without a fight."

"Come on."

"Try and pick her up."

"Well I... I... don't..."

"What?"

"I don't want to freak her out."

"Here's the impasse, then," he says. "We need to get her out of here. She's not going voluntarily. And you won't grab her. One of those things has to change."

"Why can't we stay here?"

"I think convincing Persephone to help you is going to be hard enough without getting her to make a house call. Why not knock her out?"

"What? You're crazy."

"This will work a lot better if she's unconscious."

She starts to make those creepy peeping noises again. I guess it's a good sign—she at least kind of understands what we're talking about.

"Maybe Pete had some of that stuff that makes people pass out?"

"Chloroform?"

"Yeah, whatever."

"Don't you think he'd have used it on her?"

Good point.

Ambrose drops into Pete's chair and puts his head in his hands. "Look," he says, staring down at the floor. "If you want, I'll do it."

"You mean…?"

"I'll knock her out. You go upstairs, you won't have to see it."

"You're not going to hurt her?"

"*FUCK!*" He jumps to his feet and his scarf sags, those big animal fangs are showing and I've never seen him lose his cool like this before. "*Yes! Yes I am going to hurt her! You think I can knock her out without hurting her? Go upstairs and let me do this and I won't KILL her, okay?*"

"NooooOOOoooo!"

"Shh, it's, you're going to be okay…" She doesn't listen to me. I don't know what to do.

I go upstairs.

I'm halfway up when I hear thumps and her screams change, she's just yelling in short bursts, no words… and then it gets muffled down to a squeak.

I can't move. I'm in the middle of the steps and I can't bring myself to go any further, but I can't seem to go down, either.

And then the door at the bottom opens, there's a wedge of light coming out of it. Then blocking the light, it's Ambrose, carrying her in his arms, like she's dead.

"Is she…?"

"She's breathing," he says. "I choked her out. You happy now?"

We put her in the backseat, I do up the seatbelt around her and we drive. Partway there, we stop to make a call.

"Raphael?" Ambrose says. Then he waits. "Yeah, look, do you have a number for your friend Persephone?" More wait. "Because I want to talk to her." Another pause, a long pause. "It's about that." Then he's quiet some more—man, Raphael sure can talk. Ambrose is starting to look impatient. "Look, I need her help. Do you want to help me too, or just give me her number?" Pause. Ambrose is rolling his eyes. "You're sure you want to help? Okay. We'll be over in a minute."

He slams the car door getting in. "That guy doesn't know what the hell he wants," he mutters.

We pull in the back of Raphael's house, and she's starting to stir and mutter as I carry her up to the back door.

"What the hell are you *doing*?" Raphael hisses.

"Can I bring her in?"

"No! Jesus, I don't see you for months and now you want my help with a kidnapping?"

"It's not..."

"Let us *in*, dammit." His scarf has slipped again and Ambrose is actually snarling. With those teeth, he can really snarl. Peaches barks and Raphael steps aside.

"You got duct tape, or better, some chloroform?"

"I've got Rohypnol," Raphael says.

"Mmmm... nah. Too little, too late. I need something to knock her out."

"What did you guys *do*?"

"Sir Drinks-a-Lot here was riding around on his white horse and he interrupted the Black Knight trying to buttfuck the damsel in distress," Ambrose says, heading towards the bathroom. He raises his voice as he rummages through the medicine cabinet. "So after valiantly besting the Black Knight in single combat, he's rescued her and driven her insane."

Raphael's been staring after Ambrose this whole time. Now he looks back to me, raises his eyebrows.

"Well," I say, "I guess. I mean, that's kind of, it." Ambrose returns. "You didn't need to be so sarcastic about it," I tell him.

"Don't you have any downers?"

"What for?" Raphael asks.

"Right, you do everything with charm." Ambrose sighs. "Maybe it's just as well. The dead guy could have loaded her up with God knows what. Something as simple as a Sudafed could put her in a coma." He narrows his eyes and glares at me. "And we can't permit a *tragedy* like that."

"So what do we do?"

"Duct tape?"

I don't like it, but Ambrose is kind of right. We can't have her yelling all over the place so Raphael's neighbors might hear. She's starting to come awake so we move fast to get her tied to a chair.

"Let's not put tape on her mouth, guys," I say. "I bet that stuff hurts."

"You're all heart," Raphael says.

She wakes up as Raphael ties the gag in place, and he steps back behind her.

"I don't want her seeing my face," he says, and his voice sounds funny.

"Why are you talking like that?"

"Because I don't want her to identify my voice, genius." We've got her facing into Raphael's empty kitchen pantry—nothing really memorable to see there. She starts twisting her neck, trying to see behind her, but I step up so that all she sees is my stomach.

Peaches squeezes around in front of the girl and lays her head in the girl's lap. I don't have to tell her to or anything.

"You're okay," I tell her. "I'm going to... it's all gonna get better."

"You see how he is?" Ambrose tells Raphael.

"Give him a break." Raphael is still talking in his funny voice.

For a minute, the three of us stand there. The girl isn't making any noise, but she's awake, she's looking around.

"Okay, I'm going to go dump the dead guy," Ambrose says. "You guys got it from here on out?"

"Wait, you're just... just leaving?" I ask.

"No, I'm 'just' going to go get rid of evidence that *you* did a murder, all right? After that, exactly what do you want from me? If you want her choked out again, you'll have to do it yourself." He shakes his head as he goes, but pauses in the doorway to say, "See you tomorrow. I'll leave your car at the usual place, all right?"

"Okay. Hey Ambrose... thanks, man."

He stays still a minute, but doesn't turn to look back at me. "You're welcome." Then he goes.

So it's me and Raphael. And the girl, of course.

"Right," he says,

"So, Persephone."

"Don't forget your funny voice."

He goes into the living room, gesturing for me to stay with her.

I get around to the side. "You're okay," I tell her. "I'm... I'm sorry. Sorry about all this. I didn't mean for... I'm sorry that we had to do all this stuff. Tying you up and... and choking you and... aw hell." I pull up another kitchen chair and lean in.

She leans away.

"Look. I really *am* sorry. I'm gonna try and make this right. I mean, you're better off with us than with Pete, right? None of us *want* to hurt you. We're... we're really trying not to."

Peaches, her head still in the girl's lap, looks up. I turn and see Raphael standing in the doorway.

"Bruise," he says. "Are you all right?"

It's weird. His voice isn't sharp. For once, he doesn't sound annoyed.

"Yeah, I'm... I'm okay."

"It's just that... you lost your cherry tonight, huh? With the 'Black Knight.'"

"Yeah. Guess I did."

He nods. "How do you feel?"

I think about it a second.

"I'm hanging in."

He just looks at me for a second and he nods again. "Okay. I talked to Persephone, she's at this club called Irony. You know where it is? Well, I can give you directions, you can go get her."

"Me? Go into a *nightclub*?"

"You don't have to go inside, she knows my car and she'll watch for that."

"Why don't you go pick her up? You know the way."

"I think I should stay here. You know. Just in case someone shows up. It'd be better."

"What do you mean? I could take care of someone."

"Bruise," he puts his hand on my shoulder. "You're a good guy, you're a brave guy and you know what? Even if Ambrose doesn't understand what you're doing tonight, I do. Okay? But you are not persuasive. I am persuasive. I can make people like me. You know this. You can't. That's just... the cards we were dealt."

"...Yeah."

We fart around for a couple minutes, Raphael programming the club into my PDA, giving me his car keys and bugging me about driving careful. As I turn to go, Raphael says, "You're not taking the dog?"

"I didn't think you'd want her in your Alfa Romeo."

"Good point. Can't you... y'know, send her to the yard?"

"He keeps the girl calm. You want that, right?"

"Yeah." He looks at Peaches, looks at me.

I turn back to the girl. "You're going to be all right." And I look at Peaches and grunt, "*If Raphael tries to hurt her, kill him.*"

Raphael's car is nice, with a lot of pickup, but it idles kind of rough. I should talk to him about that. Barry's old PDA shows me a little colored map on how to get there. Man, it's like something out of Star Trek. Then I pull up and see the people outside the club. None of them are wearing parkas with flaps over their faces. That's for damn sure.

greg stolze

Out comes Persephone. Wow.

It's like… I don't know what it's like. When I was a young guy, I'd all the time think about women I'd want to lay, right? I'd, you know, imagine meeting some woman in a bar, or on a beach, or, you know, on a cruise ship or I'd help her when her car broke down or I'd rescue her from a mugger or some damn stupid thing. Like guys do. And some of the time I'd picture myself in really expensive clothes and a nice car—like an Alfa Romeo, like Raphael's car. But all the women I imagined getting into my imaginary nice car, none of them were like Persephone. No, none of them were in Persephone's *league*. Because I'd think about girls from the swimsuit calendar or girls from TV or girls from gym class who looked good running, but never someone *classy*, like her. Never someone who seemed so smart. Never someone who wore dressy clothes, not because she was trying to look good, but just because those were what she always wore. Like, what's dressed up to me is just dressed to her.

I don't know. It's just strange, her walking towards the car, towards me. It's not something I ever could have imagined.

Halfway across the street to me, she starts to glare, and she makes a little arm motion like she's turning a wheel. What the…? Does she want me to roll down the window?

I roll down the window.

"Open the door for me, you clod!" She hisses it while she's still four steps away.

"So, some nice car, huh?" We've been driving a couple miles and she hasn't said anything.

She turns her head to look out the window. "I hear Jaguars are notoriously hard to get fixed."

I think about telling her it's not a Jag, but I guess there's not much point.

"Uh… well, first off, thanks for, you know… Helping. Helping me out."

"I haven't done anything yet."

"I know, but, I mean, being willing is... it's a help. It helps."

"Can you get some grip on what you're trying to say before you speak? I think *that* might help."

We drive on a little further, in silence.

"I'm sorry I didn't get out to open your door quick enough."

"Oh for Christ's sake..."

"Well *sorry*, I'm trying, okay? I mean, I just, I'm not a door opener. The first time I tried it with my wife, she laughed her ass off. She, uh, considered herself an enlightened woman."

"What's that supposed to mean?"

"What, enlightened woman? That she was, I guess, you know, a feminist or whatever."

"No, I mean..." She turns and glares at me. "You think I'm not a feminist? Not an enlightened woman?"

"Uh..."

"I've passed the *bar exam*. I held a four-point GPA through college *and* law school and I had a great career afterwards, certainly a better career than *your* wife. You want to know why I wanted you to hold the door?"

I don't, but I think she's going to tell me anyhow.

"I have a position to keep up. People *notice things*. They notice that tonight I'm in an Isaac Mizrahi and they'd notice if tomorrow night I showed up in gothic lace with a fake lip ring, okay? I have got *layers and layers* that I'm working and you can't even... look. The people I move among? They *pay attention*. They want me because I'm wanted, all right? So if they see me get into a car with some, some *dork in a parka* who expects me to hop in like a streetwalker... what do you think that does?"

"I'm sorry."

"I can open my own damn door, I don't need any man looking out for me, but those people, that's where I hunt, and hunting's not so easy that I can just piss away advantages, *any* advantages."

I don't say anything for a while. This is like fighting with Nina: sometimes it's best to just pipe down and see if she's run out of steam.

I drive.

Okay, so maybe she's said her bit. Try something nice, something to give her a chance to get back to normal.

"I'da thought it'd be easy, for you."

"What?"

"You know, looking the way you do. Being able to, you know, just zap people."

"You think I just 'zap people'?"

"What do I know about it? Nothing. Sorry again, I just... You just made it look easy. Y'know?"

"You don't have a clue," she says, but her voice is a little more calm, and when I sneak a glance over, she's got a little tiny hint of a smile.

Chapter Eight:
Persephone

Bruise Miner is different in his parka.

I never realized just how much of my reaction to him was based on his face. I mean, I should know better than to judge on looks, right? Seesawing between the Linda wardrobe and the Persephone gear like I do.

(Last night I tried mixing some pieces and I wasn't sure if I was going to laugh or throw up. I mean, I didn't just look stupid, I looked... *wrong*. Almost the way Bruise looks wrong...)

Bruise looks like something out of one of my brother's old horror comic books, and that affected me. I'm sure he genuinely *is* dumb, violent and pathetic, but the fact that he's repulsive on top of all that probably made me more impatient than I'd usually be. Less pity, more irritation.

When you think about it, Bruise is a pretty sad case. My Embrace was no picnic, but at least my sire stuck around to explain things and take care of me afterwards.

(My Embrace. There's a euphemism for you. I talked about this stuff with Bella before our falling-out, and she made hers sound like the best one-night-stand ever. Like she was *jealous* I had that with Maxwell. But Dubiard, he said his was rape. That was exactly the word he used. And me... mine was different from both. It wasn't horror or delight, but something related to both. There isn't a word for what I felt. There isn't a word for what Maxwell did to me.)

Part of me wonders what it would be like to be unbound, like Bruise. Loki calls them slackers and says they're good for exactly nothing—hell, when he talks about them, he

greg stolze

sounds like a sheriff from the south in the seventies, railing about the hippies. But why not live night to night, worry about feeding and safety and nothing else? When I think about Solomon, Bella, Norris and Tobias (not to mention Maxwell), the idea of an existence without politics sounds like an incredible luxury.

But they'd never let me get away with it. Loki would never forgive me, Solomon would declare victory and Maxwell… I don't know what he'd do. Part of me thinks he'd let me go, maybe not even notice. Part thinks he'd hunt me to the ends of the Earth.

No, I'm stuck. And if I don't want to spend an eternal unlife with *no* life, being the designated whipping girl of the whole city, I'd better get some friends on my side. Friends with pull. Like Norris.

I still haven't found out who Miner's sire is, which means Norris still thinks I'm an idiot. Would he really do me that much good as a patron? (I don't think he'll ever be a friend. He's not the type to be or have friends.) He'd be better than nothing. People fear him, and that's *something*. It would be better than running off to Maxwell again, better than being weak and dependent.

(I didn't tell Maxwell about my suspicions… my *stupid, childish* suspicions. Norris spared me that at least. Nothing's happened. That evil bitch Bella was just blowing smoke up my ass, trying to get me to do something stupid. And on cue, I did.)

I need to show Norris I'm not a dope. I need to prove my worth to Maxwell… not to mention myself. So I need to get to the bottom of the Miner mystery, and it looks like the only way to do that is to get Miner on my side. However distasteful that may be.

And now we're at Raphael's house. Oh, and *this* time Miner gets the door for me. Perfect.

I don't know why *anyone* would expect him to remember who sired him. Or remember anything. He's a moron.

"So what's the problem, anyhow?"

Before he can answer, Raphael comes trotting, holding out his hand and giving me a wide grin.

"Thanks *so much*," he says, and I suddenly feel like it's something awful. It must be, if they're so effusive when all I've done is *show up*.

"What exactly am I doing?" I ask.

He turns to Miner. "You didn't *tell* her?"

Miner, the sad sack, just shrugs. He starts to say something, but Raphael cuts him off.

"I'm really sorry but, you know how it is sometimes," he's rolling his eyes, giving me an expression that I think is supposed to communicate how much better he and I are than Bruise and that sometimes cool folks like us just have to give breaks to the dorks. Like he wants me to take up the hip man's burden.

"Do I?" I turn to Bruise. For just a moment I worry about keeping Raphael on my side, but I know his kind. He'll adore me as long as I treat him like crap. The instant I acknowledge that he's my equal, he'll start trying to surpass me.

"Bruise, why don't *you* explain things."

"Well, you see... uh..."

Then there's another interruption. A sound, a voice from the kitchen. A thin, hurt little voice.

No. It's not an interruption. That sad sound has been in the background since I arrived. It's just that I didn't hear it until Bruise had trailed off into tongue-tied silence.

I follow.

In the kitchen... Jesus Christ. He's got a girl, some tiny little kid, all tied up. His dog's got its head in her lap, probably ready to bite off her fingers if she moves a muscle. Only she's not going to move a muscle because her hands are tied behind her back, and her thin ankles above too-small Keds are taped to the legs of a chrome kitchen chair.

"What did you *do?*"

"Well..."

I go to her and someone's put *makeup* on her, mascara and badly-done eyeliner and that had *better* be lipstick on the corners of her gag. Then I look at her neck and see the oval purple marks on either side of her windpipe, four on the left and one on the right. A handprint.

I turn to face him, this ridiculous snowman in his parka, this blob, nothing visible of him but his outline and his eyes. Eyes as blank and stupid as a shark in a tank.

"What *happened*?"

"I kinda found her. You know." He looks away, shifts from one foot to another, God, he looks like a ten-year-old getting scolded by mother.

"And you couldn't bring yourself to finish her off, is that it? Got too full?"

"Hey, I *never* planned to kill her! I'm trying to…"

"Oh shut up. You make me sick."

"I didn't want to hurt her at all!"

I look down at her again and realize she's wet herself.

"Too late," I tell him. "She's hurt. What do you want me to do?"

"Look, I didn't…"

"Do you want my help or not?"

"Yeah! I mean, of course I do, I went and got you and, you gotta understand…"

"If you want my help, you'd better knock off the self-justifying *crap* and tell me something practical!"

I know what he wants, of course. He wants me to wave my magic wand, go zap, and clear out all the blowback from his monstrous lack of self-discipline.

"I hoped you could… fix her."

Fix her. Yeah. Like I'm mommy and the wheel came off his wagon. Fix it please.

There's a part of me, a tiny selfish sliver, that wants to just blow these two assholes off, walk out the door, head down to a taco joint and call a cab. Just leave the girl, let them clean up their own mess.

But I can't do that.

Because she's not just a mess, is she? She's not just a punishment for Bruise's dumb behavior. She's a person, still. A mess of a person, but still.

God, I could barely manage to make *Scott* forget, I bungled that so badly that he nearly went out of his mind. Maybe he *did* go out of his mind, maybe no one got to him but me and *that's* why he

(killed himself)

did it. What's going to happen when I start mucking around with a girl who's clearly already badly, *severely* traumatized, who's already got her brain locked up in knots? Is there any chance this could work, any chance at all?

Fix her. Sure.

But what are the other options? I can't leave her with these clowns. They'll screw around and dither and debate and, eventually, take the path of least resistance. No, if anyone's going to make this right, even halfway right, it's going to be me. Shit.

And looking at the expectant faces on Bruise and Raphael (okay, I can't really see Bruise's face, but his posture says it all), I can foresee a *stream* of this kind of crap, a river, a torrent. If I fix this, they're going to be calling me like a building superintendent. "Can you…?" "I kinda need…" "This guy, could you make him forget…?" Why not? They think I just *zap* people.

If I don't do this, she's doomed. If I do, they're going to call me like mommy every time they skin their knees.

Fuck.

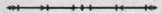

So I look at Bruise and Raphael and I say it. The slogan for Kindred everywhere.

"What's in it for me?"

"Persephone, look…" This is Raphael, trying to pour oil on the waters, and I'm not in the mood. I glare and he zips it.

Bruise just looks at me with those dumb animal eyes. "You don't…" He's whining. Then he stops and he says,

"Anything you want." Says it without the self-pity and raw-ness. He's resigned.

For a second, I wonder about him. But then I glance back at the girl, tied up until she wet herself and sobbing around her gag, and no.

"Big words, from a bum in a cheap overcoat," I tell him. "What could I possibly want that you could possibly get?"

He shrugs. Worthless.

And then I have a thought.

"Tell you what," I say. I take off my coat and sling it over a chair, undo my cufflink and roll up my French sleeve. "There's one thing." Then I raise my wrist and rake it across my teeth.

(It hurts. Of course it hurts, and I know it hurts but... the pain doesn't seem to mean anything, any more.)

"Don't," Raphael says, and for a minute I think he's whining at me not to hurt myself... but no.

He's looking at Bruise.

But Bruise is coming forward.

"So that's the price, huh?"

"One tonight, one tomorrow."

"Bruce, don't *do it*," Raphael says, and he actually plucks at Bruise's sleeve. He doesn't grab it, doesn't pull it, but he gives it a few little tugs with his fingertips.

"No," Bruise says. "It's okay."

He's right by me now, he unsnapping the hood and drawing it back. Once again, I see his boils, the skin pulled so taut it shines, the ripples and crevasses where his flesh has roiled together. It almost doesn't look like a human face, but instead like some wild rock formation from deep underground. But it stretches and shifts like skin, or rubber, as he speaks.

"If this is what I gotta do."

Then he drinks me.

How do I describe what this is like?

I remember when Maxwell drained me, the insistent pulling and me beating on him but only weakly, no real strength in my fists because there was no real drive to stop it, rather the hope that I could go on being killed forever and never die. I was a mortal then, and I felt the thrill of the edge of mortality before it pulled me over.

But this isn't like that, because I'm no longer outside that edge.

There are all the feeds I've made, all the times I've been the one whose pull has mesmerized the living, the times I've been the door through which they glimpse dark eternity...

But this isn't like that, because Bruise is not alive.

He draws from me and it is a trade among equals. We're both on that thin gray border between the warm red light of life and the cold infinite black of demise. While he drinks, we anchor each other. While he drinks, we move through each other and we mingle, I can feel my *self* flowing into him, into that strong and twisted frame, so different, so big and clumsy and filled with shame and hurt.

Then it's done. He pulls away and looks at me and he just looks like Bruce to me now. He's no hideous monster. That's just him.

There's a little bit of me looking back from behind his eyes. Not a lot. Just enough to make him grateful.

While my blood lasts within him, he'll be less alone.

That's why it's so addictive.

He kisses the injury closed. Gently. I brush my hair back, and then realize Raphael is still there.

This irritates me for some reason. It's like making out in a dorm room in college, and then your roommate walks in.

"Right." I start fixing my cuffs. "Untie her."

As the gag comes out, her cries get louder, more pronounced, and when her hands are freed the first thing she does is bend forward to hug the dog and pull it close.

"Get her some clothes, a towel... stuff to clean herself up. C'mon people, *think*."

Like Laurel and Hardy, Bruce and Raphael hop to it.

I Push Out at her. I'm no genius with sculpting it—I know some can fine-tune the emotional response, bending it towards maternal affection or lust or paralyzed shock and horror, but I'm doing well to just project it. Still, I try to be gentle, try to lure her with kindness, caring and a sense of trust.

"Can you look at me?" I ask, and she does.

Good. I lock gazes with her—she has hazel eyes, green along the iris rims shading to brown. I need eye contact to climb around in her memories, and I was worried about getting it. But she's staring at everything. Too afraid to look away, I guess.

"Whenever I ask you to, I want you to look in my eyes," I tell her.

She nods. Her poor mind is a fragile thing, trembling and fluttering. It isn't hard to control, but it's complicated. I can feel the frailty and know that it will snap incurably if I'm too rough.

"I want you to trust me."

She nods. I ease off the stern power of command and return to cajoling and charm.

"Tell me your name?"

"Valerie," she says.

"Valerie. That's a pretty name. Where do you live, Valerie?"

Her lower lip starts to tremble. "I ran away from home."

"Shh! Oh, don't be sad." Adoration isn't working. She's tearing up, she's slipping away. I'd better use control again. "You feel calm," I instruct her. "You're aware of your memories, but you know that they are just thoughts and that they have no power to harm you. You are safe now, here with me. You can discuss what has happened to you without losing control. You acknowledge your feelings, but they are set aside for now. You can talk to me without crying or becoming hysterical."

"I feel calm," she says. I smile a little and get a little weak smile back.

"How old are you, Valerie?"

"I'm sixteen."

I've never seen such a tiny sixteen-year-old. "Tell me what happened. You ran away from home?"

"Mom has a new boyfriend. Ian. He hits."

The simple way she says this makes that deep vampire anger flare up inside. I want to find Ian, break his arms and suck his blood until he dies. That'll teach him. But not now, no time for that now, I have a little girl to save and heal.

"So you ran away. How'd you do that?"

"I saved up my money from working at the 7-11. It was hard, because I had to lie to mom about not getting hours so that she wouldn't take it. But I told her I got a remedial math class after school and she said I'd just have to walk home, so I'd secretly take the bus home like always, then change at work, and come home late."

Poor kid. "That's a very clever plan. You must have needed a lot of courage to do that. What did you do next?"

"When I had enough money, I got on a train to Chicago to go meet William."

"Who's William?"

"He's this guy I met on the Internet."

That's how Raphael preys. He's got at least a dozen fake identities reeling in the lonely for him. Maybe this isn't Bruce's fuckup. Maybe Bruce came in to help his buddy.

"I called him from the train station and he told me which bus to take and how to get to his house. Only when I got there, it wasn't William."

"Who was it?"

"I don't know. Some old guy. William had sent me a picture on email and he was young, but this guy was old and fat. He said he was William's older brother and that William would be home soon, I should come in and wait." She swallows hard.

"Then what happened?"

"At first he was okay. He asked if I was hungry, and I was, but I didn't want to eat in front of him. And he asked if I wanted a beer or a margarita, but I told him no. Then he asked if I wanted to wait in William's room, in the basement, and I told him the kitchen was fine, and then... then..."

"Yes? It's okay Valerie. You know it's all right."

"Then he grabbed me and pulled me down there, he pulled me down the stairs. He had his hands on my arms and they were behind my back, like in a full nelson, and he threw me on the bed."

I swallow hard too, but it feels fake, like I'm acting. I'm trying to feel like I'm about to vomit. In my head, I know this is awful, and I feel terrible... but it's a distant terror. To the new part of me, the part Maxwell put in me, the part Solomon awakened,

(the part that wants to hurt Ian)

this is just business as usual. To my vampire, Valerie's story is as moving as the directions on a jar of makeup remover.

"He kept touching and grabbing me and I was trying to... to not let him, and then I heard someone coming down the stairs. I thought it might be William, but it wasn't."

"Who was it?"

"It was a man in a coat. Or I thought it was a man. The others called him Bruise."

Jesus Christ. All this time I thought Bruise was the old guy, the predator, the fake William.

"The... man in the jacket. What did he do?"

"He hit the fat guy, hit him real hard. And then he pulled him up off the ground. He'd knocked the fat guy out and then he bit his neck."

For a moment she's quiet, and her eyes drift away from mine. She's not looking around Raphael's kitchen, she's looking back into her memory, and once again she's too scared to look away.

"That must have been frightening."

"He was so gross!" She's starting to breathe heavily again. "The fat guy was bad, but Bruise was just... like, *sick*! And when he bit into the fat guy, he, he like dug his face in, like he was at a pie-eating contest, he was..."

"Shh..."

"...and blood went everywhere..."

"Shh, it's okay, it's over now..."

"And then when he was done he dropped the fat guy and he *looked* at me."

"I know Valerie. You were very brave. It's over now."

Then she breaks my gaze again and looks in the doorway. She points.

"And he's *still here!*"

I turn in time to see Bruce slinking away.

Eventually I get her calmed down again, get her under control and get the rest of the story. Lord. I really misjudged Bruce on this one. Granted, he wasn't exactly delicate and poised, but still.

In time, Raphael comes back with some clothes that just might be tiny enough to fit her. God knows what happened to any luggage she had, and her purse or whatever. I tell Raphael to wash out her old clothes and dry them well, I send her to the shower and then I go to talk with Bruce.

"What next?"

I wish I knew. "Well, I'll... uh, I'll have to come up with some fake story of what happened to her. Something plausible."

"Are you going to hand her over to the cops?"

"I think I have to."

"And they'll give her back to her mom, who takes her money and has a boyfriend who hits."

I sigh. "How much did you hear?"

"I heard it all, I guess." He's put his hood back up, and sitting on the couch next to me I cannot see one inch of his ruined flesh. He's slumped forward, hands limp in his lap.

"Bruce... you know you saved her, right?"

greg stolze

"Yeah?"

"That guy probably would have killed her."

"I guess."

"Maybe not for a long time, too. You know? What I mean?"

For a moment he's silent. "You know what gets me?"

"What gets you, Bruce?"

"That *I'm* what scares her. I mean, shit, that guy I killed was a *rapist*, a fuckin' sex criminal, and *I'm* the one who makes her... go all spacey. I'm *that* ugly."

"Bruce, your ugly is only skin deep. That other guy's ugly went right down to his soul."

It feels corny as I say it, but it gets him to turn and look at me. He's got big brown eyes, just like his dog.

"Maybe it doesn't matter," he says.

"Maybe what doesn't matter?"

"Whether she... you know, likes me or not. Maybe what matters is she's alive and he didn't get her."

I pat him on the back. Then I hear the shower turn off and tell him he'd better go hide again.

I'm not proud of it, but I used to be a real bitch. Back in grade school, actually, I was a bully. I don't mean that I was a big girl who knocked the other kids down and took their lunch money. No, I was a talky bully, the one who came up with nicknames that made kids cry. I don't know why I did it. I just liked it.

There was one boy I picked on a lot because there was a lot of material. He had goofy teeth and his upper lip was always, *always* severely chapped. I think now it might have been a medical condition, because it was red and inflamed right up to his nose sometimes, like a bad-skin moustache. He had glasses and he was poor. His name was Charlie something.

I remember once at recess when Charlie and I were way back in the corner by the parallel bars. The bell rang, but I wasn't done with him. I kept on making fun of his dorky glasses and uncool clothes while everyone else ran into the building. I don't know why he didn't go too. I think he tried, but I got in his way and called him a crybaby, and said I wasn't done talking to him yet.

And then he punched me in the stomach.

It hurt, and I crouched down, doubled over, but it was more the surprise of it. That he dared to hit me. I waited for him to get in trouble. I waited for the teachers to grab him and chew him out.

Nothing happened. He just stood, looking down at me, and then he turned and went back into the school. I waited for a teacher to come and make me feel better, so I could tell on him. But no one came. Eventually I stood up and went inside to my classroom, where I got a reprimand for being late.

Now that I think about it, that was when I stopped bullying.

I guess I'm thinking of it now because I've got a little of that same feeling about Bruce. That feeling like everything I counted on turns out to be nothing. That there's a new reality, and I'm going to have to be a new person.

Persephone isn't going to cut it for this. Unless it's time for her to grow up too.

Not long after that, Raphael and Valerie and I get in his car to get a ride back to where I'm parked. Immediately, Raphael starts politicking me.

"I'm glad you put the Vinculum on Bruise. He'll be a lot more manageable now," he starts. I give him a glare. "No, seriously. I'm glad."

"Raphael, I was *right in the room*. You know I'm the one who rewrites memories, so why are you even trying?"

"Come on. Bruise is mad at me, his buddies have been running me down when I'm not around. Of *course* he's going to accept the drink if I tell him not to. You have heard of reverse psychology, haven't you?"

He says all this like he can't possibly imagine *why* Bruise's friends talk trash about him. "Give it a rest, Raphael."

"Look, I just don't want you to get the wrong idea..."

I wait for him to glance over, and as soon as his gaze touches mine I say "Silence!"

He frowns, and twists his lips around a bit. It wears off after about a minute and he says, "That was a dirty trick."

He drops off the two of us and speeds away without so much as a good-bye. But I know his type. He wants to impress me more than ever now.

I have the dead molester's address from Bruise and I drive around the neighborhood until I spot a nearby gas station. I keep right on past it and pull into a dark parking lot behind a coffee shop.

"Valerie. Look into my eyes."

She does.

"Listen to me. I am going to tell you what really happened to you tonight, and you are going to believe me."

"I'm going to believe you."

I quit the enslavement trick for a moment and turn on the adoration trick. "You want to believe me, don't you? You trust me that it's for the best? You'll be safer and happier if you believe me."

"Uh huh." She bites her lip—nervous, as if she's worried that she might not trust me despite all I'm doing to cram it down her throat.

"Okay then. Here's what *really* happened. You got to the bus stop, just like you planned. The fat old guy picked you up—that part is right. But when you went to his house, you were sleepy. You told him you were tired and he said you could go downstairs and take a nap on William's bed. You were uneasy about that, because you thought he was kind of creepy, but you were really tired and you hoped that maybe you'd fall asleep and when you woke up William would be there and everything would start to get better." Her mind is like butter. She's been trying to find a dark hole to stuff these memories into, and it's pathetically easy for me to poke a deep one in her and help. "So you went down onto the bed and fell asleep. You had a dream—a strange dream about a dark-haired woman and a man with short hair, and two very ugly men. But they aren't important. They were just dreams. Bruise, Ambrose, Raphael and me—we're only dreams. We don't matter because we're not real. We're just people you saw in a very strange dream, a dream you'll forget and never have again. But when you woke up, William wasn't there. The fat old guy was there and he started touching you. No, shh, it's okay, this is the worst part but it gets better. He started touching you and he's the one who put his hands on your neck and choked you, but you rubbed your thumbs in his eyes and kicked him in the balls. That made him let go, just for a moment, and you ran up the steps and out the door. That happened just a few minutes ago, you fought your way free but he still might be after you! The only safe place is that gas station down the street. If you run there, you might be safe! Run, Valerie! Run for safety!"

I hate doing it to her, hate having her eyes get wider and more afraid and then she's out the door, running. As I start the car and drive away I hear her start a long, loud keening shriek.

When I get back, Bruce and Raphael ask me if she's going to be all right.

"I think she'll be just fine," I tell them.

The next night, I pick up Bruce. It's weird. It's like a date. I even ask if he's eaten.

"Yeah," he says. "Plus I'm, you know, still pretty full from last night."

Last night.

"So. You want to get a hotel room?"

"Uh, sure. I guess. If that's what you want."

Almost a perfect parody.

I thought about taking him back to my new place, a loft I got cheap because it never ever gets direct sunlight (if only my landlord knew!) but I decided against it. He doesn't need to know where I sleep. Even if he never betrays me, and I don't think he will, he could be followed. He could be used.

"You come to this place often?"

"This is my first time."

"Oh. Do you…? Ah, never mind. It's none of my business."

So much for the small talk. Time to get down to business.

I start rolling up my sleeve, and this time I have a kitchen knife for the bloodshed. Watching me, Bruce slumps a little.

"So we're doing that, huh?"

"That's the deal."

"Okay." He sounds resigned.

"What?" It's out of my mouth before I even think about it.

"I just thought that… maybe, because of, you know, Valerie… that you wouldn't make me…"

"A deal's a deal."

"Yeah, I guess."

I make the cut and hold it out. With a sigh, he bends over it.

"I suppose soon, I won't be able to hold a grudge."

He takes the second drink. The second sip towards total slavery. And when he's done, he's crying.

"Are you okay?"

"I just…"

I help him to the edge of the bed, hoping he won't spill his red tears on it. "I didn't…"

"What is it?"

"I didn't think I'd ever feel this way again," he says.

He looks at me and I hate what I've done to him, and I hate myself for doing it. But I can't stop. There's too much danger in mercy. He's looking me in the eye and I can't miss my chance.

"Bruce," I tell him. "Whenever I ask you to, I want you to look me in the eye."

"Okay."

"Whenever I tell you to, you *will* look me in the eye."

"I will. You didn't have to order me, you know."

God, it's like kicking a puppy.

"You will never tell anyone that you've drunk from me. You will never tell anyone I hypnotized you."

"I will never tell," he says, and he doesn't have that zombie drone I'm used to. It doesn't sound like mindless obedience, but like a promise.

"You will never harm me, and if you feel someone else trying to control you, you will immediately look away. Do you understand? If someone else tries to take your will, you look away. My strength is in you now, you will have my strength helping you resist."

"Anyone but you," he says.

"You will never tell anyone my secrets."

"Of course not."

"And you will always…" I can't say it. I can't say "always be loyal to me." I don't know why.

I look away.

For a moment, we just sit. Then, hesitating, he puts an arm on my shoulder.

"Are *you* okay?"

I can't stand it. I just chained up his mind and he's concerned about *my* mood. I start crying too.

For a while, the two of us just cry together.

After that, we hang out. It's kind of strange. We're certainly a mismatched pair, but… I don't know. I like it. I like being around Bruce, even though he's no genius and no prize pig. He's a real change of pace from clubs and expensive restaurants and space-age bachelor pads.

He's got a fresh perspective, too. One time I asked him if he'd consider taking part in the Chicago scene, if I were to make the right introductions. He said "What for? All you guys ever do is sit around being dicks to each other."

He makes a persuasive case.

He introduces me to Don, a blood freak who's apparently like the village bicycle for Cicero Kindred—everyone's had a turn, ha ha. Bruce takes me to the lousy little den that he rents with Don and a couple other Kindred, and tells me he's suspicious about Raphael.

"Don't you worry about Raphael," I tell him. "He won't mess with you now that you're on my side."

It feels a little like bravado when I say it, but I kind of mean it too.

Then one night, I find out who sired him.

Here's how it happens: I'd gotten a dog for him from an animal shelter (because the strays are pretty thin on the ground in winter, and I figured the mutt would just wind up dead anyway—it was a mean, ratty thing, no one was going to take it home) and we'd gone up to the apartment so he could eat it. He kills it in the bathroom—he knows how much I hate to watch—and then he cleans up and comes into the living room. For a while, we just sit.

This is actually the least comfortable situation for us—just sitting, not doing anything. Other than matters vampiric, we don't have much to talk about. And so I finally say, "Hey Bruce. You ever wonder who gave you the Embrace?"

"Huh?"

"Who made you Kindred. You know."

"Yeah, I... I know what you mean. Oh totally. For a while I tried to find out, but... you know. I couldn't. No one seemed to know anything. Everyone seems to think it was this Anita character, that she did it for... I dunno, some reason... then skipped town." He shrugs. "How would I find anything out?"

"I've been thinking. I might be able to help you remember. If you want me to, that is."

"Really?" He sits forward on the edge of his chair. "You really could do that?"

"Well, I'm not making any promises, but I could *try* to do it."

"Sure! Yeah, why not?"

"Okay. Come here and look into my eyes."

He moves his chair close, saying, "I mean, I was totally wasted that night…" and then he looks up into my face and falls silent.

"Think back," I order him. "Tell me what you remember."

"I was drinking at Pitchers & Pool with Tony and Spence and Leo, the new guy from Lawn…"

I get the spiel, an intimate glimpse into the barfly lifestyle, and it's boring until the point where he leaves the bar.

"I'm walking down the street and someone hits me," he says.

"You mean, you got hit by a car?"

"I don't know. One minute I'm walking and then something hits my head."

This doesn't sound promising. Too slickly done—whoever it was clearly didn't want to get spotted.

"What happened next, Bruce?"

"I woke up and I was… different. Really hungry. Hungry in a different way. And then the guy slammed a stake into my chest."

"Who did?"

"I don't know the guy."

"It's a man?"

"Yeah."

"What does he look like?"

"Short, *real* ugly—thin nose, fingers like claws, all decayed and shit…"

He just described ten percent of the Nosferatu, but it's a start. I've got a gender.

"...wearing this weird old-timey suit, it's like bright green."

Before I can stop myself, I lick my lips. "What do you mean, an old-timey suit?"

"It's like... I dunno, you know in old Bugs Bunny or Mickey Mouse cartoons, there's always the big bad wolf, and he's wearing a suit? A suit like that, with a fancy hat and shoes with those white things on the side and, you know, maybe a pocket watch on a chain? Like what a pimp would wear."

"You mean a zoot suit?"

"I don't know."

He doesn't know, but I do.

I've found Bruise's sire. I've got something for Norris. Unfortunately, that's not the end of his story.

"I blacked out—you know, the stake and all—and then all of a sudden I was awake again. And I was real hungry. There was this homeless guy there, and he'd pulled the stake out. I was so hungry..."

Oh no. Poor Bruce...

"I just jumped up and bit the guy on the neck and I drained him dry right there." Bruce is still in a trance, his voice stays calm and even, but I can see a change in his face, in his eyes. At some level, he knows what he did, what he's just remembered. "I killed that guy and left him and then I ran off."

"Why did you run?"

"I was scared of the guy in the suit. And I didn't want to go home because of what I'd done to the bum, so I just ran and kept running. Then the sun came up and it burned me." He says this with more emotion than describing his first murder. "It burned so bad... and I panicked, I ran into the nearest building and tried to go as far from the fire as I could."

"And you didn't remember any of this when you woke up the next day?"

"No... not until right now..."

"What the hell is this?"

I jump. I didn't hear the door open, didn't hear footsteps, and now Ambrose is staring down at the two of us. He looks pissed.

Bruce blinks, turns to look at him. "Hey man," he says. "Persephone was helping me remember..."

"Yeah, I'm sure 'helping' you was the first thing on her mind." He turns to me and glares.

Bruce's eyes have gotten wide and he has one diseased hand covering his pustule-rimmed mouth. "Oh God," he says. "I remember now. Shit, I killed that guy!"

"Nice one, Princess," Ambrose tells me. "Yeah, it looks like you helped him a *ton*."

"Shut up!" I don't just say it—I *command* him.

It's like trying to poke a feather through cinderblock wall.

"Don't play that crap with me." Ambrose gives me the finger.

"How could I have killed that guy and not, not even remember it?" Bruise is still shell-shocked.

"If you want to forget, I can help you."

"Could you?"

He turns to me and I meet his gaze, and then suddenly I'm seeing stars and lying sideways on the couch.

Ambrose hit me!

"Hey!" Bruce jumps up and stands between the two of us. "Man, what are you...?"

I sit up, head sore, and you know what? Fuck him.

I get past Bruce and sock Ambrose in the gut, as hard as I can. He staggers back and a loud "Ooof!" escapes his mouth. I go in for another swing and then my feet leave the ground. Bruce has hugged me from behind and picked me up.

"Quit it!" I yell, "Put me down!" But I'm not looking in his eyes and I can't make him do it.

"Not till you get a grip," he says.

"Hey, he's the one who hit *me*!"

"And now you've hit him back, so you're square."

"It's okay," Ambrose says. "Let her go."

Bruce lowers me and I turn to Ambrose with my fists clenched. Then I notice that his fangs are bared, and holy shit, he's got a three-inch claw tipping each finger. Suddenly I'm not so goddamn sure I want to fight any more.

"Ambrose man... it's cool, right?" Bruce steps between us. My knight protector, God.

"Ask her," Ambrose rasps.

I straighten my clothes. "I think you owe me an apology," I tell him.

His laugh is hard and ugly.

"C'mon man," Bruce says. "What gives? You know you shouldn'ta hit her."

"Bruise, *wake up*! Don't you get it? Don't you understand what she's *doing* to you?"

"It's not like that man,"

"No, it's *exactly* like that, man." He looks me right in the eye and I can't help it, I flinch back. "I'm sorry I took offense when you were brainwashing my *friend*," he says, and he's still wearing his scary face.

Fuck. I'll take it.

"Apology accepted."

"Ambrose..."

"Get out," he tells me.

"No, man, you gotta..."

"Bruise, you can either stay here with me or get out with her."

Bruce looks to me for guidance, which gets a disgusted snort out of Ambrose.

"It's up to you," I say, turning to the door.

"Look, I..." he shifts back and forth, looking between me and his buddy. "I'll catch you later, okay?"

From the pleading tone in his voice, I know he's talking to me.

I go, type up a letter to Norris, and start an elaborate postage routine. Then I get to a phone, a Raphael-approved landline, and call Loki.

"Hoy hoy," he says, and I can hear this week's slammin' dance single blaring in the background.

"Do you have a phone number for Scratch?"

"What?"

"A phone number for Scratch?"

"Who is this?"

"It's Persephone!"

"Yeah? I think I've got something that'll work. Hold on, I'll text-message it." Probably wants to spare his vocal cords. I look down and watch the numbers unfold, making a mental note.

"Thanks!"

"That's not his direct number, it's one of his guys, but that guy can put you in touch."

Great. I get the secretary. I suppose I should expect that, I'm just a little piss-ant.

"Thanks anyhow!"

"Yeah yeah, gotta go. See you at Sound-Bar, 'kay?"

Getting through Scratch's flack-screener takes more persuasion than I'm used to, but I invoke Norris' name and, eventually, I play the "I'm connected to Maxwell" card (though I *hate* it). After what seems like a decade, I get forwarded.

"What's shakin', Martini?"

Yeah, he sounds a hundred years old.

"Hello, Scratch. I thought you and I should have a little talk."

"You coulda come to me face to face. I'da thought you'd prefer it."

"I'm calling as a courtesy. I want you to know your judgment is unclouded."

"You've got a pretty high opinion of yourself and your cloudiness. I like that."

"I just sent a letter to Norris," I say. "It's got directions to one of those UPS Store locations?"

"Oh boy. Letters to spies about post-office boxes are never good news."

"Just hear me out. This could work out fine for absolutely everyone. It's win-win."

"Uh huh." He doesn't sound convinced. "Everybody likes winning. I'm all ears."

"Norris asked me to find out who sired Bruce Miner."

Silence.

"And you did," Scratch says. His voice is perfectly calm, level and cool, and yet I cannot escape a wave of knowledge, the absolute certainty that I'm talking to something old and dead and deadly, something that I may be threatening. I shouldn't need to swallow, but I swallow hard.

"The letter tells Norris where to find that little trivia fact if I haven't been seen around for a week or two. He won't get the letter for a while. I have plenty of time to put... any name that's convenient in there."

"Like Anita's name, for example."

"Anyone who wouldn't make trouble."

"Like Anita." He speaks with a very final tone.

"That's very easily done."

"It would help me out a lot," Scratch says.

"I'm sure. And it would help you even more if Bruce believed Anita was his sire, and could clearly say so to all and sundry."

"Yeah. And in return?"

"All I ask is your friendship."

There's a pause.

"No, come on now. Put the screws in. Get serious."

"You have nothing I want more than your esteem. Come *on* Scratch, you know how Solomon and his lackeys have been treating me."

"Well, yeah, I've kind of noticed that..."

"You're an elder. You're a *Priscus*. All it takes is a few words from you—as long as they're the right words, in the right ears." Christ, I can't believe I'm sucking up for social status to a guy whose face looks like a mosquito crossed with a cancerous growth. But there it is.

"Heh. I start to see your point. Consider it done."

"Thanks."

"...as soon as Bruisey boy tells everyone the news about Anita."

"I'll arrange it soon."

"I always liked you, Persephone."

"Maybe next Elysium, you can show me that giant octopus."

After a while, I get a call from Bruce. He's at his car and wants to know if he can come and pick me up. I tell him where I am and wait.

While I'm waiting, my phone rings again. I flip it open without a thought and say "Persephone."

"I… I'm sorry? I must have the wrong number."

I feel cold all over. It's my father's voice.

"What… number were you calling?" I change my voice, just a little.

He reads me my phone number and I tell him he's gotten one digit wrong. Then I hang up and take a deep breath before he calls back.

"Hello?"

"Linda?"

"Yeah, is that you Dad?"

"Yes. How's it going?"

"Just fine." There's a little pause. "How are things with you?"

"Well, your mother has that sciatica thing acting up again, and you know how I get that cough every winter. But we're well, thanks. We're doing just fine. Um…"

I'm getting a weird vibe from him. "Is something wrong, Dad?"

"Well…"

"Is Andy okay?"

"Andy's fine, Emily's fine, everyone's fine. Actually, um, if there's anyone in the family we're worried about, it's… you."

"Me?" I laugh and it sounds forced. "Me? I'm fine. Why wouldn't I be?"

"Well, your mother tried to call you at work. She wanted your advice about… something, I don't even remember. But anyway, they told her you'd left the firm."

There's an awkward, expectant pause.

"Yes," I tell him, "I have left the firm."

More silence.

"Weren't you happy there, honey?"

"I... well, I felt there were more opportunities else-where." I swallow, hard. "You remember Scott Hurst? You remember me telling you about him?"

"Mm... you know I'm not good at names." Dad's apologetic. Yeah, he's sorry he's having trouble following my lies. I'm sorry he's buying it all.

"I interviewed with them when I first got out of law school, and I actually liked his firm better, but Barclay, Mearls and Shaw offered me a better package, and... I don't know. I guess after putting in the actual years, I figured I wasn't going to make partner any time soon, and maybe I would be happier at Scott's firm, even if it is smaller and means less money." I'm warming up to the story. I brush hair back around my right ear and switch the phone to that side.

"Can you give me a number for this Hurst place?"

I sigh. I don't even have to fake this part. "That's where it gets complicated. Scott passed away recently."

"Oh no!"

"Yeah, so now the whole firm is... whopperjawed. "*Whopperjawed* is one of Dad's words. I never use it with anyone outside the family.

"Gee, Linda..."

"Oh, I'll be fine. I might go back to Barclay, Mearls and Shaw, I might look for something different, I... I'm at a real, I feel like I'm making a lot of changes..." Man, Dad has *no idea*. "I just want to step back and take stock for a little bit."

"I see." He's silent again, and I can mentally *see* his expression, the way his face twists to the side when he's thinking hard. "Why don't you come home for a while?"

I'm at a loss.

"Oh, Dad, I don't know."

"C'mon! Your mother and I haven't seen you in so long."

For just a moment, it sounds like a great idea. I could go home, see my parents, get away from the city and Norris and Solomon and scary guys with fangs and claws... and, yeah, sure, I'll explain everything to my parents and *they'll* understand, right. I might as well rub their necks with melted butter and lock them in with Norris.

"I dunno Dad, I'm pretty busy with the job hunt and, you know, the re-prioritization."

"Then we could come up there!"

"Uh..."

"I'm sorry. I'm being pushy, aren't I?"

"No, it's just..."

"I am. I apologize, I just... you're my little girl, you know?"

I'm his little blood-sucking freak.

"I haven't seen my baby girl in so long... I miss you. That's all."

"Maybe for Easter," I tell him. Then I see Bruce's junk-wagon cruising out of the slush. "Oh, I gotta go Dad, my... date's here."

"Anyone interesting?"

"I don't think there's a future in it, but we'll see. Gotta go! Love you! Bye!"

I get in the car. It's a hunk of crap. The back seat has holes patched with duct tape and the heater doesn't work. If we were alive, our breath would steam in the frosty air.

If we were alive. God, I just lied to my father about the suicide of a friend. I've never felt more dead in my life.

"You okay?" Bruce asks. Even Neanderthal Man over there can tell I'm upset.

"I'll be fine," I say.

"You're not too mad at Ambrose, are you? He was just, you know, trying to protect me."

"It's hard to fault him for that." I'd like to kill that dusty old fucker. Would Scratch do that for me? Probably not.

"He's got a tough row to hoe. He's a carrier, you know."

"A what?"

"A carrier. An HIV carrier."

"Poor baby."

"C'mon, it's a, you know, a serious thing. How would you like it if you couldn't feed on anyone without maybe giving 'em AIDS? I mean, he can't even give Don a dose when the poor guy begs for it."

"Would you mind pulling over here?"

He does. "What's on your mind?"

"Look into my eyes."

I take my time rewriting his memories—I want this to stick. Scratch gets deleted and replaced with—"Anita," whom I don't even know, but I come up with a plausible story, an introduction, et cetera. If Anita comes back and denies it, it's not my problem. Let Scratch worry about it. He seemed confident that this Anita character is a good fit.

As a kindness to Bruce, I also cover up the death of his homeless rescuer. Bruce shouldn't have to beat himself up about that. It's not his fault. Everyone's crazy with hunger when they're empty, and never more so than right after the Embrace. Maxwell had made preparations for me. I didn't have to kill anyone. I would have, though.

Poor Bruce. At least I can help *him* out.

When we're done I ask him to drop me off by my car, I wave at him as he goes and when he's out of sight I call Norris.

"Hellow?"

"Norris?"

"Persephone! I'm so delighted to hear from you."

"I've got news for you…"

"And I can reciprocate, but you go first."

Huh? Never mind, I'm not going to waste time with Norris' unfunny head game jokes. "Bruce's sire: It's some Nosferatu named Anita. Do you know her?"

"I've heard of her, yes. One of the ne'er-do-wells in Cicero. Hasn't been around much lately, so perhaps she fled Chicago after her... indiscretion. Mmyes, how intriguing. But we have bigger matters to contend with, my dear."

We? "Such as?"

"Well, it seems I owe you an apology. Solomon has made his move against Maxwell."

A week later, Bruise and I have our first encounter with one of Solomon's pets, one of the Brigmans.

Chapter Nine:
Maxwell

When I wake up, Robert is waiting. He has been with me for thirty years. He carries my blood of life in his veins—not the weak, sentimental tie of an ancestor, but the mystic bond between Kindred and thrall. He has tasted of me, and through me, immortality. As long as he can beg, borrow or steal the Vitae, the Life, our potent blood, the ravages of age and time pass him by. Even as they pass by me.

As every night, Robert carries a steaming, moist towel, a pair of electric clippers, and a fresh safety razor. Formerly it was scissors and a straight blade. How times have changed.

Robert is the only one privileged to see me when I first awaken. It sounds like a bad morning-after joke, doesn't it? But the Kindred of Chicago, who see me as their Prince with his natty, *au courant* moustache and goatee... how would they react to me as I was upon my Embrace, as I appear every nightfall, with the broad, wild whiskers of a mountain trapper, my hair kinked and wild, just waiting for a handful of rancid bear grease to keep back the insects?

The rumor among my people is that I was born in 1800. It's not true.

I was *Embraced* in 1800. I haven't smelled rancid bear grease for over a hundred years, yet my memories of it—you needed it in the summers, if you had to travel near the swamps, otherwise you'd get eaten alive—often seem more vivid than the smells I catch today—my cologne, my shampoo, my aftershave and soap.

First Robert uses the electric clippers to remove the bulk of the beard. Then I bathe. Then he shampoos and styles my hair while the hot towel warms my face. Once it has done its work, he applies fragrant lotion and uses the safety razor. He believes he shaves me perfectly (and after decades, he ought to know the terrain) but in truth he still sometimes leaves a nick or burn. I don't mind. I heal before a drop of my precious blood can seep free.

Tonight the usual goatee, and is it even *à la mode* any more? Robert keeps track, but even he may someday become a creature out of time, like me, to whom sideburns and nasal piercings, mullets and bell bottoms and wraparound sunglasses all look equally odd, equally new, equally affected and foreign.

Last night he told me he's started watching *Queer Eye for the Straight Guy*. I have no idea what that is.

It's a Wednesday, so my clothes are casually uncool. Tonight's role: 40-something SBM goes to college class for personal enrichment. I'm a major benefactor at one of the local liberal-arts colleges, and I'm taking a night school pottery course. Wheel thrown. For this I wear jeans and a plain T under one of Robert's weathered old flannel shirts. Just the thing for playing in the mud.

I enjoy being an amateur, doing something at which I am expected to be clumsy. I need the break, honestly. Solomon has challenged me—supposedly it's Justine Lasky, but the whole Primogen knows the truth. I'm a little surprised it's not Norris, but...

No. I'm not going to think about that now. There's nothing to be done. I am going to my college class and I am going to learn how to make clay bowls.

I drive myself in the Mercedes. I hate driving. I've been doing it since cars became common, but modern vehicles... they have too much speed, too much pickup, too *much*. They always remind me of the film *Metropolis*: soulless machines into which humans fall. Usually Robert drives me, but tonight I can't have a chauffeur.

I'm the oldest student, of course, but even my *role* is older than the others. I think there's one woman in her thirties who keeps smiling at me, and I smile back. Even our professor can't be more than thirty-five as she patiently teaches us to center the clay, to press evenly.

We are all of us beginners and the knack of making an uneven wad of earth into a smooth shape while it's centered on a turning wheel—it's not the sort of task they're used to learning. They are intellectuals, used to mastering spreadsheet programs or new marketing paradigms, and to apply themselves to something that will not listen to reason… it's hard, frustrating.

For me, it's difficult for different reasons. I've worked with my hands for centuries, and I have far more physical strength than any of these modern people. But mere force will not center the clay—indeed, uneven force makes it distort, skid, slide away and bulge into ungainly lumps. It is all a matter of control.

I am the first of us to learn how to do it.

People wonder why I gave the Embrace to Persephone. Solomon wonders *how* I could.

I lost control.

I go over it in my mind, almost every night. Certainly, she was my type—and when I use that phrase, it's not like a mortal man expressing a preference for slender thighs or bulging breasts. Women—young *smart* women— I feel an affinity to them. They draw me. I have had 200 years to refine myself, to study and shave and earn until I'm no longer a backwoods hick who was valued only after the fashion of a scent hound or a sled dog. And yet, I look on them and they are my *anima*. They embody everything I still lack, for how much can I really change? I'm a dead man. How can I grow?

I know, with my reasoning human mind, that I can learn and have grown. I am as educated as any. I'm a sophisticate with clean fingernails and informed opinions. Yet every sundown I rise as that hairy rustic, the kind who'd think a manicure is something you eat at a fancy restaurant.

Every nightfall, the monster inside whispers to me, tells me that what I really need is *them*, the women, that only by consuming them can I know what it means to be delicate and calm and wise. Only stealing their lives can fill up the void within me. Only their blood can paint over my flaws.

For 200 years I have pursued the type, and Persephone—"Linda"—was so perfectly its expression. Young, but confident, and deservedly so. Clearly intelligent and accomplished, but keeping still the sweet patina of youthful promise. We met on behalf of others to discuss Meigs Field, she speaking for her clients, me for the Mayor's people, and I was enchanted. I knew that I would have her, I made my arrangements and, like any good predator, I did not hesitate to strike.

How did she die?

I lost control.

Why did I bring her back?

Solomon claims to love his little family, but I think he truly sees them only as containers for their precious, priceless *genes*. He does not know what it means to see someone who is your lost half, and then to kill her.

How could I *not* preserve her? Even half-dead, marred by our curse, she is still more vital and alive than most of the sleepwalkers stumbling through the city on their way to bland homes and TV shows and service-sector jobs.

I brought her back because I could not let her go.

After class, I chat with my fellow students. The most interested one is the woman in her thirties, although she's white. A couple other women give me looks, shy smiles. They might suffice. They're young enough. The white woman is too old.

"I have to ask," she says.

"Your accent... is that French?"

"Québécois," I reply. One of the nice things about the "Maxwell Polermo" persona is that I can relax into my normal speech patterns. Americans are suckers (so to speak) for anyone with an accent.

"What do you do?" she asks.

"I'm a management policy consultant." This is, I have decided, the best lie for me in such instances. It's close enough to the truth, but more importantly it sounds lucrative, complicated and dull. Very few ask for details.

"Yourself?"

She launches into a lengthy explanation, the meat of which is this: She assembles gift baskets for a large department store. She starts listing celebrities for whom she's assembled hampers of wine and cheese ("...oh, and I did one for John Cusack, you know?") and I just listen. She's horribly boring, which makes me feel much better about my problems. At least having jealous vampires angling for your job is *interesting*. More, she makes me feel better about being undead. We Kindred tend to sentimentalize life, only to forget how often it is half-lived.

"So why are you taking this class?" she asks, jarring me out of my reverie.

"I don't believe the intellect can be motionless," I say. She looks blank. Before it can grow to an embarrassing pause, I explain. "If my mind isn't improving, it's declining. I'm always trying to learn new things, new skills... learning just fascinates me. It's what I do for fun."

"Yeah," she says. "I kind of want to improve myself too, express my artistic side—though I get a little of that doing the baskets..." and we're back to her job again.

It's sad.

Eventually she excuses herself and I set off across campus to meet the college president.

President Melville Figge is always glad to see me and not, I think, solely because I'm a benefactor. Nor is it because I have used some sanguine trick to seduce or bedazzle him (I haven't). He likes my company because we think alike, we agree on the course Chicago higher education ought to chart and we are both worldly enough to do something practical about it. But tonight my business is not Figge, nor am I his. He has just finished presiding over a dinner for early-admittance scholars, and I (as a firm supporter, not to say fundraiser, of the scholarship program) have an opportunity to meet some of the youngsters to whom our kindness shall flow.

"This is Kelly," he says, ushering in a tall, slender young woman with deep black skin and excellent posture. I stand.

"Pleased to meet you," she says. Firm handshake, good elocution.

"Likewise. Thank you for taking a moment to speak with me."

President Figge slips out as Kelly and I seat ourselves. She's a senior at a high school in Bloomington, top honors three years running and a onetime national debate competitor.

We chat about Bloomington and why she'd want to come to school in Chicago instead of the University of Illinois. She gives cogent reasons—better potential for internship, a more prestigious program in her field of choice (political science). I sound her out on a desire for independence and she graciously admits that she's interested in being away from her parents—not to break ties, but to mature and become her own person.

She's so poised. Her neck is straight, proud and slender, like the tender stalk of some rainforest flower.

"Come here," I tell her. "Unbutton your sleeve."

I want to take her throat, but I content myself with the crook of her left elbow. When sated, I look into her eyes and tell her how she met me briefly, we discussed schools and public speaking strategies, and when we were finished there was a gap in her schedule, so she went and participated in the blood drive downstairs. I question her, making sure there are no flaws in the story—she's not anemic, she has no blood conditions, she's donated before. Nothing to arouse the suspicions of her parents when she meets them again briefly before going to stay overnight in the dorms with another highly intelligent woman studying political science.

I even put a sticker on her sweater. It depicts a blood drop with happy human features, and has the caption CHARLIE CORPUSCLE SAYS: *BE NICE TO ME, I GAVE*

Little details count.

I speak with several other students, but only one of them merits another Charlie.

Two nights later I am hard pressed to remember Kelly's name. I have many enterprises which require my attention: Tending to my "well," as they now call it, assuring myself a steady blood supply; watching over *mes débrouilles*, my little scams, the tricks and maneuvers that keep me wealthy; and tonight, dealing with the Primogen, the challenge to my rule and all the fascinating maneuvers of Kindred politics.

Yes, I may try to pretend it bores me, but when I am honest I admit that it is one of two things that can truly hold my attention. There is much hand-wringing in the media about the short attention span of the younger generation, but speaking as someone whose attention span has gotten longer and wider and now covers decades, I can see how the ability to be diverted and entertained by transitory phenomena would be a great blessing indeed. I try to be flighty and sometimes it even works, but by and large my mind drifts inexorably back to my two great fascinations. Ah well.

It's a bitterly chill evening. Without vitality to warm me, I must resort to artificial means to keep my muscles from freezing like a side of beef. Fortunately, in the modern age of forced-air furnaces it's simple to stay supple. Thinking about such issues is an essential trait, being aware how they cut both ways. If a bystander saw the five of us walking along jacketless, showing no discomfort from the cold and with our speech unaccompanied by steam, it would be very suspicious indeed. But by the same token, we can meet on a building rooftop and be assured that no nosy human is eavesdropping on us. In the summer, the "tar beaches" are clogged with people who can't afford air conditioners, and even in autumn or spring one might get young lovers, an erstwhile photographer, a hopelessly optimistic amateur astronomer, or the sadly more common simple voyeur. But not tonight. It would take a peeping tom of unusual dedication to be out this evening. The ice crunches under our boots and the wind rakes along rooftop aerials, moaning in time to our words.

Before, the high and mighty of the undead met in comfort, soft strains of music supported idle chatter and gentle perfumes masked the air as the Kindred waited for my predecessor as Prince to appear. Then one night, as several counselors chatted unconcerned, the doors locked and gasoline fell from the ceiling, the entire room became an instant fiery tomb for the three the Prince thought were traitors.

The real traitors were Norris and Solomon, whom the Prince had warned away. Since that night, the Primogen has often met out of doors. Providing security is difficult, but they still feel safer this way. For that matter, so do I.

"Solomon," I say, greeting him as he arrives.

"Maxwell," he says in return. No honorific. I let it pass, this time.

Solomon's resources are significant. His mortal contacts are less wealthy than mine, less established, but more numerous. That family he rules is widespread and he takes a decisive interest in many others who fit in with his notions of genetic quality. Most important, his control of his church, the Lancea Sanctum, is formidable. Many of its more lackadaisical members would probably remain loyal to the city Prince over their Bishop if it came to that, but the nature of this crisis throws my princely status into question. And the hard core who would obey him no matter what… they tend to be older and more powerful, and they have delved deep into the mystic secrets of the Vitae.

Solomon has the hunger of a shark. Sharks never sleep, but cruise the oceans with the dead-eyed arrogance of an animal that anchors the food chain. Nothing can scare them, control them or drive them off once they catch the scent—and they can smell blood in the water for miles. The only force that can overpower a shark is its own rage, its own hunger. That's Solomon. He can face fire and the sword unblinking, as long as his appetite is not thwarted.

"It's come to this, then," I say.

He shrugs and shakes his head. "I hope…." He trails off. I know this is a gambit. I know he planned to leave his phrase unfinished before he spoke the first word, so that I can draw him out, so that he can look reluctant, so that I can feel he's sharing an intimacy, so that he can make a better pose of sincerity. We have danced this dance for decades and I know my steps as well as he does.

"What?" I ask him.

"Whatever happens… tonight… I hope our friendship can endure."

The damnable thing is that I know he hopes just that.

"It has outlasted all trials so far," I say, and my tone is one of comfort, but my words give no certainty. The damnable thing is that I share in his hope, but I cannot offer assurance.

"My Prince."

Miriam comes from the sky, a great black bat one moment and the next a short black woman. She offers me respect and loyalty, and I'm not surprised. She is the youngest, after all. But more, we have always been good to each other because we are so different.

Though she takes the form of a bat or wolf, Miriam has a hunger more like a snake. Her soul has none of a bat's darting impatience or a wolf's ragged cruelty. It is not for her to run her prey down, snapping at hamstrings until it falls, exhausted, having bled on the snow for miles. No, like a snake she lies in wait, cool and collected, finding the perfect branch on which to drape until some morsel steps beneath and she can drop upon it.

Snakes move without the appearance of movement, and so it has been with Miriam in Chicago. One year she arrived, an unremarkable neonate. Presently she became an elder of her type, by simple virtue of survival and remoteness. Respected for her disinterest, she gained influence nearly by default. Her followers are the wild ones, the loners, and it is a rare skill to forge power by leaving others alone. Yet she has managed it. I could not really guess how widespread her influence is. Not so wide as mine, I'm sure, from the few times I have had to counter her interests. But snakes are cold blooded, with unblinking patience. If she is to betray me, she wouldn't disrespect me first. Pythons don't need to taunt.

The three of us stand, equidistant, the points of a triangle.

"This is a wretched night," I say. Miriam grunts an assent, her eyes on Solomon.

"Don't take it personally, I beg you," he says. "All things are impermanent, and none more so than a Kindred's reign."

"I meant the weather," I lie.

"Oh." A pause, just enough to be a jest, not enough to be an insult. "I hadn't noticed," he lies in turn.

"I don't care what you say, I *feel* the cold," Norris grumbles as he emerges from the doorway.

"I'm glad you came out regardless."

"Nothing could keep me away... my liege."

An expression of loyalty, but guarded, delayed... does that mean conditional? Norris introduced himself so casually, in a spirit of easy conversation. Of all of them, I have worked most closely with him, of late. Of all of them, I have dealt him the most setbacks, reining in his ambitions. Norris does not understand that often, less is more. He does not trust charm and gratitude, so he must spy and verify. He cannot imagine that anyone would want to help him, so all his informants and agents and slaves serve from fear, ambition or addicted necessity.

Norris keeps his secrets, and those of his blood-warlock ilk. He keeps secrets from me, though not as many as he thinks. I, in turn, am sure I believe some lies he has told me. But each of us compliments the other's lacunae: He is loathed, and I am adored, and neither envies the other his role.

Norris is hungry though, hungry for power, hungry like a rat. Rats cringe and scuttle and elicit disgusted cries, but they are always there, they always survive and in time their jaws can gnaw through anything. They lurk in the filth and dine on rancid scraps, but eventually every nobler creature feels their teeth. He would betray me, and take his resentful witches and secret police with him. I know this. He would betray God or the Devil, Longinus or the Crone, if rewarded for his treachery with some power he desires.

Has Solomon made a better offer? Norris' loyalty comes down simply to that.

"How is, hmm, everyone this evening?" He asks it and shoots sly little glances between myself and Solomon.

"Fine." Bishop Birch doesn't even bother to return his gaze. What does that mean?

"I think I've found a good stock to graft to the Brigman family."

"Indeed? Would that be to, aah, Diane Brigman?"

"Her or her daughter Margery."

"Is the daughter even old enough?"

"Sixteen is a fine age. Healthy and hearty for birth."

"But what of the scandal?" I ask, half a smirk on my face.

Solomon makes a petty gesture with his hands. "Pah, what of it? In ten little years no one will even care. What's that against a good merger?"

"What if she doesn't want to?" Miriam asks, her voice quiet.

"You have some very old-fashioned ideas," I tell her.

"I'll not force her," Solomon says. "If not her, her mother. But Diane isn't as young and there were complications with Margery."

"Diane's husband won't care?"

"Ian is well in hand. He knows what matters."

"Where the devil is Justine?" Norris seems to have tired of Solomon's husbandry. He's huddling in his coat and rubbing his mismatched hands for warmth.

"Anxious?" I ask him.

"I'm sure he just wants this over with," Solomon says.

"As do we all, no doubt."

"Sorry to keep you waiting." Justine emerges from the stairwell.

"It's worth it for your dramatic entrance." Solomon says it with a wink.

She is dressed from hood to ankle in a glossy black mink coat, so thick it nearly doubles her diameter. It encloses her completely, save for her pale face and the black ankles of her high-heeled boots. Very *au courant*. I'm sure climbing the stairs in those was no treat.

Ms. Lasky is the second youngest of the Primogen, and the most lovely. There is a starkness, an aggression to her beauty—her angular features would be ugly if they were worn with less pride, if they were less balanced by her startling eyes and alabaster skin. Our Mistress of Elysium is a hawk, balanced on airy currents that seem to be nothing but still can hold her regally above us all. Justine cruises our world, all majestic beauty and aloof stillness... until, like a hawk, she drops to prey. In a moment, the calmly soaring hawk becomes a falling bullet from the sky, keen eyes locked on something small and hapless below it. When you see her strike, you realize that the beauty is incidental: This is a creature designed solely to kill.

What is Justine's power? Words, air, laughs and lusts and petty grievances, style and discretion and popularity. Things that seem meaningless next to my riches, or Solomon's occult might, or Miriam's silent army of fierce allies. But like the wind, like a whisper, Justine's power moves unseen and creeps into the smallest, tightest places. Like Norris she is feared and like me adored. While not so deep as the fealties owed the others, she is perhaps the only one of them who can speak freely to'*any* of the Kindred in Chicago, and give a natural proposal of mutual advantage.

Solomon has chosen well. Of all of them, she is the only one who could truly rule in my stead.

The five of us stand in the chill. We are motionless as corpses.

"As all members of the Chicago Primogen are present, I call this meeting to order. Is there any old business?"

We have nothing but old business. Questioning who will rule—that is the oldest business of all.

"New business, then?"

More silence, still and absolute. I look at Justine. Slowly, the rest of the Primogen does as well.

She is as lovely and inscrutable as a butterfly or a forest fire.

"Ms. Lasky? Any new business?"

She takes her time, but I see the subtle shift beneath her coat. She is drawing in breath. She does not need it to live, none of us live. She needs it only to speak.

"There is one thing."

"Yes?"

She makes us wait. Very dramatic.

"I regret to inform you, my Prince, that one of our number has conspired against you."

I do not smile. I must not smile. This still could be a trick.

"I'm shocked. Are you certain?"

"Regretfully—yes."

I don't turn my head but I steal a glance at Solomon. He's absolutely still. He looked like that just before the last time he frenzied, the last time he let his frustrated wrath get the better of him. It was a man, that time, a Rabbi who had simultaneously struck a blow against a clique of Lancea Sanctum "devil worshippers" and won the heart of one of Solomon's eugenic prize pigs. Solomon tore him to pieces, not even bothering to feed.

But this time he remains silent as Justine expands her accusation.

"I beg your protection from Solomon Birch, your own advisor and my fellow Primogen."

"Solomon? What have you to say about this accusation?"

"Accusation? This is no accusation, merely a... bald insinuation." He smiles, but all four of us hear his teeth grind and grate. "If she produces any semblance of substance to her... tale bearing, I'll reserve my right to reply."

"Of course. Primogen Lasky? You have made a serious accusation."

"I know, and I shudder to consider the grave charge of sedition... but I am more afraid to break the laws of my Prince."

She is, perhaps, laying it on a bit thick, but she can carry it off.

"What is the substance of the charge?"

"On January twentieth, Solomon Birch approached me and suggested that I rebel against you..."

"I said no such thing."

"Solomon?" I raise my hand. "Please. In the spirit of dignity with which we have always operated, allow her to completely finish her statement before you disagree."

"The Bishop suggested that you were unfit to rule, and that your actions in Embracing Persephone Moore showed that you were losing control of yourself. A Kindred who cannot control himself, he said, is unfit to control a city—especially when his breech of our law is so dramatic and causes so great a loss of the vulgar Kindred's prestige. 'Vulgar' was his word, not mine."

"I understand completely."

"He then flattered me, saying that I alone had the power needed to take Chicago from your grasp. I will not narrate his individual insults to the rest of the Primogen," she says, her eyes sliding particularly to Norris—a masterful fillip. "Suffice to say, he felt that I alone was held in sufficient esteem by my peers to maintain control in a time of unrest and uncertainty."

"Did not Solomon suggest himself in the role of my successor?"

"He said—and again I quote—that he could not in good conscience replace you and maintain his position as Bishop of Longinus. Rather than face personal conflicts of interest, along with resistance from the Circle and others who do not espouse Lancea Sanctum philosophy, he chose to retain his religious position and avoid additional political duties. He did make a point of assuring me that

I would have total support in my bid for praxis from the Lancea Sanctum, however."

"I see." I turn to Solomon. "Do you dispute this account?"

"Need I dispute it? Where is the evidence? All we have are her assertions."

"The charge that a Primogen is a liar, particularly about such an important matter, is a serious one as well. Either we harbor an insurgent or a character assassin. I would be derelict in my duties if I failed to scrutinize both possibilities." I turn to Justine. "Would you submit your will to my gaze, that I might compel truthfulness?"

"Of course, my liege."

"I object," says Norris. "Respectfully, my Prince... we all know the limits of such forces. What one mesmerist pulls forth as truth may, heh, be only a skein of lies, faithfully trusted by the teller through no fault of her own... but in truth, only the product of, mm, a previous entrancement."

"Yes," says Solomon. "Perhaps Justine is but some other Kindred's tool in this matter, someone who has bent her weak spirit into service. Given fifteen minutes, my Lord, I'm confident I could make her believe that... say, Primogen Norris here... had conspired against you, or me, or even that mortal mayor you so favor."

I'm "my Lord" now. "This is problematical, then. Solomon, would *you* submit to such questioning, that I might learn the truth of this matter?"

"Respectfully, I will not."

"Indeed? You're wise in the ways of the Blood. Surely *you* would not be taken unaware by the entrapping glance? Surely the judge of Longinus' law cannot be so... readily bent?"

"It is my position as Bishop that forces me to resist. My will is pledged to the service of the Lancea Sanctum. I cannot lend it to any other, even to my Prince. If you believe her over me, punish me as if I was guilty. I accept that over the loss of my volition."

And the ball is back in my court. Do I believe her? Oh, I surely do. Not that Solomon was so crude as to directly suggest insurrection, but I've no doubt he agitated to oust me. Now I have an out. I punish him without officially condemning him for his crime, I punish him by his choice because he would rather be punished than be untrue to his faith. Very clever. He admits no wrong, satisfies me through vengeance, buries the situation and appears as a spotless, blameless martyr to his religious brethren. It's far less damning to him than a decision of guilt.

Shall I let my old friend off the hook?

"The question of whom to believe is a tricky one. To resolve it requires... delicacy. May I cross examine you on this matter?"

"But of course."

"Do you pledge to tell the truth?"

"I swear on the blood of Longinus that I will not lie to you about this matter."

"Did you tell Ms. Lasky to challenge me for the title of Prince?"

"I did not."

Indeed.

"Did you imply that my reign was weak?"

"We discussed politics. I admire you, but I do not think your position flawless. Of course I mentioned some problems I perceived."

"Did you suggest that she might be a better ruler than I?"

"I enumerated strengths she has that you, perhaps, lack, ways that emulation of her might improve you. If she interpreted that as some disloyal invitation..." He shrugs his shoulders.

"And Persephone," I say, and this time he meets my gaze. This is the core of it. The bone of contention. "What do you think of her?"

"My liege?"

"What is your position on her Embrace?"

He frowns. "You know my position."

"What is the *church's* position on the creation of childer?"

This time, there's a long pause before his answer. "It is forbidden."

"Do you agree with this position?"

"You know where my loyalties lie."

"Do you agree with the Lancea Sanctum position on the Embrace?"

"I do." It's barely audible.

"And those who perform the Embrace? What of them."

Another long pause, but there's no way out.

"They are sinners."

He's defeated. He can't escape this without renouncing his faith. I've won.

"How serious a sin?"

"It is a grave sin."

"Should so severe a sin be tolerated in a leader?"

He says nothing.

"Solomon Birch, Primogen and Bishop, I demand a reply! Can a leader who Embraces be tolerated?"

"Yes!" He looks up, meets my eyes and I see a plea within them. "If that leader repents. It is not too late, Maxwell! Set aside your madness! Admit your wrongdoing and be cleansed. Admit that Persephone is an abomination, a monster, a walking sin and *your* sin in particular. She cannot be lawfully killed, but break her foolish will, bend her to humility, slave her at least to the point that she is no longer an adornment on folly's arm. Make her an example of misery, that others might not know temptation. Make yourself an example by begging my forgiveness, and that of the church, and the forgiveness of mankind for your part in expanding their curse! Admit that *you were wrong* and all can still be made well!"

There's a pause. The others seem uncomfortable, the way a child might when he visits a friend's home just in time to see the parents argue. They look at me, or at him, or at their toes or out over the horizon.

"Have I shown regret, Solomon?"

"It's not..."

"Have I shown regret?"

He sighs. "No."

"And that makes me, up to this point, unfit to rule?"

"Yes."

"Did you give Justine reason to believe that was your position?"

"I... cannot say."

"Have you made a secret of your faith?"

"No."

"And any true Bishop of the Lancea Sanctum would condemn me."

"Yes."

"I see." I turn to the others. "I think we've heard enough. Are you ready to vote?"

They all nod.

"I propose a secret vote, excluding Justine and Solomon due to their... profound conflict of interest. If you believe Solomon has indeed shown himself guilty of inciting rebellion, write 'Treason.' If you believe Primogen Birch has been slandered by Primogen Lasky, write 'Falsehood.'" I consider giving them an out, allowing abstention, but no. This was too close. "I'm afraid I must insist on one of those two votes. Clearly, it is one or the other and I must rely on your judgment and wisdom to determine which."

I open my cell phone. "I'm summoning my seneschal, who is several floors below. As he does not know the matter of the vote, he cannot alter the outcome. Do you all agree to be bound by this vote and by Garret's administration of it?"

The "ayes" are unanimous.

Garret arrives after an interval that would be appropriate if he *were* several floors down (though he was actually immediately beneath us). Norris, Miriam and I carefully write out our votes and, within clear view of all present, hand them to Garret.

He holds them carefully, so that we can all see they do not move and are not switched.

"The votes read: Treason; Treason; and Treason."

Unanimous against Solomon. Pity. Had there been one dissenting vote, Norris and Miriam could each have claimed it to him. He'll make matters difficult for both, I reckon.

"Solomon Birch, you have been found guilty of conspiring against your Prince. It is my prerogative to decide your sentence." He raises his head, calm and collected, but in his eyes I see a smothered holocaust. I'm within my rights to have him exiled (possibly to plot against me), staked (possibly to be rescued by his followers in ten years), maimed (from which he'd eventually recover) or even destroyed (which would prompt vicious reprisals from the Lancea hardliners).

Besides which, he is my friend. And if I try anything too severe, he's quite likely to lose it and mangle someone, probably Justine, but maybe Miriam or Norris. Or me, for that matter.

"You have given me years of wise counsel, judicious support and genuine friendship. I honestly believe this current problem is surmountable. You have shown a dearth of loyalty, true…"

I roll up my sleeve and run a sharp fang along my wrist.

"But loyalty is easily come by."

For a moment, I think he's going to fight. His refusal to match my eyes was mostly a ploy, but his belief in free will is genuine. And a blood oath is far more potent, far more intimate.

But at the ultimate, he trusts me. He drinks.

Two nights later, Garret is behind the wheel of the Cadillac, I'm dressed in black and musing once more on Persephone.

Why did I give her the Embrace?

True, I lost control and killed her. True, I brought her back primarily from sentiment. Or at least in part from sentiment.

(I have known myself for two hundred and forty years, but still I question my own motives. Indeed, as the power of the Vitae within me has grown, I question them, and their real source, more and more.)

Sentiment is not blind. Mine isn't, anyhow. I have centuries of experience with foresight—that's how one gains centuries of experience.

Looking at Linda as she sprawled dead on the couch, robbed of her life's grace, part of me knew horror, shock and a desperate urge to mitigate my crime. But another part was cool and calm and considered what would happen if I brought her back. What would be the outcome? The repercussions? What I believe they now call "blowback"?

I knew Solomon would be aghast. I knew his shock would eventually sour into rage.

Did I Embrace her despite that expectation? Or because of it?

Solomon has been at my side for years, my most dependable advisor, my most stalwart companion. There is little with which I have not trusted him, and few of my secrets that he could not learn.

Our differences make us complimentary, but we are still very different. Part of me—that calm part—knew that I had become too close to Solomon. And of course, if I knew a thing, surely Solomon knew it as well.

By placing all his faith in God's plan, Solomon has lost the ability to fully rely on anything less than the divine. I've long felt that his own nature would, eventually, compel him to test his confidence in me. I, in turn, felt much the same discomfort in being so reliant upon him.

Perhaps we are not so very different.

In any event, when I considered Embracing Linda, I knew that it would take that spark between Solomon and myself, the merest inkling of a need to test our bond... and fan it to burning life.

As I feared and expected, Solomon chose to sacrifice me to his principles. Fortunately, I'd been anticipating that since the moment I bled into her mouth.

Having my blood, my Life, within him will tame Solomon's opposition to me for some time. When it wears off, we will drift apart into mutual mistrust, but by that time conflicts with other Primogen will have eroded his power base. If both of us survive long enough, we will find grudging common cause on some issue and, eventually, bury the hatchet.

Persephone played an unfortunate role in this matter, of course. I knew he would vent his spleen on her first, before I was ready to truly draw his ire. I tried to protect her as best I could—instructing her on the fundamentals, introducing her to Bella, finding her an apartment and even leading her towards a Guilford. (I knew one was empty and hoped she would find it. She did not disappoint me.) Many of these advantages she lost or wasted, but I tried. I did the best I could.

Now Garret is driving me to her funeral.

"I'm so sorry," I say, shaking her father's hand. She got her looks from him—he's tall, elegant, dark hair turning silver. His wife is much shorter, coming only to his shoulder and topped by a mop of gingery curls.

I exit the receiving line and look at the other mourners. I'm the only black face present.

The program is on a nice ivory stock, and the picture on the front is printed in color. She's standing in front of water, smiling, her hand raised to shield her eyes. Her hair is longer in this picture, blowing in the wind, and in the sunlight it shows subtle red highlights. I never noticed them. I never saw her in the sun.

It's a small funeral home, tasteful, filled with religious-themed pictures in gilt frames, antimacassars, miniature statuary of sleeping sheep. Everything is sober-colored, dark plums and browns and the deep tones of varnished wood. It reminds me of nothing so much as the Brigman house, where Solomon resides. I glance over at the closed casket, the rows of folding chairs, filled with her contemporaries and family. The older look sad, but resigned. The younger look shocked, aghast or simply empty. I turn my head to catch pieces of conversation.

"...so young. It seems like just yesterday she was giving that speech at her high school graduation, you remember?..."

"...said it was an accident."

"What do you mean 'said,' Steven?"

"Well, you heard the rumors. You know."

"You think she overdosed? Fuck, why don't you just pry up the coffin lid and make sure?" She should be careful. Her voice is not as low as she believes. If their exchange becomes more heated, the relatives will hear.

"Damn Pamela, don't get..." I walk over by Steven, casually, just getting in his line of sight so that he remembers others are about. He lowers his voice. "I mean... so soon after Scott."

"You're not going with the idea that they were... you know..."

"Nah, that's crazy." They're back to whispers. My work is done.

"Did you know her very well?" This query is addressed to me.

I turn. The speaker is a short, stocky man with sandy brown hair and a tidy beard and moustache. His eyes are red and he wears his dark suit with discomfort.

"Not terribly well," I reply. "We... sat on opposite sides of a few bargaining tables."

He smiles. "I bet she was a terror."

"A terror? No. A skilled negotiator though. She practiced the art of compromising without being compromised."

He smiles. "That sounds like her. I'm Andrew."

"Max. How did you know Linda?"

"I'm her brother."

Leaving the funeral home's reception area, I step down a side hallway. There are three doors, two to lavatories and one unmarked.

Through the unmarked door I enter a short corridor. Bruce Miner leans against the wall, his parka still on, arms crossed.

"How's she doing?" I ask.

"See for yourself," he tells me. As an afterthought, he remembers to say, "Your highness."

"Do you think that'll be okay?"

His posture bespeaks confusion.

"I can't... I mean, I'm not going to stop you if you want to talk to her."

"I don't want to intrude."

He shrugs.

Clearly he's not one for the subtler jobs of social interaction. I slide past him into a plainly decorated room where Persephone sits, watching her memorial through hidden cameras and listening to microphones in potted plants. This is why this funeral home was specified. Many of our kind choose it for such occasions.

She is sobbing.

"Persephone?" I say. When she doesn't reply, I try "Linda?"

"Linda's dead," she says.

I sit beside her on the loveseat. She's watching her parents.

"I'm never going to see them again," she says.

"I know." I put an arm around her and she leans into me. Her flesh is cold.

"I always thought, you know, how *great* it would be to see your own funeral, to see everyone sad at losing you, to hear all the nice things they say…"

"It's a pleasure better contemplated than experienced."

"I wish I could tell them I was joking! I wish I could tell them it's a mistake, a hoax…?"

Her voice holds out slim hope that I'll run with this, tell her it's okay, suggest a way to make it happen. It's sad. This is not the strong, confident Linda I Embraced.

I unwind myself from her and say, "You know it's not possible."

She sighs. "This will protect them, though. Right?"

"Persephone, you are a monster in a monstrous world. How protected is anyone? Kindred have less cause to torment them now, but their best protection is to be far from you and far from Chicago."

"And telling them I'm dead drives them away. I know. It's just hard. It's hard to let go."

Wait until your family has been dead for a century, my dear. See how much better you feel then.

Tomorrow a full coffin will be sent on a train to Indiana, where it will be buried in Linda's name. I killed the girl inside myself, then had Robert run over it with the Hummer. She wasn't the type who appeals to me—some nobody with black hair, a runaway—but I felt I owed it to my offspring. In Linda's grave, she will get more flowers and tears than she would as Jane Doe. I hope to speak to the Moore parents alone before then, ensuring that the city of Chicago forevermore fills them with sorrow, so that they never return here, never risk the vengeance of the Kindred or the weakness of their daughter.

It's the least I can do.

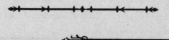

More days pass, I become more skilled with the molding of clay, and then comes the first Saturday night of a new month. The night before Elysium, the night I have set aside to spend with my beloved.

When I rise, Robert carries no razor for me. The clothes he offers are layers of stained rubbish, tossed aside and foul with grime. Thick-bearded and wreathed by a grayish cloud of floating hair, I dress as a bum and set out into the early evening darkness.

Ersatz homeless, I prowl the streets. I see the trashcan fires and hear the drug vendors chanting "Rocks, rocks, rocks...." I drift past police cruisers and wander the shadows of skyscrapers. I speak to no one. It is such a relief to ask no questions, get no answers. Such a relief to be nobody.

I sit for a while by a lion on the steps of the Art Institute. I watch people pass. It's early evening still and there are tourists heading to the Magnificent Mile, urbanites headed to Water Tower Place to look for marked-down fashions, women leaving the galleries with sketch pads tucked under their arms. One is dressed with the zany color of a Dr. Seuss creature, and I can't help but feel her personal appearance will catch more eyes than her painting (or whatever) ever will.

This is our night, my love, my Chicago.

Kindred politics are endlessly intriguing, as the ploys of the undying can uncoil for decades, perpetually snarling themselves upon the blink-fast movements of mortal toil. But Chicago, the quintessentially modern city, the open-air museum of the finest architecture the New World has to offer... Chicago is endlessly *delightful*.

It is easy to become wrapped up in the Kindred side of Chicago and forget that we are only a thin dark shadow on a vast and magnificent edifice. They style me her Prince only because they cannot perceive that it is she who is majestic and I who am ruled. One night a month, I can emerge to refresh myself upon her, drink in beauty that nourishes the man in me no less than blood nourishes the monster. One night only can I spare.

This is *why* I am Prince. Not because I'm oldest (though I am) or most powerful, but because I remain in touch. Because I love this city in all her ever-changing, ever-renewed grandeur. That lets me feel the movements of mankind more than Solomon ever will, with his technology briefings from his blood-addled slaves. It hones my intuition sharper than Norris can know, for while he scours the darkness for secrets and treachery, he forgets that some things can only be learned from beauty and life. I am unstinting in my adoration, as bowled-over and love struck as I was when I saw the White City, when I saw the Sears Tower rise, when I first heard the Chicago blues. The other elders may grudgingly maintain their cold and disdainful touches upon the pulse of current affairs. I embrace it with the clumsy eagerness of a young lover.

And once a month—it seems like so little, but if I let myself I would forget everything else—I walk the streets. Sometimes as a beggar, sometimes like a prince, sometimes as a shiftless urban shark. I probe her public places and her secret ones, I walk the neighborhoods of the Ukrainians and Poles and Assyrians and Greeks. I play my role and I wait for the city to show me something unique, something completely human.

"Hey buddy. You okay?"

I look up at the cop. I know him.

"I said, you okay?"

"I'm jus' sittin'…" I mumble it intentionally, I act spacey and lost. It's officer Grundy, he of the hockey-star son. He cannot possibly recognize me.

"I can see you're sitting, *sir*, but according to our anti-loitering law, *sir*, what you oughtta be doing is walking." The sarcasm on each "sir" is worthy of Justine herself. I stagger to my feet.

"Why you gotta be all tough wi' me?" I mutter.

"I'm sorry, *what*?" He's got a mean edge on his voice.

"I axed why you gotta be all tough, badge an' gun an' club..." I'm enjoying this far more than he is. He's the one who has to feel the cold, and I'm the one who gets to see a decorated police officer's cruel side.

"Do you have a place to sleep tonight?"

"Sure I do, sure I do..."

"A place with an *address*?"

I mumble incoherently and start to shuffle away. Grundy glares... and then he sighs.

"Christ," he says, his voice coming out on a puff of steam.

"It's gonna snow, y'know? C'mon, let me arrest you."

"I don' wanna go to no jail!"

"It's a hot meal and a chance to scrub down," he says, his voice an exquisite mix of pleading and disgust. "Come on. You want to end up frozen on some sewer grate?"

"I ain't no jailbird! I'm a US citizen! I got me rights!" I start to stagger away at a good clip.

He grabs my sleeve and I yank it from his grasp, I continue to move, wondering if he'll follow, hoping for something and not knowing what...

I hear his second sigh meld with the whispers of taxis through slush, and as I look back he's standing, watching me shuffle off, resigned... defeated.

Sometimes, my mistress Chicago is harsh with me.

Elysium is merry the next night. Chicago's Circle of the Crone celebrates February eighteenth, for some reason that I can't be bothered to recall at this moment. Bella has bedecked herself in black and silver finery and, with my permission, invites all Chicago's Kindred to her mortuary festival. We are to come in costume, and the site for the party is a recently de-consecrated Catholic church down south near Halstead.

"There shall be games, and sacrilege, and music," she promises. She has put so much effort into her appeal that even I feel I could make love, if only it was with her. "There will be so much to see and learn and do, so much to have done to you. Bring your friends, your enemies, your ghouls and fools and lovers and tools. Come! It will be as it always is. It will be something you have never known before."

I've got nothing to top that, and neither does anyone else. I dismiss the formal court and we loiter, conversing, snickering, politicking and bickering.

As I exchange pleasantries with Rowen, I keep one ear honed for gleanings in the field of polite babble. I smile and nod at her, with only half my mind on our conversation.

Justine and Norris are off to the side. It can't be anything he considers important or he'd have taken her to the restaurant: *He's* well aware how keen our senses can become.

"...employed in, heh, minor matters solely."

"See that she stays a 'minor' agent, please. Her loyalty is all over the map and you know it. Cicero, her sire, her Carthian friends... about the only group she hasn't courted is the Lancea Sanctum."

"Mmm, you overestimate her, heh, esteem for the Circle. There is some, ahem, bad blood there..."

"Really?"

"If you listened to her... if she was *loyal* to you... then you would know."

Ah Persephone. She's gotten her wish: They're paying attention. Lowering my head as part of an indulgent chuckle, I glance at the impressionist reflections cast in the windows. Spotting her solely from her damaged reflection is nearly impossible, even for eyes as keen as mine... Ah! There hulks Bruise Miner, her perpetually-parka'd pal. He's easy to spot for that *dog* of his. Persephone, always the lawyer, convinced Loki that there's no rule against bringing animals to Elysium and, indeed, many who know their feral speech carry a crow in a pocket or a serpent as a garter belt. But a dog? It's quite the affectation for a newcomer. Already people talk. Of course, he seems genuinely oblivious.

"...sure she's okay?" Miner asks.

"I told you, I took care of it." She's impatient with him, I don't need to see her to know she's looking around. But for whom? I cast my ear wider and hear Solomon and Bella.

"...had only supported me, you'd have your recognition."

"That's not fair and you know it!" She's passionate. "I did all you asked and more."

"You attempted all I asked and failed at much of it. I see no reason to cast my lot in with failures."

"You arrogant..."

"Excuse me?" This is Persephone's voice. My nod to Rowen becomes a little brittle as I strain to follow my own conversation (something about disturbances at the Morton Arboretum) while simultaneously eavesdropping on my childe's.

"Persephone," Solomon purrs. "To what do I owe the pleasure?"

"I was hoping the two of you could clear something up for me."

"It's always my pleasure to instruct a neonate."

"It's more a question for her. Bella, were you involved in Scott Hurst's death?"

"Who?" Bella sounds genuinely nonplussed. Of course, if she really didn't know anything, she might well pretend knowledge in order to cover what might be a weakness. So this could be a ploy, feigned ignorance. Or I could be starting to think like a clinical paranoid.

"Scott Hurst. My lawyer friend."

"I thought he was a suicide," Solomon says, cruel joy making his voice positively oleaginous.

"I'm sure he thought it was too. But we know, don't we? Bella, tell me the truth!" Oh my. It sounds like Persephone managed to catch Bella's eye.

"I... I was the lure. But I didn't know they were planning to kill him!" Again, she sounds convincing. The ruling gaze is notoriously hard to use on our kind, however. Persephone may well have overestimated her control, allowing Bella a chance to fall back to a more plausible lie.

"Then you'll get yours, too," Persephone says. Oh, I hope that's empty bravado. Otherwise she's being very foolish, to telegraph her intentions.

"Get her what?" Solomon asks.

"Her punishment."

"Just like I will, no doubt."

"Just like you *have*."

There's a pause.

"It must be, heh, a subtle revenge indeed if I haven't noticed it."

"How are the Brigmans these days?"

There is a pause, filled by the hum of other conversations.

"Excuse me," I say to Rowen. "I see Garret signaling me. Can we continue this discussion later?"

"Of course."

I turn towards Garret and, with a nod of my head, indicate that he should head to the back, where a suddenly dangerous conversation is occurring. I tune back in.

"...one of them with flu-like symptoms? Of course, it is the season for colds, isn't it?"

"The Brigmans are a hearty family," Solomon says.

"Oh, I'm sure they are. But there are some things that can kill even the strongest mortal. Say, something that preys upon their autoimmune system."

"Persephone, if you have something to say, say it. I grow weary of your childish insinuations."

"As you wish." Dubiard steps in front of me, mouth open to speak. I drive him back with a shake of my head. "A member of your Brigman herd is HIV positive. The antibodies should be at testable levels by now. At least, they should be in the *first* victim."

"If you have done this thing, I swear that you will…"

"How many of them have you fed on in the last month? How many have you given your blood, your so-called 'life'? Only it's not, is it? If you're a carrier?"

I'm getting closer and I start to prepare. I withdraw from my flesh, making it hard, cold, dead, an instrument only, a thing that cannot be harmed because it has known the ultimate harm. I can't tell what Solomon's doing, but from the blankness on his face I suspect he's bracing himself as well.

"What's the matter, Bishop? Cat got your tongue? Shocked and appalled that mortal friends and allies, like *Scott*, are now in play on *your* side? Amazed that some-one finally had the courage to act against you?"

"Your family…"

"My family is gone! They're dead to me and I'm dead to them! I can't stop you from killing them but I'll never know if you do! No, that threat's played out, Solomon. Your beef isn't with them. It's with *me*. And your own rules won't let you kill me, will they? Or will you? Why not do it right here? Right in front of God and everyone, just like last time? You want to. Don't you? Don't you want to give in, be weak, and lose your mind, *again*?"

The blows are brutal, just a blur of fists to her face and body. She shudders with the speed of it, like a rag doll in a terrier's mouth, and then a figure in a parka slams into Solomon's side.

I don't need magnified hearing for the rest of this. I let it go least it deafen me.

"Hey!" Bruce must have expected Solomon to fall over, but the elder is far too strong. Instead, Solomon

greg stolze

lifts him like a child, then slams him hard into one of the concrete benches. Pieces of stone flake off the bench and Miner's body breaks.

The dog lunges in, biting, and Solomon kills it with a single backhand.

"Stop!" I shout, and now Garret and I are close enough, but Solomon is so fast, too fast for me, he falls on Persephone with a savage stomp to her chest, everyone is fleeing, screaming, and I finally get my arms around his shoulder.

"Stop now!" He's beyond reason, he howls like an animal and tries to break free, Garret reaches for his legs and gets a punch and a kick for his efforts, and then I wrench him backwards, I trip him over a bench and Christ, he's so much stronger than me and much faster, he breaks his arm to free it, he howls and jerks the bones straight but I get a chance, a look in his eyes.

"Freeze!" I tell him.

There are limits to my powers of command.

They work poorly on our kind. I always keep that in mind, I always remember that seeming obedience may be a ruse. But Solomon has my blood within him. Part of my soul, perhaps. Soul reaches to soul and I try to drag my friend, my mad wayward friend, back from the depths of his own curse.

"Solomon, you don't really want this. Killing her is against your faith. It is a sin before Longinus."

I see his reason painfully return. His muscles relax beneath me.

Now, of course, everyone has arrived to help me. Just a moment too late for it to matter.

"Banish him," Justine says.

"This is the second time in a year he has defiled Elysium. If you won't banish him, I will, and if you won't back me..."

"Yes," I say. "Solomon Birch, you are banished from Elysium for one year from this date." I can't look up from him, I have to judge my actions solely by the murmurs of the crowd.

It's not enough.

"Additionally, your actions show that you are unfit to serve in the Primogen. You have one week to appoint a replacement or I'll do it for you."

Still not enough. I hope he can forgive me.

"As an insurance against any ill-conceived notions of revenge, I'm afraid I must place my Vinculum tighter upon you."

"NOOOO!"

This time he resists, but Garret has one arm, Loki has another and Rowen throws herself on his legs.

"Open your mouth!" I tell him, but I cannot compel him, his resistance to this is too profound, so I need Garret's help to pry his jaws apart so that I can bleed into him for a second time, poison him with my will again, betray his trust once more.

I see nauseating loyalty mist over his eyes, and as I stand I can see fear and disgust on many faces around us. Good. I've done a disgusting and fearsome thing. It's better that they know how far I will go to preserve order.

The only ones not looking are Persephone and Miner. She has put herself back together, somewhat. Enough to hobble over to him and pull him off the bench. He, in turn, is crawling towards his dog.

"Bruce? Bruce? Are you okay?"

"Peaches," he whimpers. "Aw, Peaches..."

Persephone never appreciated what the Brigmans were to Solomon. Poisoning them wasn't just a move in the game. They were a thing of beauty, to him. His testament to the potential of humankind. His gift to the future. His apology for being what he is.

Ruining that took away his reason to be anything other than a monster. I, in turn, have left him one taste away from being nothing but a slave.

Why did I Embrace her?

Solomon's hunger is like a shark, and he frenzied when pushed. We all have our hunger to face. Mine has always been a human hunger, a hunger for completion, a hunger to have what I lack. Or so I flattered myself. I always thought mine was less base, less corrupting than those other, animal thirsts.

But the thirst is keener, now.

I lost control with Persephone because as I drank her, it did not abate. I took more and more and was no nearer to being satisfied.

This happens, as we age. As our hungers mature. At some point, we unliving cannot cheat death when armed only with human blood. We need to rob our fellow thieves.

We start as human, become something else, and steal humanity to survive. Given enough time as vampires, perhaps we change again and must steal from Kindred to survive.

When old enough, only our Kindred blood sustains us. Our addictive, enslaving blood.

Since Persephone, I have fed, successfully, from mortals. It doesn't happen every time. But I've seen the path. It will happen more and more.

I have heard a legend that the blood of one's offspring is not addictive. That it does not form the bond that enslaves, the bond I have placed on Solomon, the bond I ordered Scratch to put on Miner's child, the one I suspect Persephone has used upon Miner himself.

If my feeding needs are to change, I must prepare. I must be ready to remain in control of myself.

All of us run from fire. It is one of the sure ways to destroy us. But now I feel the fire inside me. I feel my hunger growing into something that mindlessly consumes, that grows hotter and crueler when fed. I find myself looking on Kindred necks with a longing I once

reserved for my fine refined ladies. I find myself wanting to drain them all dry.

Perhaps that is why we fear fire. Not because it de-
stroys us, but because it is so similar to what we become.

Epilogue

"Are you sure this will work?"

"No."

For a moment, the pair don't speak. The only sounds are the sobs of the men in the open-topped cages, two men no one will miss.

"How do we find out?" The speaker is the taller of the two, and thinner. He wears a T-shirt and jeans.

"We try. Then we wait. We expose someone who isn't infected. We wait a few more months and test her for the antibodies." The second is shorter, heavily muscled. He has stripped off his shirt, and has it neatly folded with a change of pants inside a metal suitcase.

"Her?"

"Or him, it matters little. If she doesn't have the antibodies, we know we succeeded. We know we purged the infection."

"Where'd you hear about this?"

"It's an old church secret. AIDS isn't the first disease we've carried, you know. In the dark ages, some from the Lancea carried bubonic plague willingly, risking themselves in long journeys to better bedevil mankind."

"That's pretty hardcore."

"We reversed our policy when people started complaining to doctors."

"The Masquerade."

"Of course."

There is a pause.

"Shall I start?" asks the shorter one.

"If you want."

"I hope you appreciate the trust I'm showing you, outlaw."

"I understand."

greg stolze

The so-called outlaw chains up the muscular, scarred monster, cuffs his wrists and his ankles and suspends him upside down.

"What're you guys doing?" whines one of the caged men, but they ignore him.

The tall one takes the other's chained form and drapes it over the edge of one cage.

"Here goes nothing." He draws out a jackknife, opens the blade, and slits his companion's muscular throat.

The men scream. The bleeding vampire doesn't, at first. But as his blood pours down, he shudders. Then he writhes. And when he opens his mouth, he shows fangs and howls.

"Oh God! Oh God!" The man in the cage is now badly spattered with blood.

With a loud creak, the handcuffs snap. Like a fish on a line, the creature bends up, scrabbles at the ankle-chain, and breaks that too. He tumbles down into the cage but twitches to his feet and lunges at the human. The man tries to fight, but it is brief.

When he's drained the man dry, the vampire regains his composure.

"I have recovered," he said. "You can release me."

The other vampire does.

As this second vampire gets tied up in turn (with rope, not chain), the second man screams and screams, huddling with his eyes covered. The two vampires have to shout to hear each other over it.

"After this," Solomon bellows, "We should talk about Persephone!"

Ambrose knows that she'd been terrified when she made Solomon a carrier, and that she'd been pissed, and that Solomon was no saint. But still. He couldn't accept that she'd spread the disease, just for revenge.

"Yeah," he yells back, as Solomon hauls him aloft. "We'll do that!"

About the Author

Greg Stolze's mind is a swampy morass of perverse imagery and violent resentment. Humankind should be grateful that his natural cowardice prevents him from attempting to inflict the sick fruits of his rotted narcissism on the real world, leaving him instead to impotently create imaginary characters to torment.

If you're interested in more of his bizarre fantasies, as of this writing you can buy his novel *Godwalker* at http://www.danielsolis.com/godwalker. His previous novels **Demon: Ashes and Angel Wings**, **Demon: The Seven Deadlies**, and **Demon: The Wreckage of Paradise** were published by White Wolf in 2003. If you're really dying to exchange ideas about *this* novel, start a thread at http://www.worldofdarkness.com.

Acknowledgements

Tremendous gratitude to the Eola Community Center branch library in Aurora, where huge chunks of this novel were composed. (I still wish you'd move one of those chairs with the swing-arm platforms for laptops into the Silent Adult Reading Room. That would be *awesome*!) Thanks also to the Eola Community Center Babysitting Room, for making my toddler happy to be there while I write. Thanks to Ken Hite, for invaluable and heartfelt aid with Maxwell's love song to Chicago. Credit and love also go to my son Nick, for making it easy to write horror. (All I have to do is worry, which comes naturally to the parent of a fearless toddler, and then focus that on the paper.) Most especially, thanks to Martha, Mom and Mike, who have always been a great help and support in my work. (Mom, I remember you reading one of my short stories, probably twenty years ago, and saying something like "It's very good but… couldn't you write something a little more *nice*?" I've thought it over and the answer seems to be "Not right now." I turn on my mental faucet and out comes drunk and abusive vampires. That's what I get.)

world of darkness novel contest

$20,000 in prizes

The World of Darkness is home to vampires, werewolves, mages and other supernatural mysteries not so easily labeled. While we're delighted for you to join us as we recount some of these stories, we'd also like to hear your own. And we're going to make it worth your time with a $20,000 World of Darkness Novel Contest that will help us find the best new novel.

The contest will take place in three rounds. One hundred winners in Round One will be invited to participate in Round Two, and five winners of that round will be asked to complete their novels for consideration for the grand prize. Here are the specifics:

1. **Round One:** The contest opens on January 1, 2005. The deadline for round one is March 31, 2005. You may enter the contest by email only. Send a synopsis of your proposed novel to <novelcontest@worldofdarkness.com>(*).

Your synopsis must:

- be no more than 250 words (about one typed page);
- include a brief description of the novel's protagonist;
- include an overview of the plot of the novel
- involve one of the **Vampire: The Requiem** or **Werewolf: The Forsaken** signature characters — these characters are described at <http://www.worldofdarkness.com/novelcontest/>; they do not need to be protagonists in your novel, but at least one of them must play an important role.
- demonstration of knowledge of the World of Darkness.
- be imbedded as part of the email itself, *not as an attachment*
- include your full legal name, street address, phone number and email address
- include the following legal statement (which does not count toward your 250 words):

I submit my idea voluntarily and on a non-confidential basis, and I understand that this submission by me and its acceptance by White Wolf Publishing, Inc. does not, in whole or in part, establish or create by implication, or otherwise, any relationship between White Wolf and me beyond consideration in Round One of the present contest. I agree that this synopsis becomes the property of White Wolf Publishing, Inc. I further understand that the acceptance by White Wolf of this synopsis neither creates nor implies any confidential relationship, guarantee of secrecy, nor any recognition or acknowledgment of either novelty or originality.

The authors of the 100 best submissions will each receive $50 and an invitation to enter Round Two.

2. **Round Two:** Those 100 winners must all write the first chapter of their proposed novel and submit it prior to June 30, 2005. The five best opening chapters will earn their authors $1000 each as well as in invitation to enter the Final Round. More details will be provided to Round One winners.

3. **Final Round.** Five winners of Round Two will enter the Final Round, which requires the completion of a first draft of your novel by January 31, 2006. The author of the best of the completed novels will win a grand prize of a $10,000 advance for the publication of their novel in November 2006. All other completed novels will also be considered for publication under the terms of our standard novel contract.

The following rules apply:

1. Applicants must be at least 18 years of age on January 1, 2005.

2. The contest judges may at their sole discretion refuse to consider any entry for any reason. Submissions that do not follow the instructions (synopsis too long, sent before the start date, etc.) will be not be considered.

3. These are horror stories, so horrific elements are expected, but the synopsis, first chapter and novels should not contain pornographic and tastelessly explicit material.

4. Only one entry per person is allowed. Former and present employees of White Wolf, Inc. may not enter, nor may freelancers who have been published in White Wolf, Inc. products or are currently under contract with White Wolf, Inc.

5. All entries must be accompanied by the full real name of the author as well as the author's physical address, email address and phone number.

6. Only novels set within the World of Darkness will be considered.

7. All submissions become the sole property of White Wolf Inc.

8. Submission of a synopsis constitutes acceptance of these rules and conditions.

9. These rules may be amended on <http://www.worldofdarkness.com/novelcontest/>.

(*) This email address is solely for submissions. For questions and FAQ, please see <http://www.worldofdarkness.com/novelcontest/>.

"The atmosphere of [Soulban's prose] cannot be praised enough... [His] writing is truly alive."
—Brand Robins, RPGnet

THE REQUIEM

Continue the story of the Kindred of Chicago in the second novel based on Vampire: The Requiem . Duce Carter is a firebrand among the Damned, fanning the flames of revolution against the Prince. But when his allies turn on him, the only person he can go to for help is none other than Persephone Moore, the Prince's only childe. Is Persephone the friend she claims to be, or out to destroy Duce?

BLOOD IN, BLOOD OUT
by Lucien Soulban

WW11237; ISBN 1-58846-866-6; $6.99 US

AVAILABLE IN FEBRUARY

White Wolf and Vampire are registered trademarks of White Wolf Publishing, Inc. Vampire Requiem and Blood In, Blood Out are trademarks of White Wolf Publishing, Inc. All rights reserved